Discard

THE SIGHT

THE
SIGHT

DAVID CLEMENT-DAVIES

FIREBIRD

AN IMPRINT OF PENGUIN GROUP (USA) INC.

ACKNOWLEDGMENTS

The author wishes to thank the following for permission to reproduce copyrighted material. All possible care has been taken to trace the ownership of all quotations included and to make full acknowledgment for their use. If any errors have accidentally occurred, they will be corrected in subsequent editions, provided notification is sent to the publisher.

Extracts from "The Second Coming" and "Upon a House Shaken by the Land Agitation," from *Collected Poems* by W. B. Yeats (Macmillan), by permission of A. P. Watt Ltd., on behalf of Michael B. Yeats. • Extract from "The Song of the Little Hunter" from *The Second Jungle Book* by Rudyard Kipling by permission of A. P. Watt Ltd., on behalf of the National Trust for Places of Historical Interest or Natural Beauty. • Extract from *Murphy* by Samuel Beckett originally published by Calder Publications. • Extract from the prologue to *Demian* by Hermann Hesse (Peter Owen Ltd.), by permission of Peter Owen Ltd. London.

FIREBIRD
Published by Penguin Group
Penguin Group (USA) Inc., 345 Hudson Street,
New York, New York 10014, U.S.A.
Penguin Books Ltd, 80 Strand, London WC2R 0RL England
Penguin Books Australia Ltd, 250 Camberwell Road,
Camberwell, Victoria 3124, Australia
Penguin Books Canada Ltd, 10 Alcorn Avenue,
Toronto, Ontario, Canada M4V 3B2
Penguin Books (N.Z.) Ltd, 182-190 Wairau Road,
Auckland 10, New Zealand

First published in Great Britain by
Macmillan Children's Books, London, 2002
First published in the United States of America by Dutton Books,
a member of Penguin Putnam Inc., 2002
Published by Firebird, an imprint of Penguin Group (USA) Inc., 2003

9 10 8

ISBN 0-14-250047-X

Printed in the United States of America

FOR POD

With love and thanks to Chloe and all the strange and generous folk of Periana. A special wink to John and Sherrie, Katie, Soraya, Antonio and Theda, Manolo, El Alcalde, young Raphael, Isidro, Bea, Shane and Poppie, Salva, Emilio and family and last, but not least, Balloo, quite the nicest black dog in Andalucía. I hope they've realized I'm not quite insane.

I'd like to thank, too, Roger Palmer at the Wolf Trust in Berkshire for introducing me to six very friendly and very smelly wolves. I'd also like to recommend Brother Wolf, *Jim Brandenburg's stunning photographic and poetic study of these extraordinary, much abused and misunderstood animals.*

CONTENTS

PART ONE
THE CAVE

PART TWO
THE CHILD

PART THREE

THE CITADEL

THE SIGHT

PART ONE

THE CAVE

I
THE STONE DEN

I cannot tell my story without going a long way back.
—HERMANN HESSE, *the prologue to* Demian

IN THE BEGINNING WAS A CASTLE high on a craggy precipice. The air around it was so cold that it seemed the sky itself would crack like ice. Night was starting to fall around its walls and the great stone stairway, which rose up and up toward the castle through the vaulting pines. The huge weathered steps disappeared into darkness, and the shadows reaching out from the forest far below clawed their way toward a little village, nestling just beneath the cliffs.

All around the sky was draining of color, the air growing pale and bloodless, as the dying circle of the sun finally disappeared behind the crags. Beyond the castle, the range of the Carpathian Mountains rose into the distance, like mighty clouds frozen into lonely monoliths below an infinite heaven. The conifers climbing the valley slopes were laden with snow, and their tops smoked eerily in the coming darkness.

Now and then a mound of snow would topple to the forest floor with a muffled thud that quivered through the air like the boom of distant thunder. It was the only sound in the wood. The stillness that settled now across the country was as deep as the blackness beginning to swallow up Transylvania, the land beyond the forest.

But there was life in the wood: a single pair of hungry, searching eyes. They were moving rapidly through the twilight, glittering furiously in the shadows as they came. Their intelligence, the ancient cunning of the predator, and their febrile, nervous brilliance made them seem thoroughly human. But they were far from human—for they belonged to a Lera, a wild animal. There was a longing and profound curiosity in those strange, semitransparent orbs, and as night swelled they became even more aware of the shadow world around them.

As the darkness thickened, the wolf's pace through the trees grew even faster and its pupils opened wider, seeming to draw in the last rays of light. Then, as it came to a sudden stop at the edge of the wood and peered out toward the glow of fires from the village at the edge of the valley, those eyes changed color. For wolves have a power that Man himself has always longed for, the power to see in the dark. Gold suddenly turned to a brilliant greenish-yellow.

It was a gray wolf, common to Transylvania, but its strength and size was unusual. It was clearly a Dragga— an alpha male, dominant in its pack—but it was bigger than most. Its fur was a beautiful glittering silver gray, and its tail was tinged with red. It had a strong, handsome face, with brilliant white fangs and gums as pink and healthy as the flesh of a new plum.

From where the wolf was standing he could just spy humans moving around on the edge of the village, stooping in the night to collect wood for their fires, and his nose curled into the beginnings of a snarl. But suddenly a wind raked the forest, and in the surrounding air giant flakes began to flurry from the heavens. The wolf swung up his head and there was fear in his eyes.

"It's starting again," he growled bitterly. "The cave. I must find the cave."

The wolf started to run once more. To ordinary eyes he was almost invisible against the snow line and he seemed to float as he came. His ears were up and his senses so alert that his muscles quivered as he ran. But he had hardly gone any way at all when he heard the snap of a twig in the wood. He swung around instantly and the snarl that came from his jaws had a killing threat in it. But as another muzzle appeared through the trees, the wolf relaxed a little, although his eyes were still blazing.

"Palla," he cried angrily. "Don't ever sneak up on me like that. I thought you were a Night Hunter."

The female coming toward him was a dominant also, or Drappa, as wolves call them, and she had a beautiful sleek muzzle and bushy silver ears. She was as lean and graceful as a mountain leopard. Only her swollen stomach and the exhaustion in her tread spoke of the cubs that now lived in her belly. Palla was close to her time.

"I'm sorry, Huttser. You don't think they're still following us?"

"No, Palla, I think we lost them long back. But there are other dangers for the wolf now, with Man so close."

The wolves' fierce yellow eyes had become wary and attentive as they flickered like little lights in the darkness. This was before the time, some three hundred years later, when Man would hunt the wolf and the forests almost to extinction, and there were tens of thousands of Grays still roaming wild and free through the trees. But the wolves had learned from birth to fear Man above all the predators, for he was a merciless hunter of their kind. And all too often the wolves had suffered, too, when Transylvania was caught in the grip of his frequent and terrible battles.

Transylvania was the ancient name for a region that lies in the very heart of Europe. A strange and mysterious country, rich in folklore and tales of darkness and superstition. A country of soaring mountains and fertile valleys that borders the lands that men know as Russia and the mighty forests that once edged the realm of Hungary. Since the ancient Dacian empire had fallen into decline, Transylvania had been invaded and fought over by a seemingly infinite variety of peoples and cultures. The Romans had come here, and after them the succeeding tides of nomadic conflict. The land beyond the forest was still bitterly disputed by the Magyars from Hungary, by the Saxons from the German lands, and by the Vlachs, who owed their allegiance to none.

Palla was nodding her head as she stared back at Huttser and they both thought of Man.

"Yes, Huttser," she growled. "When you left us to scout, Brassa's paw was caught in one of their traps."

Huttser's eyes widened in alarm.

"She managed to pull free, Huttser. But we should get her inside as soon as we can. The cave is just far enough away from the humans' dens to be safe."

"We should get you inside, you mean," said Huttser.

Palla seemed to be looking through her mate rather than directly at him. Wolves rarely look at each other directly in the eye for fear they might raise each others' anger. But their muzzles lifted in agreement. Their flight had been a harsh one. Since they had mated unusually early, they both feared their cubs would be born in the deathly grip of winter, before spring would come to warm the world and drive back the killing snows.

"The Stone Spores and the den on the mountain," growled Palla suddenly, looking toward the giant stairway and the castle. "It means we're close now, thank Tor. I've never known weather this bad."

"At least it'll be impossible for the Night Hunters to track us in this, Palla. Even if Morgra has told them to follow us."

Palla winced and the unborn cubs kicked in her belly. Morgra was Palla's half sister, and it was Morgra, not Man, that the wolves were fleeing now. Though Palla had not seen her in years, Morgra always stirred painful memories in the Drappa. When Palla had been little more than a whelp, Morgra had been driven from their pack for killing a cub, and wolves believe that once a wolf tastes the blood of its own it gets a liking for it. And now that Palla was coming back home to where it had all happened, Morgra's presence seemed strangely closer than ever.

Morgra lived far to the north, over the great Carpathian Mountains. She had always been a fighter, and with her exile she had sought a new role among the wolves of Transylvania. She had managed to win control of the Balkar, which in the wolf's language meant Night

7 *The Stone Den*

Hunters, a group of six wolf packs made up entirely of fighting males that had been formed to defend the borders of the land beyond the forest. With the leadership of these guardian wolves came the title of "First of the Wolves," and never before had a she-wolf laid claim to it.

That past autumn Morgra had also put the seal on her power by ordering the free wolves, as the rest of the wolves in Transylvania termed themselves, to present their new-born cubs to her. None knew what her strange edict was for, but Palla could not forget what Morgra had done to the innocent cub in her pack. So Huttser and Palla had decided to flee south toward the Stone Den, which marked the valley where Palla had been born. But Morgra's Balkar wolves had followed them. Huttser had finally managed to lose them in the deep gullies and snowy defiles of the Carpathian Mountains.

"But Huttser," whispered Palla suddenly, "if Morgra really has the Sight, then couldn't she follow us in any kind of weather?"

As soon as Palla spoke of the Sight there was a strange frustration in Huttser's look.

"Hush, Palla," he growled nervously. "I've told you a thousand times before, it's a foolish superstition, nothing more, and we have left Morgra and the Night Hunters far behind."

Huttser prided himself on being a clear-thinking wolf, and he hated the superstitions that were spreading once more through the land beyond the forest. Dark rumors had grown up around Morgra, which she was carefully fostering, and she was known to dabble in the black arts. Some said she was trying to enchant the animals and sought allies among even the wolf's bitterest enemies, like the bear and the mountain lynx. Others said that she possessed the gift of the Sight, an ancient though largely forgotten myth among the wolves. In essence it was the power to see far-off visions beyond one's own body, though few gave much credence to the fable anymore. In days gone by it was said that many wolves possessed the power, and other animals, too, in the times when magic and witchcraft ruled their lives and darkness dominated their stories.

"Huttser," said Palla suddenly, "I'm tired and our cubs—"

"We must keep moving. Where are the others?"

"They should be close. I ran on a little to find you."

The fur around Huttser's muzzle glittered as he threw up his head. The wolf's powerful howl quivered on the air, climbing higher and higher until the sound seemed to hover like some winged bird above the forest. Suddenly there was an answering call, and they both swung around to see three more wolves springing across the white. The pack was coming through the trees toward them. There were two females and a male.

At the back a proud old she-wolf was limping badly, and she kept lifting her paw in pain. The right pad was very swollen, Brassa's blood still matted thickly around the fur. Luckily the trap's angry metal jaws had been left in the wet too long and rusted through, so she had been able to escape. It had been dangerous for the whole pack, though, especially with Huttser scouting ahead. Wolves are fiercely loyal and will rarely abandon their own in times of trouble; Brassa's accident had slowed them up badly.

9 *The Stone Den*

Just in front of Brassa came Kipcha, Huttser's sister. She was smaller than Huttser but had her brother's boldness in her tread. Kipcha looked exhausted, though, and her heavy coat was thick with snow and frost. Beside her ran Bran, the Sikla, or Omega wolf, the weakest in the pack. Bran had a particularly wary look as his tongue lolled from his mouth. His features were distinguished by a ring of black around his right eye.

There was a frantic whining and dipping of heads as the wolf pack was reunited and the others greeted Huttser. The wolves rubbed their flanks together tenderly as they wagged their bushy tails. The Dragga spent a while inspecting Brassa's paw and whining in sympathy as he licked the wound above the pad. When Huttser was satisfied it was not too dangerous, he lifted his head again.

"Very well. Did you see any Lera?"

Suddenly the pack heard the angry screech of a bird somewhere high above the clouds.

"A while back," answered Bran immediately, "I saw a set of pads in the snow."

"Dog or Varg?"

As Huttser used the formal word for their own kind, Bran raised his tail proudly.

"Varg," he answered. "They weren't meandering about like a foolish dog's, Huttser, but moving in a straight line, like the hunting wolf. At first I thought it was Khaz, but it was traveling in the direction of the village."

"Good. It's probably just a loner, looking to scavenge."

"But I don't like this place, Huttser," sniffed Bran mournfully, peering up through the snowy air at the strange castle, high on the mountain.

"No, Bran, and we must keep a sharp eye. But it's too cold for even Man to hunt."

"Man," growled Palla scornfully.

Kipcha was looking toward the village. A wolf has a powerful instinct for danger, but it is a highly intelligent and inquisitive animal, too, and Kipcha's interest was suddenly roused.

"The humans fascinate me, Palla," admitted the she-wolf almost guiltily, "and I've never been this close to them before."

"And you don't want to get any closer, Kipcha," snorted Brassa beside her, whining and licking her wounded paw. Palla nodded immediately.

"Brassa's right. My parents only chose the cave because there is so much game around here, and in their day the human dens below the mountain were far fewer. We always kept well clear as cubs. Men may live in packs like us, but they are not Lera."

"Man isn't a Lera, Palla?" growled Bran with surprise as the wind rose and made the forest shake around the Sikla.

"Don't be foolish, Bran, every Varg knows that Tor and Fenris made Man different from the Lera."

As Palla spoke of the wolf gods, Tor and Fenris, Brassa nodded approvingly. They were the makers of sky and stone, the wolf gods of the Varg's formal religion, which had long wrestled with ancient cults and superstitions like the Sight and was far older than the oldest of the trees in the forest around them.

"Tor and Fenris gave Man a gift," Palla went on gravely, looking about her in the snow "that set him forever apart from the animals. The gift of intelligence.

Though he doesn't have the power to see in the dark, or scent a thousand flowers on the breeze and listen to the falling leaves, his mind makes him strong and cruel. And evil too."

Brassa lifted her head to the heavens, and for a moment, through a breach in the thick cloud, she saw a single star, shining so brightly above the castle and the village and the returning wolf pack, that it looked like a beacon light. She shivered and Huttser noticed how cold she was becoming. He was frantic to be moving again.

"Come, Palla," he cried. "You must lead the way now. If you don't find the cave soon we'll all be carrion by the morning."

Palla looked back gravely at her mate.

"If I can remember where it is, Huttser."

Palla sprang forward in the freezing blizzard, and the ground dropped suddenly ahead of them as they came to a river. It was wide, but its surface was completely frozen over. Soon the whole pack was moving across. Palla and Brassa went very slowly, fighting the wind and careful not to trip, as Palla looked desperately for any natural feature she might recognize from her youth. Although wolves have better memories than many animals, they share the general forgetfulness of the Lera, and for suns Palla had been trying to remember the best route back to her birthplace. But soon Bran was running at Kipcha's side as the pack followed the Drappa along the river's sweeping course.

"Kipcha," cried the Sikla as he fought the bitter wind. "It's been so strange, fleeing like this with the Drappa pregnant."

Kipcha struggled to keep a grip on the ice. "I know, Bran, but Morgra can never get her paws on Palla's cubs."

"Why does she want our pups, Kipcha?"

"It's not just ours she wants. But I don't know. I've heard such strange stories lately, Bran. Perhaps it's to do with the legend."

"Legend?" said Bran, thinking to himself that it was certainly a night for legends.

"Of the Sight," cried Kipcha. "I was told about it when I was a cub, but I had quite forgotten it until I saw that horrid castle and Palla started talking of Man's evil."

"Why?" growled Bran nervously.

"Because the legend speaks of both Man and the Varg."

Bran suddenly remembered a story that always frightened him as a cub. Of a wolf whose side was pierced by one of the man pack's sticks during a harvest moon and so, when the moon fattened, he underwent a terrible transformation. His muzzle withered and his fur fell away to leave him pink and bald. His teeth and ears shrank, and he stood up on his hind legs like the two-feet. Instead of talking in the voice of howling song, he began to voice in Man's strange grunts and whines. His tail shriveled away and he could no longer run like the river, or scent for miles. He lost the power to see in the dark and had to go down to live with the man pack, feeding on meat shriveled by Man's burning air.

"You don't mean the Wolfman, Kipcha?" whispered Bran, shuddering.

"No, Bran, that's just a cub's story," growled Kipcha, shaking her head scornfully. "The legend tells of a time when a wolf with the Sight will steal a human child."

"A wolf steal a child?" said Bran in astonishment.

"And rear it as his own, to teach it the ways of the Sight," Kipcha went on.

"Who ever heard of such a thing?" growled Bran.

Kipcha had come to a stop below the looming castle. There was an air of loneliness and violence about that craggy place, of some profound mystery, too, that even the bats wheeling above its battlements could not fathom with their piercing senses. But Huttser was more interested in the icy ground where he was nosing a set of huge paw prints.

"Bear," the Dragga grunted as the rest came up. He sniffed the spores with distaste. "It seems wolves are not the only Lera treading through the forest tonight."

Suddenly, ahead of them, Palla gave a delighted howl and turned to lead them up off the river. She had remembered the way after all. The she-wolf's relief was plain as she spotted a small frozen waterfall and a birch tree, beyond which she knew lay the cave they were hunting for. Soon they were standing outside a low entrance in the slope of the hill, below a great boulder. The cave was partly shielded by a trailing willow, its mouth yawning into the blackness beyond.

"Thank Fenris," cried Huttser as the wind shook the branches.

The cave was low-ceilinged, so that Huttser had to drop his head as Palla led him inside, but it stretched well back into the mountain and, despite its proximity to the stream, was also remarkably dry. The air was fresh and cool, but the wolves found it far warmer than the world outside.

"It's good to be back," growled Palla with pleasure, and the she-wolf's voice began to echo around the rock chamber. "This is where I was born, Huttser. My birthing den. We could fit the whole pack in here when we needed to."

"A perfect place to rear our pups in safety," sighed Huttser, nuzzling his mate tenderly.

Palla lay down and Huttser licked her beautiful face. His heart was full of worry, but Palla could already begin to feel the numbness leaving her limbs as she lay in the warm, dark cave. Yet the she-wolf was desperately hungry and her head felt light and dizzy.

As Brassa prowled into the cave, she began to look around her fondly. "Huttser, I nursed Palla here myself," she said proudly, "and her brother, Skop, when their parents were off hunting food for them."

As Brassa mentioned Palla's brother, the Drappa looked up, worried about what he was doing on such a terrible night. Skop had long departed to find his own pack, and Palla hadn't seen him in many moons.

"It brings back such memories," whispered Brassa.

"Not all of them good," murmured Palla. "You nursed Morgra here, too, remember?"

Brassa looked strangely wounded. She fell silent as Kipcha settled on the edge of the chamber as well. As Bran padded inside, he pushed accidentally against Huttser, who turned and snarled at him. Bran jumped sideways, creeping back to the edge of the wall in submission and showing his throat to the Dragga. They were all exhausted and hungry, and Huttser's worry for Palla had strained his patience to breaking point.

"Try and get some sleep, all of you," Huttser muttered

sullenly, turning away from Bran. "Without sleep how can a Varg go on?"

Bran whined miserably. "Sleep? How can I sleep with this ache eating at my gut? And it's so cold, Huttser."

"I know, Bran," said Huttser gravely. "We must pray to Fenris for this storm to stop."

Brassa smiled as Huttser spoke of praying to Fenris. She was already praying to Tor, but that was as it should be. Fenris was the Dragga god of the wolf's faith, and a male would always invoke his name if he felt threatened, just as a female would call to Tor.

"Besides, Huttser," Bran went on, "I'm bound to have nightmares about that Stone Den. It's horrid."

Palla looked up. "My parents said the castle was deserted, Bran," she whispered as if to reassure the Sikla. "But they used to tell dark stories about it too. They say Morgra climbed up there once. But she was always inquisitive. She asked so many questions about the Sight."

Huttser immediately threw Palla a warning look, but it was too late to stop Kipcha.

"The Sight," she whispered excitedly, her breath stroking the others. "Tell us more about the Sight, Brassa."

Brassa was the pack's adviser and keeper of stories, but the old she-wolf suddenly seemed rather nervous. As she stared around the cave, the others' eyes had locked on her, though, and Brassa turned to Huttser, for she knew he disapproved of discussing such things. But there were so many rumors already circulating around Morgra now that the Dragga let her speak. Perhaps the nurse might allay some of their darker fears.

"Most say that the Sight is pure myth, Kipcha," growled the nurse quietly in the darkness. "The Varg's belief in it died out long ago, thank Tor, although it was the way of seeing that the predators have believed in since the birth of the sun. The seeing that comes through the forehead. The sense beyond sense, drawing its strength from the energy in all things. They also say the power has not reappeared among the wolves for generations, except among the fortune-tellers, who keep its secrets. Until now."

"Why had it disappeared?" asked Palla.

"Who knows. Perhaps it faded because the Varg began to look to reason and their wits, though the Sight was always a very rare gift. That, too, made it feared. But some believe that when it reappears, it will come to more than one."

Bran gulped.

"In the old days, Brassa," growled Kipcha, "what did the wolves use it for?"

"That, too, little is known of. Some say it helped the wolves survive the Great Trek, when we first came out of the Land of the Northern Snows. Others that the old Seers, the fortune-tellers, cultivated it as a way of telling the future. Still others argue that it was a gift from heaven to help the wolves in their search for Truth."

"The stories, they frighten me," growled Bran.

Brassa nodded coldly. "Yes, Bran. It's frightening. There are many powers associated with the craft of the Sight. One is to see through the eyes of birds, the Helpers."

Bran stirred unhappily.

"Another is to look into still water and see things there

of far-off realities, of past, present, and even future. This is the fortune-tellers' special skill."

The wolf pack all looked up, not simply because of the strangeness of the idea, but because a wolf fears nothing more than death by water. If a wolf is drowned then it is believed that the soul can never find a true resting place in the skies with Tor and Fenris.

"But the truest power," whispered Brassa, "that is the most fearful, although it is said that none have reached it. It is real power wolves with the Sight sought for so long: to touch the minds of others directly and control thoughts and even physical actions."

The wind outside was screeching now, moaning and howling around the cave mouth. As it pushed the clouds across the sky, light from the strange star Brassa had seen shone in the cave. The wolves were all thinking fearfully of Morgra, and they hoped more than ever that they had left her far behind. But Bran, whose eyes were still fixed on Brassa, fancied she was keeping something back.

Seeing the others' distress, suddenly Huttser sprang to his feet. "All this is nonsense," he cried irritably. "The Sight is nothing but a myth, as Brassa says. And besides, doesn't the wolf have senses enough to master the world without black arts or some hidden craft?"

Even as Huttser spoke, a shadow suddenly spread across the wall of the cave. It swayed gently, and though it looked something like a wolf, its muzzle was strangely extended and misshapen. Huttser swung around, growling threateningly, and even Bran raised his tail in challenge, although he drew backward too. But as the pack recognized the handsome face that suddenly appeared through the darkness, they all sighed with relief.

"Khaz," cried Kipcha, wagging her tail delightedly.

The wolf that trotted into the cave was only a little smaller than Huttser, though distinguished by a great bushy red tail. The others looked proudly at the fine wolf standing before them, for Khaz was both brave and kindly, and they all trusted him deeply. His strong eyes were sparkling as he acknowledged Kipcha and dipped his head to the Dragga, for in his mouth he was carrying a hunk of fresh meat. It was this that had distorted the shadow thrown onto the cave wall from the world outside. As Khaz threw the meat on the cave floor, he shivered and shook the snow from his thick winter coat.

"There," he cried, "not much I'm afraid, but enough to give strength to Palla and her little ones. This cold could freeze the claws off a bear."

"Good for you, Khaz," growled Huttser. But he was thinking, too, of those huge paw prints in the snow, "I was wondering where you'd got to."

"I would have caught up with your tracks sooner," panted Khaz, lying down and nuzzling up to Kipcha for warmth, "but I was checking for Night Hunters. No sign at all, thank Fenris, though I met another family fleeing the edict."

The freezing wind began to whistle through the willow tree now and its movement sent swaying shadows dancing like crabbed fingers across the cave floor. Palla began to gnaw at the flesh, chewing at it with the side of her powerful jaws. It was tough, but her teeth were very sharp and to an appetite enlivened by hunger, it tasted delicious. Bran's eyes looked longingly at her across the cave.

"And I saw other things to worry us, Huttser," growled Khaz, though there was little fear in his strong voice. "Humans, hunting near the village."

"Man," snorted Brassa, lifting her paw as if in evidence of what she was saying. "They are evil. They are cruel and kill without hunger."

"So do we, Brassa," said Khaz rather cheerfully, staring at Palla, too, as she fed. "For we are Putnar also." Putnar was the wolves' word for a predator. Among the titles Morgra's Balkar gave themselves to intimidate the free wolves was "First Among the Putnar." Khaz bared his teeth. He couldn't hide the saliva beginning to drip from his jaws as he gazed at Palla. Although he had made the kill and eaten a little himself, it was only a small calf, and he hadn't lingered to feed properly.

"Some things not even the Putnar can control," Khaz went on, growling to himself thoughtfully. "I got into one of their sheepfolds last spring. I wasn't hungry by the time I left, but I . . . I couldn't help myself. I killed them all."

"The blood lust was on you, Khaz." Huttser smiled indulgently, "That's all. And when they bring so many tamed Lera together in one place, it's difficult to resist."

As the wolves thought of Man's strange habit of taming the Lera, they all nodded gravely. It was fundamental in Varg lore that the wolf was the only Lera that could never be truly tamed. Freedom is a wild wolf's birthright. Palla finished her meal and licked her lips as the others tried to swallow nothing but their disappointment. It wasn't really difficult because, though they were all bitterly hungry, there are few bonds in nature as strong as a wolf pack, and their cooperation is remarkable, especially when the Drappa is pregnant. They will all hunt to feed the expectant mother and nothing is allowed to get in the way of the pack's future, now symbolized by the life stirring in Palla's belly.

"I'm glad of one thing at least," said Bran mournfully, promising himself that tomorrow he would take the very fattest snow rabbit he could find, "that the humans are always fighting one another. Just think if they really turned their attention on the Lera."

"Coward," muttered Khaz under his breath. He didn't have much time for the Sikla.

"Hush, Khaz," said Huttser.

The Dragga turned to Bran and his expression was meant to make up for his anger earlier. "Which is why the wolf should walk as a shadow when Man is about," he said softly. "Why he should remember the oldest law, never to meddle in human affairs."

Bran suddenly thought of what Kipcha had said of a legend, but Huttser had laid his head gratefully on Palla's paws. The Dragga was desperately thankful that they had reached warmth and safety at last. Palla could give birth any sun now and the last thing he wanted was his pack out in the open. Outside, the snowfall was already beginning to stop. The winter had been unusually long, for it was late February, but it had almost run its course. Now the secret earth, which lay hidden beneath its pure white shroud, had sensed the coming thaw and was preparing to throw forth new life.

But Huttser was mistaken if he thought their arrival

had gone unnoticed. Something had seen the wolves enter the cave. Its trail in the snow led back through the forest to the castle on the mountain, and its eyes were watching the cave mouth intently. In their glittering gaze lurked the flames of longing and of hate, and above its head hovered two black wings.

A small herd of red deer was grazing in the grass on the edge of the forest at the valley bottom, munching happily on the lush spring stems. It was fifteen suns since the pack had returned to Palla's birthplace beneath the gloomy castle, and most of the snow had already thawed.

"Now," snarled Huttser in the woods, "now is the time of the Putnar."

The fur on the Dragga's back seemed to quiver as he dropped down like a cat and began to edge forward through the grass, scenting the air as though tasting it. His ears cocked forward, his eyes suddenly full of a sly cunning. The wolf's instincts were fully engaged, and though his awareness of the deer was not held in his conscious mind, all his senses were at work, reading the patterns of the herd. But suddenly one of the deer lifted its head and the herd bolted. The wind had changed.

From the darkling cover of the woods, three sleek gray shapes came shooting toward them. The wolves moved as fast as darting swallows, but springing in a clear, straight line across the grass, covering the space between the trees and the deer in a matter of seconds. One deer, with a back leg that was slightly deformed, began to trail behind the rest as they fled, and as the wolves closed they swerved toward it. But Bran leaped forward on his own, making toward a stag that carried a full head of antlers.

"No, Bran," cried Huttser angrily, "not that one!"

Bran was far too excited to heed Huttser, and his jaws were almost within biting distance. His heart was racing as the wind raked his ears and the scent swamped his nostrils. But the stag had the measure of him. It waited for Bran's head to come a little closer and let out a vicious kick, catching Bran full in the muzzle. Bran shied away, yelping in pain, as both his front legs buckled and he spun helplessly in the grass.

"Don't let them get into the trees," cried Huttser frantically.

Kipcha hardly needed to be told as the she-wolf raced after the rest of the deer. She was coming from the left and she made straight for the slower deer, trying to split it from the herd. Huttser was with her. The two wolves working together instinctively, seamlessly, as they had done on so many hunts before, closing in steadily and swerving to shadow the living contours of the herd.

Closer the wolves came, and closer to the crippled deer and, just as Kipcha snapped at its right hind leg, Huttser pounced. He was around its neck and, as the deer rolled, his huge mouth closed. The wolf bit deep, drinking the hot, sweet blood as it flowed between his teeth, his jaws snapping like a trap around the warm fur. The bite was fatally accurate and, as the young stag tumbled in the grass, it was dead before it even stopped moving.

Huttser held on to make sure of his quarry though, shaking the deer's neck back and forth like a broken twig.

Its body went limp, but still Huttser worried the dead stag, proud of the kill and feeling the power and guiltless glory of the wild hunter. Only when he was certain it was dead did the wolf raise his head and howl with pleasure. But as soon as he saw Bran coming toward him, Huttser's eyes narrowed angrily.

"A pack works together, Bran," he cried. "Don't ever forget that. If we don't have that, what by Tor and Fenris do we have?"

Bran drew his tail between his legs.

"Besides, Bran, this was the weakest Herla," said Huttser, using the formal word for deer.

Huttser and Kipcha stared accusingly at Bran, and now embarrassment drove the Sikla to speak.

"The weakest," he snorted, "I could take any one of them, Huttser."

Huttser snarled and took a swipe at Bran. "You could take nothing of the kind, you fool. Besides, we hunt the weakest not just for the ease of the kill, but so that the Herla may go on, too, and feed us in the future. That is the law of the Putnar."

Bran knew the law as well as any, though his own thoughtlessness, his desperate excitement, and the intoxicating smell of the deer had made him suddenly forget it.

"Very well, then," snapped Huttser, "let that be an end to it. Now let's eat, we've earned the Putnar's right."

Bran edged forward, but as Kipcha came up he slunk back again. In the pecking order of the pack, Kipcha had the right to try the kill before the Sikla.

The deer hovered by the trees beyond as the sounds of the ravening wolves came to them across the grass, their own senses almost frozen in impotent horror. But they all knew that this was the law, and at least for another sun the danger had passed. It was a law as old as the rocks that littered the giant mountains, and a law just as hard.

After a while the wolves' hunger began to abate. Kipcha was licking her paws like a giant kitten, as Bran cracked and crunched on bits of bone to get to the delicious marrow and suck out the last bit of goodness, when Huttser lifted his muzzle.

"Now we must take meat for Palla."

Although its ribs were open to the sky, nearly a third of the deer carcass remained intact in front of the feeding wolves.

"Shouldn't we bury the rest?" asked Kipcha.

"No, Kipcha. Listen."

They lifted their ears to the south, and a familiar sound filled the air. Soon they saw wings flapping toward them across the forest, and Kipcha growled and dipped her head in defense of the carcass.

"Kipcha," said Huttser quietly, but this time with little rancor, "today we all seem to be forgetting the law. Let the birds scavenge it, with a free heart."

As the birds flapped toward them, though, Bran growled. "They look like Wolfbane's Helpers." He shivered.

Huttser smiled and shook his head indulgently.

In wolf lore Wolfbane was a demon spirit, in human terms the equivalent of Satan himself. It was said that long ago Wolfbane had made a blood pact with the scavengers of the air. Like the Sight, the cult of Wolfbane had been popular in the ancient days, when wolves believed that specters and demons haunted the land beyond the forests and the packs had lived in fear and ignorance. Before the coming of Sita. Sita was the she-wolf who had been sent down by Tor to bring the light of truth and goodness into their lives. Tor had sacrificed her own daughter for the wolves' sake, and because of her the wolves had begun to talk only of the power of Tor and Fenris, who made the world and kept the light of truth shining into the Varg's lives.

Though Sita's coming was believed by many to have banished the cult of Wolfbane forever, parts of the old superstitions had mingled with the new beliefs, and some wolves still said that Tor and Fenris would send Wolfbane to stalk the earth whenever the wolves betrayed them. Until the courage and strength of the wolves could drive him back into the shadows. Wolfbane was now known as the Evil One and the Shape Changer, since some thought he was a giant wolf, with terrible yellow-black eyes and teeth the size of trees, while others thought that he could take on the shape of anything that ate meat: a lynx, a bear, or very occasionally a man. It was said that he walked with the dead, and if young wolves misbehaved, their parents would warn them that Wolfbane was coming to gobble them up, for Wolfbane was said to love to feed on the flesh of cubs.

Huttser left the carcass to the birds now and led the others back in the direction of the den, but as they crested a high slope, Kipcha's muzzle began to quiver. At the top of the hill, the wolves looked out in amazement. His thoughts still on the Evil One, Bran began to tremble violently.

They had visited the plain below them already, and seen game here—deer and sheep and even water buffalo. But now, as the wolves looked down, they could hardly believe their eyes. There, before them, were humans. Some were on horseback, while others marched wearily through the grass. There were nearly a hundred of them. They were moving in columns, their sweating horses snorting and pawing the earth. Several of them carried long branches in their hands, from the top of which fluttered brightly colored skins, each marked with a cross.

Huttser noticed that the sharp sticks at their sides glinted like teeth in the sunlight and that the men riding the horses were clothed in the strangest way. Their chests and heads sparkled and glittered brilliantly, as if they were made of the same hard material as their shining sticks.

"Man," growled Huttser, setting down Palla's meat.

"What are they doing here?" whispered Kipcha nervously.

"They have the look of Putnar. I think they're hunting."

"For wolves?" shivered Bran, and he thought of Kipcha's words in the forest about a legend of a man and the wolf. A twinge of fear gripped Huttser's stomach too.

"No, Bran. They seem to be on the move. I think they are traveling south."

Huttser was right, for this was the time before the coming of Stephen the Great, the Hungarian king and a fabled defender of Christendom, when a new threat had arisen like a specter in the East. Even now the Ottoman Turks, who came from the southern lands and adhered to nothing of the Christians' beliefs, pressed hard at the haunches of eastern Europe and belief fought belief, as power wrestled power.

The wolves watched them warily until Bran began to growl again.

"Huttser. What Brassa said about Tor and Fenris making Man's mind stronger than the animals," he whispered. "They are wolf gods. Why would they do such a thing, for, like Wolfbane, Man brings nothing but evil?"

Huttser shook his head, picking up the meat again.

"The stories have an answer for that, Bran," said Kipcha at his side as they watched the columns sweating below them. "Some believe that Tor and Fenris put all kinds of evil in the world so that the wolves would have a choice. Others that they lost power over the predators, over their own creation."

Bran found the idea very strange.

"Some even say that Tor and Fenris made Man because even they did not understand where they themselves had come from and longed to see further."

The wolves slunk away at this talk of evil, and Huttser was suddenly filled with worry for his pack. He quickened the pace and, as they neared the den, led Bran and Kipcha hurriedly up the hill toward the cave, the kill still dangling from his mouth. He only paused at the stream to drink, lapping his tongue in the sparkling mountain water, his stomach rippling as it filled. Despite what they had just seen of the humans, Huttser felt strong and alive and free.

He could see Brassa sitting on the slope above, her head up and alert, looking out across the valley in the coming evening. But Huttser suddenly felt the strangest sensation.

It was a sense carried to him from somewhere he could not fathom, but as real to a Lera as the evidence of any eyes.

Huttser leaped up the slope, leaving the other two to drink, and as soon as he padded into the cave he heard a snarl. Palla was trembling in the shadows, and the she-wolf's eyes glittered dangerously in the semidarkness.

"What's wrong, Palla?" cried Huttser anxiously as he dropped the meat. "Has anyone—"

"No, Huttser. But you may not come in here."

Huttser was startled by the hardness in Palla's voice, especially since he'd come to protect her.

"But, Palla—"

"It is my time," snapped Palla. "You may not see this."

Huttser bridled, for though they had never actually fought each other, their strong temperaments were well matched and they often argued. But Huttser resisted the temptation to growl at Palla. Her belly was very heavy, and every now and then her pupils would dilate, as twinges of pain gripped her stomach and shook her body.

"I've brought you food, Palla," said Huttser, nudging the kill toward her. "Is there anything else you need?"

"No, Huttser." Palla's tone softened as she sniffed the venison. "I'll call you when it's time."

Huttser turned sullenly and padded back outside. He stretched himself out next to the old nurse on the hill. Huttser did not try to disguise his worry and irritation. They all trusted Brassa implicitly and rarely hid their feelings from the nurse.

"She won't let me into the cave, Brassa."

"Into the den, you mean," said the nurse kindly. "She's ready, Huttser, and she must do this alone. The law allows no Varg into the den during birthing. Don't worry. Palla will summon you when she's ready."

Huttser knew she was right, but he was not used to feeling so useless. The two wolves lay there for a while, Huttser scratching himself and nibbling at fleas, gazing about him irritably. But after a time the wolf noticed that Brassa was looking at the large boulder, on the slope above the den.

"What is it, Brassa?"

For a moment Huttser fancied he saw something almost secretive enter Brassa's eyes.

"Nothing really," she answered after a while. "It's just that's where they passed judgment on Morgra."

Huttser had never met Morgra, and he only knew the story vaguely, but as he caught Brassa's scent next to him, he realized that she had begun to shake, and he could suddenly scent fear on the air.

"Why did she kill the cub, Brassa?"

Brassa swung her head away, and as she spoke her voice was quivering. "Morgra always longed for pups of her own, Huttser, but even as a youngster there was something odd about her. Many said she had the evil eye and it made it hard for her to find a mate. One night she stole into the den and carried off a cub. It may just have been the way she carried it, or it may have been her own bitterness, but when they found her, there were tooth mark's in the little one's neck. She'd killed it."

"So they drove her out?"

"For moons we would see her ranging the hills, watching the pack. Then she vanished. They say she tried to join other packs, but none of the wolves would take her in.

They say she kept talking of Wolfbane, of the Evil One. It was after that the rumors of the Sight really began."

"You fear Morgra, don't you?" said Huttser.

"Yes, Huttser, I fear her."

"Well, Morgra is far away," growled Huttser, getting up suddenly. "And what's past is past. Now if Palla won't let me inside, at least I can stand guard."

Brassa nodded as she watched Huttser padding off farther down the hill. Male wolves become fiercely protective of the den during birthing, and Huttser would be no exception. But as Brassa looked back toward the rock, she shook her head strangely and shuddered.

That night the pack crowded around outside the den, nudging Huttser and whispering together, listening for any sign from Palla inside the cave. Every now and then they would hear a whine or a low growl, which made Huttser more and more anxious. But if any of the wolves strayed too close, the growl of pain would grow into a warning snarl, which made the wolves retreat instantly.

The pack lay down by the boulder, where they could see clear to the western edge of the valley. In the darkness they suddenly heard sounds drifting toward them on the spring breeze. In the village the humans were celebrating, and their fires were sparking with life, for they were only just beginning to mark the birth of one of their own.

A sun passed, and as another night of waiting came in, Huttser laid himself down at a slight distance from the den mouth, from where the wolf had the best vantage point to protect the cave. He had hardly slept in two nights, and at last exhaustion overcame him. As he slipped into dreams, filled with running deer and strange moonlit shadows of an angry she-wolf that seemed to float in the air, he felt a brooding sense of disquiet.

"Huttser. Wake up, Huttser."

Huttser sprang up, growling angrily, but it was Palla standing there in front of him. In the half-light his mate looked exhausted, but as Huttser gazed at her in the coming brightness, her beautiful eyes sparkled.

"Come," she said softly.

Huttser was shaking furiously as he followed Palla into the den. The Drappa stopped near the entrance and whined. There, at the side of the cave mouth, lay two little bodies. They were motionless in the dust and their fur was caked with grime and grit.

"No, Palla," gasped Huttser, scratching the ground in front of the dead cubs.

"The journey must have done it, Huttser," she said softly.

"Morgra's to blame, and if I ever get my paws . . ."

But Palla knew now was no time to look back. "It is nature's way, Huttser," she growled firmly. "And we must look to the living now. The pack must survive."

As the voice of the law echoed once more in his ears, Huttser gazed proudly at his mate. He remembered the days he had first started to court her and, silently, he thanked Tor and Fenris that she had chosen him.

"Over here, Huttser," whispered Palla.

Set back well into the cave Huttser saw the leaves, twigs, and molted wolf hair that Palla had used to make a more comfortable bedding for the birth. But Huttser gasped as his eyes grew accustomed to the shadows, and he looked at the cave floor. On the ground was a little ball of fur, rising gently up and down.

"Just one?" he asked, hardly daring to breathe.

"Look closer."

There were two beautiful newborn wolf pups. Their miniature bodies were curled around each other, and their foreheads nestled together peacefully as they lay sound asleep. One's fur was a smooth bluish black, while the other's was much lighter, and their stubby little tails were as bald as worms. They had tiny ears on their blunt wolf heads, which seemed absurdly large for their bodies. Their faces were deeply wrinkled around their eyes, which were clamped firmly shut. Palla's tail was wagging furiously.

"When, Palla?"

"The morning after that first sun."

Huttser felt annoyed at having been kept waiting and worrying so long, but now Palla lay down, positioning herself in an open arc around her cubs. Suddenly there was a frantic squeaking and the heap of fur erupted like a mole-hill into a frenzy of tiny moving limbs. They scrambled over each other to get to Palla's side, pushing and shoving their way forward instinctively. Although they couldn't see them, both were soon positioned proprietorially next to one of the she-wolf's teats. They started to guzzle greedily and Huttser could resist no longer. He bounded forward, yelping and covering Palla in great slobbery licks.

"Stop it, Huttser." Palla laughed, pushing him away with her muzzle. "It's enough with these two pulling me apart, without you all over me too."

Huttser pulled back sheepishly, but he could see the sheer delight in Palla's face. He lay down beside her, and together the Dragga and Drappa set about grooming them and whispering excitedly. The day had grown old when Palla lifted her head.

"Well, then." She smiled. "What shall we call them, Huttser?"

"I . . . I don't know, Palla. What are they?" Huttser was a hunter and unfamiliar with the ways of family life; he hadn't even asked yet.

"A dragga and a drappa. That one, the light one, that's the girl."

"How about Larka?"

The Varg's word for newly fallen snow seemed perfectly appropriate for such a light coat.

"Well, my little Larka. How do you like your name?"

The tiny she-wolf couldn't have heard her mother, for she was still blind and deaf, but her tail went on shaking.

"And the dragga?" asked Huttser.

"I thought of Fell, after my father. Ouch. He bites like Fenris."

"Fell and Larka." Huttser nodded delightedly, but as Palla looked down again her eyes grew grave.

"They're so very little, Huttser."

"I know, Palla."

The parents fell silent for both knew the harsh laws of survival and how much danger faces young cubs in the wild.

"Well, we shall have to feed you up, Palla," said Huttser tenderly at last, "so your milk is as rich as sunlight."

"We'll bury the others outside the den, Huttser, beneath the birch tree, and then you must fetch the pack. It's high time they were introduced to their future."

Outside Huttser and Palla laid the unnamed cubs gently down on the earth beyond the cave. They scratched a shallow hole in the ground below the birch tree, and rolling the little corpses inside with their snouts, the wolves turned their backs on them sadly and began to kick the earth over their bodies. The giant sun was setting behind the Carpathians, turning the ridges of cloud to fire and lighting the deep valleys and dark ravines with a last luminescence.

"My poor little ones," whispered Palla when it was finished, "you never saw anything of the world."

But Palla was a she-wolf and, as Huttser went off to summon the pack and the sun finally vanished behind the castle, she turned without another word. Palla trotted back to her living cubs waiting in the den, leaving the dead to the tree and the stream and the cold, uncomprehending earth.

There was a happy chorus of whining and yelping as the pack crept into the den that evening. Brassa was allowed to look first, as the oldest pack member, and the she-wolf beamed as she gazed down at the little ones. Khaz and Kipcha came next, and Kipcha licked Palla tenderly on the snout and whined longingly at Khaz. Though it is unusual for any but a Dragga and Drappa to mate in a wolf pack, Kipcha adored Khaz, and she had long dreamed of pups of their own.

"I shall hunt for them, Huttser," Khaz cried, "and catch the fattest deer in the forest."

"And I shall teach them to scavenge like Fenris, Palla," nodded Kipcha, "and to run as straight as Tor too."

"I'll show them cunning and wisdom," said old Brassa gravely, "and tell them all my stories, just as I did Palla when she was little, so they will be safe from Wolfbane and all harm."

Despite his usually skeptical nature, Huttser smiled and nodded. It was also a given in wolf law that stories are an essential part of a wolf's training, and that to know as many of the old tales as possible was in itself protection against darkness and evil. It was why the wolf loved story-tellers so highly, and partly why the pack so loved old Brassa.

Bran bounded up to say something, but as he stood there, the Sikla couldn't think of anything at all, so he grinned instead and wagged his tail furiously. Khaz began the call as the pack stood around the children, and they all took up the note. Palla and Huttser stood proudly together over their cubs as the howl of celebration echoed around them. Huttser's heart could have burst with pride and joy. As he looked at his newborn children and at his pack, the wolf felt he had achieved something gravely important, and he felt almost invulnerable. But Huttser suddenly noticed that Bran had broken away from the group. The Sikla's muzzle was nosing the ground toward the cave mouth and his jaws were beginning to slaver.

"What is it, Bran?"

As Huttser began to scent, his whole body went rigid.

"Blood."

Huttser swung around to the back of the cave where Palla and Brassa had begun to groom the pups and, as soon as Khaz caught his look, he and Kipcha followed them outside. Night had come in, and over the castle on the mountain, bats were flapping through the dark, still air.

A dead lynx was lying on its side in the grass in front of them. It was small for a lynx, and from the blood oozing from its torn throat, it was clear that it had only just been killed. The fresh scent in the air came, strong and sweet through the dark, and made the fur on the wolves' backs tingle and stand on end. Huttser began to growl, his upper lips curling backward to show the pink gums and hard white teeth.

"Who comes without Tratto's Blessing," cried Huttser.

Khaz snorted in agreement as Huttser spoke of Tratto. Tratto was the wolf who had first brought together the Balkar packs, to resist the incursions of southern Varg, driven by human warfare to seek new hunting grounds in the land beyond the forest. He was a brave and bold wolf from the high mountains, and in fighting off the invaders, it was really he who had managed to unite competing packs for almost the first time in Transylvania. Tratto, above all, had insisted on suppressing superstition in the land beyond the forest. He had made the Balkar pray regularly to Tor and Fenris and outlawed any talk of cults or dark crafts. When Tratto had brought peace again, he had kept the Balkar together as his personal army, but he had asked little of the free wolves, except allegiance and the occasional gift of game.

Many of the wolves had been happy to give it, and it was Tratto's strength and leadership that had long prevented the wolves from turning once more on each other within Transylvania. But now that Morgra led the Night Hunters and was demanding allegiance, too, it was a very different matter. Apart from her obsession with the dark arts and her unwelcome edict, Morgra had already allowed some of the Balkar to openly break the law. In Tratto's day, pack hunting grounds were shared freely, but wolves wanting to cross a boundary were careful to ask the permission of the pack Dragga occupying a territory; "Tratto's Blessing" it was called, a way of formalizing the natural relationships among the wolves.

Before Huttser could say any more, something flashed past his eyes. It had dropped from above and now, lying in the grass next to the lynx, lay a dead wildcat. Huttser swung around angrily.

"Gifts," cried a voice just as he turned, "for the newborn."

Huttser's hackles came up as they saw a she-wolf standing on the slope, watching them from the shadows above. She looked old, maybe six or seven, and her eyes glittered as she gazed down. Her right ear was missing, and her muzzle had grown strange tufts of fur that had clearly sprouted over the deep facial scars underneath. Around her jaws were the dark stains from her kill.

"Who are you?" snarled Huttser.

"Just a passing Kerl," answered the stranger coolly, and she began to pad down the slope straight toward them. Her voice was soft and reassuring, but Huttser thought it ripe with cunning too.

Huttser shivered. There are many Kerl—lone wolves who either leave or are driven out of packs to survive on their own in the wild. But to a pack wolf like Huttser, their status carried connotations of sadness and even fear, for above all a pack wolf dreads loneliness.

"What do you want here?" he said as the stranger reached level ground in front of them.

"Want? Why to share a little of the love that I heard in the den. I hope a stranger has a place at the feast."

Suddenly a bird hopped out from behind the she-wolf. It was a raven, coal black and beady-eyed, and even as it did so, the pack heard Palla's voice.

"Morgra," she hissed furiously.

Palla had frozen at the den mouth with Brassa standing next to her. Palla's eyes were flashing like flint. She had swung her whole body around to protect the den and was baring her teeth. Bran and Kipcha shrank away toward the den immediately, and Huttser and Khaz prepared to spring, ready to defend the pups in the cave against the cub killer. But Morgra just smiled coldly as she advanced on the pack.

"Come, sister," she whispered. "There's no need to show your teeth. I wish you no harm. I don't want to spread discord through your pack." Morgra stopped and now she was looking at Brassa, her eyes glittering in the darkness.

"So," she growled, and to Kipcha's ears her words seemed tinged with bitterness, "I see the nurse is here to guard the den at least. Such good care you take of cubs, Brassa. Such good care you always took."

Strangely, Brassa couldn't hold her gaze, and she looked away guiltily.

"What do you want, Morgra?" growled Palla beside her.

Morgra turned her head slightly to face her sister now, and an odd melancholy look suddenly came into her eyes.

A look that might have been mistaken for sadness. The old she-wolf paused and then answered quietly. "Want? Why, Palla, to join your pack, of course."

The pack could hardly believe their ears. The Balkar leader, the First of the Wolves of Transylvania, the wolf whom they had fled in the bitter winter, was suddenly before them and asking to be accepted into their midst. It was so strange Huttser couldn't think of a thing to say.

"Join our pack?" stammered Palla, "but you . . . the Balkar . . ."

"The Night Hunters are not a family," snorted Morgra immediately, "and to lead a pack of draggas is no satisfaction to a she-wolf. But now you have little ones . . ."

There was something almost tender in Morgra's gaze. She had stepped forward again, and her eyes were searching now beyond Brassa and her sister, trying to penetrate into the darkness of the den.

"Keep your distance, Morgra—"

"Won't you let me come home, sister?"

Palla felt her guts clench as the pleading note came to her ears. It was many suns since Palla had thought of Morgra as a sister.

"Home?" Palla muttered, amazed by the strangeness of it. "Do you think I've forgotten what you did?"

Morgra's lips curled up to show her teeth, but when she spoke her voice was soft and almost sad.

"Forgotten?" she whispered. "But you were too young to even remember, Palla. They were mistaken."

"Cub killer," growled Khaz suddenly.

"I am no cub killer," hissed Morgra, rounding on Khaz. "And one sun I shall have justice."

Morgra's voice was so angry that the whole pack flinched, but as they moved closer to protect the den, her tone changed immediately.

"But even if you can't bring yourselves to believe me," she went on in a wheedling voice, "can't you forget the past, Palla? Let it go. Together we can all make a future. Such a glorious future. For so long now I have wanted cubs of my own, but I am barren, Palla, barren."

Palla and Kipcha looked up in horror. For she-wolves, there could be few fates more terrible than being barren.

"For years I lived as a Kerl, Palla, without family. Now I am old and before I die I want to run with a pack again, like the Varg should. And you, my sister, my own blood . . . I could be a boon to you, Palla, for I have learned many things."

Palla hardly knew what to say, but she felt a pity stirring in her for her half sister. Next to Palla, Bran shivered. His eyes were on stalks.

"You come here," Huttser said, stepping forward, "without even asking Tratto's Blessing." Although he couldn't have explained why, Huttser suddenly felt that Morgra was lying through her teeth.

"Tratto," snorted Morgra. "Tratto is dead. I am the First Wolf and now my word is law. And, Huttser, as a Dragga you should know above all that we need leaders in the land beyond the forests. It is strength that keeps us from turning on one another."

Bran thought he heard something cold and secret in Morgra's voice.

"And is it your love of cubs, Morgra," said Huttser angrily, "that led to this edict? That forced us to flee through the snows to protect our little ones. That killed two of my pups."

Morgra growled softly, but she didn't give way a whisker, and her face showed not the slightest remorse.

"I, kill your cubs?" she said coldly. "More accusations, Huttser. Be careful how you throw around blame, it may come back to you."

Huttser remembered what Palla had said in the den about their journey and survival, but he didn't like Morgra's tone at all.

Morgra was looking up toward the castle now, silhouetted on the craggy mountaintop. It suddenly looked more sinister than ever to the pack, though Morgra's eyes were amused.

"So you fled to the shadow of the Stone Den, to escape the edict," she growled. "A strange place to seek safety. When I was a cub they used to say Wolfbane lived up there. They said that the Evil One lived in the earth and only rose with the setting sun. That at night Wolfbane would come to drink blood with his great fangs."

Bran shuddered and he remembered what Palla had said in the cave the night the pack had returned, about Morgra climbing to the castle herself. A thin crescent of moon had risen, and it cast a ghostly light on the distant castle and the great stone stairway. There was a slight breeze now, sending clouds drifting across the face of the moon and casting huge shadows over the forest. Bran could already see a shape rising from the earth, floating down toward them from the castle, its giant fangs dripping with blood, its hungry, bloodshot eyes searing into him.

But Morgra suddenly paused and shook her head. "The

edict was to make a census of the free wolves," she went on calmly, turning back to Huttser, and again Huttser fancied she was lying. "Nothing more. But now I am here to offer you my help and protection. There is much darkness below the Stone Den, and Man is on the move again."

As she spoke of Man, Morgra's eyes began to dance, and Kipcha suddenly thought of the humans they had seen in the valley.

"In fleeing my wolves you have brought yourselves back within Man's shadow, and he throws a mighty shadow across the world." The she-wolf was unable to hide the admiration in her voice. "For like the wolf, he is a creature of legends."

Kipcha's ears came up, and Palla noticed that Brassa had started to tremble. Bran, too, had cocked his head and the Sikla's eyes looked suddenly very alert. Huttser wanted to drive Morgra off, but the thought was leaping through his brain that if there were Balkar with her the pack might be in real danger. With newborn cubs he couldn't afford to take any risks. He looked over to Palla, but his mate, too, seemed uncertain.

"Your hesitation is understandable," said Morgra scornfully. "Don't let me rush you. You must choose for yourselves, as all things must, and I have work here myself. Such work." Morgra paused. "Besides, I would hunt in my own home once more and see the old boundaries. I'll visit you again after two full moons have returned. That should give you enough time to conquer your doubts. So watch for me, sister."

Morgra turned scornfully, and she was moving back up the slope when she suddenly stopped and swung her scarred muzzle around. Now the tenderness in Morgra's voice had vanished completely.

"But be sure to make the right choice. Though the free Varg are too stupid to believe in the old stories, many strange powers haunt these mountains. We wouldn't want their eyes to turn on you, Huttser, and I am a better friend than an enemy. In the meantime I give you all . . . I give your blind cubs a blessing."

Morgra smiled coldly. "May Wolfbane protect you."

She turned and vanished over the hill, and the pack noticed the raven take to the air and flap off noiselessly into the distance after her. As they followed its flight, they had no idea that in the forest below it two more wolves were moving swiftly past them through the darkness.

The first was a female and the second an old gray dragga. The fur whitened sadly around his muzzle and his eyes had a mournful brilliance. There was a complicity in their look, and it was clear they were hunting for something.

"We're nearly there," whispered the female as they ran.

"Yes," growled the old gray wolf, "and it must happen below the Stone Den. We must find it before she does."

"But when, Tsarr?"

"At a time when the humans go to war once more."

"And how shall we know him?"

"Skart's eyes shall watch for him from the air, Jarla," answered the old wolf, looking up. "He has a special mark, as is only right. For he heralds a legend."

2
STOLEN

Through the jungle very softly flits a shadow and a sigh—
He is Fear, O little Hunter, he is Fear!
—RUDYARD KIPLING, *"The Song of the Little Hunter"*

THAT SAME NIGHT Palla lay at the back of the cave, suckling her blind cubs, as the pack rested in a circle around the Drappa. Huttser had called an urgent meeting and they were talking gravely in the shadows. They were avoiding one anothers' gaze, just as Palla had done when she had first seen Huttser in the forest, for the wolves could all sense a dangerous tension in the air.

"Perhaps she really wants to help," muttered Bran cheerlessly, trying to break the silence. "She offered us her protection and she is the First Wolf now, as she said. Whether we like it or not."

"Protection?" snorted Khaz loudly, showing his teeth in the darkness. "A cub killer who gives us Wolfbane's blessing. Why should we want her protection?"

"But if there truly was some mistake," Palla whispered sadly. "It must have been terrible for her, to be barren.

45

And then to wander as a Kerl, only to lead this pack of fighting males. It's not natural. And she is my sister."

Brassa was suddenly staring at Palla.

"What are you saying, Palla," growled Huttser on the edge of anger, "that we should take her in? Your parents saw what they saw, Palla. They were right to drive Morgra out. And if she already has a taste for cubs . . ."

Brassa's ears twitched. She seemed to want to speak, but she changed her mind. Palla dropped her head guiltily and licked her little ones.

"You're right, Huttser."

"She said she had work to do here," said Kipcha suddenly. "What do you think she could mean?"

"You heard what she warned," whispered Bran, beginning to growl, "about powers haunting these mountains. Did no one else see that there was a bird with her? Think of the Sight—the power to see through the eyes of birds."

On the breeze outside they heard an owl hooting mournfully above the forests. The shadow of the woods seemed to steal into the den.

"If we don't take her in, perhaps she could—"

"Stop it, Bran," snapped Khaz. "So what if she does have the Sight? How can the power of seeing hurt us, anyway?"

The pack all nodded, all except Brassa who was suddenly looking away.

"Brassa?"

"What is it, Palla?" muttered the nurse, turning back nervously.

"You know more of the Sight than we. Do you think she could hurt us if we refuse her?"

"I . . ."

"Tell us, Brassa?"

Huttser was looking intently at the nurse too. "Why do you fear her so much, Brassa?"

"Not her," muttered Brassa, "but maybe the Sight."

"Why?"

"The power of the Sight draws its strength from the energy in all things," said the nurse slowly. "And so some say the craft brings control over the elements themselves, and so the power to curse."

"Curse," gulped Bran.

The shadows around them seemed to swell in the cave. A wind suddenly blew through the den, stirring the hackles on the wolves' trembling necks.

"But I've never believed it," added Brassa halfheartedly.

Huttser sprang to his feet and turned to address them all. "Did we return to the Stone Den to succumb to foolishness and lies?" he cried, his voice echoing so loudly through the cave even the deaf cubs seemed to hear him. "I won't let superstitions frighten us. The Sight is a thing of dreams and fables, just like Wolfbane."

"She looked up at the castle, too," said Bran miserably. "And if she's been up there, perhaps Wolfbane really does live—"

"Silence, Bran," snapped Huttser. "I do not fear Morgra for her magic, and my pack at least will not be ruled by stories and superstitions. But the Balkar are quite another matter. If the Night Hunters have followed her, we may have something very real to worry about."

"Huttser," growled Khaz gravely, "do you think they're here already?"

Before Huttser could answer, the cubs at Palla's belly began to squeak as they struggled at her milk, and the pack's attention was gratefully distracted from thoughts of Morgra and her strange request.

When the pack was on the move and hunting constantly, they cooperated naturally, but now that the pack had new cubs, an even stronger bond was forged. They all worked for the safety and nurture of the infants, and internal rivalries were suppressed. As Palla began to teach her pups, Khaz and Huttser were soon off hunting for food for the Drappa, or scouting for signs of Morgra and the Balkar. At the den the female wolves drew even closer to Palla, sitting with her in the cave and telling her all they knew of grooming and feeding or trying to take her thoughts off her half sister.

But it was Huttser who was lying at the back of the cave a few suns later when Fell suddenly dislodged himself from his mother's side, got up, and trotted straight over to his father. The pup stood there watching him, wagging his tail.

"Look," said Palla happily, "Fell's eyes have come."

But Huttser was startled when he looked into Fell's little face, for his eyes were still firmly closed, yet he seemed to be able to see his father. As Brassa drew nearer, the black cub raised his head and looked up at her too. Although his eyes were clamped shut, Fell seemed to be perfectly aware of everything that was going on around him.

"Is he asleep?" whispered Huttser, but as he did so, Fell swung around and trotted straight back to Palla's side and started to suckle again.

Thankfully, the cubs' eyes both opened that night, and

though they could hardly focus, Huttser felt a thrill of wonder for, like those of all newborn wolf cubs, they were a limpid blue. Except that Fell's right eye had a tiny flaw in it, just below the center of the iris, a sliver of green, like splintered emerald. Palla looked proudly down at her pup, for wolves believe that a special mark or even a flaw can be a sign of great character. But Brassa seemed strangely unsettled. That night she lay outside the den, muttering to herself.

"It can't be," she kept saying in the shadows, "not again."

"Larka," said Fell irritably, "budge up, Larka."

The cubs were already quite large and their paws were huge. They had all their senses now, and both had been fully weaned. But with Morgra around and possibly the Balkar, too, they still weren't allowed outside the den, which frustrated them both. They were eager to run outside and explore, but instead they had been made to stay in the dark listening to Brassa's stories.

"What can we do?" said Larka excitedly at her brother's side.

Just then, Brassa's huge muzzle appeared above them. Brassa had given Palla a break from tending to them so the Drappa could go hunting with Huttser. Palla was happy to leave her cubs with the nurse for a time, for what she now lacked in hunting and fighting ability, Brassa more than made up for in knowledge and experience. Wolves, more than most animals, value age in the pack, for though it brings sickness and failing faculties, it also brings its own wealth of insights into the world.

The pack had seen no more of Morgra, but Bran had been left by the boulder to help guard the den, while Kipcha and Khaz had gone off on their own, as they often liked to do these suns.

Larka suddenly noticed that the evening was coming and moonlight was already creeping through the mouth of the cave. Larka was very fond of trotting to the edge of the den herself and peering outside at the world.

"Brassa," she whispered, "what is the moon? Why does it grow in the sky?"

"Because the moon is the goddess Tor," answered Brassa softly, smiling down at Larka, "looking down on us all. As some say, the fury of the sun is the hunter Fenris, snarling at the Varg, so they say the moon is the wolf goddess, opening her eyes wider and wider and stroking the world with her kindness."

But Fell's eyes had sparkled at the mention of Fenris.

"One day I'll hunt," said the black cub hopefully. "Won't I, Brassa? Like Fenris. I can't wait to kill something," he added, wrinkling up his little nose. Brassa looked down at him tenderly too.

"That will come, Fell, all in good time. You've yet to learn quite what lies out there in the wild, even for the Putnar. To face that you will need not only courage, but wit and cunning. The cunning of the hunter. Now, pay attention. I'm going to tell you a story."

"A tale of Wolfbane," yapped Fell, "a story of the Evil One. They say he lives in the underworld, don't they, in the Red Meadow where the dead live?"

The cubs wagged their tails at the old nurse, and Larka settled again. They loved listening to the rhythms of

Brassa's voice and plucking out familiar sounds and phrases. Each sun, Larka and Fell seemed to know more and more words and, though they longed to be gone from the den, like all the grown-ups, they loved stories.

"No, Fell," whispered Brassa, "not a story of Wolfbane."

"Of a horrid Grasht then," piped Larka, "a vampire. Cursed and drinking blood."

Fell nodded enthusiastically. Now here was a story he could really get his teeth into.

"No, Larka," answered Brassa, looking very nervously at the white wolf. "Let me see. Perhaps the story of Sita."

Brassa peered closely at the cubs and shook her head. "No, you are too young and first things first. It was in the beginning, when the wolf gods Tor and Fenris created the world and so brought light out of the darkness. When, in the shape of the moon and the sun, the great gods made Dammam, the first wolf, to rule over the whole earth. Then, because she loved him, Tor took one of Dammam's teeth and out of it she fashioned the she-wolf Va, to be his mate. As Tor and Fenris stood over Dammam and Va and looked down on them from the heavens, they were glad at what they had done."

Fell yawned for he had heard this part of the story before, but as Brassa spoke of Tor and Fenris standing up there in the clouds, he suddenly thought of Huttser and Palla towering protectively over them in the den.

"Why?" asked Larka suddenly. Larka was always asking things of the grown-ups and, though she rarely listened to the answers properly, her favorite question was always "Why?"

Brassa licked the little she-wolf. "Because Dammam

was very lonely as he wandered through the forests, Larka. So Tor let Va give Dammam a beautiful litter—"

"But who made Tor and Fenris, Brassa," growled Larka irritably. "What was before them?"

"Stop interrupting," snapped Brassa, though she was deeply impressed by Larka's question. Brassa shook herself and tried again.

"So, as I was saying, Tor let Va give Dammam a beautiful litter of thirty-three pups, made up of every type of Varg in the world: timber wolves and red wolves, chancos and arctic wolves, all of whom lived and grew and spread out through the forests. But the oldest of these cubs was the gray Varg Fren, who was Va's favorite."

Fell and Larka stirred excitedly. Depending on who was telling the story, and especially whether it was a male or a female, Fren was either the greatest hunter and fighter in the forest, dark and mysterious, a loner and something of a villain, too, or the kindest father and the best defender of the brood. Brave and cunning, and always at odds with Tor and Fenris, Fren was the hero of a thousand wonderful adventures.

"One sun Fren was fast asleep in the sunlight," growled Brassa, "when Tor came padding slowly by across the clouds. Now Fren heard Tor, but he pretended to go on sleeping, for he guessed what was coming next. Tor was furious with Fren because he was always disobeying her and stealing things from the wolf gods: food and magic and the secrets that they forever kept hidden in the den of the night. Above all, he had tried to steal the golden deer pelt that once worn would bestow not only freedom, but all knowledge and wisdom on the wearer. It hung from an ancient branch in a forest of almond trees."

The children's eyes were glittering.

"Just as Fren had expected, Tor grew angrier and angrier as she saw him sleeping there, and in order to wake the wolf, she let out a howl that rose to the stars."

As Brassa told her story, Huttser and Palla were padding slowly down the hillside side by side, matching each other's pace and trying to enjoy the warm evening. The hunt hadn't gone well, though. Palla was tired, and again her thoughts were occupied with Morgra. She was looking up at the heavens. "Huttser, it's almost full again. Do you think . . ."

But Huttser wasn't listening. For the last few moments Huttser had grown deeply unnerved. He stopped as the valley opened below them. From where the wolves were standing, they had a perfect sweep of the forest, clear to the castle on the mountaintop. Its great black walls loomed above the endless pine trees and not even the gentle glow of the setting sun could soften its battlements. The wolves could see the river and, through a break in the trees, the little waterfall. At this angle they could not see the entrance to the den, but Huttser's heart began to pound as his eyes ranged back and forth across the hill above the cave.

"Where's Bran?" he growled suddenly. "I told him to stand guard."

"There," sighed Palla with relief, but the she-wolf's tail came up and she began to sniff the air. Palla's eyes were not as good as Huttser's, but her nose was telling her more of the faint shape she had spied in the distance. A Lera was moving back and forth across the hill right by the big boulder. Its head was down, scenting the ground, and its tail was wagging. But its coat belonged to no Varg that Huttser or Palla knew. It was a light beige color and perfectly svelte.

"A dog," snarled Huttser.

But suddenly the dog turned away from the den and ran straight back into the trees.

"Do you think he found it?" whispered Palla.

"He'll have picked up the scent all right, but perhaps Bran scared him off."

In that moment they heard a sound lifting over the valley that made the wolves tremble to their bones. In the distance, among the trees at the base of the Stone Spores, voices rose in a baying frenzy. Not one voice but ten, twenty voices, crying together. Now, through the woods, the wolves could also see strange orange lights flickering about the branches, like little eyes of light, moving up the valley from the direction of the village.

"Man," cried Huttser desperately. "Man is hunting and that dog is one of his hounds."

Palla began to shake. A wolf's instincts are perfectly balanced between the need for fight or flight, and a she-wolf will sometimes abandon even her own cubs if the threat to them is too great. Palla was wrestling with her own nature.

"My pups," she cried suddenly, "hurry."

Huttser could hardly keep up as the she-wolf bounded down the slope. Palla's springing limbs were seized with a furious energy and every muscle was trained toward a single purpose: reaching her cubs in time. Night came down and the hungry darkness consumed the forest, but the wolves' desperate eyes began to glitter in the shadows as they ran. The dog pack's frenzied barking sounded nearer every moment, and Palla's heart was beating so hard it was ready to burst.

Brassa was finishing her story. "But Fren had howled so long and so hard that his call had filled the whole world. And there was plenty of howling left over for every wolf in it. And for every kind of feeling, too—the howl of the hunter and the mate, the howl of friendship and of loss, the howl of danger and of mourning too. Which is how, my dears, Fren stole the secret of the howl from Tor and Fenris, and how he showed his cunning too."

Brassa was smiling down at the cubs, but she swung around immediately as Palla bounded into the cave.

"Brassa. Quickly. We must move the den."

The cubs leaped up, their tails going and their voices breaking into delighted barks. Brassa could see Palla's desperation, and she was immediately nervous that the cubs were already grown so large to carry.

"What's happening?" cried Brassa.

"A hunting pack," snarled Huttser from the cave mouth, "and humans are on their trail."

Larka and Fell didn't really understand what a hunting pack was, let alone humans, but they immediately sensed the tension in their father's voice. Larka looked nervously at her brother, but the black wolf's eyes shone.

"Then we must hurry," growled Brassa. "Follow the stream and the river and use the water to cover our scent. Farther down the river to the east, there's an old badger's set by the big oak."

"Good, Brassa." cried Huttser, looking gratefully at the nurse. "Take Palla there. I'll draw them off and try to get to you when I can. It'll be quicker if you carry them."

"But, Huttser," cried Palla.

"Don't argue with me," snarled her mate.

Huttser sprang out of the cave, and as soon as he emerged into the evening, he saw Bran running up the slope toward him. Bran had picked up the scent of a squirrel near the den a good while earlier, and it had made him completely forget about his charge of guarding the entrance. His face was full of guilt as Huttser spotted him.

"Huttser, I'm sorry, I just wanted—"

"Silence, Bran. Follow me."

In the den Palla grabbed Larka. The pup was quite heavy, but as Palla held her by the loose folds of fur around her neck, the young wolf instantly went limp, and Palla found her easy enough to carry.

"What is it, Brassa?" whispered Fell as the old she-wolf dipped her muzzle to pick him up too. "Is it that cub killer?"

"Hush, Fell. You must be quiet now, and as brave as you can."

"I'll look after you, Fell," growled Larka suddenly as she hung from her mother's jaws.

The she-wolves sprang out of the cave, splashing into the stream, with the pups swinging from their mouths. As they followed the stream down the hill, Palla turned to see Huttser and Bran watching them from beside the boulder. Huttser nodded gravely and then sprang straight toward the sound of the approaching dogs.

◆ ◆ ◆

Little Larka's thoughts were consumed with fear as her mother ran through the deep black night. Yet she was excited too. She hardly knew what was happening. But one thing was for sure, this sudden adventure had carried them beyond the confines of the den, and as she peered about at the looming trees flashing past them, her very first taste of the outside world thrilled the young wolf to the marrow.

"How far?" panted Palla in the darkness. They had stopped to put the cubs down. Suddenly the air quivered. Behind them, through the dark, came furious barking. Palla's hearing seemed to have become even more acute with the adrenaline pumping through her body, and now she could even hear paws churning through twigs and leaves.

"Hurry," she cried, "they're on to us."

For a time the pack had followed Huttser and Bran, moving so fast that they had left their human masters far behind, but after a while they had split into two, and half of the hounds had turned back to the den. They were furious when they discovered it empty, but they had wandered around by the river and one of them had stumbled on the scent of the she-wolves by an elm tree.

They had followed it silently, noses locked to the ground, sniffing the pungent, feral odor of the wolf and losing it in places where the she-wolves had crossed the water. But they had just picked it up again and set up a chorus of barking. This was the sound the wolves could hear now, and they knew there was no time to lose. Brassa grabbed Fell again and bounded ahead, searching desperately for the badger set. As the dogs called behind them, she was almost at her wits' end.

I'm just a forgetful old fool, Brassa kept thinking bitterly to herself.

At last Brassa spotted the big oak and then a wide hole high on the far bank and mostly obscured by a log. She waded into the water with Palla behind her, and soon they were on the other side. The set went a good way back into the bank, and it was certainly wide enough for a wolf and two cubs, but Brassa realized immediately there would be no room for her.

"Hurry, my dear." She trembled. "Go as deep as you can. It's their only chance. Keep the little ones quiet, and I'll try to make it into the mountains until it's safe again."

"Don't leave us, Brassa," whispered Fell.

Brassa dipped her head and licked Fell's nose. "Don't worry, you'll be safer with your mother."

There was no time to argue. Palla began to back into the hollow, pulling the cubs after her.

"Good luck, my dear," cried Brassa, and the old she-wolf sprang away.

Palla drew Fell back into the darkness behind Larka, and the moist walls closed around them. The air smelled heavily of badger.

"Mamma," growled Larka. "Why are they chasing us, Mamma?"

"Quiet, Larka."

Palla was terrified of alerting the dogs outside and besides, how could she ever explain why animals chased one another? Larka and Fell could hear the dog pack drawing nearer and nearer across the river, and suddenly the full terror of their situation dawned on the cubs. Larka began to tremble, and as a reflex to her fear, although she was well beyond suckling, she tried to get to Palla's milk.

"Keep still, Larka," whispered Palla angrily.

But Fell had noticed a beetle scurrying across the low roof of the den, and he let out a squeak that turned into a growl, and finally a little howl. Fell clamped his mouth shut again, startled at the extraordinary sound that had just popped out of his throat and terrified that he had just given away their hiding place.

The dog pack was far enough away for the sound to be muffled by the earth, but two of them heard something and looked across the river. They saw the log, though not the mouth of the set, but while the others discussed what to do next, they splashed across the water and climbed the slope. Palla's blood froze. She could hear the sound of the dogs' footfalls just above them, through the thick earth, coming nearer and nearer to the entrance.

They would have discovered it, too, if one of the other dogs hadn't called out to them from across the river.

"What have you got, Vlag?"

"I don't know, boss," answered the larger of the two. "There's something here all right. Smells like badger."

Beneath them the cubs looked up, for they were amazed that they could understand most of what the dogs were saying. Palla readied with her claws as Fell and Larka squeezed closer to her warm belly. If they had been able to they would have climbed back inside.

"You don't want to waste your time on stringy badger meat," said the dog across the river. "Not with delicious wolf cubs about."

Larka and Fell shuddered.

"He's right, you know," agreed the dog next to Vlag. "It's wolves we're after. That's the scent the humans gave us in the kennel. They say there's a pack around here again."

"I don't know why they keep coming down from the mountains," said Vlag. "You'd have thought they would want to stay well clear of our masters. And with so many trees up there to hide among too."

"Hmmm," snorted the other dog, "I know. Perhaps the winter forced them down for game. But whatever they're here for, wolves are our quarry now."

"I suppose so," muttered Vlag irritably. "But sometimes I wish the humans would just let us hunt what we want. Always chasing after wolves."

"I heard there's a reason behind it this time, Vlag."

In the set below, Palla's ears came straight up.

"What do you mean?"

"Don't you know? One of their own pups has been taken. A human child. Stolen by a wolf, from the village below the castle."

Palla's eyes opened in astonishment, and it was all she could do to stop howling herself as she listened to the dog's strange tale. A wolf steal a human. Would even the bravest of the Putnar dare to do such a thing?

"Taken a human?" growled Vlag, almost as startled as Palla shuddering below him. "But why, there's plenty of game around here?"

"That's the odd thing. And there was no blood. For several suns that loner, the old female, was snooping around the village."

Morgra, thought Palla nervously.

"Then this happens and now the humans want their revenge. They're fond of revenge."

"Then we should give it to them," cried Vlag.

He dropped his head again and was about to nose in the direction of the set when a mink that had her den nearby shot past him, straight across the river and almost through the legs of the pack hounds. The dogs saw her and, completely forgetting about their intended prey, bounded after her, barking and snapping, eager to make up for their lost quarry.

Palla's mind was on fire, and she couldn't stop shaking as she thought of what she had just heard. Whatever it all meant, now that the humans were roused, her cubs and her pack were in greater danger than ever. She was desperate to tell Huttser the news, but it would be a long while before it was safe to venture outside. As the sounds of the dogs disappeared into the night, Palla looked tenderly at her little ones, trembling helplessly beside her, then laid her head down on the damp earth. They were all exhausted, and it wasn't long before sleep had folded them in her gentle paws.

Palla woke suddenly. Light was filtering into the badger's set, but it wasn't the morning that had roused her. Again something was moving about above their heads. Palla heard a scratching and she thought that the dogs had returned. Again her claws opened, and she readied to attack as a huge muzzle appeared in the tunnel mouth.

"Huttser," cried Palla delightedly.

Huttser was standing proudly in the sunshine. Bran, Khaz, and Kipcha were with him, but Palla gasped as she saw them. Huttser's right flank was covered in blood, and Bran was shaking badly. Kipcha's face was terribly scratched, and Khaz had a deep gouge on his back.

"We had a scrape with our friends," growled Huttser. "And it was lucky for us these two turned up when they did. Though you didn't fight badly, did you, Bran? I tell you, even a Sikla can fight when his back is really up against it."

Bran wagged his tail proudly.

Huttser's eyes suddenly glittered, too, as he caught sight of Brassa, limping toward them along the riverbank. The whole pack was safe. There was a yapping and growling behind Palla now and the wolf pups popped up the riverbank. As soon as they saw their father, they bounded forward in the grass.

"Children," cried Huttser as the cubs jumped at his legs, barking and biting at his fur, "I bet I look worse than Morgra."

Palla growled as soon as Huttser mentioned her sister. "Huttser," she whispered, "there's news."

The pack was exhausted and dazed by their battle, but Palla's tale made them all gasp. Khaz snarled and Kipcha began to tremble. Brassa's ears came up too. But it was Bran who was most affected by what he heard.

"Palla, Huttser, don't you realize? It's the legend," he said.

Huttser and Palla swung around to face the Sikla. He suddenly looked very nervous and turned to Kipcha for support. Brassa was shaking her head.

"Legend?" whispered Palla.

Huttser began to growl angrily as Kipcha told Palla what she had heard of a wolf with the Sight stealing a human.

"Brassa," Palla said suddenly. "You know more of this than you are saying, don't you? Why don't you tell us what's going on?"

The nurse was pawing at the grass. "I heard a rumor about it once, Palla." She shrugged. "The legend of the Man Varg."

"Man Varg," gasped Palla.

"But it's rubbish. Just a bit of foolish nonsense," said Brassa.

"Foolish nonsense?" growled Palla angrily. "But a wolf has stolen a human child, Brassa. That is not nonsense. What is this legend?"

"Tsinga told me about it once," muttered the nurse reluctantly. There was something strange in Brassa's voice.

"Tsinga?"

"You were probably too young to remember Tsinga, Palla," said Brassa almost hopefully. "The old fortune-teller who lives in the valley beyond the rapids?"

But Palla did remember, if only faintly. As cubs, they had known the valley as the Vale of Shadows, and although she had never actually been there, the place was surrounded with stories that had always made the children shiver excitedly in the den.

Her father had told her once, only half jokingly, that it was guarded by a huge wolf with two heads and a furious river that let nothing cross, and whose hungry waters were formed from the saliva of a thousand feeding packs. Palla had met Tsinga once as a cub when the fortune-teller had come to visit the pack. She had scared Palla and her brother, Skop, half to death. Tsinga had strange ways and some thought her quite mad, but others believed that she could see the future.

"Go on, Brassa," said Palla coldly.

"Tsinga's kind, the fortune-tellers, they have always guarded the beliefs of the Sight and its secrets. They have limited power themselves, gained through training, but they know as much as any wolf about the Sight. They were keen to keep the secrets to themselves and really shared them only with one another. Yet long ago, one of the fortune-tellers gave the wolves a legend, in a verse. It tells of the coming of a Man Varg, as Kipcha says."

"What does it say?"

"I have never heard the ancient verse, Palla," growled Brassa, dropping her eyes. "But I believe it tells of a time when a wolf with the Sight will steal a human child. That together they will use the true power of the Sight—the power to touch minds—to bring forth a final power."

"Final power? What final power?"

"I don't know, Palla," snapped Brassa. "I told you. I've never even heard the verse."

Palla was glaring at Brassa. "What else?"

Again Brassa hesitated. "I do know the legend has something to do with Wolfbane's return, too," she answered reluctantly, "and with Wolfbane's winter."

"Morgra," shuddered Bran, thinking of her strange blessing to them.

They all knew the story of Wolfbane's winter. It was

said that if the Evil One ever returned he would bring a terrible winter with him that would shroud the whole earth.

"Then Wolfbane is the Man Varg?" asked Bran, confused.

"No. But the verse says their coming shall coincide. Because in the stories Wolfbane, too, had the Sight. It was once his proudest power."

"Is this child the Man Varg then?" growled Bran.

"I believe it is a wolf that shall become the Man Varg," answered Brassa, "with the help of a human child."

"So that's the work Morgra talked of," whispered Khaz disgustedly. "Stealing humans. Whatever else that cub killer's done, she's broken the oldest law."

"Then Morgra is trying to fulfill this legend," growled Palla. "That's why she took the child."

"Stop this nonsense," cried Huttser. "How do you know it has anything to do with a legend? With Morgra's tastes, more likely than not she's eaten it."

"They said there was no blood," Palla replied. "Perhaps it has something to do with us, Huttser. Perhaps that's why she wanted—"

"Stop it," snarled Huttser. "If Morgra wants to fool with legends let her. At least it should take her mind off joining the pack. And one thing's for sure, it's made up *my* mind. I'll drive her away myself if she comes back. Balkar or no Balkar."

"But now the humans will want our blood even more, Huttser," growled Khaz. "We should get far away from this place." Khaz's tone was grave, but his bold eyes were gleaming too. As the pack stared at their friend, they knew that he liked a challenge and would give everything he could to defend them.

"We can't, Khaz," said Palla. "The children are still too small to travel any real distance. We must lie low until the danger passes. We can't go back to the cave now the dogs have found it, but at least there's one boon. If we find a safe enough den, Morgra won't be able to find us either."

"Very well, Palla," said Huttser. "We'll take them into the mountains and then look for another den, until it's time to find them a Meeting Place, some proper spot in the sunshine for them to play and prepare themselves for their first hunt."

The children had been fascinated with the news of a theft of a human child, but talk of their first hunt was far more exciting to the cubs. Fell suddenly lifted his head and let out a howl, and for a moment Huttser and the wolf pack grinned. But suddenly Palla lifted her head too.

"What is it, Palla?" asked Huttser, seeing the look in her eyes.

"Can't you hear it?"

Huttser could hear nothing, but it wasn't long before he caught the scent. Fell and Larka both started to sniff the air too. In that moment the stillness was woken again with a call. Palla's tail rose, though not fully, for she had recognized the note.

"I think it's my brother, Skop."

The pack didn't have to wait long to find out. Soon a male wolf came padding up the riverbank. Larka and Fell wagged their tails excitedly as they spotted a wolf cub trailing wearily through the grass behind him.

"Skop," cried Palla delightedly, for his surprise appearance had lifted the specter of the dogs and of this strange legend too. "I thought it was you! It's good to see you again."

Skop was no bigger than his sister, and he had the same strong, intelligent face. The little wolf with him was very handsome, with the beginnings of a true Dragga's muzzle, though he looked rather nervous as he peered about.

"Thank Fenris I've found you, Palla," growled Skop. "I've been hunting for suns and suns. I tried the old den, when I finally remembered where it was. But you'd gone."

"Humans have been hunting," growled Palla, "but where are you going, brother?"

"Northeast," answered Skop gravely. "There's a rebel pack there, Palla, hiding out near the mountains. They're preparing to fight Morgra."

"Fight Morgra," said Palla with surprise, and Khaz strained forward. The whole pack was listening intently now.

"They're led by a bold Drappa named Slavka. She has called for the free Varg to join a Greater Pack. To fight Morgra and the Balkar."

"A Greater Pack?" growled Huttser.

"What are rebels?" Fell piped up suddenly.

Skop smiled down at the black cub. Skop was a brave wolf, and though not a Dragga himself, like Khaz he was a natural fighter.

"Rebels are wolves that live in the hills," he said cheerfully, "and fight for freedom and howl songs to the moon all summer long. For centuries there have been rebels in the land beyond the forest. Fighting power and opposing the will of the First Wolf."

Khaz was nodding happily, but now Huttser began to shake his tail disapprovingly.

"A Greater Pack, Skop?" he snorted. "But I thought such ideas had died out long ago. And now the rebels have picked it up too."

"These are strange times, Huttser. The rumors around our half sister grow with each sun. Perhaps Slavka is right to call on us all to join her."

"But what should wolves have to do with a Greater Pack?" growled Huttser. "Our pack's size should be determined by our territories alone, and by the ties of family and blood. Freedom lies in the bonds of the pack, and the only true freedom runs with the Varg. That is the untameable spirit of the wolf. That is our birthright."

The pack felt a thrill as Huttser used words spoken to them since their very earliest days as cubs. Skop, too, knew that the life of a pack was a thing determined by nature alone. A wolf pack's size normally grew like its boundary, swelling or decreasing according to the amount of game. When game was scarce the territory would have to grow, and this naturally increased rivalries between neighboring packs and competition for food. Very often, rather than spreading into another's territory, wolf Draggas would drive out newer members of their own clans.

In this world of keen competition, some wolves had evolved the idea of a Greater Pack, where all the free wolves might come together as one and so competition would be carefully controlled. Even Tratto had begun to talk of such a thing. But, as Huttser's response had shown, it was an idea that was fiercely resisted, too, because it seemed so unnatural and because wolves are so attached to their family structures.

"But why do these rebels want to fight Morgra?" asked Palla. "What is happening?"

Skop's eyes suddenly grew grave, and they heard the grumble of early summer thunder in the heavens. It made the children's bellies quiver and, as the pack looked up, they saw that above the castle, storm clouds were ribbing the sky.

"Children," said Skop, nuzzling his young companion forward, "this is Kar. Why don't you take him over there and play for a while."

"I don't want to play," said Fell, dying to hear what Skop had to say. "It's silly."

"Oh no," growled Skop, looking down at him wisely. "There's nothing more serious than play."

"I won't!" snorted Fell.

Suddenly, Huttser leaped at Fell and grabbed him by the scruff of the neck. He meant it mostly in fun, but the cub was not ready for it and, as Fell found he couldn't escape, he felt a furious anger burning inside him and a pain that ran down his spine and made him feel sick. It was as though a shadow had just passed into him, a shadow of his father's power. Huttser let go and he was smiling blithely, completely ignorant of what he had just done. Fell glared up at him.

"Why don't you share that hunting call I showed you, Kar?" said Skop.

At this, Fell turned jealously to Kar. "He doesn't look like he'd know a hunting call," he said scornfully at the newcomer.

"Stones are raw, they blunt my claw," said Kar straightaway, "but words will never hurt me."

Larka liked the newcomer immediately. Kar liked Larka, too, for her eyes were twinkling mischievously at his response. The pup was about the same size as Larka and Fell, though his coat had the classic gray coloring of a wolf and he had a long, thoughtful muzzle like Huttser. He stood there, peering timidly between the two of them until Larka suddenly stepped up and touched his muzzle with her nose. The three of them trotted off to play.

It was only when Skop was sure the children were out of earshot that he swung around to address the pack again.

"Things grow dangerous, Palla. The Night Hunters are crossing heedlessly into pack territories now, breaking Tratto's Blessing wherever they go. They murdered Kar's parents."

"Poor little thing," gasped Kipcha.

"That's why I brought him here. I don't know what else to do with him."

"But why are they attacking?" asked Khaz.

"To spread hatred and fear among the free wolves. But they wanted the cub too. They took his brothers, and it was only because he was playing beyond our Meeting Place that I managed to get him away at all."

"What does she really want with them?" growled Huttser angrily. "It has nothing to do with a census, that's for sure."

Palla shuddered as she thought of how close her half sister had come to the den and her own cubs that night.

"The talk gets darker and darker," said Skop, lowering his voice even further, "of the old evils and of the cult of Wolfbane."

Bran looked up and they all thought of Morgra and this child. The legend had said that Wolfbane would return. Bran wished he knew what it all meant.

"What of it?" growled Huttser.

"Think about it, Huttser, is not the Evil One said to feed on cubs?"

The pack shuddered as they listened, and now they all turned to look at the children. The three of them were chatting happily together.

"Skop," said Palla suddenly, "Morgra is around here somewhere. She tried to join our pack."

Skop turned to his sister in amazement and his muzzle curled into a snarl.

"And now this human, too," said Kipcha. "This legend of the Man Varg."

"Hush, Kipcha," snapped Huttser immediately, but Skop's ears were quivering.

"I know about it already, Huttser," said Skop. "Word is spreading through the forests."

"If Morgra has taken a human child, maybe this legend has something to do with us," Palla said anxiously.

"But I don't think Morgra has stolen it," growled Skop immediately. "On my way here I heard a rumor that a dragga has taken the child."

The pack looked at each other in bewilderment, but

Huttser seemed pleased. "I would believe anything of Morgra," he growled. "But this sounds like wolves hunting, that's all."

Again came a rumble of thunder, but this time it was more muted, and as Palla's eyes turned to the castle, still visible above them, she saw the sky was clearing again. The storm had passed the valley by.

"Come," said Huttser suddenly as he saw the three cubs walking back toward them. "The dogs may return. Skop, you'll join us for a while, won't you?"

Skop nodded as he picked up Kar.

"But keep a sharp eye," growled Huttser. "Tonight is the full moon."

It was Kipcha who grabbed Fell in her jaws now, more carefully than Huttser had done, and Palla went to pick up Larka, but Khaz stepped forward.

"No, Palla. You're tired. Let me."

As Khaz approached the she-cub, she looked up at him gravely. "Khaz?" she asked softly. "Wolfbane and this Man Varg, are they really coming? Are they both coming to gobble us up?"

Khaz smiled and shook his head reassuringly. He was looking at Kipcha, and as he saw her holding Fell, he suddenly wondered why he had never told the beautiful she-wolf how much he cared for her.

"No, Larka. No one's going to gobble you up. And if anything tries they'll have to get through us first. For we will all give our lives to protect you. You are the future."

Next to Huttser, Khaz had the strongest jaws in the pack, but as he bent to pick up Larka, so carefully did his teeth grasp her fur that the cub hardly felt a thing.

But suddenly Skop stopped and put down Kar again. "I've just thought," he cried cheerfully, "it's something I remember hearing once, but it convinces me this legend can't have anything to do with your pack."

"Why not Skop?" asked Palla. She hardly realized that Skop was now trying to help Huttser reassure the others.

"What I heard about the legend, Palla—it can't begin here. Not in a place where we were safe and happy as cubs. They say that the legend could only happen in a place where some great crime or injustice had been committed."

The wolves trotted on, though Brassa kept looking back down the river. In her old eyes there was a terror stirring. And a secret too.

The pack had been traveling all day, but frightened of the humans and their hunting dogs, they had threaded slowly east through the forest, stopping often to rest, and now and then letting the cubs walk along on their own. But at last the wolves had left the cover of the trees and begun to double back.

Although he knew the best spot for a den and a Meeting Place was by the river, Huttser didn't want to take them anywhere near the cave until he was sure the dogs had gone, so they had taken a path toward the hills. Evening found the wolves and their cubs high in the mountains. A mist had come down as the night thickened, and they were padding along a winding mountain path that climbed above a ravine, almost parallel with the castle. The ravine plunged toward the river below, and as they walked they heard the distant growl of thunder in the heavens. The storm seemed to be circling, and as they thought of the legend and Morgra's threat to return, their pace quickened.

The river had swollen greatly in places as the snows in the high mountains melted, and it rumbled angrily far below. All around the wolf pack the air was sharp with rock and stone, and the full moon had risen. They all thought of Morgra as they looked into its sallow face, and in the distance storm clouds began to gather. As the storm began to swell above them, flashes of electricity rippled through the sky, forking and branching through the heavy air and suddenly illuminating the valley in hard blue light. The wolves' fur began to tingle with the energy pulsing about them.

The lightning suddenly lit up the castle ahead of them, and Bran shuddered as he thought of the stories of Wolfbane living up there among the weird stones. This legend of a Man Varg was already mingling in his mind with tales of Wolfbane, and as he remembered Morgra's blessing to them, he felt a sickening churning in his stomach.

Around them, jagged cliffs and craggy promontories butted from the mountain, among a welter of stranded trees and clinging scrub. In the night the plants began to take on strange and mysterious shapes. Here would suddenly seem to be the shape of a wolf or a lynx, there the form of a bird in flight.

The wolves knew this country well. These were the Carpathian foothills, an impression of the giant ravines and thunderous, pine-strewn gorges that rucked through Transylvania, growing into towering precipices as the Carpathians curled like a sleeping dragon across the country's wide, flat plains. Normally the pack would have felt safe here, but they grew more and more nervous as the night and the mist and the coming storm fed their imaginations.

Huttser was leading them in single file, and the air had grown strangely still as the mist furled about them. On the wolf pack went, with Huttser peering into the gloom ahead. Then the lightning flashed again and there, on a ledge above him, stood Morgra.

She was holding a bleeding rabbit in her mouth. The moon was behind the old she-wolf, breaking through the thickening clouds. In the half-light her fur seemed to ripple and shimmer as the mist clung like smoke around her head. She looked larger than when he had first met her, and her eyes glittered savagely.

"Morgra," snarled Huttser.

Kipcha put Fell down in the mud, nudging the cub behind her toward Khaz. Fell blinked up in horror at the strange apparition as Khaz dropped Larka and stood towering over the children. Skop was trailing behind and as he put Kar down, the young wolf tried to crawl under his legs. Fell and Larka were standing side by side now, and in the sky the storm was above them, yet beyond the edges of the cloud the night was still perfectly clear, glittering with starlight. It seemed for a moment that the heavens had been split in two.

The pack felt the first spatterings of rain on their muzzles and then, the thunder closing around them, the downpour began. Soon the wolves were drenched in the deluge.

"I have come again, Huttser, as I promised I would," cried Morgra, dropping the rabbit. "I always keep my word. Where are you going with the little ones?" Morgra's voice was full of cunning as it rang out above them, and Huttser gave a dangerous growl.

"Trying to hide them from me perhaps?" snorted Morgra, smiling at the threat. "It's impossible, Huttser. I wield the powers of the Sight."

"We are not trying to hide," lied Palla angrily, coming abreast of her mate. "The humans have been hunting and their dogs uncovered our den."

"Then let me help you against the humans and the many dangers that face a pack in the wild. For I know much of Man. We shall be allies, you and I, and as an honored member of your pack, your poor barren sister shall give you Wolfbane's protection and aid you to survive."

Huttser's eyes narrowed in disgust, but as he looked over to Palla, he could see that she was confused by her sister's presence again, and he turned back to Morgra.

"You would help us against Man?" he cried scornfully. "Yet you rouse his wrath by creeping through the night to steal a human cub. Where is it now, Morgra? Or are its little bones already whitening the earth to feed the crows?"

As soon as Huttser said it, Morgra's angry eyes fixed on Palla.

"What is he saying, sister?"

"You deny you are a cub killer," answered Palla coldly. "Are you also denying that you stole it? A human child?"

"A human child?" gasped Morgra. "When did this happen?"

There was something in the she-wolf's surprise, some ring of startled truth, that made Huttser wonder.

"Tsarr," whispered Morgra suddenly, lifting her head to the skies. "That old fool, Tsarr. But he found it sooner than I had imagined. The Marked One. It is the ancient verse. It is the legend of the Man Varg."

The rain was stinging Morgra's eyes, and the storm seemed to have reached a fever pitch as rolls of thunder crashed against the clouds. Morgra broke from her thoughts.

"Well, then," she whispered coldly, the rain whipping off her muzzle, "you have more need of me than you think, for dark forces are at work, Palla. Forces none of you can understand."

"We don't need your aid, Morgra," cried Huttser. "We can deal with Man on our own. We just ask you to leave the pack in peace."

"Peace? And when Wolfbane comes again, Huttser, when the Evil One returns to summon the dead?"

Bran shivered behind the Dragga and Drappa.

"What is she talking about?" growled Palla.

"These are stories to frighten cubs," snarled Huttser. "And my cubs have been frightened enough."

"Mamma," whispered Larka suddenly, shivering next to Fell, "tell her to go away, Mamma."

"Hush, Larka."

Larka's sudden terror had a startling effect on Morgra as she saw the cubs standing side by side in the moonlight.

"Let me touch them," she hissed. "Let me smell them. I come to protect the cubs. To help them grow. Come here, children. Come to a mother worthy of the name."

Palla could bear it no longer. She sprang forward,

growling, her paws splashing through the mud and her muzzle raised for an attack.

"Get out of here, Morgra," she cried bitterly. "Haven't you done enough harm? You can never be a member of our pack. Fooling with legends! Spreading rumors and superstition. Go back to the Balkar and your secrets and your lies. Go back and leave my family in peace, or I shall kill you myself."

Morgra drew back a little, but there was no fear in her eyes, only the steely glint of hate. But those eyes began to flicker too.

"Your family?" she hissed, and Huttser fancied he heard a note of genuine fear in Morgra's voice. "And only a family . . ."

Suddenly, there was a crash in the heavens and a bolt of living electricity forked past the wolves. It struck a tree above Morgra and the darkness blazed with fire. The whole pack shrunk back, and Larka and Fell looked up in astonishment at the burning branches.

"So be it," cried Morgra, smiling delightedly, the shadows from the burning tree dancing around her scarred muzzle. "You have chosen your own destiny, Palla. And since you cannot forget the past, then let it return to haunt you—as Wolfbane always returns, the friend of the dead. For you shall truly learn of the past, Palla, when the Searchers are summoned. When Wolfbane's army of the dead come. For they are waiting, Palla, in the cave of the dark, now and always. They are with us here. They wait in dreams and in nightmares, watching and judging. They prowl angrily through the shadows, at the gates of death, waiting to pounce on the living."

The pack thought Morgra had lost her wits, but they were too terrified to do anything but stand gawking at her in the pouring rain. The flames on the tree were dying again, fizzling into silence.

"You talk of bones whitening to feed the crows. Then let them be your bones, scavenged by the creatures of the air. When Wolfbane comes and when the final power is unleashed."

Suddenly there was a flapping of black wings above Morgra's head.

"And let this be my real birthing gift to you, Palla. For I curse your family and your pack."

"Huttser," whispered Brassa, stepping forward now, "for Tor's sake stop her."

"By Wolfbane I curse you. By the power of the Sight, the power that has cursed me all my life, your little ones shall grow, and as they do, you shall all suffer. One by one your pack will be broken, until you are ready to give me the cubs. And if you do not, they too shall reap your fate."

"Stop her!" cried Brassa again.

Before they could do anything, Morgra threw her head up and let out a howl that seemed to rock the ravine. Then, in a voice full of malevolence, she cried, "May the past that's dark with crimes, bring revenge in future times!"

The words sent a strange shudder through the old nurse.

"The Sight," Brassa snarled as though she had been bitten, turning her face to the clouded moon and the drenching heavens.

"Morgra," whispered Palla. "Please, Morgra."

Huttser and Palla started to move forward. The pack came, too, and as she spoke, Morgra began to back away. She was set at a slight angle to the path and now her hind legs were getting closer and closer to the drop. Her eyes took on a glassy, faraway look, as though she were no longer addressing the pack, but talking to the whole world. The others were horrified as they watched. Horrified and entranced. She paused for a moment and then, as she looked at the wolves coming toward her, the light of triumph woke in her eyes and she cried out again.

"Fear and guilt—here begun, let them break you, one by one."

Morgra gave a violent snarl and the words "one by one" turned into a howl that shook through her whole body. Then suddenly she turned. Before they could follow her, Morgra had vanished into the dark. The pack stood trembling and shivering in the deluge, the cubs curling around themselves in terror, and Morgra's curse seemed to hover above them, broken only by the distant screech of a raven as it circled into the deepening night.

3

HUNTERS

The courtyard of a vast, ruined castle, from whose tall, black windows came no ray of light, and whose broken battlements showed a jagged line against the sky.
—BRAM STOKER, *Dracula*

IT WAS SUMMER PROPER and so hot that even the trees seemed to sweat. The river shrugged through the valley below the strange castle, alive with gnats and gadflies, wheeling and flitting over the lazy waters. The only sound to disturb its course, the sudden plash-plop of a fish as it burst from the gloomy depths to take a bite and disappeared again into the murk. It was as though the river itself contained some strange secret as it wound through the valley. A secret held in its waters and the creatures that lived within it, in the earth banks that formed its course, and among the wolf pack that now lived on its edge.

Huttser had found the cubs a Meeting Place, near an abandoned fox den in a mound of raised earth by the river, shielded by a small copse of poplar trees. Here they had begun to learn their first real lessons about adult life, scouting after ants and beetles and going on mock hunts. They were even nearer to the castle than before and on the same side of the river. For a long while the cubs had not been allowed to wander farther than a hollow log near the riverbank, though, and they were all thoroughly bored with the place.

Kar was lying by the river, and Fell and Larka were asleep together not far off. While Kar looked like a normal gray wolf, Fell's coat was a pure black, in striking contrast with his sister's. Larka's coat had lightened and just a few streaks of black and gray muddied the white. All the children were now the size of large dogs.

The sun after Morgra had cursed the pack, Khaz had climbed high into the mountains and spied a wolf traveling north again. He was certain it was Morgra, for he had watched the raven flapping after her. Since then, they had seen no more of the old she-wolf. Khaz had not noticed the raven suddenly wheel around in the air and head south once more. The news that the First Wolf had left their hunting territory had done something to settle Huttser, and he had told the pack time and again that they had nothing to fear from her words. Indeed, he had forbidden them to discuss the curse at all.

But this legend of the Sight, of a Man Varg and some final power frightened the others, especially Brassa, and for a while a sense of foreboding hovered like a vulture over the pack. The nights would bring thoughts of Wolfbane and of Morgra's terrible threats, like unseen specters padding from the trees. And Palla could still not understand why, if Morgra had come to the Stone Den in search of human prey and some strange legend, she had asked to join their pack at all.

The Drappa had begun to think that this legend had something to do with them, and that it was the reason Morgra had wanted to get to her cubs. Palla could not figure it out, but she remembered what Brassa had said of the powers of the Sight reemerging in more than one, and she kept arguing with Huttser as she watched the children carefully. As the days drifted on and the cubs grew, Palla noticed nothing odd about either of them, though, and gradually her fears began to abate.

As for the rest of the pack, with the exception of Brassa, the summer itself had largely dispelled the sense of ill omen. The wolves had seen little more of Man and there was no sign of the Balkar at all. Huttser had begun to mark the pack territory, too, with Khaz, Skop, and Bran, leaving their skats and scent wherever they could to warn off other wolves. This had helped to reassure the Dragga.

From the mountains the male wolves had looked out across Transylvania onto the wide flat plains to the south, which stretched from the great rock chasms of the Iron Gates as far as the Danube delta and, climbing higher and higher, even to the great Transylvanian Heath. There in the far distance they saw walled Saxon towns and Magyar strongholds, strange onion domes that glinted like the sun and pretty Vlach villages strewn like flowers across the plains.

Skop would often look out longingly as they did so. He had plans to move northeast again in search of Slavka and the rebels, and the wolf loved nothing more than ranging free through the wild, but for the moment he had decided to rest with his sister's pack. He could see that a normal family routine was doing Kar a great deal of good. Skop had found it hard to look after the youngster on his own and he still didn't know what he would do about him when he set out. Palla was very tender with Kar, for in some way she felt that he was a replacement for her unnamed pups, but Huttser, with his worries for his pack, was less tolerant of the young wolf. Kar was not his own bloodline and the Dragga would often growl or snap at him despite himself.

What Larka had heard of Kar's parents made her feel very sorry for him and she was particularly attentive, especially since he seemed so frightened by the curse and the legend. Though his features had the strength of a Dragga, Kar was often timid and submissive; what had happened to his parents had clearly affected him deeply. Larka and he had become firm friends, though, and Larka would often sit with him in the long grass and ask him all about his home. Thankfully, Kar had been too young when the Balkar attacked to remember much about what had happened, but it comforted him somehow to talk of the past and of his brothers, Cal and Grell. Larka was always complimenting Kar, too, which made Fell furious because Kar was always making mistakes in the lessons at the Meeting Place and was much less capable than Fell. Fell thought him a bit of a coward, and he often teased him, but whenever he did Larka would step in to defend the timid pup.

Now a noise woke Kar from his nap by the river. Next to Fell, Larka was struggling desperately in the grass. Her paws were fighting with the air and she kept whining and scratching at her own forehead as a dream shook through her body. Though her eyes were still closed, her muzzle was snapping and biting at some imaginary opponent.

Ever since the terrible night Morgra had cursed them, Larka had begun to have nightmares.

"Larka," said Fell, opening his eyes, too, and nudging his sister roughly with his muzzle. "Wake up, Larka."

The she-wolf blinked nervously. She seemed to calm down as she saw the river and began to remember where she was.

"You were dreaming, Larka," said Fell more kindly.

"It was horrid, Fell," Larka said, lifting her pretty white muzzle. "I dreamed that the whole pack had gone and that only you and I were left. But the curse was following us and Wolfbane was coming to kill us. Though the Evil One came in the shape of a human, he had huge wings, too, like a giant bat, and he lived in the Stone Den just like Bran said, surrounded by human cubs that he feasted on every night."

"It was only a dream, Larka," said Fell cheerfully, wagging his tail and getting up. "Come on, Kar. Let's play a game."

"What game, Fell?"

"A game of stares," said the black wolf, taunting. "We have to stare at each other for as long as possible and the one who turns away first loses."

Kar didn't like the sound of it much, but as Fell peered at him, he tried to stare back. In no time at all Kar had looked away and Fell snorted scornfully, "Well, really, what good are you?"

"Fell," said Larka, still thinking of her horrible dream, "you don't think this legend will come true, do you? And you don't think the Sight really brings the power to curse?"

Kar shivered.

"No, Larka," growled Fell. "The Sight is just a stupid lie. And the human child has probably been eaten. I wonder what they taste like, though," he added mischievously.

"But Mother says there are more things in the world than even a wolf can understand, Fell," said Larka. "I heard Brassa saying one sun that perhaps to leave the old pack boundaries was a way to break a curse."

"She-wolves are superstitious, that's all," snorted Fell, "and Father hates it when Mother talks like that. He says that we must believe only in the truth and what we can see with our eyes or taste with our teeth. He snarled at her again last sun."

Larka's eyes grew strangely sullen. Though they had tried to keep it quiet from the cubs, Huttser and Palla were often arguing. Larka winced when she thought of their angry voices in the night, for Larka hated nothing in the world more than when her parents quarreled.

"We are Putnar," said Fell proudly, seeing his sister's distress. "The forest fears us and we shouldn't be afraid of anything. Not legends or stupid curses. They're just as silly as Brassa's story of the golden deer pelt."

"Which golden pelt?" asked Kar, wagging his tail.

"The one that Tor and Fenris put in the forest. They told Fren that it was the source of knowledge and freedom, but if he ever tried to steal it they would strike him stone dead. I mean, why put such a thing in the world and then not expect a wolf as clever as Fren to be tempted by it? It's crazy."

"Maybe they did expect him to be tempted by it," said Kar.

"What do you mean?" growled Fell.

"Free will." Kar shrugged.

"What on earth are you talking about?"

"Skop says that Tor and Fenris put Wolfbane in the world so that the Varg would have a choice between good and evil and so have free will."

"Oh, shut up, Kar," said Fell.

"That's also why Tor sent Sita down among the wolves."

"Sita," whispered Larka. She liked the name, and she had long wanted to hear the story from Brassa.

"You mean you haven't been told the story of Sita yet," said Kar with a mixture of surprise and disapproval.

"No, Kar. Tell us."

"It was when Tor and Fenris had quarreled again, and Fenris was so angry that he had made the wolves fight bitterly among themselves. So bitterly that it seemed there could never be peace. Tor's heart grew sick and, at last, she sent down her own daughter, Sita, to stop them. The daughter she loved above all else, for Sita was gentle and kind."

"But how did Sita stop them?" asked Larka.

Kar paused. "First she went through the world healing the Varg and telling them stories and spending her time even among the lowliest of the Siklas. She told them, too, that they mustn't be afraid and that there was no death but only joy and that love was the greatest courage. She said that they should send her their children, for she knew that children can really see the truth and she loved children above all things."

Again Kar paused. "But that wasn't really why Sita had come among the Varg."

"Why, then?" asked Fell.

"Tor, knowing that Fenris was vengeful and had demanded tribute from the wolves to appease his wrath, let the Varg mock Sita, and spit at her. She let a friend betray her, and the Varg finally killed her."

Larka opened her eyes in horror.

"You don't mean that Tor sacrificed her own daughter?" growled Larka.

"Yes," whispered Kar, "because she loved all the wolves and she wanted them to see what a terrible thing they had done. The most terrible thing they could ever do."

"But Tor created the wolves," growled Larka. "She didn't have to do that. She could have just stopped them fighting."

Kar shook his head. "No, Larka, as I said, in the stories when the Varg were created they were allowed the greatest gift of all, freedom and the free will to do as they would. But the story doesn't end there."

"It doesn't?"

"No. After three moons Sita was brought back."

"What?" said Larka with surprise, though it made her feel strange. "Brought back from the dead?"

"Yes," answered Kar, but then he paused, "well, not exactly. You see there was no death, as Sita had said, and Sita was the daughter of a god."

The young wolves looked at one another.

"Besides, Larka," continued Kar, "Tor didn't make the world."

"She didn't?" said Larka with surprise.

"No, Larka," said Kar. "Tor and Fenris made the world."

Larka had felt a strange sense of wonder creeping

through her at this story, but Fell suddenly noticed that they had come to the edge of the Meeting Place. Some way ahead of them the river bent around toward the castle, and Fell could spy speckled trout leaping from its waters. He looked around. His parents were nowhere to be seen, and the others were lying snoozing beneath the poplar trees.

"Come on," said Fell, "let's go fishing."

Kar turned to Larka nervously.

"But, Fell," said Larka, "you know we're supposed to stay at the Meeting Place. They said we should be in sight at all times."

Larka was rather more responsible than her brother and besides, the dream had not put her in the mood for adventures.

"Don't wander off," snorted Fell. "Don't do this. Don't do that. Don't do anything at all. That's all I ever hear, Larka. This is our perfect chance, and Khaz is always going on about testing ourselves. Besides, Kar says we've got free will."

"But, Fell," whispered Kar, looking up at the castle, "remember Morgra's curse. And Kipcha saw the humans hunting again the other sun."

"So what?" Fell shrugged. "I'd like to watch them. They sound a lot more interesting than the silly Lera. But we're only going a little way off, anyway. Besides, Larka," added Fell temptingly, "haven't you ever felt the urge to disobey, just for the sake of it?"

Larka *was* suddenly tempted to disobey her parents, and she certainly didn't want to let Fell wander off alone. She had felt protective of him ever since the dogs had come, and in truth she was just as inquisitive as her brother.

"Come on."

As Fell made for the bend in the river, she and Kar followed along behind him. Soon the cubs were trotting along, sniffing everywhere and enjoying their taste of freedom. In no time at all Larka's head was bursting with questions about everything around her. The river glittered brilliantly and the trees on its edge were alive with birdsong. Everywhere fluttering shapes sported in the leaves and dragonflies flashed sparks of color through the blue. Kar was delighted, and Fell's head was soon so full of dreams and adventures that he felt he was floating through the air.

They reached the bend in the river at last, and Fell stopped to lap at the water, tasting reeds and fresh bracken on its delicious current. The trout had moved on farther downstream, but as Fell drank he suddenly blinked with surprise.

Fell had often seen his own face in the water, but now he was startled. The stories he had told himself as they walked along, full of his own heroic deeds, had gone and there he was in the river, almost a stranger. No, surely not a stranger, but Fell, a young wolf, something real and solid, far more solid than all the fantasies and dreams that swirled around in his head. It was an oddly uncomfortable feeling and he suddenly wanted to know what he was. More than that, where he, Fell, really was. Whether he lay in the dreams that seemed to float above his head or there, in that furry face.

For a moment things went out of focus and then came back again, and as they did so, he recalled something Bran had told him of the Sight and the power it brought to look into water and see things of far-off realities, of past, present, and future. Often in the safety of the den, the three pups had discussed the strange powers of the Sight. Kar didn't like the idea of seeing through the eyes of birds at all, and Larka mused what it meant to look into another's mind. And now Fell suddenly thought what a very fine thing it would be to know the future. To know his own future.

Fell heard a noise above him as he looked into the water. It was the drone of a bee and it grew louder and louder as the wolf stood there. The sound had an insistent, mesmeric quality, and Fell suddenly recalled a honeycomb Brassa had shown him one sun near the riverbank. As Fell listened he wondered what it would be like to crawl across those little transparent cells where the bees' grubs had lain, writhing and squirming and changing as they fed, and as the sound grew in the air, Fell had the most extraordinary feeling. He fancied that in the ceaseless humming a word was trying to form, and to him it sounded just like Larka's favorite word, "Why?"

"Fell," cried Larka suddenly, and Fell shook off the feeling, "remember that Brassa told us to be careful of the river. A wolf fears nothing more than death by water."

"Rubbish," growled Fell irritably.

But the river's spell was broken. The cubs wandered on and soon their excitement and the glory of the day quite overtook them. Larka began to nip gently at Kar's fur and Fell bounded up to join them. Kar started a game of tag. Soon the three young cubs were rolling around and around in the grass together, laughing and thinking of nothing but the feel of the rich earth, the warmth of the sunlight, the sounds and smells of the river, and the sheer joy and companionship of playing free at one anothers' side.

At one point Kar fancied he heard a sound and they all got up, lifting their fluffy tails and standing shoulder to shoulder. Despite Fell's sense of rivalry toward Kar, they all knew in that instant that they would fight together if anything came to harm them and that, in that moment of growth, they were all on the same journey: to learn and experience and understand. But not before they had done a lot of playing.

Fell suggested a game of hide-and-seek, and then Larka showed Kar how she had learned to dig in the soil. Kar watched her happily until he grew distracted by a frog that was making for the riverbank. He upturned it with his snout and he, Larka, and Fell were all peering down at it with fascination when they suddenly heard an angry voice behind them.

"Fell, you ought to be ashamed of yourself."

The children swung around immediately to see Huttser and Palla hurrying toward them. They were both plainly furious and Huttser, who had called out, glared at Fell.

"What in Fenris's name do you think you are doing? How dare you disobey your mother and me!"

"I'm sorry, Father," spluttered Fell, "I . . ."

As Huttser noticed the faint grin that was flickering around his son's muzzle, he snapped at him.

"Fell, don't ever tell someone you're sorry if you don't mean it."

"But, Father . . ."

"Anything could have happened. What if Larka had got lost?"

Kar was rather hurt by the fact that Huttser hadn't mentioned him and seemed only concerned for his daughter's safety.

Fell dropped his head submissively, but Huttser was right, he didn't really feel sorry or ashamed. He suddenly thought it was very unjust, too, that Huttser was scolding him alone and not Larka or Kar. He wanted to say something really clever to Huttser. Many times after Huttser had punished him for being naughty, Fell had thought up angry answers to his admonitions. Answers like, "Well, I never asked to be a part of the pack," or "You wouldn't say that if I was dead." But now he just mumbled something sulkily, something he had heard Palla saying one day about Morgra.

"What did you say?" growled his father.

"Am I my sister's keeper?" Fell shrugged.

Huttser glared down at the black wolf, but Palla stepped in now. "Don't be too hard on him, Huttser," she said softly. "Nothing's happened. And besides, they'd have left the Meeting Place soon enough anyway, with our little surprise."

Kar and Larka looked up excitedly. Huttser shook his head as he stared at Fell, but the anger was draining from him and he, too, had wanted to surprise the children.

"Very well, Palla," he said almost irritably, "you tell them."

"No, Huttser. It's your right. You're the Dragga."

"What is it, Father?" asked Larka.

"It's time, children," declared Huttser, lifting his red tail high behind him. "Fenris is ready to smile on your first hunt."

"Our first hunt!" cried Fell delightedly.

"May I come too?" asked Kar, and Fell snorted with disgust.

"Of course you can, Kar," whispered Palla.

Larka beamed at her friend and bumped Fell scoldingly with her snout. By the time they got back to the Meeting Place, the pack had already gathered around and were waiting eagerly for Huttser's lead, panting and wagging their tails furiously. Skop smiled as he saw Kar's excitement.

"Now, children," said Huttser, "stick together and keep in the background. If it's safe we'll draw you in at the end."

Huttser lifted his muzzle. As he opened his jaws, the hunting song that came thrilled the cubs. The wolf pack began to answer the call immediately, Khaz and Kipcha howling like banshees, Bran bounding up to join them. There was a new excitement in the air and a new responsibility. Only Brassa was still lying quietly in the grass.

"Huttser," she said suddenly. "I won't be coming with you."

"Is there anything wrong?" growled Palla with concern.

"No, no, my dear," answered the nurse, licking her paw. "My paw hurts, but you run along and don't worry about me. I'll be fine here. But I can do with some fresh meat. You'll get it for me, won't you Fell?"

Fell wondered why Brassa suddenly looked so old, but he wagged his tail happily, for he was deeply fond of the nurse. Larka felt a sudden pang of jealousy and she ran up to her mother, but Palla growled at her. Despite all her fears for the children, on their first hunt there would be no room for foolish sentiment. Now the cubs had to begin to learn their own way in the world.

Huttser and Palla led the pack away at a steady trot to the east along the river and away from the castle. As Brassa watched them go her eyes were fixed on both of Palla's cubs, and she seemed to be trying to make up her mind about something.

"Look after yourselves," she muttered gravely. "Please look after yourselves." Then Brassa lifted her head and called after them. "And strength to your paws."

Brassa didn't know it, but another pair of eyes was watching the young wolves from the shadow of the trees. Eyes as piercing as a knife and a fierce yellow black.

Huttser led them in a clear, straight line through the grass and immediately began to test the pace, making sure that the cubs could keep up, but still pushing their trot hard as they could. One day the young wolves' stamina would be their greatest ally; they might have to trail a kill for as many as seven or eight suns before eating.

A wild feeling of liberation gripped Fell as soon as they set out. His mouth started to water furiously, and his eyes had such an intense look that it was clear that he was already well beyond playing. Fell's excitement was almost unbearable and for some reason he suddenly thought of the Sight and wondered greedily at its final power.

But as the day went on, Fell's excitement began to dwindle, for the wolves had seen no Lera at all, and the children began to trail farther and farther behind their parents. They were running along the edge of a forest now. The young wolves instinctively felt at ease near the shadows. The sunlight cast sometimes beautiful, sometimes gloomy shapes through the firs onto the forest floor, but the pines were well spaced, and here and there as they looked toward the trees, the children could see clearings where the light glowed in shimmering golden brown pools. As they went, Larka noticed a bird sitting on a low branch above them. Although she didn't have a name for the creature, it was a lesser kestrel and it flicked its head back and forth now, for it held a little cockroach in its curving yellow beak.

"What's that called, Fell?" asked Larka.

Fell was already growing irritated that the pack still hadn't found any game. "Why ask me," he answered, looking at the bird a little resentfully, "and why are you always asking so many questions, Larka? If you were lost in a lovely woods would you really want to know the name of every tree or mushroom in it?"

Larka wondered about the question. She didn't take Fell's mood personally, and now she peered even more closely up at the creature. Its talons, too, were yellow as they gripped the bark, as were the rings around its black eyes. The bird's head was a blue gray and its wing feathers a beautiful orangey red, while its chest was specked with black. Larka thought how fine the bird looked, but as they padded past it she started in amazement. Larka thought she'd heard a voice behind her.

"Watch out," it seemed to say.

Larka swung around, but the kestrel had lifted into the air and was climbing higher and higher. Kar noticed the bird, too, as it soared above them.

"I don't know what its name is, Larka," he said as his

muzzle traced its course through the sky, "but it's flying Putnar all right."

"Flying Putnar?" said Larka with surprise. She had thought of it as a bird and little more.

"Yes," growled Kar, "as opposed to the flying scavengers. It's a hunter, Larka."

Fell was getting really bored and he suddenly wanted to tease both of them. "I know all about the flying scavengers," he growled, his eyes twinkling, "Wolfbane made a pact with them. Bran told me about it the other sun. Do you want to hear the story?"

"Yes," said Kar immediately.

Larka was not at all sure she wanted to hear a story of Wolfbane just now, but this was their first hunt and she felt too proud to show her brother the fact. "All right, then."

So Fell began as they padded along after the adults. "It was when Tor and Fenris had been betrayed once more," growled Fell, trying to remember Bran's exact words, "and Fenris sent Wolfbane down to take revenge on the Varg. But with time Fenris got tired of revenge and he longed to trust the Varg again. He had no more need of the Evil One or his darkness, so he ordered Wolfbane to return to the shadows. The Shape Changer had grown used to the world, though, and to the warming sunlight and the smell of new grass on the breeze. He was furious, and because he could do such things he transformed himself into a flying scavenger, a great hooded crow, and flew away to hide in a rowan tree in the famous valley of Kosov."

Bran had spoken of the valley being famous, and Fell said it now as though he himself had been there, even though he had no idea that the valley of Kosov was indeed a real place, banked by high mountains and far to the northeast of the castle. A terrible battle had once been fought there among the wolves, long, long ago, although its meaning was lost to time and wind and weather. Many wolves had died on the valley slopes on that ancient day. So many that the name of the place, commemorating the battle, had become legendary in wolf lore.

"For suns Wolfbane hid from Fenris in the valley," Fell went on gleefully, thoroughly enjoying the attention he was getting. "And the lesser birds like the crow and the raven, the scavengers of the air, came to help him. They fed him and fanned him with their wings and brought him news of the world beyond."

Larka felt a small thrill as Fell spoke of the world beyond.

"But at last, after Fenris had hunted among all the Lera, among the beetles and the fish, the snakes and the wild lynx, he learned that Wolfbane was disguised as a bird in the valley of Kosov and he came himself as a golden eagle to hunt him down."

Fell threw up his muzzle as he started to impersonate what he thought the god might sound like. " 'Wolfbane,' cried Fenris in a terrible voice, 'you have disobeyed my commandment, Wolfbane, and now you must pay for your disobedience.' "

Kar shivered a little as he thought of Huttser's anger at what had happened that same morning.

" 'But, Lord Fenris,' answered Wolfbane." Fell had put on a silly whining voice now. " 'I have come to love the world and the sunlight and the power I wield over the Varg.'"

Larka giggled.

"But at this," said Fell, "the god Fenris grew enraged with the Evil One, and quite understandably if you ask me, so he sent a great wind to blow Wolfbane out of his tree. Plop."

Fell gathered himself for the finale.

"'You dare to disobey me,' snarled Fenris furiously as he looked at the silly creature lying in the grass." Fell's eyes twinkled, for he was trying to imitate his father now. "'I made you, Wolfbane, and I made you as darkness. So you must stay in the shadows until I choose to summon you again. For it is my choice alone. And remember, Wolfbane, it is not you who have power over the Varg. For they are my children, and it is I who do with them as I please, for good or bad.'"

Kar and Larka were thoroughly caught up with the tale now, but Fell had paused portentously.

"Well, Fell," cried Larka, "what happened? What did the Evil One do?"

"Wolfbane knew that he must obey Fenris's command to return to the darkness," Fell said, "because Fenris was god. But before he went he made the flying scavengers a promise, because they had helped him. That one sun he would return and give them mastery over the birds of prey and over the Varg whom he now hated, and swell their craws with seas of blood, till the noise of their feeding woke even the dead."

"There," concluded Fell, thoroughly proud of the way

he had told the story. "What do you think of that?"

Larka gulped. She hadn't liked the story's ending at all. "Stop telling tales," she said, trying to sound grown-up. "Look, we're falling behind."

The cubs ran on and soon they had caught up with the rest of the wolf pack. On they went, and the sun grew in strength above them. It was a good hour before Huttser suddenly lifted his tail expectantly.

"At last," he growled.

Larka was rather startled, so soon after the tale of Wolfbane, for in the distance they saw a flock of birds wheeling and circling through the blue, flapping their black wings and diving suddenly through the empty air. The birds' hungry cawing echoed through the day.

"There must be carrion there," growled Huttser with pleasure as he watched them. "This time the birds bring us meat. They want us to open the prey."

The wolf pack bounded on and soon the wolves had reached an area of flat ground on the edge of the forest. An old water buffalo had broken its leg and perished that same morning. The flock of crows had settled plumply around it and were flapping about noisily, cawing and screeching or jumping suddenly to peck at the creature's lifeless eyes.

"Mother," whispered Larka as they approached, "do we ask their permission to feed?"

Palla almost laughed at her daughter.

"Ask a scavenger's permission to eat?" she snorted. "No, Larka, we are Putnar, we ask no one's permission."

As the wolf pack came down the slope, the greedy crows took to the air in a cloud of black feathers. They settled again around the wolves, watching and waiting eagerly for the Varg's teeth to open their find.

"A good lesson for survival, children," cried Huttser with pleasure. "When we can't find game, wolves must look to the flying Lera to aid us and scavenge a meal. Although we are Putnar, we must listen for their calls on the air, too, for as the pack works together, so all nature must aid itself."

One of the birds was set slightly apart from the rest and was watching the children intently. Its eyes were as beady and black as they had been that night it had spied the pack with Morgra. It was a raven.

"For this is the order of things," Huttser went on proudly, "as the Putnar must feed, the Dragga and Drappa must lead the pack. Come, Palla . . ."

Suddenly the reasoned look in Huttser's eyes, the ancient intelligence of the Putnar, vanished. He swung back to the buffalo with a snarl, opening his huge jaws like a cave, plunging his teeth into the still warm flesh.

The birds crowed and flapped about delightedly and the young wolves watched in amazement as Palla joined her mate. Larka had never seen such a fury in her parents before, even when they quarreled, and the sight suddenly terrified her.

Fell, too, remembered resentfully the pain he had felt when Huttser had grabbed him by the scruff of the neck that sun Skop had arrived. But as they watched, suddenly all three children began to grow angry themselves.

The blood lust was on their parents and the fur around their muzzles was already drenched with gore. Their eyes had grown almost sightless with the furious pleasure of the feast, and as the other wolves joined them, biting and snarling at one another as they found their place around the body in their natural pecking order, they all settled in to gorge themselves.

"Come, children," growled Palla at last as she saw them hanging back.

Fell leaped forward. A frenzy had woken in his eyes, and as he tugged at the meat and tasted the fresh blood, he was mastered by a wholly unfamiliar passion. That wild sense of freedom was mingled now with a strangely liberating anger. Kar joined him and Larka pushed in beside them, too, and started to tug at the buffalo. But as the crows flapped and cawed about them, Larka suddenly fancied that amid the noises she could understand words. The birds were talking.

"Tear it," one seemed to say, "crack its bones."

"Hunger," snapped another, "time to feast."

"All in good time," crowed a raven. "Let the Putnar gorge and the scavengers wait. For when Wolfbane returns and his promise is fulfilled, all nature shall rebel and then we shall feed on them too."

Larka's head was dizzy, and suddenly she grew hot all over. She turned her muzzle and noticed the raven watching her intently. Larka shivered, for she thought she had recognized it, and then something even more extraordinary happened.

For a moment Larka could no longer see and then, with a flash, she felt that she was in the air itself. Below her was the ravening pack, tugging at the sides of the dead buffalo, pulling away at the skin that contained its flesh, desperate to get to the meat and tendons and bone inside. As Larka looked down she gasped, for there was her own body lying still in the grass next to the carrion. Larka seemed to hover and dive over the bloody ritual and then, almost as suddenly as it had happened, she found herself stirring in the grass again, as the sounds of the pack came once more to her ears and the raven settled quietly nearby.

Huttser looked up. Fell was trying to push Kar out of the way, but Larka had vanished.

"Kar, where is Larka?"

"I don't know, sir," stammered Kar, looking around with surprise.

"Damn you," snarled Huttser, "are you a dragga or not?"

The pack had stopped feeding altogether.

"Something must have frightened her," growled Huttser. "She can't have gone that far. We'll follow her scent."

But as they began to nose for her, Palla grew frantic. The smell of the buffalo was so fresh in their nostrils and its blood so strong on their lips, they could not pick up any sign of Larka at all.

"Split up," cried Huttser.

Larka was in a torment. As soon as she reached the cover of the trees she had looked for somewhere to hide, anywhere where she could be alone to think as she tried to understand what had just happened. She found an abandoned hole by the bole of an old elm tree and scrabbled angrily at the soil, pulling her body inside, eased by the darkness and the warm earth. There she lay and tried to calm her breathing. The young wolf's eyes were still swimming and she felt a terrible throbbing in her head.

"What's wrong with me?" whispered Larka bitterly to

herself. "I was looking through that bird's eyes."

It was as if she had left her own wolf body and become one of the birds, flying above the feeding pack. Larka began to tremble violently.

"The Sight," she gasped. "The power to look through the eyes of birds."

As she said it, the air seemed to have been sucked from the den. The revelation so startled Larka that for a moment she mistook the beating of her own blood for the sound of an animal stalking her.

"Is this the curse then?" she murmured in terror. "Is this what Morgra threatened? Wolfbane made a pact with the birds and what those crows said . . ."

Larka suddenly heard voices approaching. Her mother was calling; Palla and Fell were walking right past the hole.

"Larka, where are you, Larka?"

Larka remembered the cold ferocity she had seen in her mother as she had begun to feed, and she felt so terrified that she pulled herself even farther into her hiding place. She was still trembling badly and now she began to shiver, too, as she heard her mother and her brother disappearing into the distance. It was getting dark when Larka pulled herself out of the hole. The forest was empty and perfectly quiet. The foliage glowed in the half-light, and the fading sun cast a web of darkening shadows through the branches like some kind of net of light.

"The Sight," she whispered again, looking about her fearfully.

Larka set off in the direction she fancied she had heard Palla going and she grew lonelier and lonelier as she went.

After a while she realized how desperately hungry she was too. Every now and then the she-wolf would stop and let out mournful howls, although no sound came to answer her. The shadows got deeper, and Larka kept looking up at the looming trees. She had the feeling that somebody or something was watching her.

"I'm a Varg," she kept saying, to reassure herself, "a wild wolf. The forest fears me and I've nothing to be scared of."

But even as she said it, Larka felt desperately scared. She might be a wolf, but what kind of wolf was she? Larka stopped. Sounds were drifting toward her through the trees. At first it was like the high-pitched scream of the she-wolf caught in some careless trap, but then it sank lower and rose again in a lilting, dancing cry. Larka was strangely drawn by the sound, and she suddenly caught a flickering, orange glow through the trees ahead.

Larka crept nearer and her ears were filled with a raucous noise she did not understand was laughter. She caught sight of a clearing. As Larka pushed her nose gingerly through the branches and saw them, she gasped.

"Man," she whispered. A terrible feeling gripped her stomach.

But the eye cannot resist a moving object and now Larka was caught. The group of humans was seated in a circle. One was holding an odd wooden object to his cheek as his arm drew a stick across it that produced the beautiful sounds drifting all around them. From the fur sprouting from his muzzle and his size, Larka guessed he must be the Dragga.

Another male was seated on a tree stump nearby, and in

front of him was crouched what Larka guessed from her soft features was the Drappa. She was holding one of the man's paws in her own and gazing intently at the palm, so intently that it seemed as though her very life depended on it. There was a fire in the center of the circle that sent out a lurid glow, which danced around their dark, leathery faces.

There was something cunning in those faces, hunted, too, for these were Roma, or Gypsies, and like the wolf they moved through the trees like shadows. Their kind had not that long since arrived in the land beyond the forest. They had drifted far from the south from a country called India, in search of freedom and land, and escaping from a system of power and belief that had made other men try to keep them forever the Sikla of their own world. But even here they had soon been persecuted and enslaved for their ways and beliefs.

In the woods and mountains some had found a taste of freedom. But they had also found fear and hate and mistrust. Because they kept apart and called any not of their own kind Gadje, they had crystallized the fear that surrounded them. They lived on the edges of society, and some had been forced to survive through crime and deceit or to earn their bread by trying to tell the future. Yet others had developed skills and adopted trades. Like the Argintari, the tinkers, and the Fierari, the blacksmiths. This little group of Gypsies called themselves Lautari, for they were musicians.

Larka's attention left the humans and was suddenly consumed by the firelight. She remembered the bolt of lightning that Morgra had dropped from the skies to burn the tree that stormy night. But this fire was different somehow. Surrounded by stones, it seemed almost contained by the circle of humans. Larka found it almost irresistible, for she could not feel its heat on her fur.

As the she-wolf gazed into it and saw the glowing red embers rippling along the wood like water, bursting here into flame, dying down again, she found her thoughts and her young memories following it, almost drawn into the dancing flames. Larka felt as if her own mind had suddenly entered a brilliant dream.

Palla, with Fell at her side, was searching desperately for her daughter on the other side of the forest when they, too, heard a sound. The ground dipped suddenly toward a deep hollow and there were two wolves standing in the clearing below them. They were strangers.

"Balkar?" whispered Palla immediately, backing behind a tree and grabbing hold of the skin around Fell's neck to pull him after her. The wolves were whispering, but the air was still and the sound came clear and true through the wood.

"I don't like it," one wolf was growling, "crossing into this pack's territory without even asking Tratto's Blessing. It's bad luck all right."

"Don't be a fool, Darm. Do you think the Balkar would ask permission?" said the other. "Besides, Slavka has given orders. Loyalty always."

Palla's ears twitched as she remembered what Skop had said about the leader of a rebel pack.

"I still don't like it, Gart, going so close to their horrid stones."

"This is where the human cub was taken from," said Gart sternly. "And it's our job to find it."

Palla's ears came up and Fell's nose quivered.

"Legends," snorted Darm in the hollow, "that's all I hear nowadays. Isn't it enough that Morgra has begun to worship the cult of Wolfbane again, without our believing in the legend of the Man Varg as well? Isn't it enough that she is trying to summon the Shape Changer herself?"

"If the legend is true," growled Gart nervously, "it is not Wolfbane we should fear, but what comes after Wolfbane. His pact with the flying scavengers and the final power of the Man Varg."

"Tell me the verse again."

Palla strained forward immediately, but his companion had paused.

"I'm not supposed to know it, and if Slavka heard me reciting it I would pay dearly. But since we're here I suppose it'll be safe. Let me see, if only I can remember it properly."

Gart thought for a while and then threw back his head, and in a deep, growling voice he began to recite. The incantation echoed through the trees and seemed to make the shadows themselves tremble around them:

> *As a she-cub is whelped with a coat that is white,*
> *And human child stolen to suckle the Sight*
> *From a place where injustice was secretly done*
> *Then the Marked One is here and a legend begun.*
> *When Wolfbane is dreamt of with terror and dread,*
> *And untamed are tamed, prepare for the dead.*

For the Shape Changer's pact with the birds will come
*   true,*
When the blood of the Varg blends with Man's in the
*   dew,*
As the Searchers are tempted, who hunger and prowl,
Down the Pathways of Death, by the summoning howl.

Then the truest of powers will be fleshed on the bone
And the Searchers tempt nature to prey on its own.
With blood at the altar, the Vision shall come
When the eye of the moon is as round as the sun.
In the citadel raised by the lords of before,
The stone twins await—both the power and the law.
Then the past and the future shall finally show,
To the wounded, the secret the Lera must know.
And all shall be witness to that which will be,
In the mind of the Man Varg, then none shall be free.

And only a family both loving and true,
May conquer the evil, so ancient, so new.
As they fight to uncover what secrets they share
And see in their journey how painful is care.
Beware the Betrayer, whose meaning is strife,
For their faith shall be tried by the makers of life,
And who shall divine, in the dead of the night,
The lies from the truth, the darkness from light?
Like the cry of the scavenger, torn through the air
A courage is needed, as deep as despair.

As soon as the wolf started to recite the verse, Palla's head
lurched up and a silent warning howl began in her brain.

She hardly understood any of these words, but Palla knew one thing all right, this verse had spoken of a white wolf.

"Larka," she said, trembling all over, "I must find Larka."

Fell began to growl at her side, but Palla shook her head to silence him.

"This family," Darm went on suddenly in the hollow, "the family to conquer the evil. Shouldn't we put our trust in them?"

Gart growled scornfully now, for he had remembered himself and he valued his leader's orders. "You know Slavka trusts only teeth and claws."

"Yes," said Darm almost angrily, "and the Combats and the Gauntlet too."

Fell's ears trembled at the names.

"Slavka says if another wolf has been born that claims to wield the Sight," said Gart, "then it is our enemy too. We must destroy anything connected to the old ways. And if Morgra finds this human, Slavka fears for us all."

"Why," said Darm, "if Slavka doesn't believe the legend?"

"Because Morgra could use the human to stir up the fears and superstitions and fool the Varg, just as she is doing with Wolfbane. It's clear it's not around here anymore, so we will travel east. That takes us toward Tsinga's valley too."

"Tsinga," growled Darm fearfully, "in the Vale of Shadows?"

"The fortune-teller was always dangerous," said Gart coldly, "and quite mad. But perhaps she can tell us more, if she still lives. Then we will track down the human cub."

"And when we find it?"

Gart's voice suddenly grew cold with cunning, "Kill it, Darm. As Slavka decrees we must kill all connected to the Sight."

Palla's eyes glittered fearfully in the darkness as a breeze stirred the leaves around their paws and made a mournful whisper through the forest.

As Larka stood mesmerized by the fire, she suddenly heard another sound, a low wail. Outside the circle of Gypsies lay a little moving bundle, in a crib made of intercrossing branches. As it turned over, Larka gasped and backed away. It was a human cub. She thought of the theft of a child. But in her belly Larka felt the stirrings of hunger and, as she looked at the defenseless creature, the wolf shuddered.

She was about to turn when she noticed that one of the humans had bent down and picked up a branch from the fire. It flared furiously at the end of his arm, and Larka was so startled that a thought flashed through her mind that perhaps Man made it and controlled it.

Larka suddenly broke away from the firelight. Noiselessly she skirted the humans and passed on as the strange music faded into the distance. The forest grew darker and darker and her spirits sank even more, for she was growing hungry. She kept looking about her for the signs of Lera, though she didn't really know how to hunt. Larka was coming toward another clearing when she suddenly caught a scent. The she-wolf looked up in amazement, for it was as if, just as she had begun to look for food, it had been provided for her.

In front of Larka stood a great tree in the center of the clearing; its branches were twisted into gnarled and ancient shapes. It was in full leaf and a chunk of raw flesh was dangling from a vine of trailing ivy below one of the boughs. As it hung there, red and raw, Larka thought the hanging meat looked like nothing so much as fruit. Strangely Fell's words about a golden deer pelt, the pelt of knowledge, came into Larka's mind.

The she-wolf felt very nervous again, for there was something else in the odor filling the air that reminded the wolf of the Gypsies. She peered about and noticed that the floor of the clearing was thick with dead leaves, though the tree hadn't shed. The place gave Larka an eerie sensation, but the meat looked far too tempting to resist. Larka sprung at it, but she was still too small and her paw missed the meat. She was going to spring again when suddenly a howl came to her that made her heart leap.

"Khaz," cried Larka delightedly. "Oh, Khaz, I'm over here."

There was Khaz, with Kipcha and Skop behind him, coming straight through the trees on the opposite side of the clearing.

"At last, little sister," cried Kipcha delightedly as they bounded toward her. Larka backed away a little for she suddenly remembered what had happened to her at the hunt.

"Thank Fenris," shouted Khaz, but as he did so, and was nearly at Larka's side, Khaz slowed and a strange expression came onto his face as he caught the scent of death swaying in the trees. Larka would remember that look for the rest of her days. The hesitation, the questioning, the fear in his brave face as he spotted the meat. Kipcha and Skop had seen it, too, and suddenly Kipcha's eyes woke to horror.

"No, Khaz," she cried, "don't."

Khaz couldn't hear Kipcha. An extraordinary feeling had just come over him. It was as though he were traveling along a deep ravine he could not escape, at the end of which lay he knew not what. He wanted to pull up, but the fear consuming his mind kept him running.

He reached the carpet of leaves ahead of the others and suddenly there was the sound of snapping twigs. Khaz's whole body contorted into an unnatural, writhing dance as the leaves rose in a flurry around him and the wolf vanished with a yelp. Larka gasped as a hole suddenly yawned in front of her. Kipcha and Skop were at the edge of the pit too. It must have been a good two branches deep, and Kipcha shuddered as she saw the vicious stakes at its bottom. Khaz was on his side and struggling furiously. One of the stakes had pierced his chest.

"Khaz," cried Kipcha desperately. "Oh, Khaz."

Below them Khaz tried to raise his head.

"Kipcha," he growled dreamily, "what happened to me, Kipcha?"

Kipcha's eyes were wrought with pain, but she shook her head hopelessly as she stood above him.

"Kipcha," whispered Khaz, struggling below them.

"The humans," snarled Skop angrily. "It's a hunting pit. The meat was a trap."

Larka was trembling terribly as she looked down at her friend kicking on the earth floor. Khaz's blood was already staining the ground.

"Kipcha," gasped Khaz, "I've been wounded."

As he said it Larka felt as though a gust of wind had just passed through her body. "It's all my fault," she whispered, starting to shake.

"Stop it, Larka," growled Khaz painfully, "Kipcha, Skop. You must get Larka away from here."

Sounds were coming through the trees. Strange cries that reminded the young wolf of the flight down the river. Then, across the ground, the wolves felt a distant tremor.

"Horses," snarled Skop.

"Listen to me, Kipcha," groaned Khaz. "Take Larka and run. As fast as you can. I'm finished anyway."

"But, Khaz," cried Kipcha bitterly, "what about us . . . our cubs."

"The pack. Look to the pack. Save Larka. You must, Kipcha, for me."

Fear had Kipcha by the throat and all her instincts told her to flee from the approaching sounds. But as she looked down at Khaz she felt as if her heart were breaking apart.

"Kipcha," whispered Skop kindly beside her, "we must get out of here."

Larka was wracked with grief and guilt as she watched Kipcha whimpering sadly above Khaz. The sounds were getting closer and Skop kept turning his head toward the trees, but still Kipcha couldn't move. It was Khaz who released them. The wolf gave a violent shudder and, with a last effort, he shook the dying voice from his body.

"Go, Kipcha," he gasped, "if Tor and Fenris had meant me to be your mate you would obey me. So now I order you. Go."

Khaz's body shuddered and his great red tail sank lifelessly to the ground. The wolf was dead. As his head flopped to the earth floor, Khaz's words by the river echoed through Larka's mind. "They will have to get through us first." Kipcha lifted her muzzle and gave a bitter howl, but the sounds from the trees were almost on them.

"Quickly, Kipcha," said Skop.

Suddenly the she-wolf turned and cried to Larka, "Run, little one. Run for your life."

The wolves' hearts beat with horror and sorrow as they sprang away. They only just vanished into the trees as, behind them, the clearing was turned to a churning fury of men and horses. The hunters had arrived.

On they ran, blindly. The bushes scratched their fur and briers and brambles cut their pads, but at last they reached the edge of the woods. The rest of the pack was nowhere to be seen, but there in the grass lay the carcass of the buffalo, and in the moonless night the birds, fattened on their gorgeous feast, had begun to pick it clean.

4

HUNTED

"The curse has come upon me,"
cried The Lady of Shalott.
—ALFRED LORD TENNYSON, *"The Lady of Shalott"*

"LARKA IS THE WHITE SHE-WOLF foretold in this verse," cried Palla through the darkness. "That's why Morgra came. That's why she cursed us all. Why Khaz died."

The wolf pack had gathered back at the Meeting Place, and now they lay in a circle around Brassa, mourning their friend and listening as Palla spoke of the ancient verse.

"I don't know, Palla," answered Brassa gravely. "But you must all set out as soon as you can. The cubs are old enough to travel now. Get beyond the pack boundaries. For a curse lingers over the place it was made and that may be a way to break it."

Huttser was shaking his head angrily. "Stop it," he cried, "Khaz's death was because of Man, not a curse. And what happened to Larka was her imagination, nothing more. We must not believe in curses or in legends."

The night was unusually clear and the sky gigantic, brilliant with starlight. As the wolf pack tried to avoid one another's gaze, they peered aghast into the heavens at the millions of tiny twinkling lights, and all felt very small.

"Don't be a fool, Huttser," snarled Palla angrily, swinging around to challenge her mate. "Larka's coat is white. She had a vision at the hunt. Our daughter has the Sight. Whether Khaz has anything to do with this or not, can't you see what it means?"

Huttser sprang to his feet and snarled at Palla too.

"Please, Father," cried Larka desperately between them, "please don't fight. Not because of me."

Her parents dropped their eyes guiltily. Fell's gaze was turned on his sister, though he wouldn't catch her eye either, and Kar was trying to look as brave as he could. Poor Kipcha's eyes were blank with pain, and Bran flattened his ears and whimpered.

"But this legend," Huttser argued, reaching for anything, "Skop said it can only begin in a place where there has been some great injustice. We have done nothing wrong."

Brassa was trembling and she seemed to reach a decision at last. She sprang up, and her voice was suddenly commanding the pack.

"Huttser, enough of this. You must believe it, for all your sakes. And Huttser, a great injustice was committed below the Stone Den."

Huttser turned to the nurse. "What in Fenris's name do you mean, Brassa? You think we should have taken Morgra in?"

Brassa dropped her gaze. "Huttser," she whispered shamefully, "I committed the injustice. I betrayed Morgra, long ago."

The pack all turned their startled eyes on Brassa. She was looking down the river toward the boulder and the den.

"May the past that's dark with crimes," she whispered mournfully, "bring revenge in future times."

"You, Brassa?" cried Palla. "But how?"

"I saw Morgra the night the runt was taken. She wasn't trying to steal it at all, Palla—she was trying to save it. The cub had crawled outside the den and a vixen was nosing nearby. But Morgra was in such a panic to protect it that when she picked it up she bit too hard."

The pack listened silently under the immense heavens, but a shadow of terror was spreading through their hearts.

"It was my fault really," Brassa went on. "I was meant to be guarding the den that night, but I wandered off. It was when I was returning that I saw it all. Morgra was so distraught that she howled until I thought her heart might crack open. Then she vanished with the dead cub and tried to bury it. When they found her they thought she had been trying to make a den for the cub she had stolen. But she didn't say a word in her own defense. The pack had already isolated her because they knew she was different, and I think pride and pure resentment shut her mouth."

"But, Brassa," said Palla imploringly, "not you. Why on earth didn't you tell them?"

Brassa shook her head shamefully. "I was afraid to own up to my own crime, Palla. But once she had killed the cub, even by mistake, I thought it was too dangerous to have her around the pups. For your sake, Palla, and for Skop's," said Brassa almost coldly. "Besides, I knew from the first Morgra had the gift, and I was a young wolf then, and inexperienced. I, too, thought it would bring misfortune on us all."

Brassa shook her graying muzzle. The misfortune she had feared all those years ago had returned to haunt her. Had returned to haunt them all.

"It was wrong of me, I know that now. But after they drove her out I swore an oath to Tor. I promised I would dedicate my whole life to cubs. To the future."

As Palla thought of Morgra and how they had driven her away a second time, something very like shame stirred inside her, and with the shame came a terrible weakness. But with it came fear, too, fear of the legend and the verse she had overheard, fear of what Morgra had threatened that night, too, about the past. Above all fear for her daughter.

"Then you knew everything all along," growled Palla accusingly. "But for pity's sake, why didn't you tell us the truth sooner?"

"The truth?" said Brassa helplessly. "I wanted to tell you about Morgra, I did. I tried to several times. Yet I was ashamed. I wanted to forget the past. And I didn't know it all, Palla, I swear it. I knew of the legend, yes, and I guessed that Morgra was trying to fulfill it as soon as I heard a child had been stolen. After Morgra came I suspected something in the den, too, about the cubs. At first I thought it was . . ." Brassa shook her head.

"I couldn't believe another with the Sight could be born so soon, even though the tales tell of it coming to several at the same time. But what Skop said about a great injustice terrified me. When Morgra cursed us I tried to tell you, Palla, to leave then."

Palla dropped her own head now. It was true.

"But even then I hoped and prayed it might all pass us by. That it was only a curse we had to fear."

"Only a curse?" growled Palla.

"There is something even greater at work," said Brassa, "as Morgra warned us that night. Now your daughter has the Sight, just as the verse prophecies, and so the legend is here, the legend of the Man Varg."

"The verse," growled Palla, "oh, the things it said, Huttser."

But as Palla tried to recall the whole of what she had overheard in the forest, the words became all jumbled up together. What rang through her mind again were the very things that Morgra had spoken of as she had cursed them.

"It tells of Wolfbane's return, as Morgra warned," Palla growled, "and the Shape Changer's pact with the flying scavengers."

Suddenly Morgra's voice seemed to be crying out over the pack again.

"It speaks of an altar, too," said Palla, straining to remember, "and the Searchers and a summoning howl. What is it, Brassa, this summoning howl?"

Brassa lay down again before the pack, shivering. "It is the very spirit of the Sight, Palla," she growled, looking straight at them, "for in its haunting cry even the dead may be raised again, to look on the world once more."

"Tell us. Tell us everything you know. Hide nothing. We shan't be angry."

Brassa nodded gravely. "The Sight brings the power to see through the eyes of birds, as Larka did at the hunt, and then to look into water and see things there of far-off realities, of past, present, and even future."

Larka felt her stomach clench.

"But the truest power, to touch minds and control thoughts and even actions, none have reached it, Palla, because it is believed that it can only enter the world if the Searchers are summoned, by the summoning howl, the ancient howl that can call them back down the Pathways of Death. The power is linked to them because they themselves have seen beyond the veil of life into the shadows. They above all have touched the energy within."

A cold breeze quivered across the river to the Meeting Place and only Kipcha looked up hopefully, for she was thinking of Khaz, and wondering if he could be called back down these pathways. She felt as if something had just padded across her resting place.

"Searchers?" asked Bran in a quavering voice.

"Spirits of the dead, Bran, and if they are ever called back into this world," said Brassa, trembling, "then the summoner can command them to do her bidding."

"Morgra," growled Palla fearfully.

"Anger and hate give the Searchers form and shape in this world, and sometimes they can appear among us for a moment or two, but only the howl shall really release them," whispered Brassa.

The pack was truly petrified now.

"And this altar?" growled Palla. "Is the human child some kind of sacrifice?"

As Palla spoke of a sacrifice, her daughter suddenly

thought of the story Kar had told them of Sita and, as she listened to the adults' fraught voices, it made her feel all the more mournful.

"Now I have told you all I know of the legend, Palla," answered Brassa, "but one thing is for certain, Morgra is trying to fulfill it. That's why she really wanted to join our pack. Not to protect us or help us against Man. But to get to Larka. She wants to become the Man Varg."

Larka's mind was ringing with terror. For the first time in her life she felt Morgra not as the shadow of fear that had haunted her parents' pack, but as a physical threat. The whole pack, too, felt the danger that was closing, like teeth, around them.

"The verse also mentioned a family, a family to conquer evil," whispered Palla. "Is it us?"

The pack was silent, wondering.

"I think that's what Morgra must have believed when we drove her away," growled Brassa thoughtfully. "Yet there is nothing I know of in the legend that says Larka's is the family. Her birth heralds the arrival of the human alone, nothing more. But there is one who might tell you."

The whole wolf pack strained forward.

"Who?" whispered Palla.

"Tsinga, the old fortune-teller. The journey will be dangerous, for there are dark stories about the Vale of Shadows and Tsinga is a Kerl. But her valley lies beyond the great rapids and a human camp, over the brow of the white mountain, and marks the eastern end of our old pack territory. Once you have sought her out, found out if ours is this family and what she knows of this final power, then you must get beyond the boundary as fast as you can."

Still Huttser was shaking his head.

"But if you are at the heart of this legend there is time," said Brassa, "if Tsarr has the child."

"Tsarr?" said Palla. "But that was the name Morgra used that night."

"I realized it was he who had really stolen it as soon as Morgra spoke Tsarr's name. That, too, reassured me a little, though I should never have let it," added Brassa bitterly.

"But who is this Tsarr?" said Larka.

"In my life I have only heard of three who possess the Sight, until you, Larka," Brassa whispered and Larka cowered. "There was Tsinga, a fortune-teller with limited power, then Morgra and Tsarr. The power was born strong in them, but now I believe it has faded in Tsarr almost entirely. Tsinga taught them all she knew, and she helped them to find their Helpers."

"Helpers?" said Huttser.

"Birds," growled Brassa almost irritably, "birds to help the gifted begin to see with the craft. Morgra's Helper is the raven. His name is Kraar, a filthy little flying scavenger."

The pack thought of the night they had seen the creature flapping away from the den behind Morgra. Larka shuddered, for it was Kraar's eyes then that she had been seeing through at the hunt.

"Tsarr's Helper, though, is a steppe eagle called Skart," Brassa went on. "He is a proud bird and one of the true flying Putnar."

Larka liked the sound of Skart immediately, especially since she had been thinking of Kraar and Wolfbane's terrible blood pact with the scavengers.

"At first Morgra and Tsarr gained knowledge and training from Tsinga," Brassa went on gravely, "But when Tsinga saw how black Morgra's heart had become, how she thirsted for power alone, she drove her away. But although Tsarr was fascinated with the legend, too, his heart was cleaner, and Skart was always determined to use the Sight for good. At one point I heard that they quarreled bitterly over the legend and what the Sight was really for. But it calms me that they are together again and have the child."

Brassa seemed suddenly to recollect herself.

"But you must be gone from here. Find Tsinga. She will tell you more if she is still alive."

"Brassa," growled Palla suddenly, "how do you know so much about the fortune-teller?"

The nurse raised her head, and in that moment it seemed all the old wolf was were her memories. "Because," whispered Brassa, "Tsinga is my sister."

Palla and Skop looked up at their nurse in amazement. Neither of them had had the slightest inkling that Brassa had a sister, let alone a sister like this: a Kerl and a fortune-teller. But Kar was suddenly thinking how many secrets grown-ups seemed to have.

"We quarreled long ago," said Brassa sadly, "but unlike Tsarr and Skart, I never made up my differences with Tsinga. I wish now I had not let so many moons rise on my anger."

"But, Brassa, you never even told me," growled Palla, though now she remembered that her father had told her that Brassa had only joined their pack shortly before Morgra was born.

"I would often visit her as you were growing, Palla, for I wanted to know about the stories of the Sight. It is stories that have always fascinated me. But Tsinga would never really trust me, for we were never close as cubs. She told me bits and pieces, threw me snippets to scavenge at and appease my appetite. But never the verse or the deeper secrets of the Sight. At last I grew infuriated with her and we argued bitterly."

Brassa dropped her head. "After that I kept hearing rumors about her. About Morgra and Tsarr and their Helpers. About the Vale of Shadows, where Tsinga later settled, away from everyone. Where you must now go."

"Brassa," growled Skop suddenly, "why do you speak as if you aren't coming with us."

"Because there is something else I must tell you all."

"Something else," cried Huttser.

Brassa lowered her old gray muzzle onto her paws. "I cannot help any of you. My time has come, my friends. I am dying."

From some distant aerie an owl screeched in the night. Huttser felt his legs go weak and he sagged visibly. This news drove out any real doubts he could muster.

"Dying?" cried Palla.

"Then we're surely cursed," whispered Bran sadly, covering his ears with his paws and letting his muzzle sink into the grass, "Morgra warned that she would break the pack, one by one."

"A lump has been growing in my belly for many suns now," muttered Brassa sadly. "But now Morgra has had her revenge for my crime, perhaps my death can make amends."

Fell had sprung to his feet, though, and he came running toward Brassa. He began scratching the ground in front of her and whining bitterly. His eyes were full of pain and incomprehension.

"Please, Brassa. Not you," growled the black wolf.

Brassa tried to smile and touched his muzzle gently with her own. "It is no real sadness, Fell," she said softly. "I'm old and have lived a full life. It comes to us all, Fell. It is nature's way. You know I will be almost glad when it comes."

Fell looked at her strangely.

"Though I have one regret," she added, licking Fell's ears. "I watched Palla and Skop grow and tended to them like my own. I wish I could see you, too, come to adulthood."

"I am an adult," growled Fell furiously, pushing away from her, "and I can fight off anything. Wolfbane and legends and curses . . ."

"Perhaps you can, my dear," said Brassa proudly. "But there is one thing in life not even you can fight. None of us can ever fight."

They all knew what Brassa meant, and the wolf pack dropped their eyes. They looked for a moment as if they were praying to Tor and Fenris.

"When, Brassa?" said Huttser quietly, staring at the ground. There was no anger left in the Dragga now.

"That is in Tor's sight alone, Huttser, yet I do not think I shall make the winter. But you mustn't worry for me. I will go into the woods on my own when it is time. You must set out as soon as you can. Some call the Sight a bane and some a blessing, but it will grow in Larka. Perhaps her powers will help you to fight Morgra's words at least, as you flee the boundaries, for if it is mastered the Sight will help her draw on all the forces of the universe."

Fell's ears twitched and there was suddenly an oddly jealous look in his eye. But Kar was thinking of the curse and how childish it made his motto seem now, "Stones are raw, they blunt my paw. But words can never harm me."

"But I don't want the powers," muttered Larka miserably.

"The Sight is not something you can choose, my dear," said Brassa softly, and she looked at Larka with warmth and understanding. "You must accept it, not as a curse but a gift. But once you have found out all you can from Tsinga, then get beyond the pack boundaries. Before it's too late."

Bran was looking up again toward the castle and, though its walls were lost in night, it towered above them once more.

"If Morgra believes you are really this family then you are a threat to all she seeks. So now, whether she gets her paws on the cubs or not, she will do everything she can to destroy you. You are cursed, but remember she has the Night Hunters at her back, too, and she will want to get to Larka again. Go. As soon as you can."

"Mother," Larka said suddenly, and as she spoke she was thinking of the story of Sita again, "let me go on my own. Then you'll all be safe. If it's me Morgra really wants."

"Hush, my child," said Palla, licking her daughter's forehead. Larka closed her eyes, relieved to have her offer so quickly and adamantly refused.

"Brassa," growled Huttser, for the Dragga felt his authority was slipping too far beyond his reach. "We will not leave the territory. We will go into the mountains, yes, and perhaps find Tsinga. But we will mark the old boundaries again with a clear, strong scent. We will live free as a pack and keep everything out. Curses. Wolfbane. Man. That is why the wolf marks its territory, so nothing may enter. But we shall not succumb to fear and we shall not run away."

But Huttser looked rather foolish as he stood there.

"You must, Huttser. For all your sakes."

"But we won't leave you, Brassa," said Palla. "The pack will not leave you to die alone."

"Palla. You must think of your cubs," insisted Brassa, "of the future." But there was gratitude in Brassa's eyes.

"Oh, Brassa," cried Palla, bounding up to her old nurse, "what shall we ever do without you?"

"Cleave to the law of the untamed wolf," answered Brassa gravely. "Survive, my dear, survive."

The pack watched helplessly as the old nurse grew weaker and weaker. The only thing that could rouse her from the painful lethargy that seemed to consume her so swiftly were the children—and especially Larka, whom she would talk to quietly of the Sight. Of the ancient days when many wolves who roamed the forests had wielded the gift, and fortune-tellers, too, had been prized among the packs. When the cult of Wolfbane had been strong in the forests and mighty wars had been fought among the Varg. It was a world that seemed to speak with the voice of the centuries.

As Brassa spoke of it, Fell and Kar would shift nervously and stare in wonder at the white wolf. They hardly understood what it all meant, but they were frightened for Larka, and their fear grew as they realized that, as her winter coat began to grow, the color of her pelt was getting lighter and lighter.

Kar would ask Skop if the curse and the legend were really true, but Skop was much like Huttser. His doubting nature was wrestling with the evidence of what had already happened. He could do nothing but shake his head and look down gravely at his charge. But after he had seen Morgra that night above the ravine and heard her terrible words, a fury had stirred in Skop's gut and his mind had long been turning back to thoughts of Slavka and these rebels, gathering somewhere near the high mountains.

Brassa expended all her remaining energy telling the children stories, too, making sure that her best tales were passed on to the future, since she above all believed that they might help to protect them. Her talk was mostly of Sita and of Tor and Fenris, the great wolf gods in the sky who looked down kindly on the Varg. She would whisper, too, that she was about to go on a great journey. Fell listened especially attentively when she spoke like this, and a new gravity seemed to have woken in the young wolf.

The weather began to change suddenly, as it can do in Transylvania. Autumn came, turning the leaves to burnished gold and fretting fire through the forests. The leaves began to fall, and in the high mountains the first snows came. Like Brassa, the country was dying, but for the old nurse, the distant seasons would bring no spring.

Fell and Larka found Brassa one stirring autumn morning. She had not gone off on her own into the forest but instead was lying beneath the trees, the falling leaves settled on her back. It was as though the woods had begun to lay a shawl across the old she-wolf to cover her passing. Fell nuzzled Brassa and whimpered softly as he touched her with his paw, but his friend would not stir. Her body was cold as stone and already stiffening beneath her coat. As Fell stared at her he could not believe that this had ever been Brassa at all.

"At least she went peacefully in her sleep," said Huttser quietly as he padded up beside them.

"What should we do, Father?" growled Fell helplessly. "Should we cover her up in the ground?"

"No, Fell. That is for unnamed cubs, but Brassa has made a true journey as a wolf, and now we must leave her for the Lera and for the seasons. For the creatures of earth and air."

"But, Father, it's too cruel," gasped Larka, looking at Brassa's body and thinking suddenly of the ghastly birds feasting on the dead buffalo.

"She is not there, Larka," said Huttser gently. "She is with Tor and Fenris and Sita now. But what she was in life is now a gift to feed nature. To feed the future."

Fell could not understand his father's words, and the thought of it made him turn angrily away. The pack padded over in turn to take their farewells of the old nurse. Palla licked Brassa's nose gently, as Larka growled sadly beside her. The strange guilt that Larka had felt over Khaz was burning inside her again, and Larka felt herself more than ever a threat to the whole pack. The children had all grown to nearly two-thirds of the adults' size, but in that moment none of them felt they really knew anything of the adult world. Palla dropped her head and the pack followed her silent lead. They were praying to Tor and Fenris, praying for Brassa's soul.

"Good-bye, Brassa," whispered Palla bitterly, and she lifted her head and howled. Apart from her brother, Skop, the last link with her childhood was gone. The call rose into the skies, and the wolf pack took it up together sadly by the river. As the mournful elegy sounded for the old nurse and for Khaz, too, its pain and sadness were in terrible contrast to the beauty of that wild autumn day.

"There is one blessing," said Palla as their call subsided. The pack followed the Drappa's gaze up to the Stone Den.

"I was happy here as a cub, but now I shall always associate it with bad memories. I shall be glad to leave."

"Are we running away, Mother?" asked Fell suddenly.

"No, Fell," growled Huttser. "We will mark the boundaries again while we go in search of the fortune-teller."

Palla looked at her mate sternly and shook her head, but it was not the time to argue with him about the path that lay ahead.

"Come, then," cried Huttser suddenly. "Kipcha, walk with me awhile."

Kipcha stared helplessly at her brother. She could hardly bear to leave the place were she and Khaz had been so happy together, even for such a desperately short time. But something bitter had got into her gut too.

"We never had a chance, Huttser," said Kipcha as she thought of Khaz.

Huttser couldn't bear to see his sister like this and he turned away. Kipcha padded slowly after him, but as she went, her brother had no notion that now Kipcha was carrying a secret with her also. Huttser looked back at the castle and its shadow seemed to be reaching after them. He tried to smile reassuringly at his sister, but his head was ringing with words that Morgra had cried out above the ravine, "Fear, betrayal, here begun," and a cloud had just passed over the sun.

The children came next, Larka in the middle. Only Bran hovered about the river. He looked up toward the castle, too, and then across to the forests where Khaz had gone. Then to Brassa lying still beneath the trees.

"One by one," whispered Bran fearfully. "One by one." As he spoke, a pheasant took wing and the startled flurry sent the Sikla bounding frantically through the leaves behind his friends.

If a bird had been circling through the blue, looking down as autumn painted its ripening colors across the forests of Transylvania, it would have spied a wolf pack weaving upward through the dying grasses. The eight of them went in single file, with the largest wolf at the front, searching the land ahead with his cunning eyes. Now and then the bird would have seen him stop and lift his gray-red tail expectantly, but for the moment at least, nothing came to trouble the pack as they fled.

Yet if that bird's eyes had been keen enough, it might have noticed that there was something especially wary in each of the wolves' treads. That at every sound, one in particular, with a smudge around his right eye, would start and look behind him. The three young wolves trailing behind the adults kept scenting the air questioningly, and two of them watched the third white wolf with special care.

As this imaginary bird watched the secret body language of the moving pack, it might have thought that there was some dark secret troubling the wolves. Yet, knowing the laws of nature and of the wilderness, it might have thought simply that the sprung tension in their padding gait was nothing more than the essence of these mysterious creatures, their perfectly adapted instinct toward flight or fight.

The wolves had been traveling for ten suns, and as they journeyed, Huttser insisted on marking the perimeter of the old territory. Palla remembered the contours of her old pack's land. She had been on many markings herself with her parents, and wolves know their territory as intimately as any human knows his home or the room he sleeps in. Palla would stop to remark on a familiar tree or brook, a glade that she suddenly recognized, or the shape of a boulder or a cairn. At these places the pack would linger, leaving a clear scent to warn off intruders, howling as they did so and pawing the earth.

Their spirits were low, but they were glad to be on the move at last, and the business of marking at least gave them something to occupy their thoughts. Larka had grown very introspective and would look up now and then to find Fell and Kar watching her nervously. It upset Larka a great deal. Kar had tried to cheer her up, chatting to her and even trying to get her to romp in the autumn leaves, but Larka hardly responded, preferring instead to pad quietly after her mother. In the end Kar gave up, and in truth he was very frightened.

Fell's feelings were more complicated. When Brassa had first talked of the Sight, he had felt a jealousy toward Larka, for he could see one thing plainly—it had made her the center of attention in the wolf pack. Now he almost wished that he had the powers himself. This jealousy was an unpleasant feeling and Fell grappled with it; he didn't want to admit it to Larka and this made it harder and harder for him to confide in his sister as he once would have. Instead he held his feelings to himself like a guilty secret.

But something else was stirring in the wolf's guts. Fell had sensed it growing in him after he had been so gripped at the hunt. It was like the fury and exhilaration that blended in him at tasting his first true meat. It was anger. At times Fell didn't know what the anger was directed toward. He looked out on the world as they went and felt an odd stirring in his belly. He would growl at the Lera around him and long to hunt again and watch the world running before his paws. Now and then he would snap at his mother and father and blame them for not paying him enough attention, or understanding the feelings of growing isolation that were coursing naturally through his blood.

At other times he would allow Huttser and Palla to comfort him and feel the peace of being a cub again. He would curl up beside his parents when they rested and listen to their strong voices and remember the stories they had told him as a pup and feel safe. But then Palla would say something to him that sounded silly or made him feel young and foolish, or he would remember resentfully how his father had clasped him by the back of the neck that sun. Then he would recall his anger and sense of freedom at the hunt and stalk irritably away. Fell grew sullen and brooding, and when this happened, he learned to direct his feelings toward Kar, another source of jealousy in Fell, for he could see how fond Larka was of him.

The wolf pack had been traveling for several suns when Skop came up behind Huttser at the brow of the rocky hill. Huttser already knew what was in Skop's mind as they gazed out at the land rolling before them.

"This is where I leave you, Huttser," said Skop quietly. "Tsinga's valley takes you directly east, but it will be quicker if I bear northeastward now, for I have traveled that route once before and I know the passes. Will you be all right?"

"Yes, my friend," answered Huttser. "We shall survive."

"I wonder why Tsinga's woods are really called the Vale of Shadows?" growled Skop as they stood looking out together.

"Well, it can't be because of a two-headed wolf," answered Huttser as scornfully as he could, "or a river that eats any that try to cross. Though we'll find out soon enough."

"Yes."

"I almost wish I could come with you, Skop. It would be good to have something real to fight."

Skop shook his head thoughtfully. "Huttser, you must guard your family now and find your own freedom. My sister does not really agree, but I think you are right. Mark your territory and keep everything out. I don't know how to fight shadows, Huttser, so I will go in search of something I can smell and taste. If Morgra seeks a power that is evil, I want to be a part of the battle. If I find these rebels all the better, but if I ever find Morgra again, I shall kill my half sister myself."

Huttser growled deeply and his eyes flickered with a cold approval.

"But, Huttser, remember what Palla heard the rebels saying that night—if they have sworn to destroy anything connected with the Sight, they are a danger to you too. Perhaps I can reason with this Slavka, if I find her—tell her what is happening."

Huttser nodded gravely.

"And, Huttser," said Skop suddenly, his voice filling with tenderness but regret, too, "look after Kar. He is all that is left of my pack."

Huttser was confused by the sight of Kar standing between his own cubs, but he nodded nonetheless. Skop padded over to Palla and stood talking quietly with his sister for a while, then he trotted up to Kar. The young wolf kept shaking his head angrily as Skop spoke to him and soon Skop turned away. Wolves hate farewells, and Kar watched him sadly as he bounded off up the slope. As Skop turned to give them a final look of parting, Palla padded up beside Kar.

"Don't worry, Kar," she whispered kindly. "He'll be all right."

"Why must he go, Palla?"

"Skop was always a fighter, Kar. Even as a cub. He wants to find this rebel pack, and with winter so close he has to cross the mountains before the snows hit."

"But why is he leaving me behind?" cried Kar bitterly. "Why can't I go with him?"

"You are still too young, Kar. But don't worry. You have us now. We are your family."

Kar looked up meekly at Palla as Skop disappeared over the hill, but as Palla mentioned a family he whimpered. He suddenly felt terribly lonely, and as the pack set off again, he ran over to Bran and Kipcha. The Sikla was whispering nervously to Huttser's sister.

"We don't know who will be next, Kipcha," Bran was growling under his breath. "Brassa said that this journey would be dangerous, so we've got to watch each other's backs. I only hope Fenris lets us escape the boundaries."

Kar shuddered, but Kipcha hardly seemed to hear Bran. Her eyes were fixed on Larka and it seemed to Kar that her look became cold and resentful.

The pack traveled on for six suns, and they were cresting another hill when the children heard a strange noise. Below them lay a river that sent up the grumbling thunder of the great rapids they had been seeking. Bran was growing increasingly nervous as they threaded down the slope, for what he had heard of Tsinga and the Vale of Shadows had almost frightened him as much as his thoughts of Wolfbane.

The noise grew steadily around them, and as the wolves got to the bottom of the slope the children bounded eagerly toward Huttser. They gasped, though, as they looked down. Palla and Kipcha were peering out nervously over the edge at the torrent tearing through the rock walls beneath them. The updraft made the wolves' fur quiver and ripple. The water crashed and boomed furiously as it fought its way down the rocky canyon. Bran could not help thinking it looked just as if it might have been formed from the saliva of a thousand feeding packs.

The mountain here was in steps, so that in the river below them, beyond two great boulders that edged the top of a waterfall, rapids had formed where the cavern narrowed and fell. Here the foaming white water was churned to a frenzy, before it reached a second massive fall and spilled down around a jagged rock.

"We don't have to cross that, do we, Father?" gulped Larka as she saw the drop. As she stared into the churning white rapids, Larka wondered what it would be like for the soul never to find a resting place. Fell thought of the power of the Sight again to look into water and see things of far-off realities. It was Bran who was remembering Morgra's curse.

Huttser began to thread carefully down the slope. The river here was calmer than elsewhere, and he saw that there were several boulders sticking above the surface and, at a point, where the jump between two flat rocks was too far to leap, a tree had fallen from the far bank and lay across like a bridge. "This won't be too difficult," he called.

In a single spring the wolf had leaped to the near rock. As he went something was watching him, high in the trees above them.

"Careful, Huttser," whispered Bran from the safety of the bank.

The next jump was greater, and as Huttser landed he felt his paws slip on the rock. But the wolf kept his balance, and the others had already begun to follow from the riverbank. Huttser crossed easily to the flat rock. In front of him lay the length of the fallen tree, one or two of its branches trailing into the water, but most stripped away by the force of current.

Huttser stepped up onto it very carefully. It felt firm under his paws, and he padded forward more confidently, stopping in the middle of the log to look downstream. Directly ahead were the two great boulders where the river plunged over the edge to the rapids. Huttser turned around again as he reached the end of the log. Palla, Fell, and Kar were close behind.

Larka, too, stepped onto the log as her mother neared the end. But as she saw the water on either side of her, Larka suddenly felt dizzy. It surprised the young wolf, for she had often run blithely across the hollow log at the Meeting Place without falling or feeling the slightest uncertainty. Even as she thought about her own fear, Larka felt herself beginning to totter precariously.

"Kipcha. Bran," called Huttser as Palla and Fell sprang onto the grass beside him, "hurry up there."

They were still hovering on the far bank as Kar, too, reached the far side.

"Go on, Kipcha," whispered Bran nervously. "I'll be behind you."

They jumped easily enough across the rocks and Kipcha sprang onto the log behind Larka, but Bran almost slipped on the last rock. He stood there, trembling furiously.

"Bran," cried Huttser angrily, "come on, will you?"

"I can't, Huttser . . . it's not safe."

"Nonsense, just jump."

Kipcha was hardly aware what was happening as Huttser shouted at the Sikla, but as she saw Larka in front of her a dark shadow crossed her mind. Perhaps it was true, perhaps it was Larka that had brought the curse down on the pack. Just for a moment, she thought how easy it might be to knock Larka off the tree. Even as Kipcha thought it, Bran closed his terrified eyes and flung himself toward the log.

"Bran, you fool, look what you're doing," snarled Huttser.

The others gasped as Bran landed heavily, and they saw the log move. Larka sprang to safety before the trailing vines holding it in place broke, but as the wet moss on the log's upper sides came in contact with the smooth stones it was resting on, it rolled and Bran and Kipcha were flung into the churning waters. Kipcha felt the horror of nightmares enfold her as she plunged into the river.

"Kipcha," gasped Huttser.

But the current overcame them immediately, and they were both swept through that churning stone gateway and vanished into the void.

"Quick," snarled Huttser, pushing past Palla.

The pack leaped after Huttser. They reached the lower bank, and as they stared at the tumbling waterfall that dropped from the high boulders and turned the river to spray, they trembled in horror at the empty surface below. Suddenly two muzzles burst into the air. Kipcha and Bran, released from the grip of the falls, were gasping for breath and fighting for their lives as the river swept them away.

"The curse," gasped Palla. "It's hunting us down."

"Hurry," cried Huttser, springing after them.

Ahead, in the path of the rapids, the river's course was cut by boulders and jagged rocks and the water careered left and right, swerving around the obstacles or smashing against their sides as it carried the wolves downstream.

"Fight, Kipcha!" cried Huttser furiously.

A boulder loomed in front of their friends, but the water suddenly swung them safely past it.

"No," growled Palla, "don't fight it. Trust the water. Let it carry you to safety."

Neither Kipcha nor Bran could hear Palla above the thunder of the gorge, but their own exhaustion came to their rescue now, for they could no longer fight the river's fury. As the wolves struggled less, only able to paddle as they kept their heads above the surface, the water, finding its own way through this gauntlet of stone, swept them left and right, past rock after rock.

"They're still all right," sighed Huttser as the rapids began to ease.

"But look!" Palla howled, trembling.

Beyond, a sudden water chute led straight to the second falls. They could hear its booming voice on the wind already, and Kipcha and Bran were beginning to spin again, moving out straight toward it.

"Fight," cried Palla, "now is the time. It's now or never."

Bran heard her and began to struggle again. His efforts had some effect and steadily the sodden wolf began to move toward the shore. But Kipcha just spun helplessly toward the second drop.

"Kipcha," cried Huttser desperately.

Kipcha was beyond fighting. The river was irresistible and Kipcha's spirits had failed her. At first she had struggled desperately, not only through instinct but because of the secret she was carrying with her, but as the rapids had slackened and she felt herself floating on the surface, a strange feeling came over the wolf. Guilt consumed her for what she had thought of doing to Larka. With guilt came exhaustion and despair. But as the feelings washed through her, the pain that had haunted Kipcha since Khaz's death lifted from her. She no longer wanted to fight.

"Khaz," she moaned faintly as she vanished over the second drop. "Khaz."

Bran had pulled himself onto the bank and the wolves leaped past him to the edge and looked down.

"No!" cried Huttser in agony. "Sister!"

The she-wolf had been thrown out toward the giant boulder they had seen from the hill, and now her sodden body lay broken across the rock. The boulder's granite side was stained with her blood. Huttser stood dumbfounded as Bran, dripping and exhausted, slunk up between them. The Sikla peered down, and when he saw her, Bran began to whimper.

"First Brassa," he whined. "Now Kipcha too. The curse is breaking the pack, one by one."

Huttser turned and snarled furiously. "You dare!" he cried. "You did this, Bran. You. It was your fault."

"Not me, Huttser," pleaded Bran. "Morgra."

Huttser sprang at him and Bran dropped on his front paws, cowering pitifully. Larka and Kar looked terrified for the Sikla, but Fell suddenly found the sight disgusting.

"Please," implored Larka, "please don't . . ."

"Huttser, stop it." Palla had sprung between them, and the she-wolf's anger held Huttser in check. He growled at Palla, but her clear eyes claimed his gaze.

"You mustn't give Morgra what she wants, Huttser. We must stick together. Not fight."

"But this . . . this coward. This Sikla."

"No, Huttser," said Palla more softly. "It wasn't Bran's fault. The vines broke."

The strength in Palla's eyes seemed to calm Huttser.

"But, Palla," he whispered bitterly, "she was my sister."

"I know, Huttser, and I am so sorry. But we need each other more than ever now. We must think of the pack, and of Larka. But your sister, Huttser," added Palla sadly, "at least . . . at least she didn't drown, and the fall made her end a swift one."

Huttser stood there helplessly, but at last the Dragga nodded.

"Get up, Bran," he growled.

The wolves stood above the gorge, hardly able to speak, the adults staring at the children as the sightless water thundered about them. Huttser looked at the sliver of green in Fell's eye and then into Larka's strong face. He did not understand the gift that had been given to his daughter, nor Brassa's words about the legend or a family to fight the evil. But if Fenris himself was hunting them, it would be Huttser's teeth that he would feel first, before a single tuft of fur on their coats was harmed.

"Father," said Larka suddenly, stepping forward and lifting her tail. "We still have one another. What stronger pack could there be?"

"But we must hurry," said Palla, looking proudly at her daughter.

Huttser paused, then for the first time, he nodded in real assent. With that there was a sudden screech through the trees. High above the gorge a buzzard had landed on a branch overhanging the rapids and begun to call. Its piercing, hungry cries shook the dying canopy, and in the distance another bird answered it.

"They are calling for us to help them open the carcass," said Palla angrily.

Larka shivered as she thought again of the powers of the Sight, and Huttser looked sadly at his sister for the final time. At last he turned away, but as he did so, none of the pack knew the secret that Kipcha had carried with her to her death. That Khaz's cubs had been stirring inside her. The cubs that at first she had fought the river to protect, until she remembered that they would never have a father to love and nurture them.

As Huttser led the dwindling pack from the rapids, another bird was watching them from the secrecy of the trees, and its eyes were not fixed on Kipcha at all, they were looking at Bran. It was Kraar.

5
THE VALE
OF SHADOWS

Eyeless in Gaza, at the mill with slaves.
—JOHN MILTON, Samson Agonistes

IT WAS ALREADY NIGHT when the wolf pack stopped suddenly, distracted for a moment from their sorrow by the sight below. In the valley beneath them lay a series of wooden structures, grouped loosely together, and from their sides an orange light was flickering faintly in the darkness.

"Man," Huttser growled.

"It must be the human camp Brassa spoke of," said Palla. "Her valley can't be far now."

Kar cocked his ears, for he had never seen a human before, let alone been so close to a village.

"Stay close to me, Larka," he whispered.

Fell swung around and suddenly the jealousy he had been feeling made him want to bite Kar's muzzle. He glared at the gray wolf instead, but Kar was gazing at Larka and didn't notice.

"We'll have to skirt it, Huttser," whispered Palla.

The wolves crept stealthily down through the trees, their eyes glinting in the shadows as they padded through the fading grass and passed like wraiths by the human dwellings. They held their fear in the silence of their paws. The pack skirted the village safely and vanished into the forest beyond, but as they went, they came to a clearing and Palla suddenly began to snarl.

There the pack saw an extraordinary shape. It was a kind of den, but it was much larger than the ones in the village had been, and of the strangest proportions. It was long and narrow, and the wooden ceiling sloped on either side to a thin ridge. On the top at the front was a wooden branch, with a second branch running across its middle. It was a cross like the crosses the human army had carried on their banners.

"What is it, Mother?" asked Larka.

"A den, I suppose."

Palla was only partly right, for though the villagers often visited the church, they never slept in its walls, except when they nodded off during one of the daily sermons. Instead, they came to talk to their god and think and pray or look at the strange carvings on its sides and smell the incense that the priest would burn on Sundays. They valued the place and feared it, too, for it was far older than any of the villagers could remember.

To the humans it looked like an upturned ship that had sailed to them across some fathomless sea, and in truth it was like a kind of earthbound ship. For the people who had built it had always lived in fear and made their place of worship so they could lift the whole structure onto logs and roll it away in times of danger, fleeing the incessant warfare that haunted the land of Transylvania. Indeed, as Huttser had seen in the valley, war was already coming once more to the forests and the plains. Soon, the people and their overlords would rise again to defend their lands and their churches, and the beliefs, too, that hovered about this place.

When the humans came to use the stave church, they would open the door and windows and light candles inside and flood it with their questions and their sorrows and their hopes, with their need to believe. But now it lay in darkness, and the door was firmly bolted. As the wolves crept past it, they saw none of the human's burning air through its windows and soon they were reassured by the silence that hung about its mysterious shape. But as they passed the church's door Bran gasped.

"Look, Huttser."

There, hanging from a metal spike, was a wolf carcass. Palla shrank back as she saw the paws, nailed flat on either side of the door, and the sad hanging head. She caught the fearful scent of death that came from the wolf skin.

"The human child," said Huttser gravely, "perhaps this is part of their revenge."

"No," growled Palla, curling up her snout angrily. "I have seen this before, Huttser, long before any child was stolen. The humans wear us like a skin on their backs."

Palla was right, for the humans' fears were not only of the dark forces that lurk in the universe but of the very creatures that were staring now at this place of refuge.

Although man had long hunted the wolf as a natural threat in the wild, there were many who had come to believe that the wolf itself was an evil spirit, for his voice haunted their dreams and made them shudder when they heard it in the trees, or calling from the lofty mountains. So they had learned to trap him and nail his carcass to the doors of their churches, as a symbol of their victory over evil, so that no dark spirits could ever enter.

The wolf pack pressed on. But they suddenly heard voices coming from the other side of the church. Huttser swung around his muzzle to silence the others.

"Which way now?" growled a wolf loudly. His voice was hoarse and tired. It was a male, and from the sound of him, a very large one.

"We'll try to the south this time. There are old rumors of it being there."

"How far, for Fenris's sake?" asked the first wolf angrily.

"Why ask such stupid questions?" came the reply. "It was lost long ago."

"But what does Morgra really want there?"

Huttser threw up his head as they listened. *Balkar*, he thought. *They must be Night Hunters.*

"It's where the altar lies," came the voice. "Only there can the Man Varg come."

"The altar," whispered Palla, looking fearfully toward the children.

"But do you think the Harja citadel really exists, then?" came the second voice.

The adults' eyes opened wider. The mythical citadel of Harja was a place all the wolves knew of, a place of enchantment and mystery, and one wrapped in fable. There was a story that though, like the Stone Den on the mountaintop, it had been built by Man, it was the place where the Varg entered heaven. But they never knew before that the mythical place was linked to the Sight.

But the citadel that the wolves knew from their stories as Harja was no myth, to wolf or man. It was a real place that had been built nearly fifteen hundred years before by the Romans, who called it Alba Mutandis. For the Romans had once wrestled bitterly to conquer the land beyond the forest, sending wheat and gold, collected from the rivers in the fleeces of lambs, back to their leaders in the west. Their soldiers had established outposts in the great mountains and the wide flat plains of Transylvania. First they had conquered the lower reaches of the Danube River and then turned north toward the high mountains where Alba Mutandis lay.

The Romans had fought their battles and lived their lives, and although their mighty empire had long passed out of the river of history, their culture had left stones in the moving waters of life far sturdier even than the statues that decked their abandoned citadels. For Transylvania, the land beyond the forests, would one day be called Roumanie or Romania, after the city that had given birth to its culture, the city of ancient Rome, and Rome's language still lived on in the voices of the people.

"Yes, I believe it exists," growled the Night Hunter beyond the church, "and when the other Balkar packs find the child we shall take it there. For only there can the Man Varg come forth. Only there can the Sight be made flesh. With blood at the altar, the Vision shall come."

"Come on, then," said the first Balkar suddenly, "let's get on."

Huttser drew farther into the shadows and his pack with him, but the Night Hunters passed away, completely unaware of how close they had just come to another of Morgra's goals.

The moon was rising as the wolf pack crept from the shadows again, wondering nervously about what they had just heard, and came to a patch of open ground beyond the stave church, bordered by yew trees. Here, they began to see shapes that filled them with even more apprehension. There were stones, flat and covered in moss or ivy, standing upright in the earth. The grass was overgrown, and here and there the wolves saw other shapes poking out of the ground; thin branches with a second branch across their upper sections like the ones on the church. They were almost the color of old wood, but they glinted strangely in the moonlight.

"What are they, Huttser?" growled Palla as they crept forward.

"I don't know, Palla," answered Huttser, sniffing the ground. "But can you smell it?"

Larka began to growl. The she-wolf had come across a bone, next to one of the gravestones. It was bleached by the sun and was very old, but rather than inspiring hunger in the young wolf, it made her tremble as it lay there in the earth.

"Look at this," gulped Fell. Fell had found a skull. The pack gazed down at it wonderingly, for it was nothing like the skulls of the Lera they knew. It was rounded and the eye sockets lay flat across its top.

"Man," said Palla.

"Mother," asked Larka, "do humans bury their dead in the earth like wolves?"

Palla thought of the little cubs she had buried outside the den but didn't answer. The pack fell silent as their shadows brushed against the weird stones. A breeze had suddenly come up, sending clouds drifting across the face of the moon that cast heavy, menacing shapes over the burial ground. The wolf pack was nearly at the end of the graveyard when a cloud much denser than the rest darkened the moon completely, and for a moment, Bran couldn't see where he was going. He bumped into Larka and Kar and they all found themselves slipping. The earth in front of them was so soft it gave way, and they tumbled forward into a half-dug grave. Bran landed on top of Kar and Larka, who started to snarl and scramble desperately at the earth walls around them. For a moment the three wolves lost all sense of what was happening and began to tussle with one another in the earth.

"Stop it, all of you," said a voice sternly from above. "It's all right."

Huttser and the others were peering down at the three of them, and for a moment, Fell found it almost amusing. There was an especially grim fascination in the sight of Kar, so helpless and vulnerable and covered in earth. But Palla felt a shudder run down her spine as Larka shook herself and they all climbed out of the grave again.

The pack rested that night near the church, but none of them got to sleep much before dawn, for the wolf carcass, the grave, and especially Kipcha's loss troubled them deeply. And they were wary of the Night Hunters. When

Larka did sleep, she had a strange dream, quite unlike her old nightmares. She was walking on her own up a steep slope and her heart was troubled, as if she had lost something and felt she would never find it again. As Larka looked on, the wild breeze strengthened and the trees shook. Then suddenly Larka's eyes were filled with a brilliant light that swelled around her, until it seemed to be suffusing the whole world. Even as she woke, she seemed to hear a voice in the forest.

"Remember, Larka," it seemed to say, "remember."

Morning light was coming all around her, but the rest of the pack was still fast asleep. Huttser was snoring loudly next to Palla, and Bran was lying on his own, dreaming fitfully and twitching all the while. Larka shook her head guiltily. She thought of waking Fell and Kar who were nestled in a pile of moist leaves nearby, but instead she got up and, without even thinking about it, wandered off.

A hunger began to rise in Larka as she went, and suddenly she caught a scent on the morning air. She crept after it toward the edge of the forest and, on a hillock beyond, saw a hare standing bolt upright in the grass. Its huge white ears shook and its whiskers twitched as it nibbled on a thick stem of grass.

Larka acted from pure instinct. Her fur began to bristle and her tail shook. As her eyes locked on the hare, they took in the Lera's slightest movement, and she knew immediately that it had sensed her and that fear was thrilling through its body. Larka could feel the tension between them almost as a physical thing, and as she prowled forward, she saw it turn its head strangely, against the natural angle of its body, which seemed caught by her gaze, pinioned by terror.

Larka's heart beat faster at the power she suddenly felt over this animal. She realized that it was feeling what she herself had felt in the forest when the hunters had come. The hare, too, was trembling on nature's delicate balance between the instinct to hide and lie motionless, to remain unseen, and the desperate desire to release its own energy and run: the ancient dilemma of the hunted.

Larka's trot turned to a steady lollop and suddenly the hare bolted. Luckily for Larka its hole was in the soft earth between it and her, so it could not make straight for ground. Where a hare has sudden spurts of speed, a wolf has stamina, and the hare quickly exhausted itself as Larka began to close. As the sun shone down on her coat and her paws sprang across the grass, the she-wolf felt suddenly happy and free. But just as Larka was on the hare, she remembered Khaz's terror at the pit and a terrible fear overcame her. There was a flash of black and Larka knew that she was seeing the grass that was rushing by, the leaves and stems, through different eyes, the hare's eyes. She felt herself springing, her claws opening and her paws reaching out, but with it she felt a horror grip her and then an agonizing pain in her own body. Larka was tumbling, sightlessly now, with the hare caught in her paws, feeling its own agony as she killed it.

There was another flash, and Larka was lying next to the hare. It was dead, but the horrible pain that had struck Larka was only just beginning to fade. She lay panting in the grass, blinking at the Lera in terror and utter misery.

"Larka. Larka."

Fell and Kar were coming down the hill toward her in the sunshine, as the she-wolf swung her bloodied head. Suddenly, filled with doubt and confusion, Larka turned and sprang away. It was a good while before the others managed to catch up with her. Fell, who had stopped to pick up the hare, laid its carcass carefully in the grass in front of Larka.

"It's your first true kill, Larka." He grinned rather stupidly. "We saw you from the wood. Why don't you want it?"

Larka shook her head angrily.

"What's wrong, Larka?" asked Kar.

"I can't explain."

"Tell us what happened."

Larka had managed to calm down a little, but when she told them they were both appalled.

"But, Larka," growled Fell, "I thought the power of the Sight was to look through the eyes of birds, not other Lera. And to feel the pain of your own kill . . ."

"Morga said the Sight had cursed her all her life, Fell," Larka whispered bitterly. "And now she's cursed us . . . me. You shouldn't have anything to do with me."

"Perhaps Bran is right." Kar nodded mournfully, dropping his tail. "He said any one of us could be next."

Fell was staring down at the hare, thinking what a pity it would be to waste it, but he lifted his muzzle immediately and snapped at Kar, "You're not part of the pack, so it stands to reason Morgra didn't mean you when she cursed us. You at least have nothing to fear."

Poor Kar looked as though he had been bitten. Not part of the pack? Kar dropped his muzzle, and he suddenly thought bitterly of his dead parents and how Skop had so recently abandoned him.

"I'll go away," said Larka with a sudden resolution, not noticing Kar's distress. "Maybe then you'll be safe."

"Go where?" growled Fell.

"Perhaps to Morgra. She and I are the same," muttered Larka, though she hardly knew what she was saying. "Perhaps I can persuade her to lift the curse from the pack."

"No, Larka. We'll find Tsinga and learn how you can use your powers to help us."

"But . . . I'm frightened, Fell," growled Larka, hanging her head.

Kar had lifted his muzzle. "No need," he whispered suddenly. "We'll protect you, won't we, Fell?"

"You?" snorted Fell thoughtlessly. "You're no better than Bran."

Kar was looking up and he suddenly caught sight of a bird, wheeling high above their heads.

"Come on, Larka," he cried, pleased with his own idea. "Wolfbane made a pact with the birds, but we'll make a pact too. The three of us. To fight for each other, come what may. To fight fear itself. If anything happens to the grown-ups we'll always have each other. No curse and no stupid talk of Wolfbane or a Man Varg can beat that."

"Fight for a Sikla?" said Fell unkindly, but he was remembering that day they had all played so happily together by the river. He saw Larka look tenderly at Kar, and Fell suddenly wished that he had had the idea himself.

"Come on, you two," said Kar. "Swear it. We'll need something to swear by, though. I know, we'll swear by the Stone Spores, where we used to play. Come on, Fell. Swear it."

Fell lifted his tail and bared his teeth.

"All right, then. I swear it. By the Stone Spores."

"And so do I. Larka?"

"By the Stone Spores." Larka nodded gravely.

"Then the pact is made," growled Kar, a little too gravely for his age. "And nothing in the world can break it. Now we should be getting back to the others."

The three young wolves walked side by side up the hill in the sunshine. Larka had been reassured and, for the first time since he had arrived with Huttser's pack, Kar felt truly proud of himself.

That night the pups felt a little less nervous as they lay around their parents, and the darkness and the wind in the trees seemed to soothe rather than frighten them. They listened to the adults, each holding their secret pact inside and finding great strength and comfort in it.

"She really tells the future?" asked Bran, licking his paws and blinking at Palla as they discussed the fortune-teller. Her valley could not be far off now.

"They used to say Tsinga had that power." Palla nodded. "Although she would always talk in riddles, as far as I remember."

"To know the future . . ." muttered Bran, peering about him into the trees and suddenly thinking of Kipcha and his own fall into the grave. "If we have a future at all."

Huttser glared angrily at Bran.

"And we must be careful when we approach," said Palla, "for there was always a madness in her."

That following sun they came to the edge of a high white mountain. The mountain Brassa had spoken of. Its great cliffs were streaked with ribs of pure marble. Bran was at his wits' end as they walked beneath its shadow. He was certain the curse would never release them now and that Wolfbane himself was stalking them through the forests. He kept wondering whose turn it would be next as he fled, but the specter of actually meeting Tsinga slowed his steps.

Beyond the mountain they started to climb another hill and, as they looked back over the terrain they had traversed, they realized that they could see the castle on the most distant mountaintop. It looked tiny now, and its human contours had faded back, making it almost indistinguishable from the natural terrain around it. It might have been nothing more than a boulder, and it was only the memory of their strange journey that gave it any dark meaning for the pack.

Twilight was coming in as they saw a wooded valley below them, and they were wondering if this was Tsinga's home when Bran pulled up in horror.

"Look," he gasped.

There were two tall beech trees ahead of them, well spaced, and between them there seemed to be a path. It might have been a goat or a deer track, but it wasn't the path that Bran was trying to draw their attention to. It was the trees themselves. Hanging upside down from the branches in each, on either side of the track, was a dead blackbird. Their beaks were missing and blood had streaked the bark.

"It must be the entrance." Palla shuddered.

"At least it means one thing," growled Huttser. "The fortune-teller is still alive."

They passed between the birds and began to descend the track. The wolves were even more nervous than before as they threaded through the dense trees, but as the pack came down those slopes, they found the evening and the forest strangely beautiful. If this place was the Vale of Shadows, apart from those grim little tokens, it hardly lived up to its name. The valley bottom was thick with fallen leaves, and those that remained on the spiky branches glowed a deep auburn in the fading light. The woods echoed with noises of Lera and birds, and thrummed with the hollow knocking of a woodpecker. Huttser was leading the pack in a straight line again when he suddenly stopped and began to scent the ground. The scent marking was faint but not that old.

Huttser howled, and for a moment the noises of the forest fell silent, its secret watching creatures startled into fear by the voice of the wolf. Huttser called again, but no answer came, so he led them on. Quickly, the trees began to dwindle now and the little valley opened. They saw a wide earth clearing at its bottom, and as they went, they began to notice that the ground was littered with bones. They were all small animals. The skeletons of rabbits and mice and voles. The bones were yellowing and well chewed, and they had long been sucked clean of their wholesome marrow.

"Stick by my side, Larka," growled Palla as the wolf pack stopped. Palla had noticed how desperately nervous Bran and the cubs were becoming. Huttser called once more, and suddenly there was an answering growl. It came from behind a heavy thicket between two pitted rocks.

"Tsinga," cried Palla, stepping forward immediately. "Is that you, Tsinga? We ask you Tratto's Blessing to enter your territory."

There was another dark growl from behind the bushes.

"Tratto?" snorted a voice suddenly. "That old fool is long dead and the Varg respect nothing anymore. Morgra and her Balkar Draggas see to that. Nothing. Except perhaps the freedom to kill."

Suddenly a shape rose from behind the thicket. The fortune-teller was staring straight at them. Larka and Fell gasped and began to back away. The old she-wolf had her muzzle in the air as she scented and her eyes were open, but they were white with the filmy cataracts that had made her stone-blind.

"It's Palla, Tsinga," whispered the Drappa nervously, trying to turn the wolf's head with her voice.

Tsinga swung up her muzzle and growled, sniffing around like a weasel and moving her sightless eyes back and forth.

"I remember a Palla from long ago," she muttered. "Before I stumbled into darkness, and before I truly saw. It is gratifying that so many of the Varg seek me out these suns, to ease me in my loneliness. Not even my trophies or the rumors I spread about my valley can keep them out anymore."

Tsinga's voice was deep and hard but sharp with bitterness, too, and Bran was reminded of Morgra above the ravine.

"Then they are just stories," growled Huttser, "about a vale of—"

"Stories." Tsinga chuckled. "Yes, they are stories. But they have truth too. For is not life itself a vale of shadows? But you are welcome, if yours is really the family."

"Then you know of us already?" asked Huttser with surprise.

"Oh yes. The rebels told me a rumor of it, though I refused to answer their foolish questions and I drove them away. I know, Palla, that you and Morgra were born beneath the Stone Den and that your daughter's coat is white. She was born there, too, born at the very same moment as the human."

"And now Morgra has cursed our family," growled Palla.

"Curses," hissed Tsinga scornfully. "Poor little Morgra. She has power, but it was always weaker than she liked. That's what she hated and feared the most. Why else throw around her curses? Why else seek out the Balkar and try to hypnotize them? Why else murder Tratto?"

Huttser and Palla could hardly believe their ears, but Bran had heard it in Morgra's voice that sun. Tratto had been respected and even loved among the free wolves, and few understood why he had chosen Morgra to succeed him. But now they knew. Morgra had murdered the leader and usurped his power.

If they had known the whole story, though, they would have been truly appalled. How Morgra had infiltrated the ranks of the Balkar and got close to the leader. How at first she had pretended that she admired him and his strong rule and the way that Tratto had suppressed superstition in the land beyond the forest. But Morgra had seen immediately how Tratto was aging, and bit by bit, she had begun to pour poison into his ears. She had played on his fears of what lay ahead for him, and as he sickened had begun to insinuate that it was the ancient ways, the black arts, that could help him. She told him things of the past, of wonders and mysteries beyond his understanding, love that had been passed to Morgra by Tsinga herself. And gradually Tratto, sick and enfeebled, had fallen totally under her sway. Then one cold night as he lay on his own, Morgra herself had come to him and, laughing at his weakness and age, she had bitten into the leader's throat.

Palla stepped closer. "Tsinga," she said softly, "Brassa is dead."

The fortune-teller hardly seemed to react at all. "Dead," she muttered, shaking her head slightly, but the years had made Tsinga hard. "Well, there may be time for private sorrow, but now the legend comes. Some say it has all happened before, but perhaps everything comes again. For generations now fortune-tellers like me have waited, passing the story from wolf to wolf. Now, at last, it is here."

"Then you must help us," cried Palla. "We have come to ask you to teach Larka of the Sight, Tsinga. To lift the curse."

"Is that all?" said Tsinga scornfully. "You have a far greater journey, Palla, if you dare make it. If you are really the ones."

As the she-wolf stood there between the pitted rocks and spoke of a greater journey, to other eyes she might have looked like some blind storyteller, standing on the shore of a far-off land, as a band of soldiers listened in the firelight, weaving tales of desperate loves and godlike wars.

"You mean if we are this family," whispered Palla, "to fight the evil. Can you tell us, Tsinga?"

Tsinga was smiling coldly. She lifted her head and her voice quivered around the clearing, but the words that came to them now seemed to return a strength and a power to the blind wolf.

> *And only a family both loving and true,*
> *May conquer the evil, so ancient, so new.*
> *As they fight to uncover what secrets they share*
> *And see in their journey how painful is care.*
> *Beware the Betrayer, whose meaning is strife,*
> *For their faith shall be tried by the makers of life,*
> *And who shall divine, in the dead of the night,*
> *The lies from the truth, the darkness from light?*
> *Like the cry of the scavenger, torn through the air*
> *A courage is needed, as deep as despair.*

As Tsinga recited the ancient lines, Kar and Larka began to back away.

"It's all right, children," whispered Palla, "don't be frightened."

"There are other cubs apart from the she-wolf?" cried Tsinga immediately, beginning to sniff again and letting her tongue loll from her mouth. "Bring them to me."

Kar looked terrified and Fell growled nervously. Palla

was going to nudge Fell on, when Huttser stepped forward slightly.

"No, Palla," he whispered, his eyes glittering cunningly. "Let Kar go. Then we'll see."

Kar glared at the Dragga, but the wolf was still too young to disobey. He padded reluctantly toward Tsinga. As soon as he did so she snarled.

"Would you test me?" she cried, lifting her nose. "This one is not of Palla's blood."

"How did she know?" said Huttser in amazement. "Does she have the Sight, then?"

"Fool," snapped Tsinga. "Do you think I do not know a scent when I smell it? For there are more ways of seeing than with the eyes. Ways we must never forget, as we must never forget what we are. With the tongue and ears, the paws and nose. And I have a good nose. Oh yes, I smell out children and thieves. I sniff out legends and lies. The wolves run and Wolfbane waits to return."

A madness seemed to have entered Tsinga, and Kar backed away, trembling.

"But he has a destiny, too," dribbled the fortune-teller as she sensed Kar go. "Perhaps as important as any. Everything has a destiny."

"Then you can see things?" whispered Palla.

Tsinga seemed to misunderstand Palla's question. "See things, Palla? With such old and evil eyes? How I long to see things again. To see the forest and the streams. To watch the sun blazing on the mountaintops and the giant clouds ribbed with breathing fire."

Tsinga lifted her muzzle to the heavens. "To see the lark climb the morning skies and dance on the air and watch spring's sap pressing green through the quivering grass, or old autumn licking the leaves with veins the color of blood. To see the shape of a young deer, joyous with fear in the lush fields. To see the terror in its eyes."

Larka was goggling at the fortune-teller. The sun had broken through the clouds, and as its chill light fell on Tsinga's eyes they looked empty and hard and cruel. But Tsinga's voice, sharp with cunning as she spoke of the deer, was suddenly full of sadness.

"But instead I must look into nothingness," she muttered grimly, saliva spattering the gnawed bones on the ground around her paws. "I must dream and talk to memories. Memories to make the gut churn with loss and longing. Yet, although the world is dark to me now, memories have power, too, such power. Such power the past has over us all."

Tsinga seemed very close to tears, and the words of Morgra's curse were suddenly echoing in the pack's ears again. "May the past that's dark with crimes bring revenge in future times."

But then a thought crossed Tsinga's mind that threw off her sadness. "Yet the Pathways of Death, they are the true pathways of the past," she hissed. "If the ancient howl ever opens them and calls to the Searchers, then the real power will begin. If the Searchers come you must never let them touch you."

"Why?" growled Huttser.

"Because they are the bringers of the power to touch minds and control wills and actions. They shall be the servants of the summoner and carry terror through the Lera. They shall tempt nature to turn on itself."

Again the words of the verse came back to Palla: "And the Searchers tempt nature to prey on its own."

Tsinga swung her head around as though looking for something in the shadows, and Larka thought of the times in the forest she had sensed something following her, and now she dropped her muzzle and began to growl at the fortune-teller.

"But come," said Tsinga abruptly. "You spoke of children, Palla. There must be another."

As soon as Fell came up, Tsinga craned her head forward and seemed to be testing the air. For a moment the pack fancied they could almost see a light in her dead eyes. Then, suddenly, the she-wolf started to shake.

"No," she cried, "get away from me."

Tsinga's jaws were beginning to foam with white froth as Fell backed away too. "I can't . . ." she gasped, "can't breathe."

"What is it, Tsinga?" cried Palla in horror. "Do you see anything?"

"Stop it," growled Huttser suddenly. "Enough of these cubs' fables. If it is true what you say then tell us simply how to defeat this evil. Tell us how to destroy Morgra."

Tsinga whirled around toward Huttser, snapping at the air.

"You think you know where evil really lies, Huttser?" she snarled scornfully. "Because you believe that Morgra is evil? But was not a great injustice done to her? Perhaps the evil began there. Perhaps it is always with us, like the Searchers."

Huttser growled boldly, but again Tsinga's gaze was blank and pitiless.

"But, Tsinga . . ."

"You believe, too, that I know what evil is," hissed Tsinga, "or how to fight it? But am I not blind? And does not my blindness make it hard for me to hunt and so make me all the more hungry? Tell me this, Huttser, when the time of the Putnar comes and the blood lust is on you, can you look into the darkness and predict the future? Can you distinguish truth from lies, tell darkness from light?"

Tsinga swung her head toward the cubs who had all huddled together. "Beware the Betrayer," she hissed, "whose meaning is strife."

Fell felt a queasy fear steal through him. Larka was petrified, but as the fear threatened to swamp her, she suddenly felt an anger bubbling up inside her too.

"Tsinga," Larka cried, stepping forward boldly. "Tell me what this final power will do then. The final power of the Sight."

Tsinga stopped dead in her tracks as she heard Larka's voice, and she seemed to be trying to read something in the sound. To see if there was enough strength or understanding in it.

"No," she growled, "you are still too young. What does a mere cub know of the world? Nothing but innocence and games."

Her parents were watching Larka. They both stood motionless as they wondered what she would do.

"I do know things," Larka growled, furious at Tsinga's scorn, and she seemed to suddenly grow in stature. "I know that Morgra is looking for the child, but that Tsarr has it. Tsarr and his Helper, Skart, the proud steppe eagle. I know that the Balkar are seeking out Harja and that

Morgra would find this cub and take it to the ancient citadel, the gateway to heaven."

Tsinga seemed impressed, too, as much with Larka's courage as anything.

"Then you know much already, my child," she whispered more kindly.

"And I know that Morgra wants to sacrifice the human on the altar, to become the Man Varg."

"Sacrifice the child?" said Tsinga with surprise, and she started to chuckle. "Oh no, my dear. Morgra needs the child."

Larka looked crestfallen and suddenly rather small again.

"But the altar must taste blood," said Palla, remembering the verse.

"Ah yes, and one must pay the price," growled Tsinga. "But Morgra needs the child to gain the power of the Man Varg."

"Why does she need the child?" asked Palla. "The Man Varg. What is this creature?"

"It is not a creature as such. If the Sight is used at the altar to look into and guide the human's mind, then together their sight shall be that of the Man Varg and a vision will be given. A vision uniting past and future. A vision containing the great secret about Man, the secret the Lera must know. A vision so startling that all nature shall be forced to behold it. A vision that shall bestow ultimate power."

"Ultimate power?"

As Tsinga's white eyes blazed back at them, she suddenly looked magnificent. "First the Lera's minds must be weakened by the Searchers. Then the trap will be sprung. For as they turn to watch the vision, frightened and ashamed, then the wolf shall touch all the animals' minds in the same moment and enslave the Lera forever. Then," cried Tsinga, "shall come forth the Man Varg, the greatest Putnar the world has ever known."

Palla swung around to Huttser in horror as Tsinga's voice echoed around them.

"Enslave all the Lera," gasped Larka, and Fell looked up.

"What?" growled Bran. "With mastery over their very souls?"

The wolves could hardly believe what they were hearing. So this was the Man Varg. The pack stared at Tsinga. Now her valley seemed truly full of shadows.

"It's what the verse said," Palla mumbled next to her daughter, though in such a choked voice Tsinga couldn't hear her. "Now I remember it. In the mind of the Man Varg, then none shall be free."

Larka's eyes were wide with fear.

The pack was dwarfed by the shadows reaching down from the mountains.

"Then this is the evil," growled Huttser, "the evil the family must conquer. Slaves, slaves to the Man Varg. Even the untamed wolf."

But even as he said it, Tsinga had started to chuckle again. The laughter rose inside her, swelling from her belly. It was as though, as she stood between those two rocks, she would have shattered the very stone with the sound.

"Still you talk of evil," she cried madly. "But some believe the Lera were always slaves. Slaves to hunger and instinct and their own blind forgetfulness. And I was a wolf once. Strong as the morning. Fast as the starling. But now look at me. Am I not a slave?"

The pack stared back at Tsinga, and she dropped her head almost shamefully.

"But perhaps you speak the truth, Huttser," she whispered. "Perhaps the Man Varg is the greatest evil. We shall see."

"Then we must help Larka defeat this legend?" Palla whispered.

"No, Palla," snarled Huttser suddenly. "We came to ask if Larka's gift could help us fight the curse, that's all. So we can live in peace and freedom and hunt wild and mark our boundaries."

"Freedom?" snorted Tsinga, starting to chuckle hoarsely again. "Boundaries? Do you think the power of the Sight respects boundaries?"

But this time the eerie laughter subsided quickly, and when Tsinga spoke again her voice was full of fear. "No," she cried, "if yours is truly this family you must find the human. Find Tsarr and Skart. Only they can teach Larka now."

Huttser began to snarl, "No, this is not why we came. We came to help our daughter fight—"

"Find the child?" said Larka, interrupting her father. "But we should have nothing to do with Man. It is the oldest law."

"There are other laws," said Tsinga strangely. "Laws far deeper than the Varg could dream up. Besides, you are linked to the child already, Larka."

Larka looked at her, surprised. "But this child," she said, "how could I find it? I don't even know where it is."

Tsinga whispered, "Perhaps the child will find you."

"But, Tsinga," said Palla desperately, "will you not teach Larka?"

"Peace," cried Tsinga suddenly. "I'm tired and you have heard enough for now. I am hungry and would have you hunt. With these eyes I must make do with vermin I catch by chance. Even those blackbirds wouldn't come to me until I'd baited the trap with a field mouse. It would be good to feed like a true wolf again. We will speak further."

Tsinga would say nothing more. She settled by her rock, among the scatterings of little bones, muttering and laughing grimly to herself. Bran and the children lay down at the edge of the clearing, wondering fearfully about all they had heard, as Huttser took Palla off to hunt for food for the fortune-teller. As they left, Palla told Bran to guard the young wolves and not to speak with Tsinga again until they got back.

Bran had no intention of approaching Tsinga. He was petrified, and as he heard the hunters howling in the night and listened to the wind stirring the trees, the moving shadows seemed haunted by specters—of Wolfbane and the Searchers and their dead friends.

Tsinga's strange words echoed in all their thoughts. Larka was greatly relieved when the first rays of morning stroked the tops of the forest and she saw Huttser and Palla returning with their kill.

"Good," dribbled Tsinga as she gulped down the last tender scraps of venison and the light swelled around her, glinting on those ugly white orbs. "Now I can think more clearly. Larka, rest near me and tell me of your journey."

The pack was lying around Tsinga again, though Bran was as far away as he could possibly get and still overhear her. As Larka settled reluctantly next to her and described what had happened during the hunt and at the rapids and in the graveyard, Tsinga suddenly threw back her head.

"This is interesting," she said, sniffing greedily. "Perhaps yours is truly this family."

Larka's heart sank. "Why, Tsinga?"

"Did you not hear? The verse tells of the makers of life, Larka, that shall test the family. Their faith shall be tried by the makers of life."

"The makers of life," growled Larka, "Tor and Fenris you mean?"

Tsinga shook her head slowly. "For fortune-tellers, who were once prized in the forests, living by soil and stream and branch, guarding their secrets and passing them only to those ready to hear them. The makers of life are the four elements, Larka: water, air, earth, and fire, the element that Man captures to make his burning air."

Something almost beautiful had entered Tsinga's voice, beautiful and full of longing. It was as though her memory was more than all she had seen in her own life, the memory of a vanishing world.

"There are few of us left now to pass on this knowledge. Indeed I may be the last. The last of a dying breed. It is all I held against Tratto, for though he was a good wolf and strong, he confused the black arts, like the cult of Wolfbane, with the fortune-tellers' natural magic. The understanding of what makes up life. The magic of the elements themselves. Your pack has already been touched by three."

"How, Tsinga?"

"Earth at the pit and in the grave," growled Tsinga, and Larka shuddered as she remembered her fall. "Air when you flew with the birds, and water at the rapids. As you go, Larka, beware of fire. But there is a fifth element, too, the source of dreams and nightmares, which you must beware above all."

"What is it, Tsinga?" said Larka, lowering her ears pitifully.

"Ice," hissed Tsinga. "The still element, that holds all in potential."

Larka let out a little whimper.

"But tell me, Larka," said Tsinga suddenly. "Just before the Sight came on you. What was happening, and what did you feel?"

As Larka described the visitations, Tsinga sniffed again, delightedly. "Yes, yes," she muttered as if welcoming an old friend to a meal. "Fear and death are the oldest gateways to the gift. Until you find Skart and Tsarr, Larka, and begin to learn to use the powers of the Sight properly—to see as the birds see, to peer into water and look on far-off realities, far more clearly than a foolish old fortune-teller. Over the centuries there have been many who could not bear to live with that knowledge. You must also learn to be strong."

Larka looked at her parents desperately.

"But you see things," growled Larka. "Can't you teach me?"

Tsinga's voice was suddenly caught between laughter and tears.

"Would you see through these eyes, my dear," she cried, "through the eyes of a mad, blind wolf? No, Larka. And I do not wield the Sight as you do. I could touch part of it once, as all fortune-tellers could. I could look into the water and see far-off realities. To do that you must first invoke the power of memory, for there lies the secret pattern of things, and then send your senses whispering out to the present and even the future."

Larka looked up; a breeze was stirring the forest.

"But I spent so long gazing and searching that it destroyed my eyes. It left me in the dark, but with the curse to know something of what must come. And it left me with my memories. But above all it left me blind, Larka, as blind as the great statue herself."

"Statue?" growled Larka.

"Yes," whispered Tsinga, "above the altar at Harja, the place of the coming of the Man Varg. The statue of the she-wolf. The very reason the Varg call the place the gateway to heaven, for it is as beautiful as the evening."

Even as she spoke, an image flashed into Tsinga's brain. There it stood before her mind's eye, just as she had spied it one bleak winter's day, so many years before. Among the ruined temples of Harja, long worn away by centuries of erosion, battered by wind and snow and shaken by the earth tremors that so frequently visited the haunches of the mountain: the giant stone image of a she-wolf and, at her belly, two suckling human infants.

Although it had grown up as an ordinary settlement, the citadel had become a sacred place to the humans who had founded it. The Romans had made it a place of worship and of augury, and a cult had grown up dedicated to that statue, for the Romans had long told a story about the founding of their first city. A story of male twins, Romulus and Remus, who had been suckled at her belly; a story that lived in their minds not so much as a truth, but with the power that myth has in the heart of an ancient people.

"Then Harja does exist," whispered Palla, "and you know the way."

"Knew the way, yet how could I find it now? But I have said enough," said Tsinga suddenly. "Perhaps too much already. I am forgetting the single most important law of the Sight. Larka must learn and choose for herself."

"But, Tsinga," Palla interrupted.

"That is the only way, Palla—" snapped Tsinga. "On her journey she must discover all she can of Man, too, for whatever she decides, knowledge alone can help her to fight. Morgra already knows much of Man, and Larka must beware of her, for those with the Sight can sometimes touch each other's minds, especially in close proximity."

The pack wondered what Tsinga meant about Morgra knowing much of Man, but it echoed what Morgra herself had said that night.

"Now you must all hurry."

"Don't worry, Tsinga," growled Huttser, "I will not let anything hurt my family. We will defeat this curse. And live. We shall protect Larka."

"Haven't you understood yet?" snarled Tsinga. "The Vision offers a power over all the Lera. If yours is the family, it is not just for your own sakes that you must survive now, but for life itself. So guard each other. For if one is lost, I fear for us all. Now go. Get beyond the boundaries as quickly as you can. Once you have done that your journey will have only just begun."

"For pity's sake, Tsinga," said Palla, "there is so much we would ask you first. Of Morgra and of Wolfbane. We must know how to help Larka."

Tsinga got up and sniffed the air. She snarled quietly as her head swung back toward the children.

"Can parents ever help their children?" She chuckled. "Well, we shall see. You talk of pity, Palla, but winter is here and with it comes death and darkness. It is as certain as the seasons themselves. But Wolfbane . . ."

Bran's ears started to quiver.

"In stories, the Evil One has always hunted the Varg, hunted through their dreams, feeding on fear and guilt. Wolfbane, the friend of the dead. For centuries his cult dominated the forests. Before Sita's star rose and the Evil One was suppressed. If the Shape Changer returns, who knows what form he will take, for may not fear come in many guises? "The verse warns of making errors. 'Who shall divine, in the dead of the night, the lies from the truth, the darkness from light.' "

The hackles rose on Bran's neck. To the family Tsinga seemed to be talking in riddles again.

"But the legend will not be easy for Morgra either. There is much that must be fulfilled before the power to enter minds could come. Above all, none have ever tried the ancient howl before. Now Morgra is almost certainly too weak and I doubt she can even look into the water. That's why she tried to join your pack, Palla. Though if she finds another to help her—"

"Another?" growled Huttser. "But Brassa told us that you only taught two wolves of the Sight."

"Yes," growled Tsinga almost bitterly, "and entrusted each with a secret about the legend. I'd hoped to make them joint guardians of the law."

Tsinga was shaking her head. "But the Sight draws on all the powers of the universe, on the inner forces of life. Though the legend speaks to the wolf, who is to say there are not others among the Lera that can touch the gift? Others that Morgra could draw on. And then, of course, there is your daughter."

Kar and Fell swung around to Larka, and Palla thought of the rumors they had heard long ago about Morgra. That she had been trying to enchant the animals too.

"But you all have a destiny, my friends," growled Tsinga suddenly. "You must help each other to guard against Morgra's hate. Your love and faith must guard against Wolfbane, and you must carry hope in your hearts, always. And Larka, remember the last line of the verse. *You* will need courage—a courage as deep as despair. Now, hurry."

The words seemed to quiver through Larka's being. The other wolves shivered in the cold, but they could see they would get no more from Tsinga and now, their minds filled with all she had told them, they turned away.

"Palla," Tsinga hissed as they went, and Palla swung around.

"What is it, Tsinga?" she answered, walking slowly back to her.

"I will tell you one last secret," whispered Tsinga. "For you are her mother. Why the verse speaks of the wounded."

"Go on," whispered Palla.

"It refers to a she-wolf, Palla. For the fortune-tellers have always known of them as the wounded ones. The Vision can only be given to a drappa, Palla."

Palla growled nervously.

"A she-wolf that has tended to another living creature. That knows the pain and love of a mother."

"But then Morgra," growled Palla suddenly, "she is barren. She has never even—"

"Perhaps," growled Tsinga, "but perhaps that was another reason for her edict. She is gathering children around her."

"But why didn't you tell Larka?"

"That secret she must discover for herself, if it is in her to do so. Now be gone. Look after your cub."

As Palla followed the pack, Bran was so relieved to leave that place and the mad she-wolf that his tail rose like a branch. But Tsinga suddenly lifted her muzzle and called to him too.

"You! The Sikla," she hissed

Bran froze in his tracks and turned fearfully. The black smudge on his eye looked like a bruise.

"Did you not think I scented you too?" Tsinga smiled.

As she held him in her blind gaze, Bran started to tremble.

"Well," said Tsinga, "is there nothing the Sikla would ask of a fortune-teller?"

"Me . . . ," stammered Bran. "No . . . no . . ."

Bran turned and bounded after the others, but as he went, he heard Tsinga sniggering and muttering to herself. Huttser led his pack up the valley, but before they reached the trees, Kar felt something fizzing on his back, melting through his fur. The cubs looked up, and suddenly the air was thick with giant snowflakes that tumbled on the bitter wind.

"And remember," cried Tsinga's haunting voice through the coming storm, "love one another. Be true. Love one another or perish."

6
ICE

To bathe in fiery floods, or to reside
In thrilling region of thick-ribbed ice;
To be imprison'd in the viewless winds,
And blown with restless violence round about
The pendant world.
— WILLIAM SHAKESPEARE, *Measure for Measure*

THE AIR WAS THICK WITH SNOW, blinding the wolf pack and obscuring the wooded mountains around them. The pack had settled on the edge of Tsinga's valley in a small, sheltering copse, but what protection it offered was sparse, and the children were shivering bitterly.

"Huttser," cried Palla, shouting to make herself heard above the wind. "Brassa told us that the Sight could give control over the elements. Do you think Morgra—"

"No," snapped Huttser. "Tsinga said Morgra's gift is weak. And even if it were strong, how can a wolf control the elements?"

But in truth the storm seemed to have an almost unearthly anger in it. Larka shuddered as she thought of Tsinga's words about those with the Sight being able to

179

touch one another, and her strange warnings of the sources of life. For a moment it was as though the very wind were echoing the fortune-teller: "It is not just for your own sakes that you must survive now, but for life itself."

"What now, Huttser?" growled Palla. "Do we do as Tsinga says and find this child?"

"I don't know, Palla. But we must reach the boundaries. As quickly as possible. We must cross the river as soon as we can."

Fell looked strangely at his father. Huttser had always inspired such courage in him, but now he knew they were running away.

"Come, then, Huttser," said Palla, suddenly trying to cheer them up. "In the meantime we must look for some food."

The children lay there, the snow heaping on their backs as the three adults began to sniff around the edges of the copse, looking for some small animal to feed on. The wolves found nothing in the blizzard, and it was growing dark when Bran finally gave up. His paws were so cold that the pads on his feet were beginning to crack. All day he had looked out into the storm and seen nothing but the shape of Wolfbane, snarling on the wind. As he slunk back to the copse, he overheard the children talking.

"Don't worry," Larka was saying. "If these powers are true, then I'll use them to help us all."

"But we're all marked," Kar whispered cheerlessly, "like Bran said."

"Bran," snorted Fell, "that coward. We mustn't listen to him. What use is he to our pack? If it wasn't for him and the spirit of a Sikla, Kipcha would still be alive."

Bran slunk down beneath a tree and laid his head miserably in the snow. Palla and Huttser had just returned, and they settled cheerlessly, too, as the night came in. Bran whined to himself as he drifted into dreams, wondering if Larka did indeed possess the power to look ahead, and thinking bitterly of what Fell had said.

Bran's sleep was troubled, and he shuddered as he woke. His coat was drenched in sweat, and it steamed in the brittle morning. Though it was bitterly cold it had stopped snowing, and now the silence of the land hung over the resting pack like a pall. Bran shivered as he peered about him, expecting some spectral figure at any moment to hurl itself at his throat. But as he waited and whimpered pitifully, nothing came at the Sikla. Instead, he kept remembering Tsinga's parting words to him: "Is there nothing the Sikla would ask?" They echoed through his thoughts like her laughter.

"I must know," Bran muttered to himself as he suddenly got up and padded off through the white. "I must know what will happen."

It started to snow again, covering the Sikla's tracks. As he crept back into the fortune-teller's valley, the thought of meeting Tsinga on his own was almost more terrifying to Bran than Wolfbane or a Man Varg.

The valley bottom was perfectly still; the gnarled bones had been covered by the snow. But as Bran crept toward Tsinga's rock, he stopped. The snow was stained with blood, a little red stream snaking out from the edge of the stone. The fortune-teller was lying on her side, and the snow around her body was covered in paw prints. She was dead. Her throat had been torn out, and her sightless eyes stared up at him.

Suddenly Bran heard a sound above and looked up. A bird was flapping high in the sky. It circled for a moment, and Bran wondered if it was Morgra's raven and if it had come to feed on Tsinga. But he saw that it was much larger than a raven. It turned suddenly and swooped toward the trees.

Bran looked at Tsinga for a final time, wondering and not without a twinge of relief, if she indeed had been the last of her kind. Then he slunk silently away. But as soon as he reached the trees again, he heard a sound and crept fearfully behind a large oak to listen. His muzzle poked around the side of the tree toward the voices. There were six large wolves lying in a circle. They were all grays, and the muzzle of the wolf who was speaking was stained red with blood.

"That's one job out of the way," he was saying. "She won't say any more about the verse at least. Now we must find the family."

Bran's ears came forward.

"We should have come sooner, though. They left the Stone Den suns back. Morgra will be furious, but I had to investigate those rumors about the citadel."

"And when we find them we kill them, too?" asked the wolf next to them.

Bran's muzzle curled into a silent snarl.

"Only the adults," growled the wolf slyly. "The children we take to Morgra. One of them is this white wolf."

One of the Night Hunters looked away guiltily. Until

Morgra's arrival, the Balkar had protected the rights of the free wolves in Transylvania and adhered strictly to Tratto's Blessing, respecting other pack boundaries. They had lived by a code of honor. Yet even before the murder of the old wolf, some among them had grown restless and discontented. Many despised the free wolves and wanted their hunting territories, while others were so used to fighting they were hopelessly lost in times of peace.

But Morgra had come among them, pretending to support Tratto but secretly spreading tales of Wolfbane and the legend, of the power that the Sight could bring them over all the Lera. She had laughed at their motto—First Among the Putnar. "No," she had said, "that prize belongs to the humans alone." Then many among the Balkar had begun to dream in the night of the altar and the coming of the Man Varg.

"But the legend," a wolf growled, "what have the Night Hunters to do with such things? In Tratto's day we fought real wolves, not dreams. But then a true Dragga led the fighting wolves, not an old Drappa."

"Silence," growled the lead wolf. "If Morgra heard you talking like that, you would pay with your life. You know what she has foreseen."

"Wolfbane," snorted the wolf who had just spoken. "She is using the threat to frighten and control us. Nothing more. Old drappa's tales that sap the strength of the dragga. Do you think I am foolish enough to believe that a story could come true? Wolfbane cannot return, because the Evil One does not exist."

"*You* are the fool," growled the lead wolf furiously. "Morgra has power, and she will summon the Shape

Changer to aid us. When he comes, you'd better know whose side you are on then."

Bran slunk back as the Night Hunters rose and began to mount the slope. The Sikla's mind was trembling with what he had just heard, but he was so frightened he could hardly move. As Bran watched them go, he realized that they were heading straight toward the pack. Bran began to shake uncontrollably. But it wasn't the words of Morgra's curse that came back to Bran now, it was words from the verse: "Beware the Betrayer, whose meaning is strife."

"Fenris," stammered Bran, "why am I such a coward? I'm worthless, just like Fell said."

As Bran thought of the children and his duty to the pack, his tail came down, and he shivered bitterly. "We're lost," he whimpered, "all lost."

But as he stood there, something stirred in him, and his mind could not stop other words from coming to him, too, words echoing out of the fury of a storm: "Love one another. Love one another or perish." Bran suddenly felt a wildness inside him and stepping forward with his tail raised, the Sikla threw up his muzzle to challenge the Balkar.

"Damn him," growled Huttser as they prowled around in the snow, looking for Bran's tracks. "Where's he slunk off to? When I find him, Palla . . ."

Huttser and Palla had been searching all morning while the youngsters had stayed behind at the copse, but there was no sign of Bran and their calls had been swallowed by the wind. Now they had come to the edge of the wood sloping down into Tsinga's valley. Suddenly they heard a painful whine. They gasped as they saw Bran struggling out of the trees. There was blood all over the wolf's coat, and his ears had been torn off. Bran's side was so badly bitten that there was hardly any fur left.

"Bran," cried Palla as the Sikla slumped to the ground in front of them.

"No time, Palla," panted Bran. "You must get away, all of you. The Night Hunters. They tried to make me tell where you were, but I wouldn't, Palla. I wouldn't betray you. I sent them west instead."

"Tell us what happened, Bran," growled Huttser softly.

As Bran relayed his story in harsh broken breaths, the Dragga and the Drappa bowed their heads.

"Morgra," snarled Huttser.

"So it got me, too, in the end," whispered Bran bitterly, the life beginning to ebb from his sad eyes. "Morgra's curse."

"Hush, Bran," said Palla tenderly, but the same fear was flooding the Drappa's mind.

"Huttser," whispered Bran suddenly, his voice so weak and strained they could hardly hear him at all. "Tell me, Huttser. What will I see when I . . . Will Wolfbane be there? In the darkness, waiting for me."

"No, my friend," Huttser said gently. "Now you go to run with Fenris through the clouds forever. Tor will be waiting, too, with her daughter, Sita, who loves all the wolves. Who sacrificed herself for your sake."

Bran's torn body relaxed a little.

"And, Bran," said Huttser guiltily, stroking him with his paw. "I'm sorry. For what I said at the rapids. Forgive me, my friend."

Bran began to shudder violently, and now it was he who could hardly hear the Dragga. Bloody spittle dribbled from his mouth and curdled with the virgin snow. The two wolves stood over the Sikla, and in that moment their hatred for Morgra was as raw as fresh meat.

"Palla," whispered Bran suddenly. "Will you tell the children . . ."

"What, Bran?" said Palla, straining to hear his fading voice.

"That I'm not a coward."

"Yes," answered Palla sadly. "We will tell them."

"And Palla," gasped Bran suddenly. "Tell Larka too. Tell her a secret from me."

"What secret, Bran?"

Bran could hardly speak now. "Tell her that it's not so terrible to . . ."

Palla was straining forward to hear the dying Sikla, and as Bran whispered the secret in her ear, Palla's eyes opened with surprise. But Bran shuddered for a final time, and the death rattle hissed out of his broken body. The Sikla was dead too.

"She is winning, Huttser," growled Palla bitterly, throwing back her muzzle. "Morgra's words will hunt us all down. If the Balkar don't get us first."

"Stop it, Palla. We are truly a family now, and nothing will break us apart. Morgra will not win, and we will escape. The old eastern boundary isn't far, is it? We will do as Brassa said. We will survive."

Palla lifted her muzzle and howled. As he watched her and the wind carried her cry down the valley, Huttser shivered and grew angry with his mate, for he knew that the elements were carrying her call straight toward the Night Hunters.

"We've got to get under cover," snarled Huttser through the snow. The little pack had come to a particularly deep drift and though the wide pads on their paws helped to hold them up, the snow was so fresh that the freezing wolves were sinking deeper and deeper as they went. The blizzard had started again, and now it was getting even stronger. Wolfbane was on their minds, and they all remembered what Brassa had once said about a terrible winter that would shroud the earth, Wolfbane's winter.

Their progress was desperately slow, and the children's coats, although thickening for the season, were soaked to the skin. The air was bitterly cold, too, and the wolves shivered terribly. But there was more than cold in their trembling progress, there was terror. The children had been horrified by Bran's death. And that morning they had heard Night Hunters nearby. The pack had moved away quickly, but Palla spotted the Balkar later that sun, in the far distance, moving after them like shadows through the blizzard.

"It'll be worse the higher we get," growled Palla, trying to spy the peaks above them through the snow and shivering as the wind bristled along her back and made her ears tremble.

"Kar," whispered Larka behind her in the angry wind. "Do you think it's Morgra trying to stop us from escaping?"

Kar trembled at her side, but he had no answer for his friend.

"Larka," said Fell, "if Morgra can affect the elements, then perhaps you can too. Why don't you try to stop the storm?"

Larka looked at her brother, and as they pressed on through the storm, she kept closing her eyes and trying to concentrate. If anything, the storm seemed to intensify.

"Keep an eye out for a cave, all of you," called Huttser, "and stick together."

They didn't find a cave, but as the wolves rose higher and the storm grew worse, Kar suddenly saw a shape looming at them through the snow. The pack crept forward and froze in their tracks.

The wind had dropped, and with it the blizzard had almost died. There, on the flat ground before them, stood a kind of castle. It was much smaller than the Stone Den had seemed on the mountaintop, and all about it were piles of rubble. It was fronted by a high arch and a wooden door, splintered and cracked, that was creaking mournfully on its hinges. The wolves knew by instinct as much as sight that it was deserted.

But the castle was made sinister by the shapes they saw ahead of them. The top of the arch was crowned with animals that glared down at them from the snowy rock. There were birds seized in the very moment of taking flight, and snakes twisting and curling around the rock. There were two snarling heads at each side of the arch, which they instantly recognized as Varg, and weird, grimacing faces that looked like humans. At either side of the archway stood two great stone dragons, and in the middle of this frozen menagerie was a Lera with a pair of wide black wings. It decorated the very center of the entrance and looked like a cross between a bird and a squirrel. It was a bat.

"It's like my dream," whispered Larka in amazement, "like the dream I had at the Meeting Place, of Wolfbane rising in the shape of a great bat."

"What do we do, Huttser?" growled Palla.

"Investigate," said Huttser immediately. "If we don't get out of this cold, Man can have us anyway."

The air seemed to freeze solid around them as Huttser led them on. The wolf pack passed under the entrance, and the children almost ducked, half expecting those stone Lera to launch themselves at them. But they relaxed as they entered the courtyard. It was deserted. There was nothing inside but piles of stones covered in snow and a few bits of rotting wood. Above all, the air had that lingering stillness of desertion about it, a tepid, empty quality, as though time itself had abandoned it. But the wolves felt the welcome rise in temperature immediately, and to one corner of the courtyard they saw a wooden lean-to that offered perfect shelter.

"Come on," commanded Huttser.

In the sky, the snow was getting thicker again. But as they crept under the lean-to, Huttser began to growl. On the ground, where the snow was sprinkled thinly, there were wolf skats.

"Night Hunters?" growled Palla.

Huttser gave no answer, but when the wolves began to investigate they realized that the skats were fairly old. There had been two wolves here, a male and a female. But Palla suddenly noticed that Larka was standing at the edge of the lean-to, sniffing the ground.

"What is it, Larka?"

At first Larka didn't answer, but then she recognized the scent from the edges of the Gypsy camp.

"Man," she answered. "Man has been here too. Perhaps it's . . ." But the wolf had no need to finish.

They settled and, though they were all cold and hungry, they were greatly relieved to be out of the blizzard. They all wondered if Tsarr and Skart and the human child had really been this way, too, and suddenly Larka thought of what Tsinga had said, "Perhaps the child will find you."

The howling wind came to them through the courtyard like voices from the dead.

"Palla," whispered Kar as they lay there, overawed by the weather and the strange little castle. "Can things really come back from the dead—like these Searchers?"

"I don't know, Kar," growled Palla. "I don't believe it."

But as Palla watched them all and saw their mounting terror at this talk of ghosts, she wanted to distract and comfort them.

"Come, children," she said suddenly. "I know a good story about things coming back to life. A story about a bird, a yellow oriole."

The children looked up hopefully.

"It lived in a land on the other side of the world, and, because of its beautiful feathers and the magic that it carried in its wings, it was loved by all who beheld it. The bird had the power to cure the sick with its song and to touch hearts wherever it flew. But there was a wolf who so loved this bird that he determined to capture it and keep it all for himself. One sun when the oriole was sleeping happily in a bush, the wolf managed to seize the bird in his jaws, though he held it carefully like a cub, and carried it off to a cave near a human den.

"The wolf lay down outside the cave, guarding the oriole day and night, and he would growl at it and order it to sing to him, for in truth the wolf's own heart was desperately sick.

"But the oriole loved nothing more in the world than its own freedom, and the power and beauty of its song was held not in the bird alone but in the joy of the free air and the glory of the changing skies. The oriole would try to sing to the wolf, for it cared for all things, but in the cave its song began to grow fainter and fainter. It grew sick itself, and at last the oriole died.

"When the wolf saw the bird lying dead in the cave, stiff and lifeless and not even worth a meal, he threw up his head angrily.

" 'It's just as I thought,' he snarled bitterly. 'The oriole was a liar. There is no magic in the world.' "

Palla was looking carefully at the cubs now.

"So the wolf picked up the oriole and carried it down to the human den where he saw the gray embers of their fire. He threw the bird scornfully into the ashes and turned away. But as the bird lay there, the embers stirred around it and started to eat up its feathers and its body. The fire burst into life, delighted at its unexpected breakfast, and the flames rose higher and higher. The fire seemed to have destroyed the oriole, but suddenly from the flames rose a shape, even larger and more magnificent than before. Into the skies rose the giant oriole, and now its wings were a glittering, shining gold, and its song was louder than ever before, for it had found its freedom again and so its love and its hope. But the wolf never saw the golden bird," finished Palla, a little sadly, "for it had not even turned back to look."

The bittersweet ending captured the interest of the children, who whispered to one another about the foolish wolf, just as they once would have over Brassa's stories.

They grew quiet again and Larka asked, "Mother, we'll be safe here tonight, won't we?"

"Yes, Larka. Not even the Night Hunters can follow us in this."

Fell growled softly at the thought of the Balkar, but he had never fought another wolf before, and his eyes suddenly grew large with worry.

"You needn't be frightened, Fell," said Palla as she saw the fear in her son.

"I'm not frightened, Mother," snapped Fell. "I'm a wolf. Putnar. Are we hunters or not? Even Bran . . ."

"*I'm* frightened, Palla," admitted Kar, from his spot beside Fell.

"I know," said Palla kindly, though she was looking at her son, "even Huttser and I are frightened sometimes."

Fell growled again, and he was suddenly tempted by a strange thought. He felt in that moment what a fine thing it would be to wield a power over all the Lera and never to be frightened again. But as the others stared at him, he was strangely embarrassed too.

"Your mother is right, Fell," said Huttser. "Fear is an instinct, like hunger or anger. We need it to help us survive, and it is nothing to be ashamed of. It tells us whether we should fight or flee."

"But, Father," said Fell suddenly, "the curse. It spoke of fear. Warned us of fear."

"Giving into fear is not the same as feeling it, Fell," growled Huttser, "and listening to it too. To learn to control fear and to face it, that's the thing. But to know when to run too."

Fell felt confused, for it seemed to him suddenly that by leaving their boundaries they were not facing it at all. Huttser could see this in his son, and he was worried. Even without the curse and the legend, or the Balkar so close behind them, Huttser knew how many dangers lay out there in the wild for a wolf. He only prayed to Fenris that they had taught the children enough in the den and at the Meeting Place to prepare them for the adult world.

"But you have nothing to worry about," Huttser went on suddenly. "We are with you. Your mother and I will protect you, whatever happens. And we will always love you."

There was something caught and almost guilty in Huttser's voice, for his words came like a promise that somewhere he knew he could not keep. One day, he knew, as surely as the others had gone, that they would not be there to protect their children. And it did not come naturally, they themselves would force their own children from the pack to confront their future. As Huttser's parents had done. As their parents had done before them. Yet even as he thought of his parents, Huttser pushed the memories from his mind. For now at least his words were true, and if it came to it, he would prove it with his own life.

Larka looked at her father lovingly, while Kar thought

sadly of Skop and felt a strange stirring in him for Huttser and Palla, a mixture of need and resentment.

Fell laid his head on his paws, and for a moment he remembered again the terrible anger he had felt toward his father that sun he had grabbed his neck. But now he needed to be comforted, and he let the warmth of safety spread like a fire through his limbs.

Huttser went on talking softly to the young wolves in the night, and his growling voice seemed to surround Fell and block out the sound of the storm. Fell was telling himself to be strong, to be fearless and grown-up, but even as he did so he wanted to relax, to sleep safe by his parents' side. He closed his eyes and let those words thrill through his mind: "We will protect you." Fell suddenly felt calm and, as his mind drifted into darkness, the young wolf gave a deep and trusting sigh.

As the little family slept, Larka felt restless. She wanted to help them somehow, and again she wished Tsinga could have taught her more of her strange powers. She got up and wandered around the courtyard. She came to a doorway. Inside there was an old trough where the animals that once lived here had come to drink. It was just warm enough inside for the brackish water not to have frozen.

Larka was going to drink, but she suddenly remembered what Fell had said about using her powers. Tsinga had told her something of the power to look into the water—of memory and sending out her senses to the present.

"I wonder," she whispered.

Larka closed her eyes and tried to concentrate. A great weariness overcame her. Though she was only a young wolf, already the past seemed to be a kind of curse, stretching from the darkness of her earliest half-formed visions. But as soon as she opened her eyes again, Larka started.

At first it was as though the water was getting blacker and blacker, and Larka could no longer see to the bottom of the trough. Then the water seemed to be swirling on its own, and from the center of the little vortex a kind of white mist began to spread out across the water's surface. Then a picture began to appear. It was neither on the surface of the water nor at the bottom of the trough, but it hung there as real as day.

Larka found herself looking at the mouth of a cave, shielded by a trailing willow. It was the den below the castle where she had been born. Larka felt a violent tugging at her heart. Then the image began to change in the moving mist, and there were Huttser and Palla on the hill when the dogs had come. As Larka watched them, she strained forward to try to hear what they were saying, but she could make out nothing at all. As the pair seemed to growl and started to run, again the image gave way. The pack was at the rapids, and Larka was looking at Kipcha stepping onto the log.

"No, Kipcha," cried Larka furiously. "Don't."

Larka would have given anything to stop her. To change that destiny and save her, but Larka felt a terrible sense of powerlessness as she realized that she could do nothing. That these things had already been. Suddenly there was Tsinga's face—old and blind and full of pain and sadness.

"The past," growled Larka. "Must it always haunt us?"

But the picture was changing again. Larka saw a great rock and a spreading almond tree. By it was a stream, and below the surface was a sheepskin, held in place by a number of stones. Larka's eyes opened wide as she saw that the fleece was a glittering gold like the oriole in the story, sparkling and shimmering with the tiny specks of yellow metal that had been scoured from the mountain by the churning water, collected in the curls of hair. Larka felt a strange sense of hope and amazement steal through her, but as she wondered what she was seeing, it vanished, and all that remained was the dirty water where the animals had once come to drink.

Larka stood blinking for a moment, transfixed by what she had seen. Then she walked back to the others, and, as she lay down by her family, she shook her head gently and closed her eyes.

The next sun, the sky was bright and brilliantly blue. For a moment, as Larka stepped from those strange walls, she wondered if she had somehow made the storm retreat. They were all glad to leave the abandoned castle behind them, and the wolves' coats glittered marvelously against the snow as they set off again.

But suddenly Larka stopped. Ahead of her in the snows, she fancied she had just seen three wolves on the brow of the slope, looking straight at her. It must have been a trick of the light against the white, for even as she looked, Larka blinked in amazement. The wolves had vanished completely.

"Larka, what is it?" asked Kar at her side.

"Nothing, Kar," answered Larka, shaking her head.

On they went briskly, and gradually Kar began to fall behind.

"Come on, Kar, try to keep up," cried Palla.

Huttser looked back at his family. It was just the sort of clear winter day for play, when a wolf should teach his children the joy of running free, gamboling through the snow and making straight lines in the powder with their snouts, just as he had done when he was a cub. But Huttser was desperate now to leave the pack boundary.

"Get a move on, Kar," he growled. "You're always lagging behind like a Sikla."

Kar caught up, though he looked very sullen. As the family neared the ridge of the mountain they were climbing, Larka caught something in the corner of her eye—in the far distance, behind them, coming over the horizon. Larka screwed up her eyes and instantly she was sure. There were six large gray wolf draggas, making straight for them.

"Father, Mother," she snarled, "Night Hunters. They're following our tracks."

They sprang forward, but as they reached the ridge their fear was lost for the briefest moment in the sheer exhilaration of what they saw. The wolves were looking out across the soaring Carpathians, vaulting over the central plains of Transylvania. The crags and slopes, the huge ravines and sudden precipices seemed to go on forever. The mountains were capped with snow, and others were bathed in red light that made them glow. The sun was sinking once more.

"Hurry," cried Huttser.

The going got harder as they ran, plunging down the slopes in front of them and climbing again up another steep slope ahead. Huttser paused again to look back, and he saw that the Balkar were coming over the ridge too.

"Keep going!" he cried desperately.

Higher the wolves climbed, fighting through the snow, and at last they came to the brow of the next slope. To the east, the mountain plunged down into a wide valley. Palla saw, with relief, the snaking river winding south, through generous snow-clad forests of glittering white conifer trees.

"The eastern boundary," she cried.

Even from here, the wolves could see that the river had started to freeze. It might be possible to cross.

Down the mountain the family leaped. Palla kept behind the children, encouraging them and making sure that none of them slipped. Fell was the fastest, though Larka almost matched him, and even Kar kept up now. They reached the tree line, and Huttser looked back once more. Still the Balkar were coming on. They had crested the second peak and were eating up the slope. As the family ran, the wind cried in their ears. It seemed to be saying one word alone: escape.

It grew darker and darker as the family threaded through the pines, moving smoothly and steadily now across the ground where the snow was less heavy. As they looked up through the trees, they could see that the sky had turned black and stars were beading through the black. A quarter moon was rising, and the air had grown perfectly still.

At last they came to the far edge of the trees, and the river lay before them. It was at its widest point here. They saw a perfect sheet of white stretching ahead and glistening brilliantly in the moonlight. Along the banks, willow and vine trees had bowed their heads over the frozen edges of the water, and their trailing branches were shawled with snow. Below them, the last residues of autumn grasses—strangling leaves and tilting bulrushes—had been seized into a static beauty by winter's grip, glittering with tiny icicles and bulbs of frozen dew that flashed liked stars.

Larka gasped at the sight, but Fell was looking up to the heavens now, and he felt a sudden gravity as he saw the full sweep of the Milky Way above them. The moon was still low, so the carpet of stars was clear and bright, and Fell remembered that Brassa had told him once it was called the Wolf Trail, for here, where the stars swept like the brush of the wolf, many believed lay the true pathway between heaven and earth, between gods and wolf.

"Come on," said Huttser suddenly. "We should cross. We've nearly made it."

Huttser felt a quickening in his heart. He could almost smell the end of the pack boundary. The end of the curse and safety for his family.

"Not here, Huttser," said Palla. "It's too wide. Look at the ice on the edges. It looks desperately thin."

"Palla, we must try."

"No, Father," objected Larka, stepping forward, "Tsinga told us to beware the fifth element."

Here and there through the film of blue, Larka could still see the water, moving steadily and noiselessly beneath the surface. Huttser nodded, and he was about to turn south when he began to tremble.

"Quickly. Back into the trees."

Another group of wolves was coming along the river-bank. Luckily, these Balkar had not seen them, for no call had come. The family slunk nervously into the shadows. The Balkar stopped about five trees away, and the fur on Huttser's back rose.

"No sign," the lead wolf was growling irritably.

"I wish we were back in camp," said another wolf. "Soon it'll be time for another cub."

"We should carry on," said a third Balkar.

"Yes," whispered the first, but as he did so, Huttser heard a sudden howl from the north along the river. The Varg began to answer, and when he finished he seemed satisfied.

"They've found nothing either," he grunted. "They're turning north again. We'll go back too. There's no one here."

Suddenly the Balkar next to him gave a painful growl, and the lead wolf swung around. The Varg was lifting his right paw, for in their journey he had stepped on a thorn in the forest, and now his paw was infected.

"This blasted wound," he growled angrily. "It'll be the death of me."

"Perhaps you should take it to Morgra," whispered the Varg next to him.

"Why?"

"When my mother taught me the old beliefs, she told me that the Sight brings the power to heal."

"Morgra heal?" growled the lead wolf with clear amusement. "Can a mountain lion become a lamb?"

The Balkar all began to chuckle, though the wolf with the wounded paw was looking around him strangely. But suddenly the lead Varg snarled.

"Enough," he cried. "This is no time for fooling."

He turned and led the Balkar silently away into the night.

Huttser stood trembling, a fury rising in him at the thought of these wolves stalking his family in his own territory. But he could do nothing now without endangering Palla and the children. They waited and waited in the shadows. At last Huttser spoke. "Come, we must try now."

"No, Huttser, not here. It's not safe."

"But we can't go north or south," said Huttser. "Trust me, Palla. I'll go first to test it. If you stay in my tracks, there should be no danger."

Palla came to see, very reluctantly, that to stay where they were was equally as dangerous as crossing the ice. Huttser led them forward, and Palla hung back as her mate stepped out onto the film of white and felt it bending and ringing beneath his paws. He took a step forward, then another, scanning the surface for the thickest part. After a while he was a good way out on the frozen water. Huttser's paws had made a fine trail in the film of powder.

"Right, then," said Palla. "Children, follow carefully in our tracks and stick together. If you feel it cracking, move away from the sound."

Larka was still shaking her head, but Palla led them nervously onto the ice. As Larka stepped out and looked down, she saw little shapes, like dots of algae, caught in its grip. She wondered what they were. The surface held, though, and after only a short while Palla was with Huttser again. The wolf pack pressed on, in single file, the cubs following carefully in their parents' paw marks. They were so close to the far bank now, they could almost leap across.

"Safety," whispered Palla. "Safety at last."

But as Fell brought up the rear, and the wolves grew more confident, he found himself looking up into the night sky again. His attention began to wander as he gazed at the stars. *The Wolf Trail, the pathway between heaven and earth,* he kept thinking, and as he did so, he started to drift away to the right.

"Nearly there," cried Huttser as he saw the far bank.

"Thank Tor, Huttser," growled Palla with relief from behind him. "You've led us across."

As Huttser turned back to Palla, his eyes flamed. Fell had swung far out to a place where the ice looked desperately treacherous. Huttser's voice carried straight to his son in the thin blue cold. It startled Fell from his reverie. Realizing he had wandered from the trail, he lifted his tail and leaped forward.

"No, Fell," cried Larka. "Don't!"

The young wolf was bounding straight for the thinnest part of the ice.

"Fell," shouted Huttser angrily. "Listen to me, Fell. Stay where you are."

Fell stopped dead in his tracks and looked around desperately. Huttser was also scanning the surface, looking for the safest place for Fell to cross. From where the Dragga was standing, it seemed thick enough.

"Fell," called Huttser as they heard the river sing treacherously around them. "Move to your left, Fell, very slowly."

"No, Father."

Huttser could not see the thin blue crack that Fell had

just spotted exactly where his father had told him to go. The young wolf began to shake.

"Fell," cried Huttser. "Trust me. Don't be frightened. Now do as I say and move to the left."

Fell hesitated, but his father's voice was somehow reassuring. His terror had closed off his thoughts, shut down his will, and now all he wanted was to be protected, to be told what to do, to be shown the path back to safety. Fell began to inch to his left. Even as he did so, he felt the ice bending beneath his paws. The young Varg froze again.

They heard it first—a fissure of sound running between them and Fell as the ice cracked and Fell disappeared with a splash.

"Fell!" cried Larka, springing forward, quite oblivious of her own safety. But her brother had vanished into the water.

"Stop her," gasped Palla.

Larka was already at the freezing blue pool, which had suddenly appeared in the moonlight. She was lighter than Fell, and the surface around the pool held as she whimpered and stared in horror at the now still waters.

"Ice," she growled. "Why didn't we listen to Tsinga? This is what she saw that sun. Why didn't she warn us properly?"

"Larka, don't move," cried Palla frantically.

Huttser and Palla suddenly heard Kar whimpering, staring down at the ice beneath his paws.

"What is it, Kar?" cried Palla.

Kar couldn't speak. He had heard it first, and the sound was getting louder.

"Palla," he choked out, "Fell's underneath me."

Kar could see Fell's face through the ice itself, his paws scrabbling desperately at the frozen surface, the bubbles of air swirling from his mouth, his claws only just preventing him from being swept downstream by the still-living current. But the surface here had grown thicker again, and Fell couldn't break through.

"Help him, Kar," snarled Huttser.

Kar was frozen with fear.

"Do something, Kar."

Kar just whimpered as Fell's body began to slide, still scrabbling, still gasping for air. Huttser was at Kar's side now, and he snarled at him furiously as he pushed him aside and tried to break through, scratching and clawing at the river. The wolf began to jump and slam down with his paws. Kar watched transfixed as Huttser fought to save his son, drowning beneath his feet. A hairline crack appeared where Huttser was slashing at the surface, but still the ice held and still Fell was slipping away.

"For Fenris's sake, help us, Palla," snarled Huttser desperately.

As Palla reached them, Fell lost his grip, and the wolves sprang after him, clawing at the thin snow, mindless now of the ice and desperate only to save Fell. The whole family was clawing at the frozen river, but it was no good. They could see Fell just beneath them, his exhausted body finding it harder and harder to fight the current, the bubbles of air fading on his muzzle.

As his claws finally lost their grip and he was swept downstream, Huttser saw a sliver of green in his son's closing eye. Palla lifted her head. She saw the sweep of frozen water before her, bending around beyond the trees, and thought of Fell drowning beneath its icy surface, his soul doomed never to find a resting place. She let out a mourning howl so loud and angry and full of anguish that the whole river seemed to shake.

The family of wolves stood there motionless, frozen with horror and despair. But suddenly Huttser swung around.

"Damn you, Kar," he cried furiously. "You should have called out sooner."

But as Huttser spoke, Palla reacted just as swiftly. "Don't you dare, Huttser. Don't you dare blame Kar. It was your fault. Yours. I told you Huttser. I told you it wasn't safe."

Huttser looked blankly at his mate as the children watched them.

"Too late," he stammered. "Too late."

Huttser's mind was suddenly ringing again with Tsinga's words: "If one is lost, then I fear for us all." At last the desperation of their flight and all that had happened to his pack overcame the Dragga.

"And now he's gone too," cried Palla bitterly. "My little Fell. Will it never end?"

"Palla," whispered Huttser hopelessly. "We must survive . . ."

"No," growled Palla furiously. "It's all your fault. If you hadn't made us cross there . . . I hate you, Huttser."

"Palla—" Huttser didn't finish. With a snarl and a sudden flash of angry teeth, the she-wolf leaped at him, blinded with sorrow by the loss of her son. In that moment, to Kar, they looked like nothing so much as thoughtless children.

"Father," cried Larka. "Mother. Stop it, please. Please don't fight. The curse. We must . . ."

But her parents could no longer hear her. As she thought of her dead brother, Larka's own mind was suddenly swamped with bitterness and grief and guilt.

It's me, she thought. *It's all my fault. It's because of me that Morgra is doing this. I have the Sight. I should have been able to foresee what was going to happen.*

Suddenly the young she-wolf turned and sprang away. Larka wanted to run, anywhere, to get away from the curse and her family and the Sight. Kar leaped after her, but Larka had already vanished into the trees on the far bank, fleeing from the terrible sound of her parents' anger. Instinct had made Huttser reply to his mate. He had sprung forward, too, opening his jaws, and for the first time since they had met and courted, Huttser and Palla were fighting.

The adult wolves tore at each other. As their snarls echoed through the snowy trees, the sound was answered only by winter's bitter silence. They did not notice that the children had gone or that the ice beneath their own feet was beginning to crack. Nor that, among the trees on the far bank, faces were emerging all around them, muzzles pressing through the branches, savage yellow eyes glittering angrily as they searched through the looming shadows.

As a she-cub is whelped with a coat that is white,
And human child stolen to suckle the Sight
From a place where injustice was secretly done
Then the Marked One is here and a legend begun.
When Wolfbane is dreamt of with terror and dread,
And untamed are tamed, prepare for the dead.
For the Shape Changer's pact with the birds will come true,
When the blood of the Varg blends with Man's in the dew,
As the Searchers are tempted, who hunger and prowl,
Down the Pathways of Death, by the summoning howl.

Then the truest of powers will be fleshed on the bone
And the Searchers tempt nature to prey on its own.
With blood at the altar, the Vision shall come
When the eye of the moon is as round as the sun.
In the citadel raised by the lords of before,
The stone twins await—both the power and the law.
Then the past and the future shall finally show,
To the wounded, the secret the Lera must know.
And all shall be witness to that which will be,
In the mind of the Man Varg, then none shall be free.

And only a family both loving and true,
May conquer the evil, so ancient, so new.
As they fight to uncover what secrets they share
And see in their journey how painful is care.
Beware the Betrayer, whose meaning is strife,
For their faith shall be tried by the makers of life,
And who shall divine, in the dead of the night,
The lies from the truth, the darkness from light?
Like the cry of the scavenger, torn through the air
A courage is needed, as deep as despair.

PART TWO

THE CHILD

7

MORGRA

And what rough beast, its hour come round at last,
Slouches towards Bethlehem to be born?
— W. B. Yeats, "The Second Coming"

Larka ran, her white muzzle up, her young face contorted with anger and bitterness and sorrow. But as she ran, someone was following her. Morgra's eyes danced brilliantly as she watched Larka run.

"Now," she whispered. "Now it really begins."

Morgra wanted to reach out with her paw and scoop Larka up. But as soon as she touched the surface of the pool, the image of the white she-wolf began to fade on the water.

"Wolfbane's teeth," Morgra snarled, and the scars on her muzzle looked like welts in the half-light.

She growled angrily as the picture dissolved completely. Once more in the water she saw the ceiling of her cave and the stalactites that hung down from above like strands of petrified hair. Morgra did not notice it, but caught between the roof and one of these stone strands was a small object, about the size of a human thumb. It seemed as though something had placed it there, but white like the rock around it, it might have been nothing more than a large pebble.

Night was coming. The shadows around Morgra crept like thieves across the cave floor, inching their fingers toward the rocky walls where a raven sat, preening himself on his perch of stone.

"What's wrong, Mistress?" asked Kraar.

"I cannot hold the pictures. My power is not strong enough. But she is alone at last, Kraar. We must find her. And soon."

"Send the Night Hunters, Mistress."

"I spared one pack," whispered Morgra. "But the rest are searching out the citadel and the human child. No, I will have to use your eyes, Kraar. We shall have to find her ourselves."

"With her power to aid you, will you be able to hold the pictures in the water?"

"This power is a mere nothing," snorted Morgra, "compared to what will come. It is the ancient howl that I really need her for. If the Pathways of Death are opened to the Searchers, the power to look into minds and control wills will enter the world. And with it the chance of final success."

"But you're already controlling the Balkar's wills, Mistress," said the raven.

"With tricks and threats, perhaps," hissed Morgra. "But when I touch the Searchers' power, then we shall truly see."

"Such genius, though," Kraar said fawningly as he flapped, taking to the air suddenly and settling next to Morgra. "To invoke the Shape Changer. To use mere myth to wield true power."

Kraar hopped nervously around Morgra's graying jaws. They had begun to dribble.

"Wolfbane must be dreamed of by all the Varg." Morgra nodded with pleasure, growling and licking her lips thoughtfully. "The wolves must fear him, it is part of the verse, Kraar, and all of it must be fulfilled if the Vision is to come. But although Wolfbane is now a game I play with the Balkar, who is to say that the Shape Changer may not really come? If enough blood soaks the earth perhaps he, too, will be unable to resist the stink and come crawling out of legend."

"Mistress," asked the raven, "did Wolfbane ever live up at the Stone Den?"

Morgra began to smile, just as she had done that day she had looked up at the castle as she stood before Palla's pack.

"Of course not, Kraar. I climbed up there after they . . . after they drove me out. That's when I first went in search of him, the Evil One. There was nothing there but the humans' stones. But it didn't stop the Lera fearing the place, and it gave me shelter for a while, and later an idea of how to enchant the Balkar."

Kraar shivered excitedly.

"What does Wolfbane look like, Mistress?"

"Ah," growled the she-wolf, "what does a myth look like, Kraar? Those that fear him for his evil say he looks like a giant toad. Others that he is an enormous bat. But I can tell you the story of what the Shape Changer looked like when he was a young Varg. Then he was the greatest Dragga of all, with a coat like a mighty bear and claws as powerful as the sun. Then, when he stood before Tor and Fenris and spat in their faces."

"Why did he do that?" asked Kraar nervously.

"Why?" growled Morgra scornfully. "Because of their commandments, Kraar. Because they would have everything obey them, like fearful little children. Because Wolfbane had used the Sight to look down on the world from the heavens and had seen all its pain and suffering, and he knew that Tor and Fenris had made it so. Wolfbane longed to revolt, to be free to do as he chose. But they had made him, too, and called him evil, and so Wolfbane went before them and spat in their muzzles and called them liars.

" 'If you are goodness, Fenris, and you made me,' he snarled, 'but won't even let me choose my own way, then how can I be evil? I am nothing but what I am.'

" 'Very well,' replied Fenris, 'then we shall send you down among the Varg to give them all a choice.'

"Tor and Fenris hurled Wolfbane from the heavens and he fell. Like a comet he plunged toward the earth, and as he hit the edges of the skies, at first his fur burned like fire. Yet as he went on falling, the air put out the flames and cold gathered around him, and it started to snow."

Kraar's little eyes were on stalks, but Morgra had finished her story.

"So what we are doing . . . it shall not cease?"

"Oh no, Kraar, and if he did come, then such an ally I should have!"

The raven's eyes sparkled with admiration for his mistress. He flapped back onto his perch and dipped his beak. When he lifted it again, there was a thin strip of raw flesh dangling from the end, like an earthworm. The raven cawed delightedly and, with a snap, swallowed it whole.

"You know it's my favorite." He dribbled, opening his coal black head feathers like a hood. "You spoil me, Mistress."

"Spoil you?" said Morgra. "Oh no, Kraar, you've earned far more than that. You opened Larka to her gift and, besides, your kind are a part of this. Have the Helpers not always been a key to the Sight? Well then, the legend shall give you your real due."

"You mean Wolfbane's promise," cried Kraar delightedly, "his pact with the flying scavengers, that he made in the valley of Kosov?"

A light mist was creeping into the freezing cave, and it seemed to wrap itself almost tenderly around Morgra's body, as the she-wolf stood over her seeing pool.

"Yes, Kraar."

Morgra lifted her muzzle and began to chant:

> *When Wolfbane is dreamt of with terror and dread,*
> *And untamed are tamed, prepare for the dead.*
> *For the Shape Changer's pact with the birds will come true,*
> *When the blood of the Varg blends with Man's in the dew,*
> *As the Searchers are tempted, who hunger and prowl,*
> *Down the Pathways of Death, by the summoning howl.*

Morgra's voice filled the cave, and above her head something inside that little pebble moved. It was alive.

"But if Wolfbane is just a story," whispered Kraar wonderingly, "how can you ever—"

"Trust me, Kraar."

"Then," said Kraar, "when you have helped us fulfill the pact, Mistress, then I, too, will wield power?"

"Of course," answered Morgra quietly, though her eyes twinkled with mischief and malice.

"All my life," screeched Kraar, flapping his black wings frantically; "all my life the Putnar have laughed at me and called me nothing but a filthy scavenger. Kraar the body snatcher. Kraar the winged thief. 'You're not a true bird of prey, Kraar, you're just a tricksy, sneaky, stealthy—' "

"Shut up, Kraar," snapped Morgra, and Kraar's head almost disappeared among his feathers with fright.

"So where were you going Larka, my dear?" growled Morgra suddenly, getting to her feet and pawing at the water. "Or are you lost in the woods?"

"What of her pack, Mistress?" Kraar asked nervously, raising his head again.

"The curse must have done its work on the rest of her brood. Did you see the look in their eyes when I summoned it? They would have believed anything and, as it is, I frightened them half to death. That lightning bolt didn't harm the effect either. But tell me again, Kraar."

Kraar began to preen himself once more. When he spoke there was a new confidence in the raven's clacking voice. "The old nurse went first, eaten up with—"

"Slowly," hissed Morgra.

When Kraar had finished recounting the manner of Brassa's passing, Morgra growled delightedly.

"So you have had your revenge," said Kraar, "on the nurse, at least."

"Brassa saw the truth and kept it hidden to her cost," hissed Morgra bitterly. "But her death is only a taste of the revenge I shall have."

Morgra looked impressive as she stood there, shaking with anger, for resentment was her birthright. Long before she had been driven out they had feared her for her strange ways, even as a cub. How she had yearned for affection and, as she grew, she had craved cubs of her own. She had ached to share so much with others, to be a pack wolf and share the secrets she was learning about the Sight. About life. She had ached to be allowed to love something. Then, on that terrible night, when she had killed the cub by accident, and they had judged her wrongly, how she hated the wolves then.

So Morgra had wandered, isolated, too, by her own gift, and discovered Tsinga and the legend of the Man Varg. In the promise of that she had found a way of sublimating her own pain and loneliness, for it was soon after that the she-wolf learned the terrible truth that she was barren. When Tsinga, too, had driven her out, she had set her powerful will and all her secret hopes on fulfilling the strange destiny promised by the legend. She had sought power in control of the Balkar, but only as a stepping-stone to a far greater ambition.

Suddenly they heard a growl from outside. Morgra swung around. The Balkar wolf waiting beyond shivered in the cold. He could hear the raven snapping and cawing inside the cave. He trembled at the noise and the thought of Morgra's strange ability to speak with the birds. But his fear was as much at the thought of disturbing Morgra at all. Although Morgra led the Balkar, they all knew how she liked to live apart and in secret, hating to be disturbed except for the gravest of reasons.

The wolf stopped at the entrance, and his tail quivered as he sniffed the air. He could see clearly to the back of the cave, for his eyes were particularly strong: all the Night Hunters had been chosen by Tratto for their ability to see well in the dark.

"Morgra," he called nervously.

There was a snarl from inside, and the Night Hunter stepped suddenly into the blackness.

"Why do you disturb me, Brak?" cried Morgra as he padded inside.

"Forgive me, Morgra," Brak said, dropping his ears. "But there is news. The fortune-teller is dead."

Kraar started to flap about as though there were hot coals beneath his feet. "Marvelous," he cried, "more carrion. That blind old fool . . ."

But as soon as Kraar said it, Morgra swung at him and her eyes were so angry they could have knocked him over.

"How dare you talk of her like that."

"But, Mistress," said Kraar, "she drove us out. You can't feel—"

"Silence. Tsinga drove us out, yes, but she taught me once and knew more than a flying scavenger like you ever will, Kraar. And she was a fine wolf herself once. Don't ever speak of her like that again."

Kraar dropped his beak.

"Morgra," whispered Brak nervously between them, "there is more news. We caught one of the rebels in the forests two suns back, another of Slavka's spies, and we . . . we questioned him." Brak grinned coldly. The rebel wolf would never answer any questions again.

"Well?" snapped Morgra.

"Slavka has summoned this Greater Pack, at last," said Brak. "With the snows, few will come until the summer, if they come at all. But there are signs that they are already stirring. Though the spy died before he would tell us where their Gathering Place is."

Brak hardly knew how Morgra would react, but she smiled at the thought of the rebel's death, and he went on. "Word must have got out . . . of what you are doing, Morgra. Perhaps it was when we attacked Skop's pack." Brak dropped his gaze.

"There is shame in you, Brak," cried Morgra immediately, trying to conceal how pleased she really was. "And shame brings weakness. Are you a killer or not? Did not Tratto himself train you to be the First Among the Putnar and to kill without mercy if called on to do so?"

Brak lifted his head in confusion as he heard the Night Hunters' favorite title.

"No Sikla here, no breath of fear," whispered Morgra, quoting the Balkar's rallying cry, too, "to train the strong we all adhere."

Brak felt a wild stirring in him. He was a powerful wolf, larger even than Huttser, though he was not the Dragga in his pack. And of the six Balkar packs, his was only the third in dominance. But they had all been trained as great fighters by Tratto, in the days of the old wars when Tratto had resisted the southern invasion.

But Brak shuddered too. There were times when he longed to resist Morgra. But, just as Morgra had said, he was too implicated in the Night Hunters' crimes. Once their terrible work had begun, there was no turning back.

"There is something else, Morgra," he whispered.

"Well?"

"The human child," said Brak nervously. "Slavka may not believe in the Sight, but you know the rumors of what happened to her and why she so hates the humans. Now all the rebels have orders to kill it, if they ever find it."

Morgra snarled furiously. "Hurry, fool. Take half the home pack with you. Find it, Brak. Find it or do not return."

"Yes," muttered Brak, but he stood still.

"Well, idiot. What are you waiting for?"

"The home pack," said Brak, dropping his ears. "They're waiting."

"You know what night it is, Mistress," cawed Kraar approvingly. "Last night Tor closed her mouth and the moon vanished."

"Very well. But go, Brak. And hurry."

As Brak sprang out of the cave, Morgra followed him slowly into the snowy air.

"So these rebels are forming a Greater Pack," cried Kraar as he flapped after her. "What will you do, Mistress?"

"Do, Kraar? I shall wait and watch, of course. Somewhere Slavka is bringing the free wolves together in one place, which can only serve our purpose. 'When untamed are tamed,' Kraar, that's what the verse says."

Kraar nodded frantically.

"When I find out where they are gathering, I shall destroy them all. Don't you want Wolfbane's promise fulfilled? And it must happen together, Kraar, if the howl is to summon the Searchers."

Morgra began to growl with pleasure. The Balkar wolves were waiting for her silently in the darkness. There were only fifteen of them now with Morgra, for the other packs had been sent out to continue their search for the citadel and the child. But the Night Hunters were a fearful sight as they stood there in a circle. They were all huge male wolves, their great chests bristling with vigor and their brilliant eyes slicing through the dark. Yet even as Morgra approached, they shrank visibly before the she-wolf, and the circle broke. Suddenly Morgra's voice rang out into the steely night.

"Brothers," she cried. "Balkar. First and most fearful of the Varg. The Sight has brought me to you to fulfill your true destiny. When your beloved leader enslaves the Lera, you shall truly be the First Among the Putnar. But now there is another we must summon. Again we call to him."

Morgra began, an incantation that trembled on the freezing air. "Come, Wolfbane, friend of the dead," she howled, throwing her muzzle left and right. "Come from the shadows and fill the spirit of one among us. Those who worship your cult again do you homage. By the power of darkness I summon you. You shall hunt for us, Wolfbane, hunt down any who stand in our way. You, the Shape Changer, shall be our servant, and together we shall feed in Wolfbane's winter. Together we shall seek the ultimate power."

Morgra's howl rose, and the Balkar shook furiously and began to growl, as their muzzles also swayed through the darkness.

"By the elements that feed the Sight I summon you. By wind and snow, by storm and rain. By the untameable forces of nature and the energy that dwells in all, I summon you. I call you forth, Wolfbane. Reveal yourself to us."

There was silence as the wolves waited. They began to look around them nervously, half expecting Wolfbane to materialize among them there and then. But nothing at all happened, and at last Morgra lifted her head and turned away.

"Fetch one," she cried as she went, "as I have shown you. Fetch one of the children and use its blood to warm the snow."

Morgra walked calmly back toward Kraar, her eyes glittering, not just with pleasure, but with pure amusement.

"That should keep the fools wondering and waiting," she sniggered delightedly, "and muttering his name too."

Below the circle they came to a nursery where a group of young wolves were standing fearfully in the darkness, guarded by the prowling Night Hunters. As Morgra approached them, the youngsters slunk back, but Morgra smiled. When she spoke her tone was kindly. "Come, my children, don't be frightened."

The wolves were all glaring at her.

"What's wrong. You know that I love you, don't you?"

Still the wolves stood there. They were speechless with terror.

"Speak up. You mustn't be afraid. I won't be angry, trust me."

"Trust you," cried one of the male cubs suddenly. "Never. Let us go."

Morgra's face looked wounded, but her eyes were smiling. "Don't say such hurtful things," she growled. "I only want to protect you. Care for you all."

In her mind Morgra was reaching out toward them as she said it, but the she-wolf's bitter heart felt nothing for the youngsters. The wolf who had spoken glared back at her furiously.

"Tell me," said Morgra, straining forward, "what is your name?"

"Cal."

"Well, Cal, you mustn't have the wrong idea about me."

"I want my parents," demanded the young wolf.

Morgra grinned. "Ah. I'm afraid that is quite impossible."

Morgra turned away, but suddenly she looked back toward the orphans. "Don't worry," she called. "I'll come and visit you again soon. Then we'll all play happily together."

Kraar fluttered down onto Morgra's back as she prowled away and although she was annoyed with the cub's demand, the she-wolf tolerated the raven's touch.

"I don't understand," said Kraar. "You're always so nice to them and yet what we are . . ."

"The legend, Kraar. The she-wolf must know the Drappa's care to reach the Vision. Yet no matter how hard I try, I can't feel anything for them. They are not my own blood. Still, they are serving their purpose all right, and by stealing them we are stealing the very heart and courage of the free wolves. We are serving hate."

Kraar nodded delightedly as he thought of how many wolves had been killed to bring the cubs here.

"With her it would have been different, though," Morgra whispered almost sadly, "will be different. When I catch her then everything will be different."

"So you did want to join their pack, Mistress? For its own sake?"

A familiar confusion entered Morgra as she thought of Palla's pack and the genuine bitterness and jealousy she had felt when they had refused her above the ravine.

"I could have tended to them, Kraar. All of them. I could have protected them and taught Larka about the Sight, like my own daughter. Together we could have fulfilled the legend. Together ruled the Lera. If her stupid parents had only let me join . . ."

Morgra was thinking back again, across the long, angry years, to that sun when she had first been driven out for a crime she had never even committed. Yet when Morgra had seen her sister again, perhaps even then she could have learned to forgive and forget. To turn the power of the Sight away from darkness, back to the goodness that lay buried somewhere deep inside her. But they had driven her away too. Had betrayed her again. With that rejection had ended Morgra's last faint hope of returning to the light.

"Come, Kraar," snarled Morgra suddenly. "You were telling me of the pack."

"I left them when that Sikla died, as I said," cried Kraar, flying above her head now, "after the female was lost to the water. Huttser's sister."

"Very well then, Kraar."

"So that only leaves this young stranger . . . and the family."

Something close to fear crept across Morgra's scarred muzzle. "The family," she hissed.

"How shall we tell if Larka's is really the family?" asked Kraar.

"Larka is already alone," Morgra growled, "but we shall see. It's why her loved ones must all die."

They had reached the mouth of the cave again, but rather than going inside, Morgra turned to an area of open ground where there was fresh meat lying in the snow. Kraar fluttered toward it immediately, but Morgra barked at him. "Leave it. This time it's not for you."

The raven settled beside her. "Why do you keep feeding them?" he asked jealously.

"Because there may be one among them," growled Morgra, her eyes searching the trees, "one who has the power too. Who could help me. Who could serve me if I can't find Larka."

Even as she spoke they heard a bellow of a bear from the forest beyond and the hiss, too, of a mountain lynx. The creatures had already been feeding in the night, and Morgra was ready to speak with them. But as the bear's roar rose above the trees, Morgra noticed that the Night Hunters below had turned fearfully and were looking up the slope. Wolves are high in the food chain and have few natural enemies in the wild except Man, but a bear, and especially the giants that roam the Carpathians, is one dangerous exception. As Morgra saw the fear the sound instilled in the Balkar, her eyes glittered.

"You asked what Wolfbane looks like," she whispered coldly. "Well, I wonder."

Kraar did not understand his mistress, but Morgra turned to look back at the cubs.

"Though we need to keep your larder stocked, too, don't we, Kraar? Tomorrow, pick out another yourself and let the Balkar deal with it."

Kraar began to flap his wings excitedly.

"No. On second thought, take the one who had the impertinence to address me—Cal."

Morgra turned back inside the cave where it was dark and a breeze stirred the pool.

"Mistress," said Kraar as he settled on his stony perch, "even though the curse has broken the family, what about Larka? Might not her gift alone threaten us? Perhaps she could—"

"Never," snarled Morgra furiously. "Larka touch the Vision? She is nothing but a whelp. Who is there to teach her? Tsinga is dead and . . ." Morgra paused. She was thinking of Tsarr. But she shook off the doubt. "Besides, Kraar. Larka knows nothing of the real world. The Sight alone cannot bring forth the Vision. There must be true knowledge too. Knowledge of the humans themselves. Knowledge that I alone possess."

Morgra's face was suddenly contorted with a kind of angry self-pity. Kraar had seen the look many times before.

"You're thinking of the village again, Mistress, aren't you? Where the humans held you. Don't you want to forget?"

"Forget?" growled Morgra.

"What happened. The past."

"I shall never forget. Not a single thing, Kraar. Not like the thoughtless Lera. Every moment of my life, every injustice, every claw of pain I shall remember, and it shall make me stronger. Shall bring me to truth and power."

Morgra was quiet for a while, but when she spoke again her voice was full of cunning. "What can a mere cub know of human power? Of the glories and horrors of his mind? What can she know of the only true Putnar, the greatest and coldest killer of all?"

Even Kraar shivered, and once again, inside the little silken pebble strung to the cave ceiling above them, a tiny creature moved. It had been alive before and had wriggled up here itself to feed on the damp moss above. It had no eyes, but its senses had taken it here, and its mouth. And now it was changing.

"No, Kraar," whispered Morgra. "Let her wander, alone and reviled. Larka will find no help among the Varg, for even Slavka has sworn to destroy all with the Sight. Let her feel the strangeness of her gift and how it cuts us off from the wolf. Let her look out on the world, for what she sees there can only fill her with bitterness and anger and hate. It shall only bring her closer to me. Which is as it should be, Kraar, for those with the Sight must choose for themselves."

"But would it not be better if she were with us now? I fear Slavka and these rebels, Mistress. Even the Balkar would be no match against all the free Varg. The packs are hardly an army."

"No, Kraar," hissed Morgra. "But when I open the pathways, then my true servants shall come. They are already being summoned, summoned by the anger and hate the Balkar are spreading throughout the forests. For they feed on it, Kraar. When Larka helps me grow strong enough to use the ancient howl, then I will have an army at my back so terrible . . ."

Kraar was silent at the she-wolf's words.

"But go, Kraar," cried Morgra suddenly, "go in search of her. I shall use your eyes."

As Kraar lifted out of the cave into the freezing air, Morgra slumped to the ground. The she-wolf looked almost dead as she lay there. But, in fact, the wolf's hungry mind was using the power of the Sight, using it to look out now over the snowy trees racing below the raven's beating wings.

"Leave me alone, Kar," cried Larka angrily in the gusting snows. "Can't you see I want to be alone?"

"I won't," said Kar sullenly as he padded after her.

The wind was howling like a demon and the storm had come again. It was over a moon since the terrible night on the river and it had taken Kar a good week to find Larka. He had tracked her paw prints in the snow and, when at last he had caught up with her, she had tried to drive him away. Since then they had argued again and again.

"I'll never leave you, Larka," Kar cried. "We made a pact and nothing will come between us."

"Nothing?" said Larka bitterly. "Fell made the pact,

too, remember, and he's already dead. Because of me."

"Larka," muttered Kar gloomily, "if anyone is to blame for Fell's death, I am. You must stop this talk."

"The pact was a lie," growled Larka. "Go away."

"No."

Larka rounded furiously on Kar in the snow. "What are you doing here, anyway?" she snarled. "What do you really want? Following me like a little cub. You can't help me. Nothing can. I killed them all, didn't I? Because of the Sight. There's nothing to help me now."

But suddenly Larka wanted to blame someone other than herself—anyone. "And, anyway," she spat scornfully, "what can you do, Kar?"

But there was something else that made her push him away, something far deeper. She didn't want to be responsible for the wolf, she didn't want to be responsible for anything or anyone.

Kar felt bitterly wounded, but he was still determined to follow his friend. In that moment he didn't feel quite as worthless as Larka did.

"We must have faith in each other," he growled. "That's what Tsinga said."

"I've lost faith in us," snapped Larka. "I've lost faith in everything."

"But, Larka, can't you stop and think calmly for a while? You don't even know where you're going."

"I do," cried Larka furiously, quickening her tread through the storm.

Kar fell silent, but still he followed the she-wolf. He looked tired and emaciated, and his fur was beginning to drop out in clumps. Larka had hardly fared any better.

Her coat was already turning a yellow gray, and the skin was hanging down from her belly. The two young wolves had nearly reached their full size, but there was little of the strength and vigor in them you would have associated with healthy wolves of their age.

They hadn't eaten in at least fifteen suns, for they had so little time to learn of real hunting from Huttser and Palla. As they traveled together, they had often picked up the scents of Lera and trailed them with their black noses skimming through the snow, only to lose them again. Whenever Larka had come close to a kill, that terrible feeling had come over her again, and twice she had seen herself looking through the hunted's eyes.

Kar was wondering what had become of Huttser and Palla now, for they had spied or heard nothing of the Dragga and Drappa. When they had fled from the river they had not seen those eyes in the trees, nor the ice beginning to crack below Huttser and Palla's paws. They had seen other wolves, though, only three suns before, hunting through the mountains. Whether they were rebels or Balkar, they had kept well out of sight.

Ahead, Kar could see that Larka had calmed down a little.

"Larka," he called, "perhaps you could try to find your parents again. Use the Sight."

"No, Kar," growled Larka bitterly, though she was suddenly glad to hear his voice behind her. "Don't talk of it. What good are these powers to me? I have terrible dreams, and whenever I try to hunt . . ."

Larka kept imagining, too, that a pair of yellow black eyes were following her as the wolves threaded through the trees. But if fear was on their trail, something else was hunting the wolves, quite as frightening as Wolfbane or Morgra's curse; the most exacting and relentless predator known to Lera or to Man. Winter itself was stalking them through the land beyond the forest, and in its jaws came the pressing threat of starvation.

"I'm hungry, Larka," said Kar as his paws crunched on through the thick white.

Larka looked across at Kar, and she felt ashamed of how she had spoken to him. Though she had meant to get away from her family and find solace on her own, she, too, was hungry and very frightened, and she suddenly felt glad that Kar had followed her.

"Don't worry, Kar, we'll find something soon."

"We'll die if we don't."

But in that moment Larka hardly cared. She felt as if she had been sent into exile from her own life, from her own childhood. Ahead of her lay nothing but fear. Larka lifted her head to the skies, and in the distance she saw a tiny black shape moving toward them. But as she watched, it suddenly wheeled in the skies and turned north again.

Below Morgra's cave—except for those wolves that had been sent out to find the child—the Balkar packs had gathered again. It had taken nearly a whole moon to bring them together. Now five of the big wolves lay together in the darkness, sharing their warmth. As always, rumors of Wolfbane were circulating and the wolves were stirring restlessly, avoiding one anothers' eyes, but listening intently.

"There's news," said one of them. "A scouting party has

returned. They brought Morgra something, and they were talking to her half the night."

"What of it?" asked another.

"I don't know, but there is a change in Morgra. She seems more confident somehow."

"Yes," said a third, "I heard her talking to herself last night outside her cave. She'd been leaving out that cub meat again for the forest animals."

"What was she saying?"

"She kept muttering to herself. 'This, I never saw this. It shall serve me well.' Then she growled and started to laugh out loud."

"But what can it mean?"

"There's something else. My pack only got back last night, but we noticed a new breath of fear on the wind."

Suddenly they heard a snarl behind them. They all knew the wolf that was standing listening to them in the darkness as one of the lead Draggas and a famous fighter among the Balkar.

"Fear," he snorted, "there is only fear for a Night Hunter if he doesn't know his true loyalties. Know who and what he is."

"Why," said the wolf who had spoken of it, "what has happened?"

"Don't you know?" answered the Dragga coldly, his eyes suddenly huge in the night. "Morgra has given orders that we kill all the cubs."

The Balkar wolves growled guiltily.

"Sacrifice them?" said one.

"No," the newcomer snarled, "we don't need them any-more."

"But why?"

"Can't you feel him, fool? Feel his very teeth on the winter?"

The Balkar stepped forward and opened his jaws, and even as he did so, it began to snow. "Wolfbane," he snarled exultantly. "Wolfbane has returned at last."

8

SCAVENGERS

Seek, and ye shall find.
—Matthew 7:7

To Kar and Larka it seemed as though they had been passing through a land of fables. As they rose above the river and climbed higher and higher among the jaws of the mountains, they saw the true wildness of this jagged country. Below, the forests and woods seemed to stretch on forever. A strange, almost enchanted kingdom, swathed in white, that for a wolf offered the promise of safety, of concealment, and of seemingly endless mystery too. But it was the fury of the mountains that called to their young hearts. Soaring slopes and grave canyons, lonely peaks and beetling precipices rose around them and woke in the wolves the full wonder and terror of life.

Yet, in the high mountains of Transylvania, they had noticed that game grew sparser and sparser. In between their quarrels, Kar had persuaded Larka to drop down in search of food, despite their fear of coming closer to Man's dwellings or other wolves whose voices they often heard now on the angry wind.

From the forests they had looked out at the humans' castles and encampments, too, and seen things that made them fear the legend even more. Troops of soldiers riding out on horseback, traveling south through the winter, their bodies bound in those strange, hard skins that glinted in the frosty sunlight. Plains flecked with the humans' burning air, as human packs met beneath fluttering banners. They shuddered as they thought of the coming of the Man Varg and a power to enslave all the Lera.

Larka stopped in the snow, and now she was wondering about what Kar had said to her. Kar had been right. Larka had no idea where she was leading them, and suddenly she realized that all she was doing was running away. It made her feel both guilty and angry.

"Come on," she growled suddenly, "you must try and hunt for us, Kar."

The friends splashed across a stream, and a fish darted around Larka's legs as she waded through the icy water. Hunger and instinct should have sent her splashing after it, but the she-wolf remembered the rabbit and just stared at it stupidly. Below the stream was a ragged forest, and Larka and Kar passed into the trees. Kar was leading when Larka suddenly pulled him up. She had seen a path skirting through the forest and, though she didn't know why, she suddenly wanted to follow it.

"No, Kar," said Larka resolutely, "this way."

Larka had just had the most extraordinary feeling. It was as though she could hear a voice calling to her on the wind. Kar wondered now if he should take the lead, but as

Larka set off, and Kar recalled what he himself had said about trust, he followed her.

The wolves padded on and, as they came to the edge of the trees, Larka's tail came up as they caught a strong, sweet scent. They had reached a steeply sloping field and below them they suddenly saw a figure toiling on the hill. It was a human. Kar glanced at Larka, and she shook her head to silence him. Larka was going to back away again into the woods, yet something held her.

The human was dressed in thick sheepskin with a strangely shaped covering of brown wool on his head. He was staggering down the snowy slope, trailing something behind him, grunting and swearing violently. The sled was piled high with wood, and every now and then a branch would drop off in the snow and he would stop and growl angrily as he replaced it on the pile. The man looked desperately thin, and his skin was wrinkled and leathery. His legs were covered in deerskin, torn and tattered, while his gnarled face was covered in black stubble. He looked exhausted, and Larka's keen eyes noticed his paws as he struggled to pick up the wood. They were bent around like claws and the naked skin was turning bright blue in the cold.

They watched warily as the old man struggled on, completely unaware of the wolves' searching eyes. At last he reached the bottom of the slope and began to pull his quarry along flat ground. Beyond stood a wooden den, with a hot mist curling up from its top. From inside an old female appeared, dressed much like the man, and as soon as she saw his paws she cried out. She rushed forward and took them in her own, rubbing them furiously. Then she hugged him tightly and together they dragged the sled inside.

As Larka thought of the mythical power of the Man Varg and all she had seen of Man from the mountains, Larka felt confused. These humans seemed to be suffering in the snows as much as the wolves had done.

It was only now that Kar noticed the other dens through the trees surrounding the first. From here he could make out perhaps twenty of them. More mist was rising from their little roofs and, here and there, he saw other humans drifting like wraiths through the snow.

"Food," whispered Kar, looking very sly. "There must be some food down there."

"No, Kar. It's too dangerous. The curse will touch us again."

"But, Larka. We're beyond the boundary now, and if we don't eat soon we'll both be dead."

Larka fell silent. She was frantically hungry. What had Huttser said on the day of their first hunt, about the two ways a wolf must survive, the way of the hunter and the way of the scavenger? But there was another faint thought, too, echoing in the back of Larka's mind. A thought that was beginning to answer Tsinga's words to her. It was hardly conscious. It was more like someone whispering quietly to her as she slept. Maybe, maybe this would be a chance to learn more of these humans.

"Very well," she growled. "We will go among them."

Kar began to pad forward.

"Not yet, Kar. First we watch and plan, and wait for night to make us invisible."

The wolves lay down and listened as the wind whistled

around the brittle wood. The air was terribly cold, and Kar's stomach had begun to growl at him. He felt utterly miserable and, though it had been his idea to look for food, the thought of going among the humans made him nervous.

"Larka, are you frightened?" he whispered suddenly.

In that moment Larka wanted to be strong for her friend, yet she longed to share her secret heart too.

"Yes, Kar."

"But you're not like me, Larka. You're bold."

Larka felt anything but bold. She gazed tenderly at Kar. He had grown into a very thoughtful wolf. So much less instinctive than Fell had been, or than herself for that matter. Fell had thought Kar something of a fool and a bit of a coward too. But it wasn't true. He was just less spontaneous, less impetuous and more sensitive.

"I'm often frightened," Kar confessed. "I was frightened on the river."

Larka growled sadly, "Don't blame yourself, Kar, and don't remind me."

"I'm sorry," said Kar, beginning to drift off into melancholic thoughts. "But it's terrible sometimes. To think of what happened to Fell and the others."

Larka nodded, but Kar looked up hopefully. "What do you think comes afterward, Larka? Do you believe those stories, of Tor and Sita and Fenris?"

"I don't know," answered Larka quietly, gazing up at the darkening heavens. The she-wolf felt a strange longing stirring inside her. "Sometimes I think they're just tales for cubs."

Kar became gloomy at this answer. "Larka. What do you think real courage is?"

The words of the verse came to the she-wolf through the trees.

"Real courage. What do you mean?"

"Fell always thought courage was being a brave hunter," said Kar. "But what if you're no good at hunting?"

Again Kar seemed downcast, but he suddenly felt that the most courageous thing he could do, the most courageous thing he had ever done, was to tell Larka exactly how he was feeling. "Can I tell you something," he whispered. "Just you? Can you keep a secret?"

Larka was almost amused, for in their predicament who was there to tell?

"What, Kar? What secret?"

"I don't want to die, Larka."

Larka's young heart went out to her friend. She reached her muzzle forward and licked him softly on the nose. Kar lifted his snout and howled quietly to himself, but as the call quivered through the air toward the humans, Larka growled.

"Hush, Kar. They'll hear you."

The friends fell silent again, as the darkness seemed to steal into their thoughts. But it gave them comfort, too, for at least it offered the frightened wolves concealment. It was getting very late when Larka got to her feet.

"Well, then," she said boldly, "if we're going to do this thing we'd better get going. Stealth and cunning, Kar."

An orange glow was coming from the first wooden den as Larka led Kar down the hill toward the humans. Kar began to shiver a little under his fur, but there was no sign of life. Indeed, if the wolves had only known it, inside the den the humans were already beginning to doze.

The old woodcutter they had watched on the hill was hunched by a stove in his single room, wrapped tight in his woolen coat. His wife sat opposite him on a wooden stool, dressed in red woven cloth and slumbering too. Her face was as old and wrinkled as her husband's, and her hands were clasped together tightly around a little wooden crucifix that she always carried with her to ward off the evil eye. She had fallen asleep watching the man she had loved for nearly fifty years.

There was a bed in the room, a simple cot. Neither of them were using it, for here, under a threadbare blanket, lay a seven-year-old boy. He was asleep, too, near his grandparents, for his own parents had died of cholera not a year before, and he was dreaming fitfully. As the wolves neared the house in the snowy night, though, the boy stirred and suddenly lifted his head. The woodcutter woke too.

"What is it, Roman? Can't you sleep?"

"I keep having bad dreams, Grandfather. Did you hear them calling in the night?"

"Yes, Roman." The woodcutter yawned wearily, and he nudged the dog at his feet. "The voice of true hunger. The voice of the wild wolf."

"I saw three last spring," said the boy, sitting up in bed now. "They looked just like dogs to me. Perhaps one day I will catch one and tame it."

"Perhaps, Roman." The woodcutter smiled. "Though some say you can never really tame a wolf, and looks can fool. Survival in the wild makes them far more powerful than dogs and far more dangerous. But if you ever do, we should change your name to Wolfram and send you to live in the northern lands."

"Why, Grandfather?"

"Wolfram means ravenwolf, Roman, a great warrior's name. Odin, the god of the Vikings, always kept two giant wolves beside him that followed him into battle, along with a pair of ravens that would peck at the corpses."

Outside, Larka suddenly stopped and shivered. The she-wolf felt her senses more acutely than ever as her interest in the dens before her blended with the fear thrilling through her body. The voices came to her faintly from beyond.

"Even today some believe it ensures victory," the boy's grandfather went on inside the hut, "to see a wolf and a raven together before a battle. Sometimes they really are seen together in the wild, but then many strange legends are drawn from real facts about nature, especially in the land of Transylvania."

The boy wrapped the blanket tighter around his slender body and looked through the small window at the soaring, snow-capped mountains. He suddenly felt a mixture of fear and desire.

"I know the Gypsies think they have the evil eye," Roman said, "and Petru says they carried off a whole group of Gypsies last month. Left nothing but their boots."

His grandfather grinned. His face was as gnarled and pitted as the bark of an ancient oak tree.

"The Gypsies do have many superstitions, Roman. That to look into a wolf's eyes can blind a man, or to walk in a wolf's tracks can lame a horse. But we should not listen to Gypsy tales. As for Petru's story, I have never heard, from any but fools, of a healthy wolf attacking a human in the wild. We are not their natural prey."

The way his grandfather was talking reminded Roman of his own father, but his parents were gone, and Roman somehow knew that he had to grow up more quickly than other children in the village.

"Petru says they are hunting them again, Grandfather."

"Yes, Roman. With this nonsense about the theft of a child and the bounty, there won't be any wolves left before long. But, then, the people are frightened. The Turk is raiding again. Perhaps that has added to their anger, though men have always hated the wolf."

"Why?" said the boy indignantly, suddenly looking very unhappy indeed.

"Maybe because they see something in the wolf that they hate and fear in themselves. Maybe because wolves take their sheep and goats, as if we shouldn't all share life's bounty. For few have the imagination to see what it is really like to be a wolf. In some towns they even put wolves on trial, as if one should judge the animals."

Roman found the idea so strange that he pulled the blanket over him.

"But then haven't we always used the animals like scapegoats. Even more than one another?"

"Scapegoats?" said Roman, peering over the blanket.

"In ancient times," said his grandfather, "villagers used to take a goat and put their hands on it in the hope it would take their sins on its shoulders. Then they would drive it out into the wild as a sacrifice to their vengeful gods."

Again, Roman looked unhappy.

"But as for superstitions, not all are bad," added his grandfather, smiling encouragingly. "My favorite is of the corn wolf, a good spirit that guards the crops."

"I think the wolf we heard tonight is a good spirit," insisted the boy warmly, curling up his toes.

"I'm sure he is." His grandfather smiled. "And we should believe such things, especially at the time of our savior's birth."

Roman seemed comforted, and he settled in his bed again to sleep. As he closed his eyes, he decided that he would have a dream, and that his dream would be about a wolf. Outside the young gray wolves passed on through the creeping night.

"Look," growled Kar suddenly, "down there."

Kar's eyes had locked on a space of open ground between two pine trees. The snow around it was scuffed and melted, marked with a good number of human spores that led back to the wooden dens just beyond. Though more of the orange light spilled out onto the snow from these dwellings, there was no one about.

On the ground where the spores led, the wolves saw a great mound of discolored matter that made Larka's senses reel. It was at once delicious and acrid, with a strong scent of decay hanging from the air. Kar was the first to begin rooting through the rubbish heap, turning it over with his muzzle and snuffling after the smells that had suddenly assaulted his senses. Larka lifted her head from the pile. She had an old bone in her jaws.

"Saved," cried Kar.

Their excitement was short-lived. It was soon clear that

there was little here that was substantial for the wolves to eat, for the villagers were desperately poor and there was nothing that they could afford to waste. Larka's bone had long been stripped of its meat by humans and of its marrow by hungry rodents and insects and the tiny creatures that swarmed like an army around the rubbish heap. There was no goodness in it at all.

"Come on," said Larka dejectedly, dropping the thing again, "let's get closer."

Larka and Kar padded on again until they saw a strange den ahead of them. The orange glow they had seen from the houses was spilling out onto the snow and, as they crept up in the darkness, the wolves gasped. There were no humans about, but the building was blazing with their burning air.

"Fire." Larka trembled. "Be careful, Kar."

"What do you mean?"

"The elements. We've already been touched by four of them, Kar. Earth, air, water, and ice. Fire is the last to fear now."

The wolves had come to the village forge, and in the flickering shadows they saw a great brazier, burning with coals. On a wooden bench in front of it lay a number of strange objects that reminded them of the soldiers they had seen from the mountains, for the scythes that the smith had been mending glittered like swords. Larka remembered the fire she had seen at the Gypsy camp. As they watched, there was a great hissing sound and the fire suddenly flared up.

In the sudden blaze of light Larka began to growl. Something was moving at the back of the fiery den. A donkey was standing in the dirt and beginning to shuffle nervously. It was tethered to a pole and as it moved in a circle, the pole turned with it. Again came the sighing sound, and the forge glowed even brighter. Larka noticed that as the pole turned it moved a wooden arm, attached to an object at the base of the forge, which looked like the stomach of a buffalo.

It was moving in and out now and, as it breathed and gave out the sighing sound, the fire burned hotter and hotter. Larka was amazed as she peered at the bellows and the donkey beyond. She realized that Man had done this, that Man had harnessed this living animal to the fire to give it life. Kar was beginning to growl hungrily as he looked at the donkey, but the forge made the two wolves frightened and they passed on.

They were walking down a clear track, and both were thankful that the night was so dark. Larka kept sniffing the air nervously, though, for the human scent was strong and made her very uncomfortable. After a while they came to another of the dens, larger than the rest and surrounded by strips of standing wood.

"Food," growled Larka.

Red brown stains bruised the snow in front of them and set the wolves' senses reeling. The blood trailed under a wooden fence, and Larka could see no signs of its source.

"Human?" whispered Kar.

"No," answered Larka, licking the ground, "I think it's pig."

Only suns before the humans had indeed killed a pig, to celebrate the birth of a child, their holy savior. They had slaughtered the pig in the manner traditional to Transylvania at this time of the year, cutting its throat in the open outside their dwelling. Very few of the villagers were rich enough to own a pig, and this was one of the most important households in the village. They had shared some of the meat with their neighbors and the fat, too, that sat on the woodcutter's table.

But suddenly Larka and Kar heard a noise behind them and turned. Five humans were standing in the path.

"Hurry, Kar," cried Larka, snarling at them, "follow me."

The friends sprang away, right through the center of the village, and as a shout went up the wooden entrances to some of the dens opened and slammed shut immediately. At the end of the village lay an open field, stretching away to a small frozen lake, flanked by trees.

Larka and Kar paused, panting furiously, and looked back. An angry crowd of humans had gathered right in the middle of the path. Some were carrying clubs and others branches that flamed with burning air, casting a lurid glow on the snow, as they shook their fists angrily at the intruders. Suddenly three of their dogs came bounding straight toward the wolves. Kar and Larka leaped across the field with the dogs in frantic pursuit. The lake wasn't far and the trees offered fairly good cover, but they had forgotten just how tired they were. Kar and Larka began to slow, but as the lead hound drew near, Kar dropped his pace further and, with a loud growl, called back to him.

"Keep your distance," he snarled, surprising himself with his own ferocity. "If you know what's really good for you."

The dogs pulled up immediately, and the wolves disappeared into the trees as the sounds of the angry villagers were lost again in the snowy night.

"What a noise," cried Kar as the branches swept past them, lashing their muzzles.

"I know," growled Larka angrily. "You'd think we wanted to eat them."

The adventure had stirred Larka's spirit, but now she gradually grew dejected again. They began to slow, but crunched on wearily through the forest. The wind rose around them and Larka shivered. Again she fancied she heard something calling, that voice on the wind. On they went, but very soon hunger and cold got the better of them.

The wolves slumped down helplessly among the trees, side by side to give each other what little warmth they could. Their coats were thick with frost, and their panting breaths sent freezing steam curling around their muzzles. Larka's head sank onto her paws and Kar whined wearily.

"Larka, we've got to find food soon."

"I suppose so, Kar, but perhaps it's all for the best."

"Don't say that, Larka. Don't you want to survive?"

Larka could hardly answer him.

"I wish Huttser and Palla were here," growled Kar. "They'd tell us what to do."

But as he said it, Larka thought mournfully of her parents' terrible quarrel that night. The image of their fight on the ice was burned into her brain, and their memory brought her little solace. Once more the she-wolf took everything onto herself. What had happened to her pack. Her parents' anger. All of it. "Everywhere I go, I bring disaster with me, Kar," she growled. "Tomorrow you must set off on your own."

"Stop it. I've told you once already, Larka, and I won't say it again . . ."

But Larka couldn't hear Kar any longer. As she fell asleep, the nightmare descended. It had visited Larka before, and it always reminded her of how she had gazed into the brackish trough at the castle and seen things she could not even affect. She was standing by the icy pool in the moonlight, looking down in horror through the water at her dead brother drifting through the river, his sodden fur mingling with the strangling weeds. She was calling to Fell and then floating with him through the murk, but all that answered her was the endless tug and sway of the river. Then, suddenly, in the water, Larka saw other faces too. There were Khaz and Kipcha, and poor Bran, their muzzles lifting sadly toward her through the reeds.

"Life," they called through the gloomy water, "life has betrayed us."

Larka stirred. This time the dream was changing, the pain of the nightmare dwindling on the rapid flow of shifting visions. Now Larka was standing by a rock and there was Fell, nodding back at her, the handsome black wolf as strong and bold as he had ever been. In front of him on the rock lay the body of a small roe deer.

"For you, sister," whispered the dream, "for you. Have faith, Larka. There is always hope."

As Larka scented the phantom meat, her tired jaws began to dribble. She opened her mouth and bit deep, drinking in the succulent juices, quenching her ravening hunger, basking in the wonderful smell that was surrounding her and filling her with life.

Larka woke with a shudder, but her belly was as empty as ever. Yet the smell was still there. Larka wrestled with her longing, half wanting to close her eyes again and abandon herself to the wonderful fantasy. But suddenly the she-wolf's eyes were open wide, and staring in amazement. The smell was real. In the snow right in front of her, lay a chunk of fresh pig.

"It's all right, Larka," said Kar calmly behind her. "It's for you."

"But how?" Larka gasped, gazing at the delicious meat.

"I stole it from the human dens while you were sleeping." Kar shrugged, waving his tail proudly. "Scavenged it. I'm just sorry I couldn't carry more back."

"Sorry! But you took a fearful risk, Kar."

"Not really. They had all gone, well, nearly all of them anyway."

"Nearly all?"

"That's the odd bit. As I was coming back with the meat, there were three of them standing there, watching me. It was that old Sikla we saw pulling that wood down the slope, and his mate. Their cub was with them too. But they didn't do anything at all. Not run or shout or shake their paws angrily. They just stood there, watching. They seemed to want to learn something."

Larka's ears twitched and she wondered, but her hunger soon got the better of her. She paused for an instant, touched by a vague embarrassment at being fed by her friend. But as the fresh smell of the pig wafted up, her reservations vanished, and the she-wolf threw herself ravenously on her unexpected breakfast.

"There, Larka," Kar growled happily as he watched her tear at the pig, "we will survive."

They slept again, and this time Larka had no more nightmares. When she woke, she felt a little stronger and her belly was no longer aching. For a time at least, Kar had saved both their lives. But Larka kept thinking about the humans, and she suddenly wondered if perhaps she had something to be grateful to them for. As she half dozed and thought about the three humans watching Kar, she fancied she saw a face, looking down at her from the trees with those strange yellow black eyes. But it didn't frighten her now.

"See," it seemed to say kindly, "you are coming closer."

But when Larka woke fully a second time, she was immediately unnerved. There was a new scent on the breeze and, as she looked about her, she saw that a strange mist was settling around them. It seemed to come from nowhere and it already hung heavy around the base of the trees.

"Kar. Wake up."

Kar growled as he opened his eyes. He had caught the scent, too, and the eerie mist was getting thicker and thicker. It reminded Larka of her visions in the water.

"Morgra," whispered Larka.

"Larka," said Kar, "this isn't mist!"

Suddenly the wolves could smell it. It was the smell from the forge and, as the smoke got thicker and thicker, their eyes began to sting. They could feel heat on their fur.

"Fire!" cried Larka. "Run, Kar, run for your life."

Their eyes were smarting as they leaped away, hardly able to see where they were going at all. Suddenly a wall of flame rose in front of them. The wolves shrunk down in terror, snarling and whimpering. The trees were flaming, sparks flying in the darkness, a crackling fury filling their ears. They both felt it blasting against them like a wind, and the force of its heat was a physical power, pushing them back. The snow on the ground and on the branches had melted, and the blaze sent out a spitting steam that hissed and wheezed about them.

The thin boughs were wet with the winter and the forest would never have caught, but for the ingenuity of man. For other humans had seen Kar stealing the pig and, full of fear and hatred, fed by the strange tale of the theft of a baby, they had crept after him with the intention of smoking out the wolves. They had piled branches and kindling kept dry in their homes against the trees. With their clever hands and, working till the early hours, painted the boughs with tar and pitch and set light to the winter. The fire had caught, and now it was so hot that it might have melted stone.

"Kar," cried Larka desperately through the smoke. "Where are you, Kar?"

The wolves couldn't see each other, but suddenly Kar yelped. A spark had leaped onto his coat and, as the burning ember seared into his skin, he sprang sideways. A wall of flame jumped up around him. Larka could only watch in horror. She did not know how to fight Man's fire. She did not know how to fight a curse or a legend.

Kar swung left and right, snarling and snapping, his

muzzle illuminated by a halo of flame and his eyes burning with pain as he searched desperately for a way out. But try as she might, jumping again and again toward him, Larka could not reach her friend. The wall of heat kept forcing her back.

"Larka, get away."

"No, Kar."

"You must, Larka," he snarled, coughing terribly. "This has proved one thing at least. Yours is the family. We have all been touched by the elements now. Go, Larka. You must survive, for all of us now. For life itself."

The flames engulfed him. Larka felt a terrible burning too. Her own tail was on fire. It flared like a torch behind her and, blinded by pain and smoke, suddenly quivering with fear and driven back by the terrible heat, Larka sprang away. But the flames were catching quickly now, and as Larka ran she, too, found herself trapped by the fire. She had leaped through a blazing bush into a small clearing, and now she was completely encircled by flame.

"Man," she cried, "Man's fire."

Larka felt a terrible fury as she thought of the humans. They had killed Khaz and her dearest friend. They had blighted her life as much as Morgra's curse and, at last, they had come for her too. If only she could escape, Larka swore bitterly, she would find one and kill it for all they had done to the wolves. But as Larka realized escape was impossible, she knew that she was lost. The flames were getting higher and higher, but there was no way out. Poor foolish Kar. In his dying moments he had thought that all that had happened had somehow proved that theirs was the family to fight the evil. But Kar was wrong. *Now they are all dead,* thought Larka, *and how can the dead ever fight anything?*

"Help me," she growled in anguish as the pain in her tail gripped her like a vice. "Is there nothing to help me? Oh, Mother, Father, why did you leave me?"

But all that came to Larka was the sound of the crackling flames. In that moment, she no longer cared. Like Kipcha at the rapids, she felt a strange lightness come over her, the lightness of despair. At least with her death it would all end: the curse, the legend, everything. It was Larka who had caused it all, caused so much suffering, and now the she-wolf would pay the price. Larka wanted to walk straight into the flames. She dropped her muzzle bitterly and stepped forward.

Suddenly, in the broiling heat, Larka felt a great gust of air, and a shape swooped over her head.

"Quickly," it cried, "this way!"

Larka looked up and saw a bird above her, and something stirred in her memory, but she hardly had time to take in the sight as the bird flew for the trees. Its huge wings beat the branches, sending up a flurry of sparks that made it look as thought it were on fire too. As the creature fought the flames, Larka saw a small opening where the fire was less intense. She dived through the gap after the bird, and it hovered above her, beating down the blaze as she went. There was a path ahead and she ran blindly now, but with hope surging in her heart.

"Follow me," screeched the bird.

The she-wolf was still consumed with fear and pain as she fled through the wood, and hope gave way to something else as Larka realized that she had escaped. Hate rang through her mind as she left Kar behind her, and although she was no longer on fire, her tail was smarting furiously.

On the bird led her. They came to a stream that snaked out of the mountains and was so fast that it had not frozen in the cold. Next to it was an almond tree by a great mossed rock, and suddenly the bird dived and settled right on top of the rock.

"There," it cried with relief. "Now you're safe again."

As it closed its great wings, Larka saw that its feathers, where it hadn't been singed, were a beigy brown, speckled with black and gray and thrown around it like a robe. The strange bird fluffed them up on its thin, long body as it looked back at Larka and shifted to and fro on its huge talons. Most extraordinary of all to Larka were the bird's piercing eyes. Two points of jet-black set in little pools of pure yellow. Larka thought suddenly of Wolfbane, but she knew now she had seen those eyes before.

They were not the only thing Larka had seen before. She growled as her gaze took in the stream, and she saw it lying there, beneath the water, just as she had seen it in her first vision. There, glinting brilliantly in the frosty sunlight, lay a fleece of gold.

As Larka's eyes opened wider and wider, she heard a stifled moan, too, from a clearing just ahead. She turned from the bird and, prowling forward, gasped as she saw the little creature in front of her. It was fast asleep. A human baby, no bigger than a young cub. The human was lying wrapped in skins, on the frosted ground, next to the mouth of a wide, sunken earth den. It was unaware of the she-wolf, and though she was still far off, Larka's jaws began to slaver and she remembered what she had sworn among the flames.

"You don't want to eat it, do you?" said the bird suddenly from the rock. "You may want revenge, but I really don't believe the humans taste very good. Not like the stoat or the roe deer, eh?"

The bird blinked slowly, as Larka turned back to it, as though it was just about to fall asleep. But there was a strength and a pride in those eyes, too, and something sharp with intelligence, that Larka liked immediately. She noticed the bird's beak now, as it spoke to her, yellow and hooked forward like a claw.

"What are you?" Larka asked angrily. "Are you a flying scavenger?"

The creature opened his wings immediately and beat the air furiously. "How dare you," he screeched. "I am Putnar and one of the noblest of the great birds. Flying scavenger, my beak."

Larka prowled back around the rock, but as she came around behind him, the bird did something extraordinary. His whole head swiveled around on his body, ninety degrees, so that he was still facing her. The bird's strange blinking eyes were smiling.

"Doesn't the Sight teach us that it is just as useful in life," he shrugged, as he saw Larka's surprise, "to look backward as well as forward? Now, tell me your name."

As soon as he spoke of the Sight, recognition stirred in Larka's mind. The eagle cocked his head and seemed to be looking intently at Larka's forehead, as though searching for something.

"My name is Larka," growled the she-wolf quietly.

"And you're Skart, the steppe eagle, aren't you? Tsarr's Helper."

The eagle nodded slowly.

"You are learning quickly, Larka. That is good. But now we are here to teach you even more."

"Teach me?"

"How to use the Sight. How to fight Morgra. That's what you came for, isn't it?"

Larka blushed in surprise.

"I . . . I didn't come here, did I?" she said in a daze. "I mean, you brought me here. Though I saw this place before, Skart. I saw it in the water."

"Exactly," said Skart. "And it is strange indeed that you have already touched the water power. But then you and the child, you already have a connection, Larka."

Larka shivered. "It's all like a dream," she said in a dazed voice. "A nightmare that began when Morgra cursed us."

"And do not dreams tell us truths and secrets of the world before we recognize things with our waking thoughts?"

Larka looked hard at the bird, and she felt the strangeness of talking to another Lera.

"Yet the Sight is no dream, Larka," cried Skart suddenly. "It is a real power and you have already used it to see the future. Now it will grow rapidly in you."

Larka was shaking her head helplessly. "Sometimes I wish I could just wake up and be back in the den with my brother."

"Wake up?" said Skart, nodding his feathery head thoughtfully. "Most of the thoughtless Lera believe that their suns are simply split into two, between sleeping and waking. But my sort believe that there is more to life than those simple states, Larka, there is also knowing."

Larka wondered what Skart could mean.

"I saw that fleece," she muttered. "What is it, Skart?"

The eagle's eyes smiled.

"Just a sheepskin. There's nothing really magical about it. Though Man seems to prize the yellow metal above everything else."

"Man," growled Larka angrily, thinking suddenly of the child again. "I don't want to know about Man, and I don't want to learn anything."

"I think you'll find," said the eagle gently, "that whether you wanted to or not, you've been learning all along, without even knowing it. But sometimes all of us need teachers."

But Skart was suddenly looking past Larka and, as she turned, she saw two wolves walking slowly up the slopes toward them. The older was a male, with a long gray muzzle deeply whitened around the snout. The younger she-wolf at his side looked nervous as she spied Larka. She pushed straight past her into the clearing, growling protectively and lying down beside the baby, curling her bushy tail across its belly.

The old gray wolf came to a stop right in front of Larka by the mossed rock. "So, you're here at last," he said simply. "You took your time."

"Didn't I tell you she would pick up the scent, Tsarr?" said Skart. "Her name is Larka."

"Tsarr," whispered Larka. "Then you all know who I am?"

Larka had lost everybody she loved, but here were Lera all around her again, and Lera that knew of the Sight.

Tsarr said quietly, "Oh yes, it's the legend, Larka. Besides, Skart here has been watching your adventures for a long while now, and he doesn't miss much. Skart's eyes can spot the tiniest spider from far above the clouds."

"Then why didn't he talk to me before?" asked Larka, suddenly feeling a bitterness again for all that had happened to her. "If he'd helped us before perhaps Kar—"

"Don't be ungrateful," snapped Skart. "I saved your life, didn't I? Before you were far too young, Larka. Your eye wasn't open yet and I didn't want to frighten you away. Though if I'd realized quite how much you know already, perhaps I might have come even sooner. But, anyway, I needed to wait."

"Wait for what?" said Larka sullenly.

"Wait for you to ask for help, of course."

Larka felt as though she had been stroked by some unseen hand.

"Come, Larka," cried Tsarr. "It is high time that you met the source of so much trouble."

As Larka followed them nervously into the clearing, the baby was still asleep, curled up outside its den, and one of the fingers on its little paws was thrust into its mouth. It shivered as it lay there, but the gray she-wolf's body had given it warmth. Larka growled menacingly as she padded up and nodded her head to the other wolf nestling the human to her belly.

"This is Jarla," said Tsarr. "She has been suckling the creature for us."

"And never has a creature suckled so long," murmured Jarla, shaking her head in wonder.

"I asked her to help us," growled Tsarr quietly, "after the Balkar took her own cubs . . ."

Tsarr paused, and Jarla's eyes were full of bitterness. Larka stepped closer and, as she looked down at the baby, she shivered. "It's not natural to be so near to such a thing. I feel . . . feel so strange."

"So did we both, Larka," whispered Jarla sympathetically, "at first."

Larka sniffed at the human nervously, but she felt a sense of recognition, too, for she had seen a child once before. Yet as she caught its scent again, a hunger stirred inside her. Suddenly the baby's eyelids opened and looked up at her. Larka blanched at the creature's striking, clear blue gaze.

Larka felt almost ashamed as it looked at her, for she could hardly hold that gaze. But the child made some peculiar sucking noises, and then it reached out its little hand to touch Jarla's coat. The human was barely a tail's length from Larka now. Her tail rose and her claws dug into the ground. Its hide was so thin she could almost smell the blood beneath its skin.

"Be careful, Larka. To master the Sight, first you have to learn to master yourself. To control your instincts," said Skart.

Larka held back her hunger. The human's face was so close to Larka's muzzle that she could have taken its head off in one snap. But suddenly it turned to Jarla. It nudged at her belly and began to suckle greedily, just as Larka had once done in the den. Larka snarled at the sight. "No. Stop it. We should kill it, or at least leave it to perish in the snow."

Jarla gave an angry growl.

"Peace, Jarla," said Tsarr.

The she-wolf dropped her muzzle over the baby's body.

"We should have nothing to do with Man," said Larka bitterly. "Can't you see what they do? What they did to Khaz and Kar? What they nearly did to me?"

"At first I thought we should kill it, too," Tsarr growled quietly. "But even if the Varg decide to have nothing to do with Man, Larka, Man may have something to do with us."

"But it is the oldest law, Tsarr."

Tsarr looked sad and suddenly very old. A strange nostalgia was stirring in him. "I was taught the law, too, Larka," he answered. "But there are even older laws than the laws made by the Varg in these parts, frightened of the humans and their wars, of legends and superstitions. Laws that are contained in storytelling itself."

Larka suddenly recalled what Tsinga had said of deeper laws.

"In the beginning the tales tell of a very different relationship with Man, Larka, when wolf and Man lived together in peace. Besides, after I stole the child, I found I didn't really have the heart to kill it."

"Why not, Tsarr?"

"Perhaps because I know the bitterness of survival."

There was a tenderness in the old Varg's voice that touched Larka to her guts, and she thought, too, of her own narrow escape. But as she looked down again, the baby brought back memories of Kar.

"I hate it, Tsarr," she growled.

"No, Larka," cried Tsarr, "you mustn't hate. As the Sight connects all things, your hate will only call to Morgra, as she tries to call to you. For it is the energy of hate that she has mastered."

"But the humans murdered my friends," hissed Larka, wondering suddenly if Morgra really was trying to call to her. "They have always hunted us, always tried to make us their slaves."

"They are Putnar, too, the greatest of the Putnar," said Tsarr. "And perhaps it is their destiny to master the world."

Larka looked down with surprise at the baby, and its eyes seemed to hold a deep mystery. Some dark potential that made her think of the soldiers she had seen in the mountains. *What would this thing become if it was allowed to grow,* she wondered fearfully.

"It's marked, isn't it?" she growled.

"Yes, Larka," Tsarr answered, "that was the secret Tsinga entrusted to me and why Morgra never found it herself below the Stone Den. Look."

Tsarr tipped his nose and muzzled away the hide that was covering the child's belly. Above its little stomach was a ribbon of hair that looked like wolf fur threading in a thin straight line right down its belly.

The child began to cry, but the old wolf leaned forward again with his muzzle and touched the baby gently in the middle of the forehead. It calmed the child immediately.

"What did you do that for?"

"It is just a baby, Larka, and understands little now but fear and hunger," Tsarr explained. "But some believe that is where the humans really see from. That there is a third eye, far stronger than any ordinary eyes."

Larka felt as if she had stepped into another dream as Tsarr turned away from the child and began to tell her of their journey. It had been easy to pick the baby up by the cloth bound around its middle and spirit it away from the village. The humans were busy celebrating its birth, a birth that the pack had witnessed, without ever even knowing it, as they lay by the boulder above the den.

They had hidden the child not far from where Larka's pack had found their Meeting Place. But one night they had overheard wolves from the rebel pack stalking the mountain, too, and learned that Slavka was hunting for the child also. So they had been forced to move on with the infant, escaping yet another enemy.

During their flight, they had indeed sheltered in the abandoned castle that the wolf pack had stumbled on. At first, after one kill, Jarla had not understood what Tsarr had been trying to tell her about making a hole in the hide through which its head might push, but she had understood the need to cover up its furless skin. So the young she-wolf had sat there, gnawing away, until her teeth had cut an opening in the hide, and together Jarla and Tsarr had managed to lift it in their muzzles over its head.

They had felt the need to bind it somehow, as Tsarr had once seen the entrances to the humans' dens bound tight shut with rope, and Jarla had brought some vine from the woods in her mouth. They had managed to get it around the cub's middle, but there was nothing they could do with their snouts to lock it together. At last Skart had managed it with his clever beak.

Time and again Skart had returned to watch Larka, for only he could travel with speed above the trees. As she looked into the eagle's yellow black eyes, she felt greatly relieved, for at least it was he and not Wolfbane or the Searchers that she had sensed in the forest. But then Larka remembered the wolves who had appeared and then vanished again in the snow.

"Now you have found your way to us, Larka," said Tsarr as he finished his tale. "You must learn to wield the Sight and help us to fight Morgra. There are rumors that Wolfbane has returned."

"Wolfbane is real?" growled Larka.

"Wolfbane is fear, which Morgra uses to control the animals," explained Tsarr. "And if they follow the Evil One's ways, does it really matter if he exists or not? Besides, the ancient verse says only that he must be dreamed of by the Varg, not that the Evil One must really come."

Larka shook her head. "Is this my destiny, then? Is there no one else to fight Morgra?"

"The rebels are gathering," said the eagle beside them, "but that only makes me worry all the more."

"Why, Skart?"

"Because they would kill the child for one, and because the untamed are being tamed, Larka, as the verse warns. The wild spirit of the wolf is being tamed throughout the land beyond the forests."

"But what are you going to do with this creature?" growled Larka.

Tsarr's wolf eyes flickered, and for a moment, he looked at Skart almost guiltily. Larka remembered what Brassa had told the pack of their quarrel all those years before, their quarrel about what the Sight was really for. Tsarr was about to speak when Skart interrupted him. "You must decide, Larka," he said. "but in the meantime you must help us to protect it."

As soon as Skart used the word, Larka's eyes blazed like the forge. She swung around to face the eagle.

"Protect it?" she cried in disgust. "Why should I protect it, Skart? Why should I help this creature? Humans are nothing but killers, with no respect for the wolf. And I do not want this Vision of the Man Varg. A power that will enslave all the Lera, forever."

There was such an anger in Larka that her whole body began shaking almost uncontrollably. In that moment Larka hardly knew what to do, but, suddenly, powerless with rage, she turned and sprang away through the clearing.

"No, Tsarr," screeched Skart as the wolf rose to follow her. "She'll return. Remember the legend. Larka and the infant already have a connection. She saw this place in the water. And the legend, Tsarr, think of the legend."

There was a desperate fury in Larka as she ran past the rock. That whole sun she kept on the move, but by evening her tread had slowed. Time and again Larka thought back to the human. The she-wolf wanted to take revenge for Kar and Khaz. To take revenge for everything that had happened to her. She wanted to tear into its throat and drink its blood.

But as Larka prowled through the wood, although she

knew she hated the humans, she could not stop dwelling on the strange destiny unfolding around her. She remembered again what Tsinga had said about not being able to escape a legend. As she looked at the snows glistening malevolently around her, she thought fearfully of Wolfbane's winter.

Larka lay down to sleep. Her tail was hurting again and, as she looked around, she saw that the skin where the fur had been singed away was raw. That night her dreams were full of the shadows of the village and Kar and the human cub's strange eyes. The next sun when Larka tried to hunt, something kept nagging at her, as though that voice were calling her back.

"I cannot escape, can I?" Larka kept saying to herself desperately. "I can never escape."

Larka suddenly remembered what poor Kar had cried out as the flames consumed him.

"Very well then, Kar, my friend, for life itself," she whispered coldly.

It was midafternoon when Larka returned to the stream to find Skart standing on the rock. The steppe eagle's back was to her as she padded up. He was standing on one leg and his head kept jabbing forward in curious little jerks. Larka's hackles rose.

Skart's feathers looked so tempting as she caught his scent. The she-wolf prowled around the side of the eagle. He was holding a dead chick in one talon, and his beak cracked into it like a shell. Skart snapped his mouth shut, but a few desultory feathers remained, poking from his beak.

So you really are Putnar, thought Larka gravely, and the wolf suddenly realized how much she preferred this bird to the ravens.

"Skart," she whispered as he saw her. "I don't know what I think about this human yet, or what we should do with it. But will you teach me, at least? Teach me more of the Sight?"

Skart nodded approvingly as Larka lay down by the rock, but he was thinking how much she knew already. For now, the eagle said he would concentrate on the power to look through a bird's eyes. But as soon as he spoke of it, Larka described bitterly what had happened to her when she had killed the rabbit, and after that the feelings that consumed her whenever she started to hunt.

"It's strange," Skart murmured immediately. "I've never heard of it happening through other Lera before. You have already looked into the water too. Yet the craft has been weak for so long in the land beyond the forest, who really knows what it can do. Perhaps that is a true mastery of the power, to see through the eyes of all."

Larka pawed the ground nervously.

"What do I have to do, Skart?"

"When you sense yourself being watched, Larka, before you have even seen the watcher, that is part of the Sight, the sense beyond your physical eyes."

Larka began to growl.

"But before you can control it," said Skart immediately, "you must use my eyes, and to do that you must look at me differently. You must see the truth of what I am."

"The truth?"

"Perhaps you think I am just a bird, Larka, but in this

feathered body do I not have thoughts and feelings and desires just like you? I am energy, Larka, as you are."

Suddenly Skart swiveled his beak around, and in a single jabbing movement he plucked a feather from his wing and let it flutter to the ground in front of her. "It will help you to sense me, Larka. Now try and empty your mind, and imagine what it is like to be a bird. To see as I see."

Larka did as she was told, but her head was so filled with all that had gone before that after a while nothing had happened at all.

"You're not trying, Larka," said Skart irritably. "Concentrate, but without really thinking. Use your instincts to tell you what I am, nothing more. Draw on the living power of nature all around you too. Then look at me, but try to see beyond your eyes. Through your forehead if you like. Try to empty your mind completely and draw the energy that surrounds us all up through your paws. Feel it bubbling up through the pads of your feet. Then try to enter my body with your thoughts."

Larka tried again and, as she let her mind empty and scented the feather, she felt a tingling in her paws and her whole body grew hot. There was a sudden blinding flash of black, and the she-wolf gasped as she found herself looking out at her own body lying in the grass. Her head had slumped on her paws and her eyes had closed. As Skart turned his own head, Larka was amazed to see the stream and the clearing, Tsarr and Jarla and the human revolving before her. Larka was seeing through Skart's eyes.

Larka was trembling all over and she was quite exhausted by the effort, but the feeling was strangely exhilarating too. It felt different to her experience on the hunt, more directed and controlled. She could see more clearly and, most important, she felt no fear. Instead, the she-wolf experienced a feeling of liberation, as though something in her was opening. Larka opened her own eyes, and suddenly she was in her body again as Skart let out a screech.

"There, Larka," cried the eagle, delighted. But Larka seemed deeply troubled as she lay beside the bird.

"Skart. What is the Sight?" she asked quietly.

Skart cocked his head. "It's another way of being, Larka, of understanding and of communicating too."

"That's why we can talk to each other?"

"Yes." Skart nodded, impressed with his young pupil. "Though some say that once all the Lera possessed the Sight, and that they could still talk to one another if they could only remember how."

"All the animals?" said Larka with surprise. Suddenly that voice she had heard in the forest seemed to be calling to her again, "Remember, Larka, remember."

"Yes, and that the instincts of the animals, to sense things before they happen, or feel a change in the weather, is a residue of the power. The power that was born when everything was really one."

Larka nodded slowly.

"There is an old story of a Herla, a red deer, who could do it. His name was Rannoch, and he lived on an island to the northwest. But the Sight is linked to language too. It is a kind of language, just like touch or taste or smell, and that's how those Lera possessed by the gift can understand one another naturally."

Larka had entered an almost unfathomable world. The

wolf noticed a tiny spider in the bushes nearby weaving busily across its web. She found herself suddenly trying to imagine what the spider was thinking and feeling as it worked toward a struggling fly. But every time she tried, she failed.

"But why is it connected with so much evil, Skart?"

"Evil?" said the eagle.

"Wolfbane. Man. The Searchers."

Skart's eyes closed and he fluttered his feathers uncomfortably, and Larka was reminded strangely of Tsinga.

As she lay there thinking, Larka remembered vividly the terrible feeling she had had with the snow hare. "The Sight makes the life of a Putnar impossible, Skart. When I hunt. It's horrible."

"That is the pain the Sight can bring to the Putnar, Larka," said Skart. "But you must not fear it, as you must never fear your own nature. If you do that it will control you. But you will learn."

"No," snarled Larka, "I wasn't meant for this, Skart. I am a she-wolf. A Putnar must hunt and kill to survive. Must use its instincts and its teeth. This power is a terrible thing and it wounds me."

"The Wounded One," whispered Skart gravely.

Larka turned and licked the burned skin on her tail, but her eyes were full of pain and a bitter self-pity. As Skart looked at Larka lying there feebly, his eyes grew colder and harder, though strangely clear too.

"Larka," he snapped, "do you pity yourself more than other things? More than your pack or Kar or your parents?"

Larka dropped her head shamefully.

"You have a power, Larka, and it is high time you used it."

Larka raised her head.

"Perhaps," said Skart, "you are ready to experience the wonder of the Sight."

"Wonder?" whispered Larka.

"Oh yes, Larka," cried the eagle. "Come into my eyes."

9
TEACHERS

How do you know but ev'ry bird that cuts the airy way,
Is an immense world of delight, clos'd by your senses five.
— WILLIAM BLAKE, *The Marriage of Heaven and Hell*

LARKA LET HER MIND EMPTY AGAIN and the energy bubble up through her paws. Suddenly the wolf was looking through the eagle's eyes once more. Skart opened his great wings and lifted from the ground as Larka's sightless body lay by the rock. She gasped as the ground dropped away and her vision rose into the blue. Higher and higher Skart flew, and Larka was surrounded by billowing white clouds. A great calm suffused her mind.

Below her, as Skart glided on the currents of air, the ground opened like a dream. Larka could see everything with the sharpness of the eagle; the mountains and the forests, the rivers and the streams, the great land of Transylvania sweeping before and below her. The cold sunlight sparkled on the water and quivered in the sea of white, and Larka felt her heart lighten and her fear drop away.

It was as though the she-wolf had suddenly been transported to the highest mountaintops, hurled into the clouds. And with the glory of that vision, came feeling too. She could feel the wind on Skart's feathers, the swooping, rising pressure of the air. She felt gloriously elated, and more alive and at one with the world around her than she had ever known.

"See, Larka," whispered a voice in her head.

"Skart?"

"Yes, Larka. It's me. Talk to me with your mind."

"But, Skart," cried Larka as they flew, "it is wonderful."

"Yes," screeched the eagle, swerving and diving proudly on the air. "This is the glory of the Sight. The wonder and the freedom that the Varg may share with the birds. And it is strong in you, Larka. That's why you can hear me now and feel what I feel."

As Skart soared among the clouds, his wings catching faint thermals or tilting to let them slide down the sky, Larka could feel the air ruffling the bird's feathers and the glorious tension in his wings. On and on they sailed, and this time Larka felt as though she were lost in a wonderful dream.

"Skart, where does the Sight come from?" she asked.

"Where does anything come from, Larka?" he replied. "For the Sight is far older than even the oldest faiths. Did your Tor and Fenris make the power of the Sight, or is it just there? You might as well ask where the sea or the wind or the stars come from, Larka."

"But the verse. It talks of Wolfbane and of Faith."

"The legend of the Man Varg came far, far later than a

knowledge of the Sight, Larka. The verse speaks to newer beliefs and later ways of talking about the world."

The snows were like a great shiftless sea below them. The land lay as smooth as a sigh as they hurried through the air on Skart's soaring wings. As Skart's head turned this way and that, Larka would spy a shape moving through the white, and she felt as if, with the effortlessness of thought, she could open her paws and pounce on the Lera below her. But she felt superior to the feeling too. There was no hunger in her now. The wolf was as free as the wind. On they soared, the wolf and the eagle together, looking down on the great winter tapestry.

"Skart," whispered Larka as they flew, and she noticed that she could no longer feel the pain in her tail either. "I feel so light and free. So is this what it's like to be a bird?"

"This is only a breath of it, Larka. My brothers and sisters could show you even more, but it is winter and they have long gone south on the great migration. I was there at the delta before they went, and the skies billowed with thunder clouds of birds. The delta was a forest of fowl then, but freedom was already stirring in their hearts."

"The delta?"

To speak of the delta was a sacred thing for the birds, but the eagle began as they swooped through the wintry clouds. Skart started by telling Larka that the great delta lay at the end of the southeastern land, where the mighty river that men call the Danube splits into three and plunges out into the Black Sea. Where the hard earth turns into miles upon miles of swamp and marshland, cut with islands of silt crowned with oak and ash, and ringed by floating reed beds, stirring in the rippling breeze. He told her of the little banks that appeared and disappeared suddenly with the incessant floods, and the ever-shifting contours of mud and sand and soil.

"Skart," asked Larka as she listened, "why birds? Why are birds the Helpers?"

"When you look at the fur on your paw, Larka, does it not seem to you, so close-up, that it could be a forest or a bank of fresh grass. Yet you know it is your paw and a part of your own body."

"So, Skart?"

"If you are too close to a thing, it can sometimes fool you, Larka. The fortune-tellers believed that the birds became the Helpers because they were the first to really see. To rise into the air and look down on the land and the rivers and the seas and behold things in their entirety. As they really are."

Larka's spirit was suddenly soaring, too, and in her gut she felt that old flame of rebellion that had carried her after Fell along the riverbank, or away from her parents on the ice. But as she listened, the energy of the feeling turned to something else, a kind of humility. She suddenly felt that she could learn much from this strange bird, whose experience was so different from her own.

"And how long have you possessed the Sight, Skart?"

"Larka, you misunderstand," cried the bird, "Tsinga, Kraar, and I. We don't possess the Sight in the way that you do. It was born in you. We touch a part of it through training. We are helpers, teachers. There to aid you, if you like. We have a connection with you, but it is not through us that the power really works. Yet we were prized once, as we no longer are. When there were many, many fortune-tellers and birds like me, trained to help the wolves with the Sight. Especially during the ancient wars."

"Tell me, Skart," cried Larka, looking down on the strange land below.

"The packs have rarely been at peace, but in the ancient times it was Man's battles that set them more and more at odds. As the trees were cut down and the land swallowed up, the wolves found themselves forced into even greater competition. Some of the Draggas among them began to seek ways to steal a march on their rivals. They looked to the Sight. The craft had been practiced secretly in the forests, and though it was associated with Wolfbane, too, most saw it as a true path to knowledge and enlightenment. The power to foretell the future or to see far off dangers was too tempting to the fighting Draggas, and they offered the wolves who possessed it great incentives to help them."

"Help them?"

"Help them win their wars. When the Helpers would rise high above the great forests and use the power to spy out opponents, hunt down packs, and fall mercilessly on their enemies. It was that that really made the Sight so feared and hated. That linked it strongly with the terror of Wolfbane, the wolf slayer. His cult grew stronger. This belief in the Sight as a wholly dark art eventually led to its suppression, and then strangely to its disappearance. For there were new forces at work."

"New forces?"

"Religion. The growth of a formal belief, not only in Tor and Fenris, but in Sita too. The wolves wanted peace, and Sita had shown them the way. She was now the way to truth and goodness and offered an end to superstition. So the cult of Wolfbane and the craft of the Sight were suppressed, and not always peacefully. Many wolves and many birds died. The knowledge of the gift faded almost entirely from the land beyond the forest. Though one of the fortune-tellers, a powerful seer named Narmin, left the wolves the verse and the promise, or the warning, of how the Sight would return. She had long lived in refuge in the ancient citadel, Harja, and there she believed she had discovered great truths about the Sight, and about Man too."

They were over a great elm forest now and, in the strangle of wintry trees, Larka wondered what was moving through the undergrowth. But the mention of Man and the specter of the Man Varg made Larka wish to be free in her thoughts once more.

"Skart," she whispered gravely, "tell me more of the sacred delta."

So Skart spoke now of the land creatures that made this strange place their home—the red fox and wild boar, the polecat and the mink. But Skart didn't really like to think of the predators that came to eat his own, so instead he turned to the myriad birds that swarmed to the delta.

He told Larka how the birds always knew when it was time to travel. Like the salmon that turn from the deep oceans and find their way back to their birthplace, the birds' secret instincts could guide them through storm and fog, speeding them across tens of thousands of miles, navigating the very currents of the air to the same annual feeding grounds. He told her of the soaring white-tailed eagle and the chattering cormorants, of the shelduck and the bittern and the brightly painted kingfisher.

As Skart named these birds, although she had little idea of what they really were or looked like, Larka felt a joy stirring inside her. The hypnotic, magical naming sung in her ears like the wind, and pictures began to flash through her mind. Larka fancied she could hear the birds' cries or see the wind stroking the sedge or smell the water thyme and peonies.

"Skart," cried Larka as he finished and the wind whistled about their ears, "the other sun, you said that I wasn't ready. That my eye wasn't open yet. What did you mean?"

"The eye in the forehead, Larka. The eye that really sees. The eye of the Sight. But now it is opening," cried Skart delightedly.

"The eye in the forehead," said Larka, "like the humans?"

"Yes, Larka. Then you may understand what you are becoming."

"Becoming?" growled Larka with surprise, and by the rock her body stirred and twitched.

It was twilight when Skart finally turned in the sky and sailed for home. Before them once more, the great sun was sinking in the west, and its light bruised the ribbons of cloud a deep and angry purple. The funnel of clouds had made a kind of bowl for the sinking sun. As it blazed for a final time beyond the edge of the mountains, firing the horizon with smoldering pinks and burning oranges, it looked like a wound from which the earth itself might die, or a great furnace on the edge of creation that was trying to forge the world anew.

As they spied the rock and the clearing, and Larka saw the human child, it seemed so small and insignificant lying there with the wolves in the snow that Larka almost felt a pity for it. Her heart had lightened, and somehow her extraordinary journey with Skart had given her an even greater inquisitiveness. What could this vision be and this great secret, prophesied at Harja? As Larka returned to her own eyes, though, she felt a terrible ache, like the pain of loss.

"So that is the Sight?" she growled as she blinked back at the bird in awe.

"Larka," cried Skart, "that is only the beginning."

"Why," Morgra snarled, slicing at the air with her yellowing teeth, "why can't I find it?"

Morgra spat angrily as she glared down at the pool in her frosty cave. All she could see in the water was Kraar's face peering stupidly back at her.

"The human?" whispered the raven.

"Yes, idiot," snapped Morgra. "Brak has been out searching for too long now, and the Sight shows me nothing of any real use in the water. Fragments of the past. Bits of what might be the future. But nothing substantial."

Morgra touched the pool with her paw.

"But I fear something else, Kraar. If Larka is somehow with the child, perhaps her very presence is blocking the pictures."

"Mistress," said Kraar suddenly, "there is news from the flying scavengers."

"Well?"

"They have spied Larka and the young stranger."

"But Larka was alone," said Morgra almost disinterestedly.

"You must have been mistaken, Mistress."

Morgra's eyes flashed and she swiveled her jaws toward the bird.

"But she is alone now," added the raven quickly.

"Why, Kraar, what do you mean?"

"They lost her again below the trees," answered Kraar. "But before they did, they saw the stranger. He was almost eaten by the humans' burning air."

Morgra's cruel eyes began to glitter. "Almost?"

"It nearly burned him up. But at the last minute he managed to escape. I doubt he will survive, though, after what the fire did to him. But it separated him from Larka. It was wonderful, Mistress. The fire sent up such a blaze that my cousins could see it for miles around. They warmed their wings on it. Is it not fine? Even the elements seem to be coming to fulfill your curse."

Morgra swung her head to face the bird. "What did you say, Kraar?" she snarled.

"What's wrong, Mistress?" whispered Kraar nervously, backing away from the she-wolf's straining jaws. "I thought you'd be pleased."

"Fool," hissed Morgra. "Why didn't I think of it before. The elements." Fear had crept back into Morgra's eyes. "Huttser and Palla," she cried, swinging around suddenly, "have they been spotted too?"

"No, Mistress."

Morgra seemed to relax. "No," she muttered, "the pack is destroyed, at least. Larka may still be alive, but if they weren't with her, her parents must have perished in the snows long ago. A family that's loving and true," she cried scornfully. "What good has their love ever done them?"

Kraar flapped his wings furiously. "And if Larka is with the child," said the bird, trying to appease his mistress, "surely that would be for the better. For when you find them both, you will force her to aid us."

"Feathered idiot," Morgra snapped, "I no longer need Larka's aid. My power is swelling with each sun, as I draw on his."

Suddenly Morgra turned and sprang out of the cave. But as Kraar followed her, the tiny pebble shook on the ceiling. The thing inside it was ready. Then, suddenly, the cocoon split open. Within was a winged shape, wet with foam. It spread its wings to dry them in the cold air, and the antennae on its head uncurled like little tongues. As its wings opened, they revealed a shape on its back, something like the skull Fell had seen in the graveyard. But its finely painted living wings were utterly beautiful. It was a moth, one which the humans, linking their understanding of life together in symbols, would call a Death's Head. Suddenly it fluttered into the free air.

Morgra prowled up the hill toward the woods, by the spot where the meat had once lain for the creatures of the forest. It was all gone. As soon as she passed into the trees, her eyes swept the ground, and Morgra shivered with pleasure. Everywhere Morgra looked there were dead animals. The Lera had literally been torn to pieces. There were stoats and mice, voles and squirrels, rabbits and fledgling birds. Their entrails were strewn across the ground or hanging from the lower branches of the trees.

"Wolfbane," growled Morgra with pleasure.

The snow was thick with blood, which in the night looked black and oily.

"Good, my friend," Morgra went on delightedly in that cold, hypnotic voice. "Drink deep on the lives of the Lera. Gorge yourself on blood. And when you are full, drink and drink again. Then you may step beyond even the instincts of the Putnar. Your power will swell like the night and mine will grow with it, too, until together we open the Pathways of Death. Soon. So soon."

Kraar shivered as he hopped after his mistress, his beak clacking at the sight of all that food. They heard a sound in the trees beyond, and the raven fluttered nervously onto a branch. A shadow fell on the snow, but as Morgra stood there, she caught sight of a group of Night Hunters moving up the hill past her cave.

"I saw them last sun," whispered one as they came. "They were bear marks."

The Balkar at his side slowed nervously. "But I was coming close the other night and I heard him. A great fluttering of wings," he argued.

"Then he comes in different guises," growled the first wolf, "the Shape Changer."

"Why won't he show himself?"

"He shows himself in my dreams. But Morgra commands him and she shall protect us. The Evil One fights for the Night Hunters now, and when she finds the rebels' Gathering Place, he shall lead the Searchers into battle too."

By the woods Morgra lifted her tail. "They are petrified of him, Kraar," she growled coldly as she watched the Balkar, and read their thoughts in the language of their bodies. "They suffer from the weakness that infects all the Lera. They are ruled by their fear for their own miserable lives."

But as the shadow in the woods came closer, Morgra suddenly turned violently. "No," she hissed, "stay hidden in the woods. Trust me, my dear, you are so ugly anyway that they would simply run in terror. Or even worse, they might laugh at you."

The shadow turned away and Kraar looked up questioningly.

"Fear is a secret thing, Kraar," whispered Morgra, "so we must keep him hidden. But we shall turn him into the thing they dread most. The shadow that is already beginning to haunt their dreams and the name that shall be spoken on the mouth of every Varg."

Larka was lying by the mossed rock next to Tsarr. She turned her head toward the clearing. She could not decide what to do with the child, and she still felt uncomfortable in its presence.

Larka was full of questions now, although she had already been learning much from the old wolf and the eagle. She had soared over the forests with Skart many times, and she had started to look into the water again, too, although she had seen little there but painful pictures of the past. Skart had told her that as the Sight grew, she would be able to see the pictures more clearly and even direct her vision into the present or the future as she chose.

Larka had learned other things too. How much Skart hated the flying scavengers like Kraar, and why Tsarr's power had faded. Skart had left Tsarr for a long while after their quarrel, and it seemed that the power of the Sight, if not used regularly, could dwindle, much like the weakening of a wolf's jaw if there are no Lera to hunt. Tsarr had shaken his head bitterly as he told her of it, and looked over to the eagle almost resentfully.

"The things I used to be able to see, Larka," he had said wistfully. "I can't see them anymore."

When Larka was not flying with the eagle or gazing into the stream, her spirits were often low. She was missing her parents and her old pack more than ever. She worried frantically about Huttser and Palla, and would often howl to them in the night.

Now they heard a moan from the clearing, and saw Jarla raise her head and turn her belly toward the child.

"Why is it so important, Tsarr?" asked Larka. "Why a wolf and a human? Why will they bring forth this final power?"

Tsarr looked very thoughtful. He answered slowly. "Narmin believed that the Man Varg, more than bringing forth a power, will take a power back, Larka."

"Take a power back?" said Larka with surprise.

"Yes, Larka. That the Man Varg will take back the power that Man stole from the Lera long ago."

"What do you mean? What power?"

"A power over the whole world, Larka," said Tsarr gravely.

"How?"

"The humans now control the world with their hands and strange tools," growled Tsarr.

Larka nodded as she remembered the forge.

"But what is it that makes the Lera different, Larka?"

Larka paused and she thought of what Skart had told her of the birds. "Instinct," she answered.

"Precisely. And in the wild wolf our instincts have been honed to perfection, honed by nature itself as we struggle to survive. Survival is the law of the Putnar, and the truest law of the Varg."

Larka shivered. Tsarr's words and the chill air made her think of Wolfbane's winter.

"But at the altar, when the wolf looks into the child's mind, the Man Varg will take Man's cleverness and add to it the stronger instincts of the wild wolf. Then, as the Vision comes, the untamed shall tame all."

As Tsarr spoke, there was something almost tempting in his growling voice. Larka looked at Tsarr and suddenly remembered that piece of meat, swaying from the tree in the forest where Khaz had died.

"What is this Vision, though, Tsarr," she asked, "and this great secret that Tsinga spoke of? The Vision that will make all the Lera look up and so trap them."

Tsarr shook his head, but his eyes were shining brilliantly. "That is something nobody knows, not even fortune-tellers. But there are those who have foretold that it is the secret itself that will really enslave the Lera."

In the mind of the Man Varg, thought Larka gravely, looking back to the clearing once more, *then none shall be free.*

"Tsarr," she asked suddenly. "In the verse, it says we must 'Beware the Betrayer.' Who is this Betrayer?"

"I don't know, Larka. That you must tell us."

As night settled around them, Larka padded off to

sleep. She woke with a shudder, and from somewhere in the skies she heard a screech. Skart's great wings were lifting over the trees as he returned from a hunt. He caught sight of a single stunted bush clinging to a snowy ledge on the mountainside and settled on the outcrop.

The ground was strewn with feathers and twigs and bits of bone. Skart ruffled his wings and felt comfort returning. It made him nervous to be around the wolves so much and now, high on the cliff face, hugged by the lofty winds, he felt secure and ready to concentrate on his own thoughts. But Skart's proud, wise eyes were huge as he peered out across the mighty forests sweeping below him, and suddenly he turned his head away to the north.

"Wolfbane," he blinked as he peered into the night. "Can it really be true? Must it be like this?"

Skart shook out his feathers. "But it's you I really fear," he screeched angrily at the air. "The Scarchers. Waiting and watching. Waiting to feed on us all. Will you come, too, if the promise is fulfilled. Will you come to turn nature against itself?"

Suddenly Skart lifted into the skies once more. It was many suns before he returned and, for a while, Larka and Tsarr feared he had abandoned them. But they were sitting together one dull, cold morning when the eagle came plunging toward them. Larka looked up cheerfully, but Skart's eyes were grave.

"What's wrong, Skart?" growled Tsarr immediately.

"I have discovered their Gathering Place, Tsarr," cried Skart. "The rebels."

"What of it? You know they won't help us, Skart."

The eagle folded in his wings and walked straight toward them. "It's in the field of Kosov, Tsarr," he said quietly.

Tsarr and Larka looked up immediately.

"Kosov," cried Larka in astonishment, and she got up. "But isn't that where the story of Wolfbane's . . ."

Skart nodded and Tsarr rose too. "Then perhaps these rebels are linked to the legend as well," he growled. "And Morgra's power seems to be growing somehow. Sometimes I even think I can sense her. If Wolfbane—"

"Anything could fool the flying scavengers, yet they are coming too. I have seen them in the skies. Their filthy beaks snapping at the thought of a free meal, for they all know the story." Skart's voice rang with scorn.

"But if Morgra somehow plans to fulfill Wolfbane's promise in the field of Kosov," gasped Larka. "Then there she will try to open the Pathways of Death, too, and summon the Searchers."

Tsarr growled nervously, "No," he said resolutely, "Morgra cannot make these things happen. Think of the verse, Larka. 'When the blood of the Varg blends with Man in the dew.' How could that come to pass? We may fear the humans, Larka, but they fear the wolf too. They hunt us, but Man and wolf have never fought each other at close quarters."

Tsarr was looking down at the baby, yet there was something in his voice that told Larka instantly that he was simply trying to reassure himself.

"And we know one thing," he added. "We do not have to go anywhere near the valley."

◆ ◆ ◆

The weather was getting much colder again, and Tsarr and Jarla were growing worried, for the human seemed to be sickening. Then one night Larka was coming back toward the clearing, while Jarla had gone hunting, when she overheard Skart and Tsarr talking together in the darkness. She slunk down among the branches to listen.

"To touch the powers so young," Skart was whispering gravely. "And what happened to her with the hare. I don't know yet what it means. But her power is greater than I have ever heard of."

"But you're sure we can trust her?" growled Tsarr. "Perhaps Morgra will reach her. Turn her."

Larka's ears began to quiver, but she felt strangely confused. Could she really trust these creatures herself?

"We must trust her. We have no choice. Think of the family the legend speaks of, Tsarr. The elements have touched them already."

"And because of it her brother is dead," Tsarr replied, "taken by the ice. Most probably her poor parents too. What family is left? There are other families going to join these rebels. Perhaps there lies the true hope."

Larka began to tremble.

"Tsarr," Skart whispered, "if the rebels are in Kosov and Morgra discovers them, if she somehow opens the pathways, then Larka is the only one whose power is strong enough to seal them again. To call the Searchers back."

"And if Morgra does summon the Searchers," growled Tsarr angrily, "and sends them out to do her bidding, what hope will there be for any of us?"

"If that ever happens, then Larka must go on her greatest journey. Then Larka must travel to the realms of the dead," said Skart.

Larka lifted her head in horror. She slunk away in the night, and as she lay down to rest there was an agonizing pain in her tail. Again terrible dreams came to haunt her as she slept, and when she woke she was still exhausted. She felt bitterly lonely, and all day she kept thinking of Huttser and Palla. She longed to talk to them and ask them what she should do. But another thought opened in her mind. The others had died. Perhaps Huttser and Palla had gone too. Had not Larka been somehow responsible for the curse? Had she not somehow killed her own parents?

It was twilight and Larka was lying in the snow by the rock when she looked up cheerlessly to see Skart flying toward her. The eagle noticed immediately how sullen she was.

"What's wrong, Larka?"

Larka looked at him resentfully as she thought of what he had said the night before about the realms of the dead.

"My family, Skart. There has been so much death."

The eagle settled and strutted toward her, but Larka had laid her muzzle on the ground.

"You blame yourself, Larka, don't you?" said Skart, looking closely at her.

"No, I don't," growled Larka.

"Liar."

"I . . . I . . ."

"Larka," cried Skart, "if you don't tell me truly what

THE SIGHT 288

you are thinking and feeling then how can I ever help you?"

"It is all my fault, Skart, that I lost them," moaned Larka with sudden anguish. "If I'd never been born the legend would have been forgotten. There would be no child. No curse."

The pain was welling up within Larka and, for a moment, the she-wolf could hardly breathe.

"Go on, Larka," whispered Skart kindly.

As the eagle watched Larka, he shook his head sadly. "Perhaps I have been thoughtless, Larka. Perhaps I haven't given you enough time."

"Time?" muttered Larka.

"To grieve."

"Oh, Skart," sobbed Larka, "it's been so terrible. Do you know what it is to be lonely? To be so lonely you can't breathe? And there was nothing I could do. Nothing at all. I'm to blame for it all. I'm worthless."

"No," cried Skart frantically. "Don't ever say that."

Larka's sobs seemed to subside a little.

"You are not to blame, Larka," said Skart sternly. "Was it you who hid the truth about Morgra? No. Was it you who killed a pup, even by mistake? You were not even born when this began."

"Then why do I feel so terrible, Skart, now I'm no longer just a cub?"

"Don't children pick up thoughts and feelings from grown-ups," suggested Skart, "and blame themselves for things far beyond their control?"

"Yes," sniffed Larka miserably, "I suppose they do."

"There," Skart said, "you're feeling a little better now. Don't hold things inside too much, for feelings can hurt us, too, Larka. Just as much as rocks or hunting pits. I sometimes think they can kill us."

"What do you mean?" Larka asked in surprise.

"Your friend Brassa. That secret she kept from the pack for so long. I believe that was the real reason that lump grew in her belly, Larka, not Morgra's curse."

"As some kind of punishment?" said Larka, horrified.

"No," whispered the bird. "But perhaps because she kept something hidden too long in her heart. The body can grow sick with guilt and shame and secrets. Or even by taking on too much responsibility."

Larka was startled at the idea, and the thought that the curse might not have been chasing them, after all, cheered her immensely. But only for a while.

"They're still dead," she growled.

"Larka," said Skart, ruffling his wings, "when the sun burns and heats the waters of the land, what happens to them?"

"I don't know, Skart." She shook her muzzle sadly.

"The waters go into the heavens to form the clouds, Larka. But then return as rain to swell the lakes and the seas and the rivers, so the Lera may drink and continue."

Larka blinked at Skart; she didn't understand what he was telling her.

"Many believe that life is like that too. That the force that lives in all cannot be made or unmade, but only turned from one form into another. That the soul, too, returns time and again, in different forms."

Larka was so startled by the idea that, for a moment, she felt as if a great veil had been lifted from her mind.

"But, Larka," said Skart suddenly, "perhaps your parents aren't dead at all. Why don't you use your powers, use them to find out if Huttser and Palla are alive? Send your senses into the present."

Larka had never really thought of the powers of the Sight as *hers* before, hers to use as she chose. She got up and padded over to the stream, and as she did so, she felt a new determination. A still pool had formed in a neck of large rocks where Larka had looked into the water before, and she lay down and peered into the stream. Larka closed her eyes and concentrated. As soon as she opened them again, she cried out joyfully as she beheld the swirling vortex.

"Kar," she gasped, springing to her feet.

There were Kar's proud ears and long, kind muzzle looking back at her. But as Larka's breath disturbed the surface, the image broke immediately. There was her own face once more, quivering in the pool, staring at nothing but herself.

"No," moaned Larka. "I saw Kar die myself."

"Then you have seen the past again," said Skart sadly.

Yet there had been something about Kar's face, something that left a nagging doubt in Larka's mind. The anguish of losing that face again gripped Larka, and suddenly her tail stung her.

"Pain," she whispered bitterly. "Is that what the Sight really teaches?" Larka lay down and began to whimper as she licked her tail. This time when Skart spoke to Larka he was no longer so understanding.

"Is this the spirit of the untamed wolf? Perhaps you're right about yourself, Larka. Perhaps you could have done more."

Larka began to growl angrily, and Skart was pleased for he had meant to rouse her. But as she lay there, and Skart could see the physical pain that was afflicting her, he decided that she was ready for another lesson.

"Larka," he said, "the ancient beliefs say the Sight itself can bring the power to heal."

"How?" she asked, lifting her battered tail hopefully.

"The body is a natural healer, Larka, if you trust it and let it do its work. But it's said that the power of the Sight can move energies around the body, too, to help the process. But there is one thing alone that will make it work."

"What is that, Skart?"

"We must believe it," whispered Skart.

Larka stared back at the eagle with eyes full of doubt.

"And there is another part of us we must try to heal, too, as important as the physical body."

"What?"

"The mind."

Larka looked up. "Skart," she cried, "then tell me more of the birds and the delta. Of the freedom and wonder of the air."

Skart fluttered his wings approvingly. The eagle spoke now of time when the seasons hunted the birds from their own lands and brought them thronging from distant corners of the world to the edges of the blue river. Of the lands where the birds migrated from, China and Mongolia and a land on the very roof of the world, where the humans robed themselves in orange and yellow as they walked through the endless snows, a distant, mysterious country that men call Tibet.

As Skart talked, Larka felt what a heavy, earth-bound thing she really was. She longed to travel on and on with Skart, eating up the earth with her eyes, taking in all as she flew. But even as the wings of her thought brought her back to the great delta, where a myriad of birds set up a clamor of voices as loud as starlight, Larka saw something else, a picture painted by her own frightened imagination. A gray wolf was moving through the watery rushes. Quietly, stealthily, creeping toward the birds.

That evening they saw the humans. Far enough away from the clearing for them to be safe, but close enough, too, for the animals to feel the thunder of their horses' hooves through the earth. They were galloping south, galloping to war.

Larka slept fitfully again by the pool and stirred well before the others. Above her, the sky was still dark and the stars glittered in the heavens. The air was cold but brilliantly clear, so clear that everything seemed to have taken on a heightened reality and, for a moment, Larka felt as if she could reach up and touch the stars with her muzzle. Above the horizon hung the fine silver sliver of a crescent moon and, as she thought how beautiful it was, she suddenly blinked with surprise.

Though the glowing shape was etched perfectly into the bluey black, Larka realized that from each tip of the crescent ran a thin line of light that made a perfect circle.

She had never noticed it before, but she could see the moon behind the crescent of light, and it was perfectly full. Somewhere in the heavens perhaps it was always full.

Soon dawn began to come and the brilliant heavens started to disappear. Larka dropped her muzzle and looked into the pool. At first she thought she was seeing pictures there, but as she watched, and the slanting morning sun sliced through the water, she realized that what she was seeing was real. There were tiny creatures in the water, almost transparent, and they were wriggling around one another, moving at tremendous speed. They had no eyes or ears or anything that appeared to give them a connection with the world around them. Yet in some strange way they seemed drawn to each other.

Larka lifted her head and sighed. All that she was learning was so strange to her. Larka thought back to her childhood, to Huttser and Palla, and growled with longing. Instantly pictures rippled across the water. Before her in the water was Kraar, and next to the raven stood Morgra.

Larka snarled as she saw her aunt's torn ear and the scars, that angry muzzle. Kraar was hopping after her, snapping his beak greedily. They passed a cave and came to the edge of the trees. Larka knew that there was something waiting beyond too.

Then Larka saw it. It was like a shadow flickering on the edge of the snow; something waiting silently in the wood. A ghastly, steely-gray shape. She could see nothing more, but a feeling hit her. She felt it as a physical thing, like a wound. All around the boughs of the trees hung dead animals and, even as Larka watched, she felt her jaws begin to slaver hungrily. From somewhere within the fear came a much darker emotion, too, a furious desire. Something Larka could not understand, for Larka realized with horror that she was suddenly drawn to this thing in the woods.

Larka slashed at the river with her paw; the images broke. As she looked around at the snow, its chill white began to change. Larka blinked, but no, this was real. Around her the snow itself crept into darkness. The sky was still blue, and the thin tufts of grass that here and there poked through the snow were green, but the snow itself was as black as night.

"Wolfbane," gasped Larka. "Wolfbane's winter has come."

Larka swung back to the pool, but the images were gone. As Larka looked around her again, the snow began to turn back to white. She saw light filtering through the trees, painting the bark with color. Even as it illuminated the water, touching the eddies with shadows, Larka heard a sound echo across the river. It was laughter.

"What is it, Larka?" screeched Skart, swooping down from the tree above as they heard her coming.

"Wolfbane," Larka cried coldly, "the Evil One has returned."

"Are you certain?" said Tsarr, and Skart cocked his head oddly as he settled beside them.

"I have seen Morgra, and Wolfbane is with her. Helping her. I know it was the Shape Changer, Tsarr. There was such darkness there, such terrible anger."

Larka could not bear to tell her friends that she had been drawn to the thing in the trees too.

"We must kill the human," she said flatly.

"No, Larka," growled Jarla, but Tsarr's look silenced her.

"Must we?" he said, turning calmly to face Larka. "And will its death put an end to Wolfbane, or to the hate Morgra is spreading through the Varg? Will it even put an end to Man's hate?"

"But what if she ever gets her paws on it, Tsarr?" Larka swung around toward the eagle, appealing to Skart's yellow-black eyes.

"Tsarr," said Skart quietly, though his eyes were sad, too, "you spoke of the law. But Tsinga taught us the true law of the Sight is that Larka must decide for herself. Be true to herself and her nature. We must learn from her too. All things must learn from one another. The human's fate. It must be her choice."

Tsarr glared at Skart, but as the eagle's eyes stared back at him, Tsarr growled and dropped his muzzle. Tsarr knew that the eagle was right. "Very well, then. Jarla, come with me."

"Where are you going?" cried Larka.

But as Jarla followed Tsarr from the clearing, looking back behind her all the while at her charge, Skart took to the air too. They had left Larka alone with the baby.

In that terrible moment, Larka realized the creature's future was her choice now. The baby had crawled out of the den once more, and as Larka glared down at its little earth-covered limbs, she began to dribble through her teeth. But something held her back. She shook her head as she thought of how Tsarr had described Man as the greatest of the Putnar, and lay down beside it.

"But you are just like a little cub, aren't you?" whispered Larka. "Nothing more."

As Larka lay there and tried to decide what to do, she suddenly felt a great weariness overcome her again. The pain in her tail had returned and, as she drifted toward sleep, she tried to focus her mind on her own raw skin and pass a warmth down through her own body. When Larka woke her tail was hurting much less and she got up. The baby had opened its eyes, too, but Skart and the others were nowhere to be seen.

Larka shook herself and felt a new cold thrill through the air. But suddenly her ears twitched and she looked up. There was another wolf on the ledge of the mountain above her, and this time it didn't vanish. As soon as Larka spied him, the wolf turned with an angry growl and padded back into the trees.

In that moment of fear, Larka's muzzle swung right over the child's face. It looked thin and sickly, but suddenly its mouth broke into a grin, and it gurgled softly as a little pink paw came up and clutched at Larka's fur. Then both its little arms came up and hugged the she-wolf's neck. Larka could do nothing. The anger in her drained through her paws. As she felt its complete vulnerability and total trust, Larka remembered her mother's warmth in the den.

"Oh, Palla," she whispered bitterly, "Huttser. Perhaps you are both dead too. But I wish more than anything you were here to help me. To tell me what to do."

But a voice was telling Larka exactly what to do, a voice

from deep within her. In her loneliness and isolation, Larka suddenly felt a desperate need, the need to give. To love something and care for it.

"No, little one, I am a she-wolf," she said simply as she stood over the human and felt a strange stirring for the child. "Our destiny is intertwined. So I must protect you, mustn't I? I must help you to live."

"I must find out more of what is happening, Kraar," Morgra hissed, bending her head lower and lower over the water, as if she were about to drink.

"Wolfbane," she whispered. "Help me, Wolfbane. Help me to find the child."

Dawn was coming, thin and cold. Morgra closed her eyes. In her mind she was turning her thoughts back to all she had suffered and using the angry force of those hateful memories to call to the power to look into water. When she opened her eyes again, she growled with disgust.

"What's this?"

What Morgra saw as the vortex cleared was not the pool but the sea, pounding against a rocky shore. Even as she watched, she sensed that something was waiting below the surface. Morgra shook her head for she did not understand what it meant, but as she closed and opened her eyes again, she growled with satisfaction. She was looking down on wolves in a wide valley. Some were patrolling, while still more were sharpening their teeth on branches and stones as they prepared themselves for what was to come.

"The rebel pack," cried Morgra with pleasure. "At last." But as she spoke, the breeze stirred the pool, and now Morgra was looking directly into the face of a she-wolf. Morgra might have been looking at Larka, so uncanny was the resemblance. Yet this wolf was a gray, and she had a scar that ran the full length of her muzzle, while her eyes were hard and angry.

"Slavka," Morgra growled, "but where are you?"

Morgra paused and suddenly her eyes began to sparkle. Thoughts were rushing through her mind, thoughts out of legend. Before her, on the edge of the valley, she had spied the trees and, as she realized that they were mostly rowans, she recognized the place.

"Kosov," she growled in amazement. "You're in the valley of Kosov." Morgra drew even closer to the pool and what she saw now, the secret she suddenly spied in the water, made her mind flame.

"Of course, Kraar. Tsinga was not so blind as all that, for she always talked of the legend as if it had already been. The ancient verse is unfolding on its own. It's like a story, a story that's telling itself."

"What does it all mean, Mistress?" clacked the bird, but Morgra ignored her Helper.

"Very well, then," she snapped as she looked down, and Slavka and the rebels appeared once more in the water. "You think you are fighting for freedom and your own boundaries, but all you do is serve the legend. For he is there, too, Slavka. He is always there. Bring the free Varg together then, Slavka, in the valley of Kosov. Bring them all as carrion for Wolfbane's feast."

Morgra swung around to Kraar. "We move, Kraar."

"Now, Mistress?"

"Yes, and we must draw all the Night Hunters together again."

"But what of the child and the citadel?"

"All in good time, Kraar. First we must serve the verse. Or it must serve us."

Once more the breeze rippled over the surface of the pool. But this time Morgra began to shake furiously. There were two wolves before Morgra now—a Dragga and a Drappa. They stood near each other and, before the wind so disturbed the water's surface that the image was lost all together, Morgra hissed and a furious weakness entered her.

"No," she snarled as though in terrible pain, "you have survived."

10

REBELS

To breed the lidless eye that loves the sun?
— W. B. Yeats, "Upon a House Shaken by the Land Agitation"

Huttser's proud gray muzzle looked older as Morgra watched them in the water and he stood there in the snow, far away from Morgra's cave, in the valley of Kosov. Palla's eyes had a terrible sadness in them, too, for the she-wolf was grieving. Palla had taken Fell's death desperately hard, and at night she would often slope off and sit on her own, brooding on her son, and cursing herself and Huttser. Palla remembered his hopeful little muzzle as he played at the Meeting Place, or the brightness in his eyes as he talked of going on a hunt.

Then she would think of the ice and the river and his soul doomed never to find a resting place, and she would feel a blow to her stomach like a wound. The pain would howl through her belly and throb in her paws. "There is nothing more terrible," Palla would often think bitterly, "than for a child to die before its parent."

There were suns when the she-wolf thought she could go on no longer, and only the thought of Larka and Kar would tell her that they must continue. But even as Palla and Huttser stood near each other and watched Slavka prowling among her band of gray wolves, there was a distance between them that there had never been before.

Huttser turned his head to address his mate, but then he growled and turned away once more. They had hardly had a chance to talk to each other since their capture, but Huttser knew that Palla still blamed him for what happened to Fell. It was almost three moons since that terrible night, and Huttser, too, felt the gulf between them like a scar.

It was the rebels who had captured them on the ice that night, though the pair were so full of fury that they had hardly been able to understand what had happened to them. For suns the strangers had driven them toward the valley of Kosov where Slavka's camp now lay. Huttser and Palla had kept their identities secret, and said nothing of Larka or their own knowledge of the legend. They remembered all too well what they had heard of Slavka and her hatred of the Sight.

At first Huttser asked for free passage through the mountains, but Slavka had laughed at him and told him that the free wolves were either for or against Morgra. That there was no middle way. There was such a veiled threat in the rebel wolf's voice that Huttser and Palla knew that it would be more than their lives were worth to resist. Since then they had been kept apart, except when Slavka gathered all the rebels for an address, and it was clear that if one of them tried to escape, the other would suffer for it. Their separation was not unusual in the rebel camp, though, for as part of their training, all mates were allowed close contact only once in a half moon. But Slavka was just beginning to trust that the pair were not Balkar spies. She had given word that in another moon's cycle they, too, would be allowed to meet privately.

As Slavka padded down the slope, she looked larger than she had seemed to Morgra in the water. She passed a male wolf and stopped to address him. "Gart, take out another patrol. More Balkar scum have been spotted."

Gart dropped his muzzle and growled in assent. "Loyalty always, Slavka."

Loyalty was the watchword in the valley, for the rebel pack had been brought together almost entirely from lone wolves or pairs whose families had been destroyed by the Balkar. Without the natural hierarchies of family life, Slavka had made herself the focus to unite the growing pack.

"But first deal with Darm," she growled suddenly. "He was caught talking about the Sight. This nonsense about seeing wolves that vanish into darkness. He was spreading rumors, too, of the family that whelped under the Stone Den. There must be no more talk of it, do you understand? No more false hopes."

Slavka's voice had grown angry, but Gart's eyes were full of guilt. He remembered his journey with Darm through the forests, and he liked his comrade.

"Take some rebels and send him on a mission, spying among the Balkar. But Gart, make sure the mission fails. Arrange it so he never returns. Let the Balkar's own teeth deal with Darm."

It was forbidden to talk of the Sight among the rebel pack, but Slavka sent out regular patrols in search of the human cub. All the rebels muttered of how their leader hated Man. There were many stories drifting around camp about how the humans had murdered her whole family, though none of them knew the truth of it.

Huttser was listening carefully. He was interested in Slavka, and had begun to study her methods. He noticed that although Slavka often went among the wolves and gave them encouragement, or talked of the great fight against Morgra, she could be very cruel. Huttser could see that without a Dragga to lead them, it made her both feared and respected in her pack. He wondered now what Skop would have made of her, though they had seen nothing of Palla's brother.

There were harshest punishments for serious disobedience. Meanwhile the wolves were trained by being made to take part in daily combats. The most ferocious of these were always the fights between males and females, for when the wolves faced off against their mates, they were wrestling with an instinct quite as deep as the will to hunt and survive.

The rebels were also forced into a regimen of constant exercise and a daily sharpening of their teeth and claws on branches and stones. Sometimes they were taken off into the mountains and made to run up and down hard slopes, and to jump rocks. Or they were chased through gullies and expected to hide in caves and then double back on their mock pursuers. If they succeeded in this, they were rewarded with extra meat at the communal feeding times.

"Come," cried Slavka, suddenly lifting her muzzle.

The rebels began to drift down from the slopes into the valley to listen. As Palla watched Slavka, she shivered, for she reminded her so much of Larka, and Palla ached to know what had become of her daughter. Slavka's face was as fine as Larka's, and her brilliant golden eyes, ringed with white fur that offset the streaks of red that ran down along either side of her muzzle, searched the wolves keenly, resting only momentarily on their waiting eyes, before moving on.

"Brothers," Slavka cried, throwing up her head. Her voice was strong and certain in the cold air. "Sisters. The training goes well, but we must not let up for a moment. Our very freedom depends on it. The hunting parties report game is growing scarce, but have no fear. With the summer the Lera flock like sheep to the valley of Kosov, and we shall grow fat again. There shall be enough to eat, even when all have joined our Greater Pack."

The rebels were nodding.

"When the winter passes the families shall come, not forty but hundreds of free wolves to fight Morgra. Then we shall go on a marking the likes of which has never been seen before. Our boundary shall ring the land beyond the forest like a mighty river, and nothing shall pass. No, not even Man."

Huttser remembered cheerlessly what he had said once to Brassa about marking his own boundary to keep out the curse. He stared oddly at Slavka, though, for she suddenly looked strangely magnificent, and her eloquence always stirred the rebels.

"Very well, then, now I go on patrol."

Slavka suddenly turned toward Huttser. She had had an instant liking for the Dragga, and he had always fought well in the Combats.

"Huttser," she barked, "you will come, too, this time, and we shall hunt."

Huttser growled at being ordered to do anything by a she-wolf, and he glanced accusingly at Palla, but he stepped forward and felt the rebels' eyes lock on him. He knew that many of the rebels were deeply suspicious of him, while others had begun to grow resentful, for word was spreading of how highly Slavka thought of him. But Huttser braced to deflect their gaze, and lifted his tail proudly.

Huttser was well used to their angry eyes, for he had already had to pass muster himself in another peculiar ritual among the rebel wolves. It had not been devised by Slavka at all, but had grown up quite naturally among them. The Gauntlet, it was called. The rebels, usually only the males, would line up in a long line facing one another, and then wolf after wolf would be made to walk slowly down the line with their muzzles raised as high as possible. The others would watch them carefully and growl among themselves. If they saw the slightest sign of doubt or fear or weakness, they would pounce on the poor wolf and set about him roughly, scratching and biting.

Despite his own sense of rebellion, Huttser fell in with the patrol. Huttser decided that he would use the time usefully to find out more about the rebel leader. Soon he even felt a sense of excitement and purpose. For the first time in as long as he could remember, he was not running, and the feeling was blissfully liberating.

There were seven wolves in the patrol and, though they saw no Balkar, they soon caught up with a small herd of water buffalo. Huttser managed to gore a male's leg and split the beast from the herd, which clearly impressed Slavka. But the animal was unusually strong for the winter, while the wolves were weak and unwilling to risk the buffalo's horns. So they began a familiar waiting game for a hunting wolf, trailing the Lera's blood through the snow, never letting it rest, worrying it whenever they could and sapping the life from its failing body.

Huttser and the wolves followed it for three nights, haunting it like shadows, and soon they were all exhausted, for none of them had slept. That night as he lay in the snow next to Slavka on the slope above a shallow valley, Huttser shivered under his thick fur. The buffalo was trying to drink fruitlessly from a frozen stream, as three of the rebel wolves hovered around it. It flinched and snorted as it heard their cries, but it was beyond flight. Around them the winter seemed to stretch on forever. For suns there had been mutterings among the rebels about the bleak, unending cold.

"You know the story, Slavka," growled Huttser as he peered about him, "of Wolfbane's winter."

"Silence, Huttser," snapped Slavka immediately. "In camp I'd have to punish you for such talk. We will have no talk of the cult of Wolfbane here, and the winter will pass."

The rebels around them looked a little doubtfully at Slavka.

"But it is fine, is it not," whispered Slavka, her eyes sparkling and her breath steaming as she licked her lips, "to hunt free in the wilderness. Even in winter."

As Huttser listened to the buffalo's mournful bellows below, he suddenly felt terribly alone, and he thought angrily of Palla.

"I love the wilderness, Slavka," he growled, "but it is hard too."

"Yes, Huttser," she agreed, "as we must be hard. There must be no place for weakness or fear, for fear destroys thought. We must be strong, strong as the wilderness itself. Like the Night Hunters."

"But don't we risk turning into them?" said Huttser, thinking of the Gauntlet and the Combats.

"Never," snorted Slavka scornfully. "Those draggas claim to be First Among the Putnar, yet they are not true wolves, for they worship darkness and superstition. But we, we must be a pack that sees clearly. Sees the truth."

Slavka snarled and spat.

"Slavka," whispered Huttser, "why do you hate the humans so?"

Slavka's eyes grew cold and she was clearly angry at Huttser's impertinence, but the she-wolf said nothing for a while.

"Your cubs?" ventured Huttser.

Slavka nodded quietly.

"I am sorry."

As the wind stirred on the slope, Huttser felt a churning sadness in his stomach. He looked up at the heavens. The wind had punched a hole in the cloud and, above, he could see the stars flickering in the black. There was another painful bellow, and now the two other rebels got up to join their comrades. Slavka watched them go and very quietly she began to tell Huttser her story.

"I, too, was interested in the Sight once," growled the she-wolf, "and the old beliefs. I wanted to believe in a power to look into the past and know the future. Above all, in a power to heal. I was young and foolish, and I wanted to know what lay in store for my family too. For I loved them dearly."

Slavka dropped her eyes. She seemed suddenly embarrassed. "So one sun I set out in search of Tsinga's valley. My cubs had not been long born to me in the den, but the pack was strong and my head was filled with a wild longing. It was while I was away that they came," hissed Slavka, shaking with sudden fury. "The humans. The others went out to try and distract them, but my cubs perished. I never even found Tsinga's valley, and as I was returning, I saw my mate die on the hill. Though I got there first, their dogs were leading the humans toward our den. Toward my cubs."

Huttser was listening with a kind of grim fascination.

"I didn't know what to do, Huttser. Half of me wanted to run, half to save my little ones. I stood there trembling. Incapable of thought, incapable of anything at all."

A terrible bitterness had entered Slavka's voice.

"And in the end you had to abandon them?" growled Huttser, remembering Palla on the hill. "You shouldn't blame yourself too much, Slavka. You were true to your nature, that's all. To fight or flee. It is the law of the Varg. The law of life."

"I will tell you about life, Huttser," snarled Slavka,

"About true wildness. As I saw those dogs coming, I swore an oath. Never to think of superstition and dreams, and never to succumb to fear again. To be as strong as nature's hunger. Its cruelty."

"Before you abandoned them," whispered Huttser.

Slavka swung around to Huttser immediately. "Now, Huttser," she whispered, "now I will tell you a secret that not even the rebels know."

"What, Slavka?"

"I didn't abandon them," cried the she-wolf. "I killed them myself. I turned my jaws on my own children, so the dogs and the humans wouldn't win. For a moment I thought to save one," Slavka added, and her voice was taut with pain. "But how could I make that choice? So I destroyed them all."

The grunts of the buffalo shuddered through the night. Huttser could do nothing but growl sadly.

"But it made me strong, Huttser," said Slavka, looking up proudly. "Then Morgra came whispering words of evil. Of Wolfbane and the legend. Filling the wolves with superstition and fear, while the Night Hunters broke every boundary they could. So I determined to destroy her and the myth of the Sight too. To teach the free wolves how to master real life, to look neither to past nor future, but to the present alone, and to set up a boundary that will protect us forever from fear and superstition."

Huttser shivered, but there was something stirring in him. Below, the rebels had begun to snarl again and one was snapping viciously at the buffalo's leg. It grunted stupidly and tried to kick out, but its strength was almost gone. Huttser was silent. He was thinking suddenly that if he could have the children back he would take his family away and forget all about Morgra.

"You are a fighter, Huttser," said Slavka as if reading his thoughts. "A true Dragga. You do not flee when evil threatens."

Huttser felt strangely pleased as he looked into Slavka's face and followed the line of her strong muzzle. His admiration for the she-wolf was deepening, and he wondered for a moment what her cubs would have been like if they had been allowed to grow.

"I saw it in you as soon as I arrived, Huttser," growled Slavka, "for I have grown very adept at judging character. Perhaps it's because of what I did, but somehow it allows me to see more clearly into hearts and minds. I can always tell a coward when I see one, or the marks of doubt and confusion. So when the rebels come to me seeking promotion or advancement, I look at them and first I ask one very simple question. What is your secret?"

Huttser shifted uncomfortably, but suddenly a bellow shook the freezing air and the buffalo's legs collapsed.

"Come," snarled Slavka, springing to her feet. "It is finished."

Huttser leaped after her down the slope. The rebels had already begun to tear at the buffalo, biting into its living flesh. It grunted helplessly as the bloodlust rose in the hungry animals. Slavka's fine coat was bristling as she reached them, and she looked around proudly at her comrades. The wolves' throats quivered, their eyes wide with the instinctive fury that drove them on.

"You see, Huttser," cried Slavka. "This is what it means to be a wolf. To face the harsh reality of life and not to flinch from it. The bitter law of survival. For there is nothing else."

In that same moment Huttser remembered Tsinga's strange words. "When the time of the Putnar comes and the bloodlust is on you, Huttser, can you look into the darkness of the den and tell truth from lies, darkness from light?"

Slavka tore at the animal, and around her the wolves' savage eyes flashed like lanterns reflecting the moon. Huttser paused, but as he saw the reddening flesh, an energy began to burn in him that he could not control. As the feeling mastered him, it swept away his loneliness and fear. No longer did the stars tower above him, or thoughts of Wolfbane's winter whisper through the trees. Again the time of the Putnar had come, and with the fury of his closing jaws, Huttser felt strength and certainty once more. Slavka was right. This was the life of a wolf.

But as he fed, Huttser looked up. The wind was screeching about them, and Huttser shivered as he fancied he saw a shape among the trees, standing there looking straight at him. But even as he looked on, it seemed to vanish in the snow again, and Huttser imagined he heard a mournful voice wailing on the air. "We are almost here," it moaned. "Release us. Release us all."

Palla was lying on the edge of the valley of Kosov, gazing out pensively into the winter. Next to her lay two she-wolves. They had been among the scouts that had found Huttser and Palla on the ice, and the three of them had become friends. Their names were Keeka and Karma.

Palla was thinking of Huttser, and she suddenly felt furious that Slavka's strange regimen did not allow her to see her own mate as she chose. She couldn't bring herself to forgive him, but Palla longed to talk to him and to share her pain. She complained about the rule to her friends.

"You'll get used to it," whispered the she-wolf lying beside Palla. "We all did, you know. Wait until the half-moon comes again. Then Slavka has promised you can see him."

Keeka was very handsome and her thick gray fur was streaked with jet black. As she spoke, her voice was filled with optimism. Palla shook her head, though. There was little about life among these rebel wolves that she could get used to.

"Why should I, Keeka? It's all so unnatural."

"There is too much work to do, Palla," answered Keeka warmly. "We must test one another's strength and prepare. But Slavka will save us. She is the bravest of all of us. The Deliverer."

In the nights the rebel wolves had often gathered together to howl out a song. The "Song of the Deliverer," they called it, and it went like this.

> *Let Fenris, cry, aaa-ooooo, aaa-ooooo*
> *The Varg that's free is always true,*
> *A mountain song, aaa-eeeee, aaa-eeeee*
> *The wolf that's true is always free.*
> *When darkness fills the world with lies,*
> *She falls like snow from troubled skies.*
> *Deliverer, Deliverer.*

It was an old song that told of the coming of a she-wolf in a time of desperate need, and as Palla heard it, she, too, would feel a stirring, and for a time would forget what she and Huttser had already had to suffer at the teeth of the rebel pack.

"Slavka fears the legend above everything," growled Palla suddenly. "But why, Keeka, if she doesn't even believe in the Sight?"

Keeka looked about her nervously. "Slavka thinks Morgra is using the legend to blind us all. But others say that if Morgra takes this child to the altar and the Man Varg really does come, then none shall be free. If it's true, what greater evil could there be than the Sight?"

Palla pawed the ground almost guiltily.

"But not all the rebels agree, Keeka," said a deep growling voice. The Varg next to Keeka was a magnificent-looking wolf with beautiful, brilliantly flashing eyes.

"Hush, Karma."

"No, Keeka, let her speak," said Palla, looking up with interest. "Why, Karma, what do you mean?"

"Not all believe the Sight to be evil," answered Karma quietly. "Some are talking of this family. They say one among them has the power."

Palla looked away.

Karma went on wistfully. "And when I was young, my parents told me that the power of the Sight was given as a gift to the wolf in the very beginning of the world."

"In the beginning," whispered Palla, looking up at the skies, "when Tor and Fenris brought light out of darkness?"

Karma turned to Palla with a grin. "Tor and Fenris?" She laughed. Her voice was rich with amusement and almost as deep as a male's. "Where I come from there are no such gods as Tor or Fenris, Palla. No, my kind tell stories of the wolf god Zostar, born from the fire forests. A wolf of heat and flame that comes to us in dreams. The great Zostar, who decreed that everything in the universe was perfect."

"Stop it, Karma," growled Keeka, for she knew how dangerous it was to discuss such things openly in the rebel camp. Karma was not from the land beyond the forests, but she had come from a country far to the south. The she-wolf had traveled many thousands of miles in her lifetime, from a place where the sun was always hot and the ground did not turn white in winter. Palla thought her wildly exotic and mysterious.

"But here," said Karma almost sadly, her growls growing deeper and deeper, "Slavka will not let us talk of such things, or even tell our own stories. Not of Zostar, nor Tor, nor the Sight. She says we must believe nothing of faith, old or new, but only in fighting and survival. She thinks they are the same as freedom."

Palla thought of the words of the verse. Of the makers of life coming to test the faith of a family. Palla's own faith had been tested almost to the breaking point.

"But you don't agree?" asked Palla quietly.

"What freedom is it to believe in nothing?" snorted Karma.

"But, Karma," whispered Keeka, looking even more confused, "Palla believes in Tor and Fenris. While you believe in Zostar. They can't both be true. That stands to reason."

"They may just be stories," nodded Karma, "ways of naming and talking about the world. But my kind believe that in stories often great truths lie concealed, unconscious truths, if we only know how to interpret them."

"Truth," snorted Palla suddenly.

Karma turned quietly to the Drappa as she lay beside her. "Perhaps you no longer believe in truth, Palla," she whispered, "because of something that has happened to you. But is truth not just a word for that which is not a lie? For that which exists beyond lies?"

Palla nodded.

"But if there isn't any god," growled Keeka, working through her thoughts painfully slowly, "as Slavka says. Then to believe in one would be a lie, it would just keep us slaves."

"Slaves, what about the slavery of knowing too much, Keeka? The slavery of the obvious and the ordinary," growled Karma.

Keeka looked questioningly at her friend, but she didn't understand what she was saying.

"Look at that tree," said Karma, turning her gaze toward a rowan that stood nearby. It was still in full berry. "Where I come from we wouldn't just call it a tree, but a living spirit. Its berries would be made from the eyes of fireflies and its leaves from the wings of Zostar's moths, which live forever and fan Zostar's tail when it grows too hot. But for those who strip away the magic of stories, the magic of life, it is just a tree, and it will never be anything more than a tree."

"But, Karma," protested Keeka hotly now. "In the old superstitions some said rowan trees beaded with the blood of evil cubs. And they would make sacrifices of innocent wolves to appease the demons of the night."

"And I am glad that many of the ancient customs were overthrown," said Karma gravely, "for in blind superstition lies evil. Yet do we not lose something when we simply abandon the ancient beliefs? And are there not many truths, truths that seem to be fighting each other?"

"What do you mean?" growled Palla.

"It may be true that we fear death, Palla, but it is also true that we would be no happier if we lived forever. Besides, when we name everything and seek to see the world as one thing alone, there is a danger that we rob it of something perhaps more important than anything else."

"What?" asked Palla.

"Wonder," whispered the she-wolf, and the breeze caught the berries on the rowan tree and shook them like little bells.

"But you don't believe Tor and Fenris made that tree?"

"Slavka says nothing made the earth or the Lera," said Keeka loudly, "that it all came about by chance."

They all fell silent, but as they looked out at the rowan trees and the snow and the thin ribbons of pink light above the horizon, the idea seemed so absurd that they all wanted to laugh.

"Who knows what the truth really is," Karma growled, "but my father always used to say that in life we usually end up with exactly what we set out to find. Unless perhaps we are able to change the patterns that make us. To step somehow beyond ourselves."

"Well," said Palla, "whether it is a spirit or just a tree, I know one thing, it is very beautiful."

In the heavens above the moon fattened, and in its shining face, many of the rebel wolves began to make out the form of Tor, who they had been taught to see as cubs.

Despite the discontents that grumbled through the pack and the severity of Slavka's leadership, morale was high. And in the evenings the rebels would howl into the night defiance of Morgra and Wolfbane and the Balkar. Slavka felt that the patrols and the hunting parties were going well and was asking Huttser to accompany her more and more frequently. He felt strangely flattered, for the rebel leader even began to ask his advice.

And the moon grew in the wintry skies.

Palla was lying on her own on the edge of the valley of Kosov, when she spotted Keeka and Karma padding toward her through the white.

"Palla," called Keeka cheerfully, "Slavka always keeps her word. Come. Huttser is waiting for you."

But Palla turned to Karma as soon as she saw her. She had been brooding on all Karma had said.

"Tell me something first, Karma. If you believe in your stories, it must be hard for you here and this Greater Pack . . ."

"I am often discontented," growled Karma, swiveling her head to look about the rebel camp. "And I'm not alone, Palla. A Dragga called Rar has been secretly opposing Slavka."

"Hush, Karma," snapped Keeka. "You know Slavka's spies are always listening. Besides, what would you do, join the Balkar?"

Karma shrugged.

"But why do you stay here, then?" asked Palla, and there was an edge of scorn in her voice.

Karma's eyes flickered with cunning and amusement. "In my life I have never stopped moving, pushed from land to land by hunger or pack rivalries or the humans' wars. Like many here now I was a Kerl and, when Slavka took me in, I took on her fight. If she would have a Greater Pack, then so be it."

"But you don't really believe there should be a Greater Pack?"

Again Karma shrugged. "One must adapt to survive."

Palla saw other she-wolves trailing across the valley to greet their mates as she set out. Some pairs were already sitting down together. Other wolves were beginning to howl delightedly. Palla felt a pang of jealousy, for she could tell from their shaking tails and the tenderness with which they scented each other and rubbed muzzles, how badly they had pined for each other.

Palla's pace slowed, though, as soon as she spotted Huttser. He was standing on his own, and Palla felt a pang of regret as she saw his fine muzzle and proud, handsome face. Her tail came up slightly, but there was guilt in both their eyes, and Palla was still bitterly angry.

"Palla," growled Huttser as she approached. He brought his muzzle close to hers. "You seem well."

"I'm not so bad," lied Palla, shrugging grudgingly, though she found it hard to resist his scent. "If you fight hard, you at least have a better chance."

They had both learned that to win in the Combats was the key not only to extra food, but to earning a respite from future fights. But they shivered as they remembered their own fight on the ice.

"I miss the children," said Palla suddenly.

Palla could not say that in her secret heart she missed Huttser too. Huttser lowered his eyes. He blamed himself for leading Fell onto the ice, just as much as he blamed Kar for seizing with fear that night. But he could not admit it to Palla, although both knew that their senseless anger had driven the children away.

"I believe Larka and Kar are safe. I feel it somehow," muttered Huttser. "Besides, it's better that she is out there. If Slavka ever discovered who we . . ."

Palla bristled, pawing the ground and Huttser saw her anger.

"Slavka is not evil, Palla."

"No?"

"These are dark times. Maybe, as Slavka says, they call for dark measures. The free wolves must survive."

"Huttser," said Palla angrily, "we must find them. Tsinga told us we must look to each other to guard against Morgra's hate. What if ours is this family?"

They caught each other's eyes for a moment, and the pain that passed between them was like fire.

"That hope is gone," growled Huttser bitterly. "It died with Fell. We must face up to things as they are. I have decided to fight, Palla. Do all I can to help Slavka."

"That will not help us. Or Larka."

"Slavka must never know the truth about Larka, but the rebels are searching for the human now, not our daughter. Let's hope she has learned enough to keep well away. In the meantime I must help them fight Morgra."

Palla felt bitterly disappointed with Huttser, but it was the memory of Fell that made her suddenly whine with anguish and frustration and say what she did.

"Sometimes I want to go among these rebels and get down on my paws and beg them to stop it. To stop trying to hurt one another just because they're frightened. Sometimes I think I'd do anything to make it stop. Let them spit at me, or even kill me, like Sita."

Palla was shaking, and it was Huttser's turn to feel disappointed in his mate.

"Palla, you're forgetting yourself," he growled coldly. "Show some more self-respect. They'll see you."

"What do I care if they see me or not," cried Palla furiously. "Self-respect. What does that mean? What about love? He's gone, Huttser. Don't you care about anything? He's gone and the reason he's gone . . ."

Palla stopped herself, but Huttser snarled furiously.

"So," he cried, and the anguish of it made his legs almost crumple, "still so much blame."

Huttser turned. Palla was shaking as she watched him prowl off below the moon, but her pride had returned and it would not let her follow him. Instead, she shivered bitterly, caught between anger and need.

The snows hit that same night, settling on the rebels' backs. It was many suns before the fall eased enough for Slavka to take Huttser out on patrol again. Balkar had been sighted in the area, and the rebel pack was on edge. But as they walked, Huttser noticed that Slavka kept looking up into the mountains high above the valley. A wistfulness had come over her and, when Huttser asked her what was wrong, Slavka told him what had happened after she had killed her cubs. She had fled into the mountains above the valley of Kosov and come on a strange collection of human dens. As soon as Slavka said it, Huttser looked up in amazement.

Slavka described the strangeness of the place, and how the earth shook there. But it was where she had rested and learned to harden her heart even more. The mountains that ringed it were practically impassable, and Slavka had stumbled on the entrance quite by chance, through a narrow gorge. If anything went wrong, she planned to lead the Greater Pack up there for safety, and she described the route to Huttser in detail. The entrance lay beyond a spring, through a great canyon, guarded by a strange rock.

The wolf patrol had been out all morning, and Slavka had kept them running. Only Huttser had really kept up with the leader, and he was amazed by her vigor. For once the skies were clear and, though the sun was not hot enough to melt the deep snows, it shone down powerfully and blinded the wolves as it glittered against the white.

"Fenris is growling today," cried Huttser as he matched Slavka's tread.

"Fenris," snorted Slavka, "you can't believe that old story too, Huttser?"

Huttser had thought nothing of the remark. "I only meant . . ."

"When I took refuge among the stones, Huttser," snapped Slavka, "I would often look up at the sun and howl to Fenris and ask for his help and advice. But with time, because he never answered, I began to try and see what was really up there in the heavens. It hurt my eyes, but soon I could hold it a little longer. I do not think that the sun is Fenris."

"No doubt it's just a cubs' fable," shrugged Huttser, wondering why Slavka had grown so serious.

"Not one to teach my cubs," said Slavka, but her face contracted with the memory of that terrible day.

"But cubs need stories," said Huttser, "and children understand what they really are. Far better than adults."

"Perhaps," Slavka growled, stopping abruptly, "but as we grow we must reject lies. Were not the Night Hunters chosen for the strength of their eyes? Well, when this is finished and Morgra is destroyed, Huttser, then I shall permit the Greater Pack to breed. Strength shall be their birthright, and we shall not teach them myths about Tor or Fenris or the Sight. We shall teach them how to look at the sun and see it for what it really is. We shall teach them to look life in the muzzle and be brave and cold and true. There shall be no Sikla then, and no more fear."

Huttser suddenly remembered poor Bran and his own dead cubs, lying beneath the birch tree outside the den. He missed Palla more than ever.

The clouds had come again and, with the evening, the temperature was plummeting as they came to the slopes below the southern edges of Kosov. Beyond a pass that led out into a wide, flat plain, the wolf patrol looked out in horror. There were humans in the plain. A number of them had already begun to raise their tents and corral their horses. They were settling at the mouth of the valley.

"What do they want here?" growled Huttser angrily, and Slavka's eyes flashed with fear and hate.

The rebels were unnerved, too, though Slavka tried to

reassure them, for the humans seemed far enough away and they were clearly not hunting. But the wolves were approaching the rebel valley again when they suddenly heard a growl and looked up the slope.

"Gart," cried Slavka, "what news?"

Gart eyed Huttser coldly as he padded toward them, for he was jealous of Huttser's new place in the pack's pecking order. It was this that had sent him out in the first place, alone and traveling far, to win back Slavka's favor.

"Plenty, Slavka. There are humans on the edge of Kosov."

"We know, Gart. We saw them ourselves."

"I spied a group of Balkar, too, Slavka. They were clearly hunting."

Gart looked exhausted, for he had been traveling for suns and suns without resting to bring the news to his leader.

"For the child?"

Gart nodded, but now his eyes began to sparkle. "I have seen it myself, Slavka," he whispered proudly, "the human cub."

"Seen it," cried Slavka. "Then tell me what I long to hear. It is dead?"

Gart dropped his head guiltily. "No. There was no way down from the mountain ledge. And a she-wolf spotted me. Beyond, I saw two others and a bird. I returned the next sun, but they had gone."

"Who is protecting it?"

Gart's eyes flickered.

"A white wolf."

Huttser's ears cocked forward. It was all he could do not to howl.

"It must be the wolf spoken of in the verse, Slavka. The legend comes," continued the eager rebel.

"Damn you, Gart," hissed Slavka. "There is an easy way to stop this talk of a legend. Go back to camp and take more rebel wolves with you. Hunt them down, Gart. Kill them. Kill them all."

A terrible feeling gripped Huttser's heart. Words from long ago echoed through his mind, words about fear and guilt. Words, too, from the verse, as they had echoed in Bran's mind that terrible day—"Beware the Betrayer." Huttser started to shudder.

"What will you do, Slavka?" he asked as casually as he could. He was trying to hide the tension in his voice. "Will you set all the rebels to finding this . . . this child?"

"No, Huttser, I cannot. If I am not here when the other free wolves arrive, they will not stay for my return. No, Gart is strong and he will not fail me."

Palla, Huttser thought suddenly as he listened to Slavka. *I must tell Palla.* But standing there next to Slavka, Huttser shivered. A wind came up and, in its howling breath, Huttser felt an even greater ferocity.

Slavka looked around with a sudden cunning. The wolves felt the touch of freezing flakes fizzing on their muzzles. Slavka peered up at the skies and, though she hardly knew why, her own heart began to beat faster. A savage thought flashed into Slavka's mind. The snow got thicker and the wind colder. The flakes seemed to swell as they fell from the clouds. Down it came, and soon the sky was so thick with snow that the rebels could hardly see one another in the fall.

"Very well," cried Slavka. "The child has survived so far. But winter's anger is coming to our aid too. If this is really Wolfbane's winter, Huttser, as so many stupid wolves believe, then let their blessed Wolfbane destroy the creature for us. For nature will aid the rebels' cause."

Slavka started to chuckle, and as Huttser stood there, he wanted to spring at her for her cruelty. Down the snow came and the sky grew dark. Night came again, and still it snowed. With the morning the distant, tepid sunlight made the air glow eerily as the freezing fall continued. For suns it went on snowing, a fall the likes of which had never be seen in Transylvania.

"Dig, Tsarr, for Tor's sake, dig."

The snow was so heavy about them as Larka shouted the order that they could see nothing but one another in the storm. The child was crying bitterly, and Larka could see that its little hands were turning blue with cold. They had moved it from the clearing after Larka had spotted Gart on the mountain, and now they were desperate for shelter.

Tsarr had picked it up in his mouth as he had before, but it had grown, and Tsarr had to struggle bitterly with his burden. They had gone in search of a cave, but they had all been caught in the drift. Jarla was cradling her body around it, for they were taking turns to shield it from the storm. Larka knew that if they couldn't find it some kind of shelter, the child wouldn't last till morning.

Tsarr and Larka dug frantically at the snow, heaping the powder behind their glittering, freezing paws, but the blizzard was so thick that they seemed to be making hardly any headway at all.

"Larka," cried a voice from above suddenly. "I can't help you in this, Larka. I must find shelter myself. I wish you luck."

Larka couldn't see Skart any longer, but she shuddered as the eagle's voice wheeled above her and disappeared on the wind.

"Tsarr," she cried, "some say that the Sight can give power over the elements. Do you think—"

"No, Larka," growled Tsarr as he worked away, "how could that be? The Sight draws it power from the force within all things, but it does not control that force. There are many superstitions about the Sight—most of them false."

Larka suddenly felt a sense of powerlessness against the might of nature, just as she had felt looking on her past in the water, a powerlessness against the elements themselves. But she was a wolf, and it stirred an anger that made the fight even harder. Tsarr had reached beyond the snow to the earth. But his old heart sank. The cold had made it as hard as stone.

Larka searched about her desperately. Her mind was numb with cold, and she could feel the skin beneath her coat beginning to stretch. It was so cold she sensed that if they didn't find an answer soon, then it was not only the human child that would be dead by morning. Larka could suddenly see Kipcha struggling against the rapids, fighting pointlessly against an inevitable fate. *Death*, she thought bitterly, *it's all around us, always*. The memory made Larka sick to her very soul, and she wanted to give up, to lie down in the snow and let a numbing peace steal through her body. But even as the emptiness came on her, she remembered what Palla had cried to Kipcha from the bank. "Don't fight it. Let the water carry you to safety." Larka swung her head up as the inspiration flashed through her mind.

"The snow," she cried, "we'll use the snow."

Larka was scrambling at the heavy powder, not straight down as they had done before, but into the side of the slope. Tsarr and Jarla looked on in bewilderment, but as Larka scooped away, the icy surface held, and below it a little recess began to appear. The wolves sprang to Larka's aid.

Soon a wide cave had appeared, and they found that the ceiling was holding above their snow den. Tsarr picked up the bawling human and together the wolves crept carefully inside as the snow continued to come down. It began to heap up at the mouth of their impromptu cave, sealing the entrance almost completely as they watched, and as it did so, Larka realized that very gradually the air was growing warmer and warmer.

There they lay, the three frightened wolves and the human child, the wolves' panting breath steaming and smoking around the baby as the strange ice cave glittered. Jarla had virtually wrapped her body around the baby again, and she could feel it shivering terribly. It had stopped crying and closed its eyes.

"Larka," whispered Jarla quietly, the echo of her voice muffled by the frozen chamber. "I think it's dying, Larka."

Larka suddenly thought of the Sight. She crawled closer to the two of them, rolling on her side, and now the baby was pressed gently between the two she-wolves. For a moment there was something vaguely jealous in Jarla's eyes, but as Larka began to direct the heat through her body, the child stirred and relaxed. As the warmth from the two she-wolves flowed into it, the baby gurgled softly, and Jarla nodded her muzzle and smiled at Larka tenderly.

11

THE RED GIRL

In the beginning was the Word.
—John 1:1

"PALLA. LISTEN TO ME, Palla. You've got to try and escape."

The returning storm had at least brought one blessing. In the blizzard Huttser was able to creep unseen through the dark and find Palla. She growled coldly as he approached, but as soon as Huttser told her what he had learned, Palla's expression turned to amusement. Her daughter was alive. Palla wanted to howl to the heavens, but her terror for Larka had followed as swiftly as her joy.

"What do you mean *I've* got to escape, Huttser?"

"Slavka wants me at her side almost all the time now," said Huttser. "You have more chance of slipping away unnoticed. Find Larka and this human. Warn her."

"Huttser, I am your mate and if I escape, we shall escape together."

The fur on the back of Huttser's neck bristled, but he suddenly remembered that first sun when he had fought

330

off her other suitors and begun to court her, the bravest and most beautiful she-wolf he had ever known.

"No. You must look to the children, I order it, Palla."

"Order it?" growled Palla, beginning to show her teeth, but more in a smile than a display of anger. "Since when do you order me to do anything? Do we not run as equals, do I not hunt as well as you and did I not bear the litter? That takes more strength than a Dragga could ever know, Huttser. Or ever really understand."

Huttser dropped his gaze.

"Palla, can you ever forgive me . . . for what happened?"

Palla whined quietly. "Oh, Huttser, there is nothing to forgive."

"How I have missed you, Palla."

Palla stepped gently forward. Their muzzles came together and their tails began to wag as they whined in the cold and licked each other's faces. Months of anguish welled out of the wolves. Months of sorrow and guilt for Fell and their pack and their own separation.

"Huttser," cried Palla, "we will find Larka again and never leave her side until this is finished. I fear this legend, but if she is already with the human, perhaps Tor and Fenris meant it all to be."

"And I shall not be sorry to leave," said Huttser, looking up at the high mountains, "I've discovered something else. The citadel, Palla, it lies above us."

Suddenly there was a furious growl. Huttser and Palla swung around together. Angry muzzles appeared in the blizzard as Slavka stepped from the storm. Gart, whose departure had been delayed by the snow, was at her side, and at their backs were a group of rebels. Slavka's eyes were burning with a fury that seemed to melt the icy air. But she kept blinking almost stupidly as the snow swirled in her face. Slavka could hardly believe what she had overheard.

"Traitors," she seethed. "Traitors in my own camp."

But as she looked at Huttser, her anger was as much at the fact that she had been so mistaken about the Dragga. She hadn't been able to see his secret after all.

"No, Slavka," said Huttser. "We are not traitors."

"Silence. It was you that sired this she-wolf below the Stone Spores. This is your loyalty. I let you into my confidence and I find I have been nursing treachery in my very den. Tell me, Huttser, did Morgra send you to spy on me?"

"No, Slavka," cried Palla desperately, stung by the raw injustice of the thought. "We loathe Morgra as much as you, and we will help you to fight her. She cursed our pack, and when we found that Larka had the Sight—"

Slavka snarled. "The Sight. If your daughter claims to have the Sight, she must die for her lies. As this human must die."

Huttser growled and sprang at her, but the rebels barred his way.

"Gart," hissed Slavka suddenly. "Go, Gart, find them."

Gart hesitated. He was filled with sudden apprehension. Slavka saw it immediately.

"Why do you delay?"

"Slavka, what if we can't get to it? The human and this she-wolf. The legend does tell of them both, and if the Sight really brings with it powers, they may be powers that I can't—"

Slavka rounded on Gart. "There are no powers of the Sight," she spat. "And where is your loyalty?" But as Slavka looked at him, something glinted in her eyes.

"Very well. If you cannot kill it, then give this Larka a message, Gart," she hissed, "from the rebel leader. From all the free Varg. Tell her that if she does not deliver the human up to me by the time the summer touches the land and the free packs arrive in the valley of Kosov, then Huttser and Palla shall fight, just as they claim they want to."

Huttser turned nervously toward Palla as the snow went on tumbling about their ears.

"But her parents shall not have the privilege of fighting Morgra or the Night Hunters, of fighting for freedom and justice for the wolf," hissed Slavka, and around her the snow seemed to swell. "No. They shall fight each other. To the death."

Safe in their snow den, Larka looked down at the baby. Its little hands were squeezed up onto its chest. She was fascinated by those strange paws and the tiny pink claws. In the past few suns whenever the cub had tugged at her fur, somehow Larka sensed that a mysterious intelligence was traveling from its paws up to the creature's mind. That it was always learning.

"Jarla," Larka said suddenly, "when the snows stop, we must find it meat."

"If it lasts till then."

As they huddled together, they all felt the same bitter determination. The wolves began to doze, and when Larka woke she saw that Jarla was gazing at the baby.

Outside, the moaning of the storm came to them like the howling of a hundred wolf packs.

"Tsarr," shuddered Jarla, "can it really be true? Wolfbane's winter?"

Tsarr growled but shook his head. "No, Jarla, we mustn't believe that. It's a story."

"Why is there so much anger in the world?" whispered Jarla sadly. "Even the stories are filled with darkness."

"Jarla," Larka said, looking kindly at the she-wolf, "when I was a cub and Brassa and Bran used to tell us stories of the Stone Den, they filled me with fear. Darkness too. But I know they were false. Just as the stories about Tsinga's valley, the Vale of Shadows, were false. We are not children anymore. We must live free from fear, Jarla. Nothing can grow in fear, but hate."

Tsarr looked at Larka with a sudden admiration.

"But is it surprising the stories are filled with darkness?" he growled as they listened to the storm. "What should we tell our children? Tales of happy families, fluffy cubs, and furry friends?"

"But how can we tell," asked Jarla, "which stories are true and which are false?"

Larka shook her muzzle, but at her stomach a little hand suddenly tugged at her fur.

"Perhaps by comparing them with our own experience," growled Larka, "or by listening to something in them that has the ring of truth."

Jarla and Tsarr stared back at their friend.

"Tsarr," growled Larka quietly, trying to think of a way to take their minds off their plight, "will you tell us a story. But a different kind of story?"

"What do you mean, Larka?"

"Of Man," whispered the she-wolf, "what you said, Tsarr, about a different time. When Man and the wolf lived together."

Tsarr thought for a while before he nodded slowly. "Well, there is the story of Fren and the red girl."

"Tell us, Tsarr."

As the child lay pressed against Larka's fur and Tsarr began, she suddenly felt like a cub again herself, safe and warm and happy at her parents' side.

"Let me see," growled Tsarr. "It was after the beginning when Tor and Fenris brought light out of darkness. In the suns when they had first made Man, the humans, in their cleverness, had begun to spread across the face of the world and learned to control it with their hands and their strange tools. In those times the humans still worshiped Tor and Fenris, and treated the wolf with great respect. If a man killed a Varg, he would feel it as a great misfortune and even hold a special gathering where they would bury the wolf in the ground and water would flow from their eyes. For then the humans knew the wonder of the wilderness."

Larka looked down at the baby and there was a wonder in her own eyes.

"The humans admired the Varg as a great hunter, and they would take their cubs and leave them in the forests to be suckled by a she-wolf, for they knew our milk would give them strength. The strength of the hunter."

Jarla growled proudly and licked the baby.

"In this way some of the wolves tended to human cubs, and for a time there was friendship between wolves and the two-feet. The stories say that the first mother, Va, herself even suckled a pair of human pups, who grew into brave and strong fighters. They came to lead their pack, throwing up a huge forest of stone dens that was known throughout the world. The same humans that built Harja, the gateway to heaven."

Larka suddenly thought of what Tsinga had said of the altar and the statue of the she-wolf.

"But of all the humans, Tor had a favorite. It was a she-child who was born on a great prairie and whose skin was red like an autumn leaf, for Tor had fashioned her from the red clay on the banks of the great river that circles the world. Whenever she looked into the girl's eyes, Tor knew she loved her, for love enters through the eyes. She clothed her, too, in the pelt of the Herla, the red deer, to keep her warm, and the she-child lived in the middle of a mighty forest in a den fashioned from the trees."

The child stirred between the wolves in the snow den.

"The red girl lived alone, but although she was nearing her time when loneliness and desire would stir in her, and her body would change and she would seek a mate among her own, her greatest friend was the young gray wolf, Fren. Together they would pad through the trees and the flowers, and share the wonder of creation. There were many dangers for the she-child in the forest, from the wild boar and the rattling snake to the black bears that roamed the trees. But the gray wolf would protect his friend from harm, especially when she made her long journeys through the forest to visit an old she-human.

"But Fenris grew jealous of Tor's love for the red girl, so he took one of Fren's brothers, the chanco wolf Barl, and set him prowling through the forests. He knew that

Barl hated Tor, for though he had always been loyal and true to her, the goddess had blighted him. It happened when Barl, who was enamored of the world, asked Tor if he could live forever. This had angered her so much that as a punishment, the goddess made him lame and weakened his eyesight, so he found it hard to hunt and grew hungrier and hungrier.

"Barl wanted revenge on Tor, and Fenris prowled into his dreams and whispered to him of how the goddess loved the red girl. So Barl determined to steal her away and eat her up. One night, though, Tor met Fenris by moonlight. They quarreled so furiously that Fenris let slip what he had done, so Tor rushed to Fren. She warned him that his lame brother was in the forest, too, and might try to gobble up the girl she loved."

Larka whined softly in sympathy.

"But one sun, when Fren had agreed to accompany the red girl through the woods to visit the old she-human, he was delayed, and when he reached the red girl's den, was distraught to find that she had already set off. He was frantic when he discovered wolf tracks outside and recognized the spores of his brother Barl. When Fren reached the den belonging to the old she-human, he rushed inside and was aghast to see blood on the ground and the red child's deerskin lying discarded nearby. At first Fren thought his friend had been eaten, but as he scented the place, he realized that it must have been the old she-human that was dead. Then he heard a lovely sound drifting through the trees.

"As Fren looked back through the entrance to the den," Tsarr went on, "he caught sight of his friend in the distance. She was perfectly safe and had abandoned her pelt to go down to the stream to wash. She was quite beautiful as she stood there in her nakedness, singing happily in the sunlight, completely unaware that the lame wolf Barl had already stolen into the den and killed her human friend.

"But as Fren watched, mesmerized, and the red girl dived into the sparkling water, he growled. He had scented his brother coming back toward the river. Fren was desperate that the child should not be discovered, and he looked around frantically. But as the lame wolf got nearer and nearer to the river, Fren suddenly had an idea. He rushed over to the deer pelt lying on the ground and, tossing up his muzzle, he threw it on his own back. Then he called softly outside, 'Is that you, my friend? I'm in here, do come and see me.'

"Barl thought the red girl was calling and had mistaken him for Fren, for with his bad eyes he was always mistaking things himself. Barl leaped toward the wooden den, and when he ran inside, he found Fren standing on his back legs, draped in the girl's pelt. There was the humans' burning air in the den, which gives off warmth and light, and as it flickered across the wolf's fur, it made his coat look red too. Barl squinted, but he still mistook Fren for the she-human, and his jaws began to slaver. Fren readied, but he wanted to get nearer to his enemy's throat, so he whispered in a little voice, 'Come closer, my friend.'

"Barl limped forward and, as he looked, he found something strangely troubling about the sight. Fren hesitated, too, as he glared at his brother, and in that moment, he feared to kill him. But as he remembered the red girl in the stream, and the beauty of her nakedness, he knew that he had the courage.

" 'But your eyes,' Barl growled, 'they're so big. And your nose. It's so long.'

" 'Yes, brother,' cried Fren, throwing off the deerskin 'and my teeth. They're so sharp. For I am a wolf, like you.'

"He leaped at his brother's throat, and though the fight was furious, surprise had given Fren the advantage, and soon Barl was lying dead on the ground. Fren stood there shaking guiltily as he looked down on his own dead brother. But when the little human returned from the river and found out what had happened, she hugged her friend and stroked Fren's fur in gratitude. But Fenris came also to the den, and when he saw what Fren had done, he growled angrily.

" 'Fren,' he cried in a terrible voice, 'you have killed your brother wolf and now you are a hunter. And so you must go from here. I shall take away your memory of the red girl, and you shall search through the world forever, until you remember what you really are. And since I am a vengeful god, your sin shall pass down to your children, even to the tenth generation, and I shall give you a commandment, Fren, in words of blood. And my commandment is this: Thou Shalt Kill.'

"The wolf nodded sadly, but now the goddess Tor came to the den. As she looked between the wolf and the girl, and heard what her mate Fenris had decreed, her heart was so wounded she could not tell which she loved more, the wolf or the she-child.

" 'Fren,' Tor whispered, 'Fenris is a god, too, and I cannot overturn his commandment. But since you did this thing for the red girl whom I love, I will sharpen your claws and polish your cunning and strengthen your instincts. In memory of the pelt that you used in your deception, I shall find you herds of deer to hunt to your heart's content. And since Fenris had decreed you shall forget the red girl, I shall take memory from all the Lera, too, and I shall set a mark on you, to aid you in the darkness of your search.'

"With that, Tor placed her paw in the middle of Fren's forehead, and when she withdrew it, the red girl strained forward to see what was there. But there was nothing, nothing at all. But Fenris knew what Tor had done as soon as Tor touched Fren. In that same moment, she had given the wolf both a curse and a gift, and that curse and that gift was the Sight."

As Tsarr finished his story, Larka growled with confusion, for though this tale of the Sight and of a friendship with humans did whisper of a world far away from the fear and loneliness that had stalked her for so long, Fenris's commandment had sounded like a warning note in her mind too. Strangely, she also remembered the question Fell had once asked their father: "Am I my sister's keeper?"

"So the story means we should be friends with all the humans?" she asked quietly, staring down at the child in the fragile cave. "As once we were."

"It can't," snorted Jarla, "nor with all the Lera. If that were so, what could we hunt and how could we survive?"

"Perhaps it is just there to make us think," whispered Tsarr, "and to see more clearly."

Larka was now reminded of something Palla had told her once in the den, of Tor and Fenris putting Man in the world so they might one sun understand where they themselves came from.

"Man can see farther than the Lera, then, Tsarr?" she asked thoughtfully as she licked the baby. "Farther than the Varg?"

"Not the kind of sight that spies a Herla from the mountaintop even in the dark," answered Tsarr, "or smells a wounded fox across a distant valley. But the wolves say that Man's first gift is imagination. And that is a kind of sight. They say that some of the humans have even flown with the birds of the air in their imaginations and dived with the mighty blue whale to the very depths of the deepest seas. But it is at the altar that you could find out."

But Larka was shaking her head. "What happened to Fren?" she whispered.

"Many things, Larka. But then the stories run out. The story of another wolf became popular among the Varg. The story of Sita."

"Tsarr," whispered Larka sadly, "they say Sita was betrayed, before Tor allowed her to be sacrificed. Will you tell us that story."

"She was betrayed by one of her own. One who had followed her ways, but who in the end did not have the faith to believe in her. He gave Sita up to the Draggas who said she was a liar, and they killed her and left her for the humans, who stripped her carcass and nailed it to one of their dens. Sita never once complained. Never once turned her teeth on her attackers."

Larka nodded gravely, but as they heard the story it seemed to shine in their minds in the snow den, shine like the stars the wolves had often wondered about in the heavens.

"But it didn't matter," said Jarla, "for Sita knew she would be betrayed. For the stories had already foretold it. And that's why Tor sent her down."

"To show her love," growled Larka, and her heart ached.

For suns it went on snowing, but their cave was warm and the human baby seemed to recover a little, nestled between Jarla and Larka. Each sun, Tsarr would have to push his nose through the snow at the mouth of the den, to give them air, and somehow the wolves and the human kept themselves alive.

But one night Larka fancied she heard another sound on the wind, a growling. At first she thought it must be a trick of her imagination, but as they listened, they distinctly heard it. There were wolves outside their cave, and as the wind dropped slightly, they heard the growling right next to them through the thin snow wall.

As Larka saw their shadowy forms through the snow, she suddenly felt a fury, and the god Fenris's commandment rang in her mind. She readied herself, but then the voices of the hunters passed away again, and in the distance Larka heard a single howl on the night.

"Tsarr," she growled, when she was sure they had gone. "The ancient howl, Tsarr. How exactly would Morgra summon these Searchers?"

Tsarr lifted his head, "That was the secret that Tsinga

entrusted to Morgra," he answered. "But Morgra doesn't know that Tsinga entrusted it to me, too, when she realized Morgra's intention."

"Tell me," said Larka.

Jarla pressed closer to the child as Tsarr told Larka how to use the howl. He told her how to speak Wolfbane's name, calling to the shadows, and how the ancient howl should be made after a kill, in that heightened dream state that only those with the Sight could reach. How the howl could touch the edges of beyond and summon the Searchers.

When he had finished, the wolves began to doze, but as their breath smoked in the snow den, Larka noticed that the walls of the cave were melting slightly. She began to wonder what was going on outside in the storm and, as she stared at the ice, suddenly the water power came on her again. As the vortex cleared, Larka was startled to see the humans' orange light flickering before her as it glittered on the walls of the den.

On the wall a wide field edged by rowan trees appeared, beaded bright with red berries. The glow was coming from a number of campfires. All around Larka drifted humans, some clad in armor, others in rough cloth. They were wearing swords at their belts, or carrying staves as they wandered aimlessly around the camp. The baby stirred next to her, but Larka was mesmerized by the living pictures on the cave wall, just as she had been by the Gypsies in their camp. But in a matter of moments, the humans had faded, leaving only the shadow of the huddled wolves, reflected faintly in the ice.

"Larka," growled Tsarr, waking beside her as he felt the tension in her body. "What is it?"

"Pictures," whispered Larka. "But they vanished again."

"Don't worry. With time they will last longer and their meaning may grow clearer."

Suddenly Larka threw back her muzzle and let out a startled yip.

"What is it, Larka?"

"Kosov," gasped Larka. "Fell told me the story of Wolfbane's promise once. He said there were rowan trees there."

"Of course." Tsarr shrugged. "It means the place of rowan trees."

Larka's eyes were suddenly huge with fear.

"What, Larka?"

But as Larka told Tsarr what she had just seen, the old wolf seemed confused.

"Think about it, Tsarr. There are humans near this rebel Gathering Place, or will be."

"So what?"

"The words of the verse, Tsarr. 'For the Shape Changer's pact with the birds will come true.'"

Tsarr's grave voice completed the words, " 'When the blood of the Varg blends with Man's in the dew.'"

Larka was the first to discover that the snows had stopped. The she-wolf had suddenly felt a furious cramp in her leg and got up to stretch herself. She pushed her muzzle through the snow wall and gasped as she looked out. The sky was a brilliant blue, and the sun sparked and flashed in the white. She suddenly felt a glorious sense of liberation, as freeing as her first journey with Skart. Even as she thought of her friend, she saw a shape on the horizon. It grew as she watched. The eagle was sailing toward her and—though it was thinner, for it too had suffered in the snows—Larka marveled at how free and beautiful Skart looked as he glided through the air.

"Larka," cried Skart as he landed beside her. "Thank heavens I've found you. I've been looking for suns. There's news."

"News?"

"Varg. Trailing through the snow. They were following each other in a line and at height they looked like lost kittens. But I flew lower and they seemed to be searching."

"I know, Skart. They nearly found us in the storm. Are they coming back?"

"No, they made for the rock by the stream, but the snow had obscured your tracks. Then they moved off to the west."

"Thank Tor," whispered Larka, but as Larka told Skart what she had seen on the walls of the snow den, the bird snapped his beak anxiously.

"Shouldn't we warn these rebels, Skart, of what is happening?" growled Larka.

Skart shook his head almost helplessly. "And sacrifice you and the child? Slavka will kill you if we go near the valley."

"But the legend, Skart," Larka said resolutely.

"No," said Skart. "Perhaps what you saw of Man lay in the past, Larka. They say a great battle was fought in Kosov once. Perhaps it was with the humans."

"But everything that has happened," she growled, "it all seems to be leading in one direction. Morgra's curse came true. Now—"

"Have hope," cried Skart sternly. "We still have the child, and without him nothing can be fulfilled. And the citadel, Larka, now Tsinga is dead, none know where it lies."

Larka let herself believe him. "Very well. But with these Varg about, whoever they are, we must keep watch. And we must find the child some meat."

"Come, then. Let us hunt together."

Larka shook her head, "I'd rather just scavenge something."

"Like that filthy raven," Skart cried, blinking sternly at her. Again an old self-pity had entered Larka's eyes.

"But when I—"

"Larka," said Skart in a kindly voice this time, "the eye of the Sight. It is possible to close it, too, Larka, when it is necessary."

"Close it?"

"Come with me and I will show you how to hunt."

As Larka followed the bird, she did not try to see through his eyes. Skart flew above her, screeching encouragement. It wasn't long before they spotted a sheep, split from the fold, that had been caught in a thicket. But as Larka watched it struggling and bleating, she began to back away.

"Tell me what you're thinking, Larka," called Skart.

"There has already been so much anger, Skart, and so much death. Morgra is hunting us. Am I any better? Besides, I don't want to feel its pain."

"Larka," said Skart sternly, "as you look at the world you think perhaps that everything is trying to kill everything else. But that is not true. There is often peace. Must be peace. Does not the carp often swim past the minnow without opening its mouth, and the field mouse live safely near the grass snake? And not all things are hunters, nor all things their natural prey."

Larka still just stared at the sheep.

"And, Larka," cried Skart, his voice scything through the air.

Larka looked up at the bird.

"It is possible," cried Skart, circling right above her head again and again, "to kill without hate. To kill, quickly and cleanly, with compassion."

"Compassion?" It suddenly seemed to her the most beautiful word she had ever heard.

"And to feel compassion for other things, you must learn to feel compassion for yourself too."

The young wolf felt a lightening in her, as though she was being given permission.

"Larka, you have done nothing wrong."

Larka was so startled that the fur on the back of her neck quivered. It was as though a paw had slapped across her muzzle. She suddenly knew what she had really been running from for so long. It was guilt. The shadow of guilt that Morgra, that the legend itself, had cast like a net over the pack.

"But, Skart, when the Putnar kill . . . Why?"

"Does a cub question why it rolls in the sunlit grass and plays with its teeth against its brothers and sisters," screeched Skart, "or a chick wonder why it should flap its wings in the nest and cry for food? You have a body, Larka, beautiful and clever and strong. You have sharp teeth and fine claws. Enjoy your form, Larka, for you have a right to be what you are, as much right as anything else."

Larka felt a wonderful peace enter her as the sun shone down on her fur. As Skart spoke of the body, it was as if the thoughts that had been oppressing her for so long had lifted from her mind. She pressed her pads into the snow and felt the wonderful tingling touch of the earth beneath. She lifted her ears to the wind and sucked in the cool, fizzy air and let her eyes flicker across the beautiful day. It was as though she was sinking back into herself, becoming whole again. Larka sprang forward. The energy in her as she sped toward the lamb was like pure thought, untrammeled by notions of hate or love or right or wrong. It was purpose.

Larka fed that day without any of her terrible visions, and she felt health swelling in her as she did so. But it was Skart who brought the prize for the child: a squirrel. Larka laid it by the human's head, but the baby just gurgled and its little hands came out and clutched at the furry object like a toy. The wolves waited for the baby to do something with it, to open it with its teeth, but it did nothing, and Larka picked up the squirrel again.

"We must feed it somehow," she growled angrily.

The she-wolf gnawed at the Lera, and at last she had made the pieces of meat so small that the child was able to take it from Larka's muzzle with his tiny hands.

As the suns passed, Larka herself hunted for food again for the child, and with the meat, its strength began to return. And then something happened that brought more hope, despite what Larka had learned of Man gathering near the valley of Kosov. The snow thawed.

The voice of spring was in the air and, if the winter had been a bitter one, it had not been Wolfbane at all who had made it so. To keep the child dry the wolves carried it up to a forest of birch trees and cleared away the snow with their paws. They collected dead leaves and twigs and made it a kind of bed, and Skart was startled when he saw it, for to him it looked like nothing so much as a nest.

So spring did come, and the wolves and the bird tended to the child. In the mountains the snows melted and on the plains the high grasses bloomed. The almond trees came into blossom, painting the boughs with soft pinky whites, and the brown ribs of the mountains, burned by the cold, turned green again and purple. The flowers blossomed, and with them a thousand chrysalides burst open like little pods and sent butterflies skimming like winged rainbows through the petals.

With the meat they were feeding it, the human seemed to grow quickly. Its little cheeks gave off a fine, healthy glow, the fur on its head had become thicker, and it could stand in the forest without falling over. But most startling of all was the change in its features. Where the wolves had been looking at a plain bundle of skin and bones, they now saw character appearing in the child, tiny crow's feet on the edges of its eyes and little wrinkles puckering around its mouth. Larka thought of what Skart had said in the air about becoming, for she knew that she herself had changed too. She had grown up.

That same night she lay next to Jarla, staring at the baby and shaking her head.

"We must call it something."

"What, Larka?"

Larka pressed her muzzle closer to the helpless creature. "I know," she cried delightedly, "we'll call you Bran."

In the baby's trusting eyes there was no understanding of her, but it gurgled and opened its arms, and, then, to the wolves' amusement, it suddenly rolled on all fours and gave a little growl.

Larka couldn't let Bran out of her sight. Her naming of him seemed to have brought her even closer to the baby. Sometimes she tried to imagine what it would really be like to look into the mind of a human. But Larka could never hold Bran's gaze for very long. Each time she was forced to look away, she thought of the Man Varg's power over all the Lera and trembled.

One time, as Larka thought of the story Tsarr had told them, she touched Bran in the center of his forehead with her muzzle, just as Tor had done to Fren. Even as she did so, she felt a shock. For in that moment she imagined that she could feel an energy coming from Bran. Could it be true, wondered Larka gravely, was there really some third eye? But what kind of eye was it, for it had no lid and no iris? Nothing surely that could show it anything of the world. But Larka suddenly had the feeling that a great power lay in that forehead.

The next sun, for a change, Larka had gone off on her own, leaving Bran in the others' charge. Skart sat high in a tree looking down on them as Tsarr and Jarla talked together. Larka was returning over a hill, in sight of the wood again, when she suddenly stopped and her tail came up immediately.

She saw them first, not as bodies, but as heat and light. Instinct told her instantly they had come to do harm in the twilight. The five wolves were moving stealthily, weaving through the trees toward Bran and her friends. As Larka scanned the distance between her and the child's bed, she growled furiously. She wanted to hurl herself through the sky toward her friends, to do something instantly to protect them. But Larka knew she could do nothing.

"The Sight," she cried, "what use is it to me to see these things and be powerless?"

Larka suddenly remembered what Skart had showed her of hunting, and something Tsinga had said long ago about not fearing her own nature. She remembered, too, Fenris's cold commandment.

"No," she snarled furiously. "I am a wolf, too, and I have teeth and jaws. For I am Putnar."

She leaped down the slope, running like lightning across the grass, her ears quivering, her tail streaking out behind her. There was violence in her paws, but as she moved with a new intent, something else stirred, too—freedom.

In the woods Jarla heard them first. She caught the sound of breaking twigs. The five wolves attacked at speed, and Skart screeched in the trees and opened his wings as Tsarr and Jarla sprang forward. They were facing off four of them now, but one of their attackers called to the fifth.

"Quick," Gart snarled, "the human. Kill the human."

As the rebel leaped toward Bran, the baby began to bawl, and Jarla launched herself furiously on the two wolves in front of her. They both sprang too. Tsarr made to turn, but Gart and another Varg were on him, and the rebel was nearly at the child. Above them, Skart swooped. His talons missed the wolf's head, but they scared the rebel so badly that he turned and clawed at the air. Gart broke away and lunged at the child himself. He was almost on it, his jaws opened to slice it in two.

There was a flash of white through the air. Gart felt the breath pressed clean from his lungs as he was knocked to the ground. Larka swung around at the wolf that was trying to fend off Skart's talons, and in one stroke delivered such a furious blow across its muzzle that it spat at her and fled.

Larka looked invincible as she stood there, her eyes blazing, every muscle in her body straining with purpose. She sprang at Tsarr's attacker, and in an instant, they had driven him off too. She and Tsarr turned toward Jarla, but the she-wolf was on the ground, and the two rebels were standing over her, clawing and biting at her throat.

"No," gasped Tsarr. His pounce knocked one of the rebels over, and Larka took the other, her teeth going straight for its gullet. The bite wounded it badly, and as it also turned and ran, its companion joined him. Gart was alone. He had got up again, but as Larka saw him advancing on Bran, her voice rang through the wood.

"Don't move a muscle, if you value your life."

Gart froze, and Larka prowled toward him. Tsarr was leaning over Jarla, licking her muzzle tenderly. The she-wolf's blood was already thick on the grass.

"Why have you done this?" cried Larka. "Did Morgra send you?"

"Morgra," snarled Gart, "what does a rebel have to do

with that filth? You know more of Morgra than we. For you also claim to have the Sight. You are the same as she."

"But what harm has this creature ever done to you?"

They were both looking at Bran, and the child was utterly petrified.

"You dare ask," said Gart. "You a wolf, a Varg, protecting a human. It is against all the laws of the Putnar. Against all the laws of nature. Morgra is already seeking our leader because of this legend. The Night Hunters are on the move once more. And you ask what harm this creature does?"

Larka dropped her eyes almost guiltily, but there was another moan from Jarla. Larka turned.

"Go, get out of here."

Gart looked startled, but when he spoke his voice was hard and scornful. "I will go. But first, don't you want to know about your parents, Larka, about Huttser and Palla?"

Larka sprang again and knocked Gart on to his back. She stood over him, her jaws open and her tail high, her front paws pressing down on his chest, her muzzle swaying slowly back and forth over his throat. She might have pressed him into the earth.

"My parents are alive?"

"For now," growled Gart, "they are being held with us in Kosov."

Larka felt a sickening feeling in her stomach.

"Your father was some use to us for a time," said Gart scornfully, "spying out Balkar and humans."

"Humans?" cried Larka.

"A few are settling beyond the valley."

Larka's heart thundered. Then what she had seen, lay in the present.

"Then we found out Huttser and your mother were the real spies," said Gart. "They are still alive, Larka, but only until Slavka decrees their end."

"Tell me."

Gart delivered Slavka's message, coldly and with defiance. When Larka heard it, she began to shake furiously, and Gart felt her torment quivering through his own body as he lay beneath her paws.

"So you see," whispered Gart, eyeing Larka's teeth, "you have a choice, Larka. Sacrifice yourself and the child, or say farewell to your parents forever."

Larka hissed at Gart and, as her muzzle came closer, he could feel her hot breath stroking his fur. He closed his eyes.

"Do it then, Larka. Get it over with. Are you a wolf or not? At least I have done my duty as a true Varg."

Larka wanted to seize the rebel in her teeth, to shake the life out of his throat, for his stupidity. It wasn't just her parents' fate that hung now in the balance, she wanted to scream, but the fate of all the wolves, of all the Lera. The legend was coming true. She had seen it. But Larka knew Gart would never believe her.

Larka opened her jaws, yet something within her held her back. Gart was strong and proud and he was right, he had risked his life to do what he felt was best. Why should he die for it, what justice would quiver through the leaves below Tor's heaven if she killed him?

Larka sprang off him.

"Go, go back to your leader and give her my message. Tell her that she is wrong. That it is not the Sight that is evil, no, not even Man, but Morgra and Wolfbane. And tell her, too, that we are not the same, Morgra and I."

Gart opened his eyes. He had expected to die, and a great lightness came over him, as though he were floating beyond his own body. The rebel got up and looked strangely at Larka. *How fine she seems,* he thought. Gart was touched by a guilty memory, too, a memory of what Slavka had made him do to his friend Darm. He was about to speak again, but Larka turned her head coldly.

"And tell Slavka that if she lays a paw on my parents she shall suffer for it."

As he padded away, Gart kept looking back at the white she-wolf and wondering to himself. But Larka had swung around to Jarla, lying in the grass. Tsarr shook his graying muzzle sadly.

"It's over, Larka."

"Jarla," murmured Larka, "I am sorry. I didn't come in time."

Jarla was straining painfully, the fur around her throat torn and bloody.

"But let me try to heal you, Jarla," cried Larka suddenly. "Let me use the Sight."

"No," Jarla growled, her breath growing fainter. "It's too late for me, Larka."

Larka could feel that Jarla's life force was vanishing.

"Larka," Jarla gasped. "There isn't much time. I want to ask you something. I want you to promise me that you will care for the human. That you will do all in your power to protect it. And that one sun you will return it to its mother, for only she can truly understand it."

Larka whined tenderly.

"No, Larka, promise me. Swear it. By the Sight," gasped Jarla.

Larka remembered bitterly the pact they had all made as young wolves. *What point,* she thought helplessly, *what point is there in making promises we never keep?*

"I swear it," she said.

Jarla closed her eyes, and as the death rattle hissed from her broken body, they heard another meaning, a meaning without words whispered from her dying voice.

It was a sigh, a sigh of gratitude and relief. Larka's howl echoed around them, and Bran turned his head as he heard it. Something was beginning to stir in the child's unconscious mind, some ancient memory. As the baby looked at these creatures and his little hands clutched at earth, he suddenly felt, not in his mind but in his skin and bones, a bond of life that when he grew he could only sever at his cost.

Tsarr rested by Bran that terrible night, licking his wounds as Skart hopped and fluttered about them and Larka went off alone to think. Tsarr and Skart were worried, and they could see that Larka had been given an impossible choice. Larka's heart was full of shadows as she prowled through the woods. She had promised herself, promised Jarla to protect the strange little human. But now her parents were in terrible danger, not just from Slavka but from the legend too. Morgra was on the move, and Larka knew now that it was in Kosov that she would try to fulfill the verse and open the pathways to the Searchers.

Perhaps she could reach them first and spirit them away. But could Slavka really make her parents fight each other to the death? Larka shuddered as she thought of it, but again that image came to her, of their snarling faces on the ice. She wanted to save them, to stop it all. But if she took Bran to Kosov as Slavka demanded, then had not she herself become Morgra's servant? It was as though Morgra was asking Larka to join her.

It was dawn when Larka rose on her paws and wandered over to Jarla's body. She shivered as she saw that already the secret workers of the woods, ants and termites and beetles, had come scurrying from the undergrowth and begun to feed on the carcass. Even as they supped, they fought one another, clambering over each other's tiny bodies. But as Larka thought of how Skart had talked with such hatred of Kraar and the flying scavengers, she felt confused. Was not the wolf a scavenger, too, like these little things? Did not everything scavenge on everything else?

"Larka," said Skart quietly, "what are you going to do?"

Larka's eyes flickered. For a moment her parents' angry voices seemed to echo in her ears, but Tsinga's cry came with her memories, out of the barren snows, across the tender grasses: "Love each other, Larka, love each other or perish."

"I am going to rescue my parents."

"But, Larka," cried Tsarr, "shouldn't we wait? The Sight is growing in you still and we have more to teach."

"I have learned enough," snarled Larka almost scornfully. "I have been learning all along without even knowing it. And what use is this power if my parents are to die? All my life I have been running, running from fear and betrayal. But I am not the Betrayer. I shall not betray Huttser and Palla, and I shall no longer be afraid."

"But the rebels want to kill the human," warned Tsarr desperately, "and want to kill you. And Kosov. Morgra is on her way—"

"They shall not touch a hair on its head," growled Larka. "Nor mine. Not Morgra, nor the rebels. And if Slavka fears the humans so much, perhaps Bran will help me defeat her."

Yet Larka faltered for a moment as she thought of the soldiers she had seen gathering on the edge of Kosov.

"But you have not yet mastered the Sight. You—"

"Peace, Tsarr," cried Larka. "Skart told me once that a child picks up blame from others, for things that were not even its fault. That is true. But if I do nothing now, if I simply use the Sight to glory in the freedom of the skies and hunt wild, will I not always blame myself? We must know what we should or shouldn't blame ourselves for. I love my parents, Tsarr, and if I betray them, will not that kill something inside me? Then would I ever be able to love again? And you are forgetting I am a wolf, too, Tsarr, and there is strength in my claws."

The hackles on Tsarr's neck quivered, and Skart nodded quietly; the pupil was becoming the teacher.

"And remember," Larka added, "the family. By saving my parents, perhaps we may find that hope again. If the verse is coming true then should we not fulfill the rest of it?"

Tsarr was thinking darkly what Larka already knew in her heart, and yet her bold words stirred hope in him too.

"But how will we carry the child?" said Skart.

"I will take it on my back," said Tsarr proudly, and he lifted his muzzle to Larka's.

"Then we go," cried Larka. "We go now."

Tsarr padded toward Bran and lay down beside him. The child reached out with its paw and tugged at Tsarr's coat, but it still sat there, looking at Larka.

"Let me try," said Larka.

The white she-wolf walked over and licked the strange little creature. Then, very slowly, she sank down beside it. Bran reached out again for the soft fur. He seemed reassured by Larka, and Tsarr pushed him gently with his nose. And Bran began to scramble onto Larka's back. Carefully, the she-wolf rose on her paws as the child clung on to her.

"Come," she cried. "Summer is close and we haven't much time."

Tsarr and Skart gazed back at the white wolf as she stood there in the forest with the little human on her back. Skart opened his great wings and took to the air, and Larka and the human cub began their race into legend. In that moment Tsarr and Skart realized that they would follow Larka wherever she chose.

The rebel wolf whimpered pitifully as he lay on his side, and his parched tongue lapped at the blood around his own muzzle. He had drunk nothing in suns and he was exhausted with the Balkar's constant beatings. Though his blood tasted thick and sweet, at least it gave him a bitter moisture. He lifted his head wearily as he saw Morgra striding toward him. It was one of the rebels that had sprung on Larka and the child, that night with Gart. Returning Balkar scouts had captured him on his back way to Kosov.

"So," hissed Morgra as she approached him, "you are still alive. Then let's go through it again. You set out to kill the human, but failed?"

"Yes," said the rebel wearily. "The she-wolf stopped us."

"She-wolf?"

"Larka."

As the Balkar saw the hatred blaze across Morgra's muzzle, they felt a chill eating into their bones. When Morgra spoke again, her voice was as still as death.

"The child," she seethed. "Larka is with the child."

There was a terrible hunger in that voice.

"Who else is with her? Is there a gray Varg and an eagle?"

Morgra hissed as the rebel nodded. The sun rose in the sky as Morgra went on questioning him, torturing the truth out of him. Evening was coming in as she pushed her scarred muzzle into his face once more.

"Again," whispered Morgra. "Larka has the human and you failed to kill it, but now Slavka has threatened to kill her parents unless she delivers it up?"

The wolf began to snarl, but as soon as he did so, one of the Night Hunters stepped up and bit savagely into his flank.

"I have told you," cried the rebel in agony.

"And the Gathering Place is in the valley of Kosov?"

"Yes. Below the human citadel."

Morgra's muzzle came even closer. "Human citadel?"

"The ruined dens. Hidden in the mountains above."

Morgra suddenly felt a great sweep of energy pulse through her. "It must be," she cried. "Very well. Kill him."

The Night Hunters next to the rebel looked relieved, for even they were sick of the torture. But as the Balkar stepped forward again, Morgra lifted her head. "Stop. Let Wolfbane."

As she named him, the Balkar shivered and looked back too. None of them would go near the forest now, and in their packs, they spoke his name with terror. They had never seen him, but he was in their dreams.

Morgra closed her eyes. She was calling to him.

In the trees beyond, a shape began to stir. Wolfbane twitched as he heard the faint whispering in his head. But he could not disobey her orders to stay hidden in the forest. She had kept him separate, away from the wolves, a spectral presence among the Balkar, a presence that had grown into its own legend.

"Wolfbane. I have a present for you. Come to the edge of the woods, Wolfbane."

The Balkar were driving the rebel toward the trees, snarling and snapping at him. He was literally dragging himself along the ground on his forepaws as his broken back legs trailed helplessly through the grass. As he pulled himself into the woods, and they heard a growl among the branches, the Night Hunters slunk back whimpering. It was a pathetic sight. Such strong and healthy wolves sniveling like whipped curs, their tails between their legs. They looked anything but First Among the Putnar. There was a terrible howl from the trees. Then silence.

Morgra growled delightedly and Kraar fluttered up beside her.

"Mistress," cawed the raven. "Do we move again, Mistress?"

"Yes," answered Morgra. "Kosov is close. It lies but suns to the south. And the citadel, Kraar. The lost citadel where Narmin gave the verse, it is found again. But we must reach them soon."

"What of the Night Hunters' search, Mistress," said the bird, "for the child?"

"Idiot," snarled Morgra, "did you not hear? Haven't you learned to trust the legend yet? Besides, Slavka has given Larka an ultimatum. If she is anything like Palla she will try to help her parents and bring the child to this Gathering Place. But if she reaches the rebels before us, I fear for them both."

Kraar opened his hood feathers and nodded slowly.

"It is ironic, is it not?" Morgra went on coldly. "Beneath the Stone Spores I offered them Wolfbane's protection, and now again we shall work to protect dear little Larka."

"And her parents?"

"The family," Morgra said scornfully, "no more obstacles will obstruct my way to the altar. So far Huttser and Palla have evaded the curse, but they shall perish, Kraar. They shall perish with the Greater Pack, when we are ready to attempt the howl."

The raven opened its oil black wings, with excitement. "How soon?"

"Have you not seen them, too, Kraar? Waiting, waiting and watching? The Searchers are hungry."

The bird thrilled at her words.

"So go, Kraar," cried Morgra. "It is time: The free Varg are going like sheep to the valley of Kosov, and the Searchers shall be their nemeses. But your kind must be there for the feast too. Your cries must wake the dead."

12

THE SEARCHERS

The sun shone, having no alternative, on the nothing new.
—Samuel Beckett, *Murphy*

Two MAGNIFICENT GRAY VARG were prowling through the grass as they made for the Gathering Place in the valley of Kosov. But then they stopped and started to growl fearfully. Everywhere there were human tents spread out across the fields in front of them. When Slavka and Huttser had seen them there had only been a few, but now there were hundreds.

"What do they want?" growled one of the wolves.

"I don't know," whispered his companion, "but the valley lies beyond."

"I don't like it."

"Nor I, but we must learn what Slavka has to say."

"But some say a family comes to our aid, from a distant land. A family of arctic wolves, and that to find them we should follow the northern star."

His companion shook his head doubtfully.

In the valley Slavka lifted her muzzle and growled with satisfaction. From every side wolves were drifting in from the forests in a steady stream that converged to form a shifting lake of gray wolves. They were coming in their packs from the mountains and the forests. Now many of the wolves stood apart from one another, the families whispering nervously among themselves. But Slavka would teach them. She would separate them all into male and female contingents and train them in the Combats. They would be proud and strong and free.

But even as she thought it, Slavka felt the breath of fear among the wolves. As the newcomers had arrived at the Gathering Place, the story had sent up a murmur among them. Many had seen visions as they traveled, visions of wolves watching them, wolves who had suddenly vanished again. Now the name of Wolfbane was everywhere too. Many of the free wolves had resisted joining a Greater Pack, but such fear was stirring through the land beyond the forest that they had come to hear at least what Slavka had to tell them. Slavka rose slowly on her paws and padded forward. She howled and the wolves came toward her.

"You are welcome," Slavka cried, and her words rang through the valley. "Welcome all. Our time is at hand. Since Tratto's murder and the coming of Morgra, evil stalks the land beyond the forest once more."

There was an angry growling among the wolf packs.

"But I am here to deliver you from this evil. To destroy the darkness of myth, the darkness of the Sight. To help us remain Putnar, not become slaves to superstition."

But among the wolves a little group were talking quietly together.

"But should you do this?" asked the female. "We swore loyalty always, and if we betray her now—"

"Stop talking about betrayal," growled the wolf she was talking to. "There is no such thing as betrayal. There is only breaking ranks."

The gray wolf suddenly stepped forward from the group. He was a huge Dragga, and his eyes were sharp and bold. His name was Rar and his young family stood at his back.

"Slavka," he cried suddenly, "you call yourself the Deliverer. But is a Greater Pack really the way of the wolf? And there are stories, too, Slavka. Of your own methods."

The wolves began to whisper again, but as Slavka answered Rar there was neither weakness nor doubt in her voice.

"Some may resent me, Rar," she said scornfully, "and think me cruel. Others find the separation of male and female difficult and the Combats cause mutterings. But we are Putnar, and I tell you now that we must fight strength with strength. There are rumors that Morgra and the Balkar are on their way here already."

But Rar was not to be put off. "We all know of Morgra, Slavka," he growled, "and the stories of Wolfbane too. But not all believe the Sight to be evil. And now there is other talk, of the white wolf."

From inside a circle of rebel guards, a Dragga and a Drappa stirred as he said it, and their ears came up. Since that night in the snow, Huttser and Palla had been kept under constant watch.

"You know it is not just talk, Rar," snarled Slavka ferociously. "Her name is Larka and she travels with a human.

But no true wolf travels with Man. We must destroy them both and end the lies that have always infected the Putnar with weakness and fear."

"Slavka," growled Rar, appealing to the wolves around him too. "If this Larka has the Sight, then perhaps she can help us against Morgra. Some say that she herself is the Deliverer. That her family has been tested by the elements. . . ."

Some of the wolves had begun to mutter again and nod, but Slavka swung up her head furiously and she gave a jealous shiver at the mention of the Deliverer.

"What are you saying?" she snarled. "That she could bring forth this Vision? This Man Varg. Man is evil, and he is close enough."

An angry growl came from many of the wolves. Rar fell silent, for he could see that Slavka was stirring them up. Even as they had come in from the mountains, they had seen the human soldiers camped at the far southern edge of the Gathering Place, and it had set their instincts on edge. Like others, Rar had sought for hope in the stories of this strange white wolf, but even he would not dare to refute Slavka as she talked of Man.

"If Larka pretends she has the Sight," Slavka went on, "she is no better than Morgra."

The dragga standing next to her looked up and there was doubt in his eyes. He had only just returned to camp and one of his number had been captured by the Balkar. It was Gart.

"But she will bring the human cub to me. I promise you that," cried Slavka. "Then, when I have killed it myself, my Greater Pack shall fight this darkness, tooth and claw, as Putnar should. We have always found our freedom in our pack boundaries and that freedom shall swell as our boundary swells. No longer separate and isolated. No longer hunting the forests alone. But together. Now is not the time to doubt or waver. Join together, for we face our destiny as one."

Even Huttser felt a tingling down his spine and, despite all her cruelty, his heart beat a little faster for Slavka.

Slavka lifted her muzzle. The note was pure and strong, and the gray wolves around her began to answer, one by one, heads lifting until the whole valley was echoing with their howling cries. Then, as the Greater Pack began to grow quiet again, another note came to them from the back of their ranks, rising in unison, low and stirring. A howling song, the "Song of the Deliverer."

The howling subsided, and as it did so, the wolves began to call.

"Slavka," they thundered. "Slavka."

Even Rar found it hard not to take up the cry now, so mastered were the wolves, so strong did they seem. As their voices carried across the air to the southern edge of the valley where the human camp lay, spread out across the plain, men leaped from their tents and seized their swords.

Only Huttser and Palla remained silent as they stood surrounded by their guards. For suns their thoughts had been filled with terror for Larka, and with the arrival of other packs, another fear was stalking the valley. The story of Wolfbane's promise and where it had been made had begun to circulate freely again. As the howls subsided, Huttser began to snarl.

"Huttser," said Palla, so the guards could not overhear her, "if only we could escape."

"They never stop watching," growled Huttser angrily.

"There are some who might help us. I heard Keeka and Karma talking. When they learned that we were Larka's parents. That perhaps our family . . ." But Palla faltered as she looked across to a nearby bush. She growled at what she saw there. There was a beady-eyed bird sitting in the nest. It was large and plump and it looked around it smugly. The creature was a cuckoo, and Palla had watched with horror how its birth had come about. For the nest did not belong to the cuckoo at all, but to a family of finches.

Palla had seen the mother and father finch weave the nest proudly and lay their little eggs. But one night when the parents were off hunting, a female cuckoo had flown down and placed her own egg in the nest too. It was much larger than the others, but feeling the warmth of its life and being forgetful, the mother and father finch had mistaken the egg for their own and sat on it with the others.

In time the egg had split open, and as soon as the huge chick had emerged from the shell, it had pushed the finches' own eggs from the nest, to fall and shatter on the ground below. Then it had begun to call for food, like a huge mouth, and so the finches had started to feed it. So rapacious was the creature, and so much food did it demand of the little birds, that with time, as the cuckoo grew fat and strong, its new parents died in the effort to give it nurture.

Palla shuddered as she thought of the horrible cruelty of it, and in that moment she wondered what a family really was.

"Most of the rebels are loyal to Slavka," growled Huttser, "and they would see us fight each other. But that shall never be, Palla. Meanwhile, we must hope and look to the future."

But the she-wolf's eyes had grown heavy and morbid. "The future," she whispered bitterly. "It's as bleak as the past."

Huttser shook his head sadly.

"Larka," whispered Palla, "do you think she will come?"

"She must not, Palla, whatever happens."

A polecat was sitting on the branch of an oak licking the fur around its muzzle. Its little fangs glistened like ivory, and it squeaked with satisfaction as it thought of the kill it had just made. It flicked its tail left and right and was just settling down to take a nap when it looked up in amazement. The creature could hardly believe its eyes. Over the past suns it had been startled to see so many gray wolves moving through the forests. But this. Never in its short life had it seen this. They vanished beyond the trunks and the polecat screwed up its eyes. But no, it hadn't been a dream. There it had been, on a white wolf's back.

But with that, the polecat heard a robin fluttering down to settle on the end of a branch, and in that instant, it forgot all about what it had just seen as it began to creep forward, stealthily along the branch, drawn by its own hunger. The polecat was not the only Lera to see the strange little family, part wolf, part man, part bird. As they traveled northeast toward Slavka in the valley of Kosov, an osprey looked down from its rocky aerie and nearly fell out of its nest. In a sparkling stream an otter poked its glistening head from the waters and promptly dropped the trout it had clasped in its eager paws. A herd of fallow deer were so startled at the sight that they began to fence with their antlers out of season. The strange apparition set up such a chattering and whispering among the animals that the forests seemed to tremble with the rumor.

But other sights had made the Lera fearful too. Sights that filled them with wonder and foreboding. Muzzles and eyes that seemed to appear from nowhere to startle the hunted, and then vanish again as if they had never been.

Larka and the others were growing worried, for Skart had great difficulty remembering the way now. But as they traveled, at least they had more success than they had done caught in winter's unforgiving grip. As spring edged toward summer, game became more plentiful; the herds of deer and cattle swelled, and the Lera lost their fear and grew lazy with feeding. Tsarr hunted for them all, and Larka's coat lost its pallid yellowy gray. She walked, graceful and healthy, through the tall grass, as white as the arctic wolf.

As she went Larka, too, began to notice more of the Lera that lived in this mysterious land. As she watched them, only sometimes did the wolf feel hunger stirring in her belly. But at other times she would look out and marvel at the forms and variety of the animals.

In the forests she saw red squirrels and stoats and weasels stalking through the trees, and fox and wildcats and otters, too, spinning and twisting through the glittering streams. She saw snakes slithering through the grasses, horned adders and steppe vipers, picking their way through life with their darting tongues, their undulating bodies so in tune with the earth that they hardly needed their feeble eyes. As Larka looked at them and thought of the promised power to control all the Lera, again she felt strangely humble.

But Larka grew frantic as the summer arrived and her friend still had difficulty recalling the best route to the valley. She hardly had a plan of what she would do when she reached Slavka, but all she could think of was saving her parents. One clear, calm morning she came to a decision.

"Tsarr," she declared, looking fondly at Bran. "I must leave you. Skart and I shall use the Sight again. I must travel by Skart's wings now."

As Larka's body slumped to the ground by the child, her mind felt a glorious freedom as Skart rose in the skies, as though her troubles were dropping away. To the north the ragged mountains climbed into the skies. But to the south, and east and west, the forests and woods had become an ocean of color below them, rippling and shrugging in a tide of branch and leaf.

But as this sea of growth swept before her Larka was startled. She realized that, though the whole looked green, now, as she looked down she could see the infinite variety of shades and colors that really made up the forests, as the clouds crossed the sun or the wind rocked the branches. As Larka thought of what lay ahead, she suddenly felt as though there was some hidden moral in the grandeur of this view.

For three suns they traveled together, and day turned to night and back into day. Larka noticed how many birds there were in the skies, for the creatures of the air had returned from their winter migrations. And when darkness came, the she-wolf marveled as they flew below a star-soaked heaven. She wondered how high Skart could fly. And if the bird turned upward whether he could ever reach those sparking eyes of light and sail through the darkness along the Wolf Trail itself, a trail between heaven and earth that for as long as the Varg could remember had been etched into their stories.

The wolf and the eagle were flapping below the moon when Skart heard a cry on the air below them. A great cloud of wings was moving steadily toward the east. There were ravens and crows and hungry buzzards. The noise sent a whispering through the clouds.

"The flying scavengers," shuddered Skart. "They are making for Kosov too."

Suddenly, below them, they recognized a single black raven. Skart dived on the air and, as they came closer, they heard Kraar's voice cawing through the night to the flock.

"Come," cried the raven triumphantly, "follow me. Soon I shall give our kind power over the Putnar, as Wolfbane promised me himself, and we shall feast on seas of blood."

Before Kraar was even aware of Skart's presence, a shadow fell on him in the moonlit skies, and the flying scavengers scattered with fright as the eagle's talons closed like a vise around the raven's wings. Kraar cawed in terror, but he was caught fast as the eagle sailed on.

"So, Kraar, we meet again," cried Skart coldly as he held the bird below him. "Flapping back to your mistress?"

"Let me go," cawed the raven furiously, "or I'll—"

"Or you'll nothing," snapped Skart, closing his talons even tighter and wheeling upward to carry the creature away from his friends. "You will be silent, or I will crush you like a fly. Now, tell me what is happening, Kraar. You're going to the valley, aren't you?"

The bird was silent.

"I will kill you if you don't tell me."

Kraar screeched on the ragged wind, but the raven knew it was hopeless.

Skart could feel the bird trembling in his grip, but he suddenly realized that Kraar couldn't speak under the force of it.

"Tell me and I will let you go," said Skart, relaxing his hold slightly. "Where is Morgra?"

"Swear you'll release me," clacked the bird. "Swear it by the Sight."

For a moment the eagle hesitated. "I swear it."

"Very well. Morgra and the Night Hunters are on their way to the valley as we speak."

"And there she plans to use the ancient howl?"

"No, I can't," screeched the bird. "Morgra and . . . and him."

Skart squeezed again.

"Yes—yes. Morgra is waiting for her true servants to come. She will send them among the Lera to do her bidding."

"But she doesn't have the child."

"She no longer cares. She says we must trust the legend itself. Is not Larka on her way to the valley too?"

Far away, the she-wolf's body shuddered as she listened, but as Kraar felt the eagle's grip weaken again with the power of his own words, Kraar said more than he had intended.

"And Harja. The citadel lies in the mountains above the valley," he cried triumphantly.

The connection between Larka and Skart almost broke with the shock of it.

"No," cried the eagle. Skart's talons nearly locked through Kraar's heart.

"Stop it," screeched the raven. "You promised . . ."

"Kraar, you are nothing but a filthy parasite. A foul, worthless scavenger. A low, black, honorless—"

"Skart," clacked Kraar suddenly, and his voice was filled with bitterness, "do you think that I choose to be a scavenger? That I like hopping after snarling wolves or taking lambs' eyes in the morning? If I had huge claws or a fine beak I would be true Putnar, too, and you would not call me honorless. What gives you the right to judge me? To have power over my kind?"

As Larka listened, she heard truth in the bird's words, and strangely she thought of the poor Sikla.

"Lies," cried Skart. "You are proud of being a scavenger, Kraar, hiding in the shadows. Or do you hate the thing you are? Is that why you serve Morgra. Because you are like her. Because she hates the life of the wolf and longs for the power of Man. Longs to be human."

Skart's talons were closing.

"Skart," called Larka's voice, "you promised Kraar you would not harm him. Whatever happens, Skart, we must not become like them."

"Very well," the eagle said scornfully, and then he dipped his beak toward Kraar and his eyes bored into the raven's.

"We will meet again, Kraar," he whispered. "I promise you that too. You are blackening the skies and the hearts of the birds, so when we do, I will not hesitate to kill you."

Skart released his talons with disgust, and the raven dropped like a stone. It opened its injured wings and, screeching terribly, wheeled into the skies. The flying scavengers had been scattered to the winds, but as Skart sailed on, Kraar turned to rally them again.

"Come back," cried his fading voice. "You've no need to be afraid. Wolfbane is with us and I, Kraar, am not frightened of the flying Putnar, I will lead you to . . ."

"It's true, Skart, isn't it?" whispered Larka as Kraar's voice disappeared into the distance. "We are caught in this legend somehow, just as Kraar was caught in your talons."

The eagle didn't answer the wolf, but as she lay by the child, Larka could hardly breathe.

"We must hurry, Skart," she said. "Somehow you must warn my parents for me. Get them away from there."

But as Skart flew on through the night, it seemed that fear itself was riding on the wind.

The sun had come again, and they were flying along the Carpathians' southern edge, directly east, when Skart began to descend. They had come at last to a plain, and Larka shuddered as they looked down. There, below them, was a human encampment. A great herd of horses was corralled at one edge and around them there was a sea of tents, and the smoking gray embers of fires wheezing in the day.

"Skart," Larka whispered, "it's just as I saw. But there are even more of them now."

Skart flew on, and in no time at all they came to a wide valley, well shielded by the trees. There were beech and elm and sycamores and an unusually large expanse of rowan trees, still bright with red berries. As Skart flew lower, Larka began to see a shifting lake of gray wolves.

"The rebels," murmured Larka, and as she said it, her heart began to beat faster. Larka felt a strange longing as she saw so many wild wolves settled together, a longing to be among her own kind again. The eagle was dropping lower still, and Larka saw a band of wolves lying in a circle. Her heart pounded as she gazed down. She would have recognized those faces anywhere.

"Mother," gasped Larka. "Father."

But some of the wolves guarding Huttser and Palla saw the bird come. They had been ordered to keep everything away, and they jumped up and began to snarl and leap in the air. Skart lifted again, and as he did so, they noticed a lone shape on the hilltop. Evening was coming down and, even as Skart's eyes looked toward the sentinel wolf, far away the hackles rose on Larka's neck. Around the powerful Dragga's body, Larka could suddenly see an angry red aura, fringed with a gray. She shivered as she saw it, and she remembered too her vision of Wolfbane and his dark halo.

"Balkar," she whispered. "The Night Hunters have already reached the Gathering Place."

The scout had disappeared into the trees again, but on Skart flew, and Larka's heart began to pound even more furiously as they soared over the forest. Among the boughs, padding through the darkness, Larka saw them even beneath the canopy of leaves. They were moving silently, in straight lines toward the Gathering Place, the Balkar's prowling auras. Then, behind them, came another aura, blacker than the rest. It seemed to swallow light itself. Again Larka felt anguish and desire, that same desire to be close to this creature. Wolfbane.

"Hurry, Skart," she cried, "we must return."

Below them, the Balkar called Brak snarled as he stood in the shadows and saw the eagle circling high above. Then, again, he looked down on the rebels in the fabled valley of Kosov. There was something in the vision of this giant pack that unsettled him deeply. For though the Night Hunters were all fighting males, all his life they had been trained to travel in small groups, like the ordinary wolf, and strike at speed. He was proud of his own power and skill, and the strength of his night eyes. He knew that in single combat there were few living wolves that could beat him. But a Greater Pack he had never seen before, and the sheer number of wolves set doubt tumbling through his brain. Only Man fought like this, not the Varg.

"No," he steeled himself, "I must show no weakness."

Brak had failed Morgra in not bringing back the child, and he couldn't afford to fail his mistress again. He began to run through the forest, his great paws springing through the undergrowth. So swiftly did the wolf move that he seemed to leave hardly an impression on the ground as he went.

Around him, the scents of summer set the wild wolf's nerve endings quivering, and as evening came down, the fading light turning the pine trees to strips of black. The Night Hunter felt a fury rising in him. His ears were cocked forward and, at every sound, the movement of a bird in the branches or the scurry of a squirrel, the wolf's running body would flex so subtly, here changing pace, there swerving left or right. He seemed to merge with the currents of air swirling through the forest. His instincts were perfectly in tune with all around him and ready at any moment to show the greatest skill of the wolf, to fight or to flee at the turning of a feather.

Brak heard a sound as he went, and on the slopes above him he saw a shadow, trailing him silently through the twilight. He recognized the gray wolf from another of the Balkar packs, but he gave no howl of recognition, for they had been told to travel toward the rebels in secret.

Together they ran, and now a third wolf joined them, and then a fourth. The wolves were moving together, perfectly in tune, delighting for a time in their true nature as they ran free through the wood. But as they came closer and closer to Morgra's camp, a change came into their eyes. A look both of fear and of need. That same mesmerized intensity that they had shown at the sacrifices and outside Morgra's cave.

Ahead of them, they could see a clearing and the other Balkar Draggas ranged about Morgra. Kraar was perched on her back as she addressed them, and her voice sang coldly through the warm air. Kraar kept opening and closing his wings as though he were orchestrating her words as she spoke. Some of the Balkar wolves looked at him with hatred, for he was always mocking them. But they wouldn't have dared touch a feather on his back.

"Very well, then," Morgra was saying as Brak and the others joined their ranks. "We attack in five nights' time. Brak, what of the count?"

"I counted two hundred ten wolves," he answered, stepping forward warily. There was a growling among the Balkar, and some of the Draggas began to shake their heads doubtfully.

"Morgra," said one, "not even the Balkar can test such odds. There are only fifty of us."

The old she-wolf's eyes were amused as she surveyed the males. " 'No Sikla here, no breath of fear?' Aren't you used to looking into the darkness?"

The Balkar dropped their muzzles in shame before the she-wolf.

"But don't worry," said Morgra coldly. "Fear is our friend now and it shall destroy this Greater Pack. For Wolfbane is with us."

"But fifty against over two hundred."

"Others shall come to help us," hissed Morgra. "We shall split their forces and drive half into the trees to die on your jaws. The night shall aid us, too, and the spirit of the woods."

"And the rest, Morgra?"

Morgra lifted her muzzle. There was something coldly brilliant in her gaze. "Slavka hates and fears Man," she said delightedly. "And now she shall have true cause. For we shall drive the others toward the human camp beyond, to die on their swords."

"But, Morgra," gasped a Night Hunter. "It is impossible."

"Silence, fool," snarled Morgra. "Are you forgetting the Searchers? Slavka has summoned her Greater Pack. Well, I . . ." Morgra paused. "Wolfbane shall summon those who no longer have need of boundaries. Who shall tear their claws through all boundaries."

The Balkar looked at Morgra wonderingly, but there was little understanding in them.

"Now be gone," cried Morgra. "Prepare. But when the killing begins, keep a sharp eye for the two I told you of — Huttser and Palla. In five nights' time, they must perish. The family must be finally destroyed."

As the wolves slunk away, they were muttering among themselves. Kraar had hopped up on Morgra's back again, careful not to let his little talons bite into his mistress's skin. As he neared her neck, his beak whispered into her torn ear, "Can it be done?"

"Oh yes, Kraar, everything is in place. The greater part of the legend is about to come true. And our strength has grown, Kraar. When the Searchers come, scenting the promise of your feast, whoever they touch shall be mine, and I shall wield the power of entering and controlling minds. But before we attempt it, I must sleep and then make a kill."

The raven cawed happily and fluttered upward into the night. "So the rebels have no future, Mistress?"

"No, Kraar. They never did have a future. All along, the past has been snapping at their heels. Driving them to this place. And soon they shall really see how hopeless is their fate, for the Pathways of Death will open, the true pathways of the past, and then they shall be consumed."

"But what do these others look like, Mistress?" cried Kraar above her.

"The Searchers?" called the she-wolf, as the darkness seemed to hiss about her, and Kraar turned in the sky to seek out the scavengers again. "You shall see soon enough, my friend."

On the plain at the southern edge, where the human Draggas had made their camp, the darkness came down like beating wings. It was four nights since Morgra had addressed her commanders and Larka had looked down on the men from the heavens. The glow of fires began to fleck through the night, and everywhere shapes were stirring as the soldiers settled about the little islands of crackling warmth. Some lay on the ground, others crouched in the shadows. Here a human was sharpening a sword, polishing its violence. There another was cleaning his armor, or attaching new flights to his bow, sharing his meager food with the others, lifting a flagon of rough wine to his lips.

The same murmur went about the camp, for there was news from the south of more raids by the Turk, and soon it would be time to do battle once more. Each of the humans was wrapped in his own thoughts, thinking of his pay or his loved ones back at home, dreaming of freedom or friendship or glory. They were drawn closer to one another, too, united again by the returning breath of fear and the most basic instinct of all, the will to survive.

In their tents, shielded from the night and the firelight by their thin walls of cloth, many of the soldiers were asleep, exhausted by their days of hard training. They slumbered now as their dreams carried them to strange, far-off places. An old veteran, lying on his simple bunk, was dreaming of his past and the days when, as a youth, he had fought so boldly. A young soldier was thinking of the future and what the journey toward the Turk might bring. His mind shuffling with the pictures of changing possibilities, of hopes and fears and anxieties made into scenes and faces by the living patterns of his own memory.

Near one of the tents, a soldier was telling a story. His voice calmed the others, for there was laughter in it. But as the darkness grew, so his tone began to change, too, and his tale turned down blacker avenues. The man was, for the most part, anyway, making it up as he went along. And even as he did so, he wondered himself where the strange voice in him that sang with invention came from and to what end it was leading him.

Sometimes, it was as if he was in charge of his story and he knew exactly to what conclusion he was coming. At others, though, it felt as if that voice was not his at all, but his father's voice, or his father's before him, or the voice out of all the many stories he had heard as a child. When that happened, he wanted to change the story, to make it new and fresh and different. Sometimes, it was even as if the leaders gathered eagerly, and he was simply telling them what they wanted to hear, and at others as if he was dreaming like his fellows in their tents. But as he spoke, a memory came to the storyteller that hurt him to his heart. In that moment, it was as if all he was saying was nothing more than the image of a man and a woman standing together in a room long before, and accusing each other bitterly of not showing enough love.

Suddenly his voice fell silent. A note came through the darkness, truer, stronger, more insistent than all the tales he had been weaving. A voice out of nature itself, carried on the black air. A call out of wildness that made him shiver to his bones. As soon as they heard the wolf's cry, the soldiers looked up and many touched their swords, for they had heard the cries before and they knew that wolves were near. Yet only the storyteller noticed something different in this howl. Something strange and unearthly.

The rebel wolves heard it, too, in their valley, and they started up in fear. Huttser and Palla heard it, and Palla licked her mate and whined as she listened. The Balkar heard it as the Night Hunters prowled toward the Greater Pack through the trees. Not five miles away, Larka and the others heard it also, and Skart opened his wings in horror.

"The howl," he screeched. "Morgra is attempting the ancient howl."

On it went, and on, searching through the Transylvanian darkness, trying to touch something with its lonely anger. The Greater Pack was up and beginning to move about, and Slavka was issuing orders. But even now there was little urgency in the rebels' tread, for they were confident of their strength.

If they had known how close the Balkar were perhaps they would have thought again, yet they were many and the Balkar comparatively few. The Night Hunters savage eyes glittered now from the trees on the edges of Kosov, as they waited and peered hungrily through the dark. Their commanders had divided them into pairs, and the

Draggas' breaths smoked gently as they licked their lips and pressed their muzzles through the branches. Everywhere in the branches around them perched the waiting scavengers.

"Do you think they will come?" whispered one Balkar.

"Wait," answered Brak at his side. "Wait and see."

But even as he said it, the howl rose higher and higher. Suddenly Brak let out a hissing growl. He feared to believe his own eyes.

There in front of him, on the edge of the valley, like a shadow it came and seemed to split the darkness. It sprang out of nothingness itself, its paws scything through the air, dragging behind them its huge wolflike body. It was a ghastly silver and its eyes were bright red and, as it materialized, others came, too, leaping from the night onto the silent grass. The Night Hunters began to tremble as they looked on, and more and more of the spectral wolves leaped into the darkness.

"The dead," hissed Brak. "The armies of the dead have come."

There must have been sixty, seventy specters before them now, their shimmering silver shapes quivering with violence, their bloodred eyes turning this way and that. But most ghastly of all was their appearance and the terrible recognition that awoke in the onlookers. As each of the Balkar looked, they seemed to recognize dead friends among them, wolves they had forgotten long ago, and it sent an anguish and a guilt racing through their hearts.

"Wolfbane," called Brak. "The friend of the dead has done this. Whatever you do, don't let them touch you."

Around them the howl went on, and it seemed to be calling to the dead. The specters had heard it and, as one, they turned and sprang toward the Greater Pack.

It was sheer terror that achieved the thing. As soon as they saw the specters advancing like a sea mist, such a panic went up among the Greater Pack that it spread like a fire. They, too, had seen the image of their dead friends, of enemies and lost loved ones, in the forms of the Searchers. But there was nothing in their appearance that drew the wolves toward them. All they inspired was horror.

Some of the rebel wolves began to run blindly into the night. Others turned to face their spectral attackers, but they gasped in terror as they lashed out with their paws and teeth only to find themselves slashing through thin air. The silver shadows seemed to pass straight through the rebels' bodies as they sprang at them, and with the passing came such terror and cold fear that a madness entered the rebels' brains.

"No," snarled Slavka in horror as she watched them come. "It can't be . . ."

"Slavka," cried Gart beside her. "We must get out of here. We can't fight this."

"Silence, Gart. It's impossible. It's a trick."

"Slavka," growled Gart angrily, "won't you even believe the evidence of your own eyes?"

All around her the rebels were fleeing and now Gart turned too.

"Loyalty," cried Slavka furiously as she saw the ranks break. "Loyalty always."

But suddenly Slavka turned in the darkness herself to see one of the specters leaping straight for her. She was horrified. The specter had the shape of her dead mate. Its silver jaws opened as it sprang, but as Slavka snarled and lifted her muzzle, the specter's shimmering form melded with her own. For a moment it seemed as if she and the ghastly apparition had become one, and then it passed on to spread horror farther into the camp.

But as it scythed through her, Slavka felt a terrible chill down her spine, like the touch of ice, and a bitter doubt crept into her brain. It was as though she could hear a wind, speaking to her.

Many of the rebel wolves were fleeing toward the trees. They had no inkling of the trap that was waiting to spring and, as they reached the woods, their minds were so consumed by fright that they hardly saw the Balkar. But as they came, they were welcomed by a forest of teeth and by the red flash of yawning gullets, fringed with gray fur, as the killing began.

But now something else happened that sent despair racing through the rebels' ranks. A rebel Dragga felt it first as he ran toward the trees. He was one of the wolves that had been touched by the specters, and he was calling to four of his comrades to stand firm when suddenly he heard a voice in his head.

"Die," it snarled, "for I have come to lead the dead. Wolfbane has come."

The rebel Varg froze. Fear had overcome him, like a great darkness.

"See your own destruction," came a voice. There was no specter near now. This voice was Wolfbane himself.

Suddenly, as the gray wolf faced the trees, the darkness was real. The wolf could no longer see. He was blind.

Elsewhere along the rebels' ranks, others had stopped moving too. They whimpered with fear as they dropped their heads and tails and confronted the sudden blackness.

"Palla!" cried Huttser as they saw the apparitions from their guard ring. "The Searchers are here. Remember what Tsinga said. Don't let them touch you."

"What are they, Huttser?" Palla's voice trembled.

Huttser was snarling furiously, but the Dragga hardly knew what to do. Around them, the rebel guards had been thrown into confusion. Suddenly, one of the specters came leaping toward them and, as it sprang, the guard ring broke. The specter pounced at Huttser and he froze. It had the form of his own mother. Just in time the Dragga dropped his body. The specter's paws almost brushed his fur and, as they came close, Huttser's mind quivered with fear and, he suddenly saw an image of Fell before his mind's eye, seized under the ice.

"Father," his voice seemed to say. "Father, why did you leave me?"

But the specter passed on, and Huttser shook himself from the dreadful reverie. "Quickly, Palla. Make for the trees."

"No, Huttser. Look."

At the tree line the Night Hunters were already making short work of the dazed rebels.

"To the south then, run, Palla, run for your life!"

Other rebels had turned toward the south, too, away from the trees and back down the valley. Slavka was there, and Keeka and Karma. Rar and Gart too. The specters sprang noiselessly after them. The maddened rebels ran on and on, whining and howling, unaware that they were being herded like lambs for the slaughter toward the humans' camp.

"So," muttered Morgra as she lay with her eyes closed in the fearful forest, "it is done."

All around her the heavy grass was wet with cuckoo spit, and the air was still and lifeless.

"Now go, my friends, out there among the Lera. Touch them with terror and open their minds. Tempt nature to turn against itself, and in so doing, bait the trap. For in hating their own lives, the only hope the Lera will look to is the Vision. Then, when their eyes turn as one to me, I shall have them."

The eerie howling rose again, and the specters chasing the rebels toward the human camp turned in the night. The rebels did not see them as they turned, for they were too frightened to look behind them. But as the terrible howling subsided, the specters dissolved into a hissing silver smoke that rolled out through the grass and the trees and seemed to carry a word on the wind like a sigh, and the word was death. Like a fog it brushed the souls of the Lera, the worms and the beetles, the fox and the field mice, and a terrible fear began to spread through the land beyond the forest.

As the humans heard the wolves coming, heard their howls on the air and saw fifty or sixty emerging at the neck of the valley, the largest pack they had ever known, they, too, thought that their nightmares had come alive. A great shout went up as they rushed for their swords and their spears, their shields and their crossbows.

Like the wolf, they were driven by instinct now, but in their hands and their minds they held a different power. Arrows flew through the air and felled many of the running wolves before they even reached their fires. But as the other wolves came on, glad at least to find an enemy that they could touch with tooth and claw, the night came alive with flashing swords and with the cries of man and beast mingling in the awful blackness.

"Dive down," cried Larka.

Like a thunderbolt, the eagle fell through the air.

"What is happening, Skart?" cried Larka as they swooped. "Hurry, Skart, we must find my parents."

The eagle opened his brown wings even wider and, with a shriek, turned in the air as dawn began to crack around them.

Larka's heart sank as Skart plunged toward the valley of Kosov. At first, the bodies on the edges of the valley were simply specks, without form or meaning. From the air they might have been stones or fallen trees. But as the bird drew nearer on the wind, and its eyes began to pick out the details of the night before, Larka gasped. Smudges of black turned bloodred. A stunted bush became a pile of dying bodies. A patch of fur, the tattered muzzle and the sad and empty eyes of a broken wolf.

Lower and lower Skart came, skimming the valley, touching the dead with the very air that quivered below his wings, his angry eyes taking in all that sped beneath him. Everywhere, the rebels lay: on the edge of the trees, contorted into unnatural shapes, some still stirring as the life left them, others alive only in the energy that decay would return to the earth.

The scenes that met their eyes were pitiful. Here a dying she-wolf had crawled through the grass toward her already dead mate and perished before she could even reach him. There, a rebel lay, the promise and hope of the trees still seized in his lifeless eyes. But what sent a shudder through Skart were the birds. They were everywhere, plucking and pecking at the dead wolves, tearing at the rebels' flesh and cawing delightedly as they hopped about like hooded grave robbers, pulling out eyes.

"Oh, Skart," gasped Larka as the skies grumbled with thunder. "Is this what the Sight is for? To show us this?"

Larka could feel Skart shaking with fury as it began to rain. "Morgra. She has fulfilled Wolfbane's promise to the flying scavengers."

"Is there nothing," cried Larka bitterly, "nothing we can see in life that is too terrible? No horror we can see that will bring peace?"

On they sailed, and now Skart turned back down the valley. As he flew over the camp, some of the humans looked up and scowled, for they wondered as they looked about if all nature had become their enemy. Among them lay the bodies of many wolves, but here and there at their sides were human corpses, too, and their blood was mixing in the earth.

"It is all coming about," Larka moaned.

But, though despair had won that sun, a question stirred in Larka's mind as the eagle flew among the dead over the valley of Kosov—a question and the faintest stirrings of hope. In all the dead faces they passed, Huttser and Palla were nowhere to be seen.

It was evening when they flew again toward the Gathering Place. As the sun began to set over the Carpathians, touching the clouds with a mournful fire, the Balkar packs were putting paid to the last of the rebels. Then, as it started to rain, from the trees stepped a single wolf. She walked slowly, but her tail was lifted and her eyes glittered with certainty. She stopped and, as she surveyed the carnage, she smiled.

"This is what comes of Slavka's Greater Pack," Morgra snarled, "of Slavka's feeble boundaries. Balkar, can you doubt me now? Doubt the glory of the Sight or the friend of the dead? Our power is growing like a forest."

Morgra lifted her scarred head and let out a howl. Her call rose again, higher and higher into the air, but it was no longer seeking. It was cold and triumphant, and the Balkar packs raised their muzzles to answer. Now, as they swayed their heads in unison, it was as though Morgra's mind was controlling them completely.

"Wolfbane," they howled. "The Evil One."

As the howling subsided again, Morgra swung around. "Hurry. I feel Larka is near, and with her the child. We must hunt them down, while the flying scavengers find the entrance to the citadel. We are so close to the final prize."

But as she spoke, a Night Hunter stepped up and began to whisper in Morgra's ear. As he did so, the she-wolf started to snarl furiously. Once more there was doubt and fear in her eyes.

"Find them," she hissed. "Find them and kill them."

Darkness came in again with the sweeping thunder clouds, and the shape of those dead souls was dimmed in the gloom of the storm and in the night. And as Skart flew and Larka looked down, a desperate compassion stirred inside her. Not only for the rebels, but for the Balkar who had died in the fight, and for the humans, too, in their distant camp.

The drizzling rain made the scene miserable indeed, for it was soaking the grass around the rebels' bodies, blending blood and sap and turning it to mud. The valley was dissected by little rivulets. Not the pure fresh waters of new life but streams of death that carried the wolves' souls weeping through the grass.

As Skart looked down on Morgra and what the birds were doing to the wolves, he felt a terrible anger. Before Larka could stop him, he plunged earthward. He was flapping furiously as he settled near Morgra, and she snarled as soon as she saw him.

"So, Skart, have you come to share Wolfbane's feast? I thought you were the true flying Putnar. Couldn't you resist?"

But even as she looked into the bird's eyes Morgra licked her lips. "Larka, you are here, too, aren't you? So we meet properly at last."

In that moment Larka wanted to leave the bird's body and run, anywhere, to be a pup again and nestle in her mother's flanks, or feel the strength and safety of Huttser as he stood over her.

"Give the child to me, Larka, and together we will complete the legend. For the Pathways of Death are open and the verse is almost fulfilled. The entrance is somewhere in the mountains beyond. The entrance to Harja."

Far away, Larka began to snarl, and Tsarr and the human looked up. But now her mind was growling, and she found the energy of her anger speaking through Skart. "Never."

"But we are the same, you and I," said Morgra coldly. "You must have felt it, my dear. The curse of the Sight. That is what it teaches you in the end. If you look properly there is nothing but pain and darkness and death. Nothing except power."

"There is," cried Larka. "There is love and hope and freedom. The freedom of the birds."

Morgra smiled as the ghastly feasting went on around them. "Come to me, Larka, and I shall soothe you. I shall teach you your true nature. The true nature of the wolf. For I have done this for you. To protect you."

"For me?" snarled Larka. "Liar. No, Morgra. I will find my parents and together we shall stop you. For we are the family."

Though Larka knew she was lying, that Fell had gone and Kar, too, for a moment Morgra's face seemed to crumple with doubt.

"I shall fight you," growled Larka. "You and Wolfbane. Always."

As Larka and Skart looked at Morgra's vicious face, they fancied her eyes were shielding something from them.

"No, Larka. Soon the legend shall carry us, Wolfbane and I, to everlasting glory."

Larka felt a tremor of terror now, and with it came a furious hate. "I will stop you, Morgra. I will look into the human's mind myself."

Morgra could hear the snarl in Larka's voice as she spoke through Skart. "That's good, Larka. Hate me. For your hate brings you closer to me. It is natural, Larka, to hate. Like hunger. Like night. You must hate me for all I have done to your pack and your friends. Remember them. Remember the pain. Remember, Fell, dying under the beautiful stars."

"No. No."

But as Larka struggled, Skart flapped his great wings, and she thought of Fell's lost soul, and she felt the hate beginning to burn in her belly. She felt it wash over her like the water that had taken Fell, and as it did so, she wanted to give in to it. To be consumed by it. To turn it, like teeth, against her enemy.

"You are barren, Morgra," snarled Larka. "That's why you can never love."

It was Morgra's turn to seethe with pain. "When your parents lie dead, Larka," she hissed, "you shall no longer talk of a family to defeat the evil."

Morgra's jaws were grinning coldly, but she suddenly threw herself at Skart, and her paw scythed the air as the screeching eagle took wing above her. Higher and higher Skart rose, and Morgra began to dwindle below them.

"We are already searching for them," Morgra cried furiously, "as we hunt for you, and now the flying scavengers will aid us. So be ready, my dear. You talk of love. Well, we shall see. For he is waiting for you, too, Larka. Wolfbane is waiting. The Evil One. Then . . . then I will make you fight love itself."

◆ ◆ ◆

"Regroup," cried Slavka in the shadow of the trees banking up the mountain. The stragglers passed back the word, but even as they did so, they felt a yawning anguish in their hearts. Only thirty of their number had come alive from the terrible valley, and all they had seen of the Searchers had almost broken their spirits.

"What now?" whispered Palla at Huttser's side.

Behind them trailed Keeka and Karma and Rar too. He had been wounded in the battle, as had Palla, by one of the human swords. But Palla had managed to save Slavka's life as they fled through the human's camp. As a soldier had raised his sword to strike the rebel leader down, Palla had knocked him to the ground.

As they fled into the woods toward the high mountains, they all began to notice the Lera, and shuddered at what they saw. Among the trees they saw a snake eating its own tail. In a stream fish had floated to the surface of the water and, though they were still alive, they just lay there, as dragonflies and gnats settled on their eyes. In the trees they saw birds, too, plucking the feathers from their own young. A madness seemed to have entered the Lera and, as they went, Huttser and Palla fancied they were watching them too. They shivered as they thought of the words of the verse; they knew that the Searchers had begun to do Morgra's bidding.

Palla lifted her head now as she saw the leader coming toward them, with Gart at her side.

"Slavka," growled Huttser as she came up. "What should we do? Hide in the mountains among the ancient stones?"

Birds were wheeling in the skies, screeching and cawing, diving suddenly toward the forest. There were so many that their wings seemed to turn the air that held them up into waves of rolling movement. As soon as she saw the pair Slavka snarled. She thought of Huttser's daughter, still out there somewhere with the human child, and anger clutched her body.

"Gart," she snapped, "why aren't they under guard?"

"But Slavka, now that—"

"Silence," cried Slavka furiously. "You think that because of what has happened Huttser and Palla shall go free? That they are on our side? No. Tomorrow it is they who shall pay for our defeat. They shall fight to the death."

Keeka looked nervously at Karma, and Rar started to growl and shake his head. But Slavka's eyes were flaming and already some of the remaining rebels had surrounded Huttser and Palla.

There was something else in Slavka's anger, though. Even now, there was a voice in Slavka's mind that seemed to be trying to control her thoughts. It had started when the specter had touched her. As she ran, the voice whispered to her, whispered of another way. It promised her things, and soothed the loneliness that had for so long eaten at her soul. That same morning it had overcome her, a terrible feeling of hopelessness that made Slavka believe there were traitors everywhere. She had heard that voice, saying the same thing over and over, just as it did now. "Kill them. Kill them both."

"Slavka," snarled Huttser, "even now you are unable to see the truth. You have become no better than Morgra. But

Palla and I shall never fight again. We will never turn on ourselves, as the Lera are doing."

"Huttser," Slavka said savagely, and it was as though all she had seen at the battle had entered her soul. "You shall fight. For a quick death at the teeth of the other will be a blessed release compared to the agony that will face the victor. Or both of you, if you refuse. Hobbled in the sun, the skin around your livers torn open to be pecked at by these birds. I will make sure that death will last for a whole moon. That is why you will fight and fight to kill one another quickly."

Some of the others looked at Slavka in horror now, but they were too dazed to oppose her will. Karma turned to Keeka and Rar, and in her eyes she held a message. But Rar shook his head. There were too few of them to help the Dragga and Drappa.

"Gart," growled Slavka suddenly, "take them away and let them contemplate their fate. In the morning call me."

That night as Huttser and Palla lay together, Slavka kept watching them and wondering coldly what they might be saying to each other. *No matter,* she thought as she did so, *all their fond words can lead to nowhere but darkness and death.* They were all around Slavka now, and as she lay there she heard that voice again, thrumming through her mind. *You are with us,* it murmured coldly.

Huttser raised his head. His mind was searching for a way to change their fate, but nothing came to the Dragga except the same terrible thought.

"Palla," he said softly, "tomorrow. You must show me your throat."

"But, Huttser."

"I'll make a clean kill, Palla. It will be over quickly."

"Has it come to this, Huttser?" whimpered Palla bitterly. "Has Morgra's curse finally won?"

"The curse," snorted Huttser, "it is not just Morgra's power that is doing this. The curse is in our hearts, Palla. In Slavka's heart. In Morgra's heart. Sometimes I think it is in all our hearts. Ours. The Balkars'."

"And the rebels, too," growled Palla, looking around her angrily.

"Rebels," cried Huttser in disgust. "For a time I thought Skop was right to want to help the rebel pack. But now it seems there is little to choose between Slavka and Morgra."

Palla looked up at the stars above them, peeking through the leafy canopy. The air was warm with summer, and a nightingale was singing in some distant tree. Its note had a mournful beauty, and Palla felt her heart stir with anger at what was to come. And anger at the massacre. Anger at the terrible injustice of life.

"It's all so wrong," she growled, lifting her beautiful muzzle to the giant night. "So unjust."

"What do you mean, Palla?"

"My sister. Was it her fault that nature made her barren? Or that the others so feared the Sight that they drove her out? That's what made her evil. And everything must fight to survive."

Huttser growled, but he had no answer for his mate.

"If there were time, Huttser, I would lead a revolt. Such a revolt that all the Lera would remember it, forever. A revolt against the sun and the moon and the stars. A revolt against Tor and Fenris themselves."

Huttser had nothing to console her with.

"I wonder where she is. And if Kar is with her," said Palla suddenly, gazing wistfully into the darkness. "What would they think if they saw what we have to do? Would Larka just be frightened away again?"

"They will never see it," growled Huttser. "For that secret I am thankful at least. Though I wish . . ."

Huttser dropped his muzzle sadly.

"What, Huttser?"

"Kar. I was never very fair to him, Palla. And I blamed him for Fell, when if anything I . . ." Huttser paused and shook his head sadly. "You talk of injustice, Palla, but it is we who make injustice. I wish I had a chance to say I am sorry. To tell Kar that I know it wasn't his fault. To make peace and ask his forgiveness."

In Huttser's heart, he was resigned and very tired. But he had one bitter solace. He believed that Palla had accepted what was to come. It was past noon when Gart summoned them. Slavka was waiting impatiently, surrounded by the rest of the rebels. They had gathered in a wide ring, and they all looked hardened by all that they had been through and witnessed, their eyes blank with misery and confusion. Keeka and Karma turned away guiltily as Huttser and Palla were pushed into the middle of the circle.

"It is time," cried Slavka bitterly, "to pay the price. When it is over, we will make for the higher mountains and hide among the stones."

The sun beat down as the wolves faced each other in the dust, and Huttser gazed sadly at Palla. But he lifted his tail and advanced.

"Show me your throat, Palla."

As Huttser stepped even closer and the rebels looked on hungrily, Palla began to snarl proudly. The skin around her muzzle curled up and her canines glinted. Even Keeka and Karma turned back to look now.

"Palla, what are you doing?"

"Do you think I would let you do this?" cried Palla, feeling as if her heart would burst open. "Let the father of my cubs be hobbled and tortured?"

"Palla, I beg of you."

The rebels' coats bristled as Huttser and Palla began to circle each other. But as they saw the dignity with which the Dragga and Drappa met, a shame stirred in them too.

"I do this for you, Huttser."

Their eyes were locked and they were both shaking furiously. As they showed their teeth and looked for the best point to spring, they felt a terrible confusion, for they knew it was anger they needed if they were to kill the other, yet it was only love that they felt in their hearts.

Huttser leaped at Palla, opening his jaws. Palla sprang, too, driven on by the agonizing energy of her feelings for her mate, and Huttser and Palla met once more. Both were on their hind legs as they began to bite and claw, desperate to save the other from Slavka's fate. They had chosen each other as mates because they could do nothing but walk as equals, and so they were well matched.

But as Huttser disengaged momentarily, Palla leaped again and missed. Her leg had been wounded in the battle, and she suddenly lost her footing. Her throat and chest were exposed as she tumbled, and Huttser opened his jaws again. His heart was thundering, but Huttser knew he had beaten Palla and somewhere it was a terrible blessing. He could see the thin skin below the fur around her gullet, and in the memory of all his kills, of the deer beneath the Stone Den, of the buffalo, he suddenly imagined he could see Palla's blood and tendons and flesh beneath. Though they were dearer to him than anything in the world, Huttser's teeth flashed.

Suddenly there was a great sweep of beating wings. Huttser looked up in amazement as he saw a huge bird sailing between them. At first he thought it was a scavenger coming to feed on Palla, but then they heard a voice, calm and commanding, ringing out around them.

"Cease," it cried. "Hasn't there been enough fighting? There must be peace."

"There," cried Gart.

Through the trees came the white wolf, and the rebels looked at her in awe as they saw the little human child riding on her back. Palla and Huttser could hardly believe their eyes. Their daughter had grown into a magnificent drappa. For a second the rebels thought that Slavka had suddenly come from the wood, so similar did Larka seem. Next to her and the strange bird was an old gray Varg.

"The human," hissed Slavka. "Quickly. Kill them. Kill them all."

Slavka snarled and, as Larka looked back at the rebel leader, she paused, for she seemed to see her own reflection.

"Release my parents, Slavka. They have done nothing to you. And now we come to help you."

The wolves were motionless. Palla and Huttser were both panting violently, their muzzles ranging around the circle as they wondered what the rebels would do. Even Gart seemed unable to decide.

"Gart," snarled Slavka, "obey me. Put an end to this evil."

Several of the rebels stepped up beside Slavka. Still Gart was motionless, and others seemed to be looking to him for guidance. But three wolves were looking to Huttser and Palla: Rar, Keeka, and Karma. Karma's eyes had touched Palla's, and there was a secret promise in them. The other rebels' startled gaze was locked on the child.

"You mustn't be frightened," growled Larka as she padded among them. "Fear and ignorance are your true enemies. We have come to help you. Help you fight Morgra and Wolfbane."

"Lies," snarled Slavka furiously. "What are you thinking? We are wolves."

But suddenly another voice fought Slavka's. "This Varg does not seem evil to me," growled Rar angrily. "And there has been enough cruelty and death, Slavka. She has risked the scavengers and the Night Hunters to save her parents and to help us all. If she has courage like that . . ."

The circle around Huttser and Palla broke as Larka and Bran came prowling among them. Tsarr growled dangerously, and again Skart came swooping through the air. As the eagle settled next to Larka, a great hush fell on the rebels. But Slavka broke it almost immediately.

"I will kill them myself."

Keeka and Karma sprang forward and stood side by side, barring her way.

"No," growled Karma proudly. For the first time in her life she was doing something she believed in.

"Traitors," snarled Slavka, backing away. "Are there traitors everywhere?"

"The only traitor, Slavka, is in your own heart."

Slavka hissed as Huttser spoke, but as she thought of that demanding voice in her mind, she shuddered too. "Gart," she said desperately, almost whining with self-pity, "you will help me. Loyalty always, Gart. Think of what the humans made me do to my cubs."

Gart was in an agony of doubt, but in that moment it was decided. If he had backed the leader more than half of the rebels would have followed him and there would have been a terrible fight. But Gart dropped his muzzle.

"I cannot, Slavka. Larka let me live."

Rar knew it was over. He nodded to some of the rebels, and immediately four of them stepped up around Slavka. The tide had turned. Larka dropped to the ground and, as she tilted her body, Bran slipped down onto the earth and sat there, smiling about him as though nothing at all had happened. As Larka backed away, the fascinated wolves began to pad forward. Bran looked up, suddenly surrounded by a circle of growling and whispering muzzles as the wildest of the Putnar gazed down at the little human.

Larka paused as she saw Huttser and Palla, and for a moment she remembered with anguish their fight on the ice. A pang of resentment quivered through her. But then she leaped toward her parents. They all came together, wagging their tails furiously and whimpering and whining with delight.

"And only a family that's loving and true," whispered Rar gravely as they watched them. "They are truly the ones."

◆ ◆ ◆

That night Larka lay watching her parents gravely as they slept. Slavka had been put under guard, though Larka ordered that she be treated with respect. But although Larka knew she had saved her parents, her heart was heavy with all she had seen at the massacre. With all that was happening to the Lera.

"You are with them again," growled Tsarr beside her, "that gives us hope."

"Hope, Tsarr?" said Larka. "The ancient verse is almost fulfilled. Wolfbane is here and death is all around us. The Searchers are abroad, doing her bidding. We are lost."

"No, Larka, we are not lost," whispered Skart urgently. "But you must try and close the pathways again. Stop what is beginning among the Lera."

"How, Skart?"

"You must howl to the dead yourself."

"You mean I should try and summon more of these Searchers myself?" growled Larka fearfully. "To do my bidding?"

"No, Larka," said Skart, flying down and hopping about them, "for in this world they bring nothing but fear. No, you must travel to the realms of the dead yourself. From there you must call back those who have entered our world."

Larka's eyes widened in horror, but she suddenly thought of Kar and what he had said about longing to know what lay beyond the life of the Varg.

"But how could I do such a thing?" asked Larka. "Morgra did not go anywhere when she summoned the Searchers. We heard her cry."

"This time the howl must be different," said Tsarr. "By howling Fenris's name, and then by carrying your voice into silence, you may follow the sound into the shadows."

"And you believe this place exists? And Tor and Va and Sita, they are there too?"

"That you must tell us."

Larka fell quiet.

"But it will take courage," growled Tsarr. His tail had come up and the wolf's old legs were trembling. "For know this, Larka. If you attempt this thing, it is fraught with danger."

Tsarr paused.

"What he means," said Skart, "is what Tsinga told him once. That you may not be able to return."

Larka blinked back at them both stupidly.

"You will need a strong root to this world," said Tsarr. "Something or somebody strong enough to bind you back. Those you love above all else, they must be with you. To call you back if the Searchers ever touch you. I am glad we have found Huttser and Palla again."

Larka was exhausted and, as they watched her, she slumped to the ground again, and gave herself up to sleep. At first Larka's dream was filled with pain. Bran was lying in the grass and, as she watched the little human, a shadow fell across its body. Larka began to shake, for in her sleep she knew it was the presence that frightened her more than anything now. It was a presence that she knew she would have to face. The Evil One.

But then Larka dreamed of Kar. He was talking to her quietly and his voice was strong and clear. "You mustn't fear, Larka," he was saying gently, as Fell had once done in her dreams. "Only fear can defeat us. Remember the pact we made. Have faith. And hope."

Larka stirred, for in her dream that face was exactly as she had seen it in the pool. Still Larka couldn't touch the nagging doubt inside her. What was it about Kar's face that made her wonder? But as Larka's mind stirred from the murky depths of sleep and rose toward the clarity of consciousness, suddenly she realized. "Of course," Larka cried as she opened her eyes and felt a thrill of real hope flow through her body. "Your fur, Kar, it was singed from the fire. You are alive."

Larka looked around, but it was raining heavily and the others were still asleep. She was thinking of Kar now and, as she thought of what lay ahead and remembered, too, all she had been through with Kar, the power of the Sight, the power to see other realities, came on her once more.

The images flashed before her eyes, leaping across the sheet rain that curtained in front of her. At first Larka saw a great sea, the same sea that Morgra had looked upon. Then Larka saw a forest and through the trees shapes were moving, swinging through the branches.

Then suddenly the forest was gone and Larka was looking at herself, but not as a reflection. She was somewhere high, high in the mountains, on the edge of a yawning chasm, filled with vicious rocks. As Larka padded along, she came to an old stone bridge that arched over the rocky void, and all around lay an eerie sight. She knew immediately they had been made by Man. The stones were regular, in crisscrossing lines that spread wide across the mountain. They were the remains of human dens. Larka remembered the castle, high above the valley where she had been born.

"Harja," murmured Larka, "the gateway to heaven."

The she-wolf could hardly take in all of what she was seeing. The stone dens lay everywhere, spread out across the rise of the mountain, stretching as far as the eye could see. In their first aspect, they gave the impression of unity and completion, but as Larka looked, she saw that most of them were broken down. Roofs had long fallen in, piling rubble among the walls of stone and the tall pillars that stood everywhere like ossified tree stumps.

Here and there among the pillars stood strange statues. Some had fallen from their plinths and smashed to pieces on the hard, formless earth. Others stood upright still, human forms that had been worked by long forgotten souls in their attempt to represent their lives. Some were so badly weathered that the human faces were worn completely flat, so that only their shapes remained, as an impression of what had been. There was something infinitely sad about these unmoving shapes. Something, too, that the she-wolf could not understand.

Larka watched herself drawing nearer to the stone bridge, and the enormous drop made the wolf's head reel. As she looked down, she felt her thoughts tumbling into the rocky abyss, spinning, falling helplessly into nothingness. Larka snarled and closed her eyes. There was a stillness about her, and everything was dark again.

When Larka opened her eyes, she was still looking at herself walking along the ravine. Larka saw herself pad onto the bridge and ahead of her was a strange statue that made her ears cock forward. It was a giant statue of a she-wolf and, at its stone belly, two suckling human infants. Larka noticed, too, a blue light all around her and, beyond, a giant moon, bright and still and perfectly full. The words of the verse entered her mind. "When the eye of the moon is as round as the sun."

As Larka watched, the hairs rose on the back of her neck, and her face curled into a snarl. Her whole body began shaking violently, and her eyes widened in horror. The pictures dissolved again, but her muzzle was dripping with rain and sweat and she was growling furiously.

"What is it, Larka?" cried Tsarr, stirring from sleep.

"Have you had a dream?" said Skart, opening his wings. "You are fretting about the path ahead."

"No, Skart," whispered Larka, "it was not a dream. I looked into the water . . ."

Skart turned nervously to Tsarr, and Larka suddenly swung her head toward Bran. She was recalling bitterly what Tsinga had once said about many not being able to bear living with such knowledge. The verse had said she would need courage. A courage as deep as despair. But not even Tsinga could know how true those words would be.

"Why, Larka, what did you see?"

"The future," answered Larka, "I have seen my own future."

In that moment the white wolf could not bear to tell her friends that the future she had seen was her own death.

PART THREE

THE CITADEL

13

KERL

I am! yet what I am none cares or knows,
My friends forsake me like a memory lost,
I am the self-consumer of my woes.
—John Clare, "I Am"

Quickly, we must travel back in time, on wings as fast as memory, back to Kar, and learn something of his own terrible journey. For what Larka had seen in the water was true. As the flames engulfed her friend, he had swung left and right growling in agony. The fire was everywhere, blinding him, burning his eyes. At last, in desperation, the wolf turned to a part of the forest where he thought the fire was at its weakest and hurled himself into the heat. The agony gripped him as his fur flamed, and he sprang through the air. But suddenly the flames were gone and Kar was rolling around and around in the snow.

The pain was rippling all over his body and practically all his fur had been burned away, but he was no longer on fire, and at least he was alive. For four suns the wolf lay there, sleeping feverishly, and when he woke he managed to lap at the snow for moisture. He got up and wandered around looking for Larka, but it had snowed again and her tracks were lost completely. For a while the wolf thought of returning to the human village to try and scavenge, but at last he set off, traveling he hardly knew where, his body still smarting with pain. It was after two more suns that Kar stumbled on an extraordinary sight.

It was a high wooden den with a sloping roof that stood on its own in a snowy meadow. Kar was reminded of the stave church, but where that had been as dark as the forest, this was colored as brightly as a spring field. Its back was painted with scenes of Man and animals, locked in some strange communion with the skies. In the heavens the people seemed to have changed into birds, for wings were sprouting from their backs, but below they had been cast into pits of burning air and flame, and around them wild animals tore at their flesh, pulling them earthward. Kar growled, but as he stood silently before the walls of the painted monastery, he understood nothing of this fable of judgment and redemption.

Kar suddenly thought of Tor and Fenris, and he wondered if they were the humans' gods, too, and if they believed that Man and Lera were connected. But as Kar looked at those wild beasts, tearing at Man's flesh, it did not seem to him that the humans who had built this place could believe that Man and the Lera were anything but enemies.

Kar padded on, and now he came to another human village, but this time the dens were broken down, charred and blackened in the snow. Though the wolf didn't know it, the Turks, pushing deep into Transylvania, had attacked one winter night and put the village to the sword. Thinking of the fire and all he had experienced of Man, Kar passed quickly on, but as he was coming to the end of the broken dens, he stopped.

Kar saw a strange den surrounded on all sides by poles made of the same substance as the crosses in the graveyard. The poles were buried deep in a line of even stones. On the hard ground inside was a shiny, rounded object filled with water. There were the last remnants of bone on the floor next to it, and the wolf blinked and growled as he looked at the prison.

Suddenly Kar heard a grunt, and a shape emerged from the den. It was the strangest dog Kar had ever seen. It was even taller than Kar, though really most remarkably thin. So thin in fact that Kar could almost see the ribs sticking out from its sides. Its legs were as slender as twigs, and fine long fur, which curled here and there into ringlets, hung about its body.

But strangest of all was its muzzle. It was so long and tapering that it seemed to go on forever, and to Kar's eyes made it look a little like a giant stoat. Yet despite the almost feminine delicacy of its body and bones, there was a tremendous vigor about it, too, a lean, springy energy that spoke both of strength and speed.

The dog was half asleep and did not notice Kar watching him through the bars. It yawned and, pushing its front legs forward across the floor of the kennel, its body dropped as it began to stretch. Its fine muzzle opened and its legs quivered with delight as it shook the energy through its muscles. Then it yawned again and opened its eyes.

As soon as it caught sight of the wolf, the dog began to growl furiously, and the barking that came from its throat seemed so loud that it could have broken open that slender frame. Another shape sprang from the den behind it immediately.

"What is it, Manov, have the masters returned?"

But the second dog spotted Kar too. Her body braced, but rather than barking, her eyes glittered hopefully.

"Hush, Manov," she whispered. "Perhaps it can help us."

"Help us?" snorted Manov. "Are you forgetting what we were bred for, Mitya? To be Putnar. We were born to drive the wild wolf from the land so that the grace and ease of the true dog may be bred into future generations."

Kar was amazed. Firstly, that he could understand the dogs at all, and secondly, that this creature had used the word Putnar.

"Oh, be quiet, you old fool," said Mitya irritably. "We can't hunt anything can we, stuck in this kennel? And if we don't eat soon there won't be any future generations. You and your breeding, Manov."

Manov seemed rather embarrassed, and he started muttering to himself. "But it's only breeding that matters, Mitya. Match the finest with the strongest. Allow only the best to survive, for the purpose they were intended. That's what our masters teach."

Mitya shook her head and came closer to the bars. "Forgive us," she said gently to Kar. "But since the humans fled the village, we've been cooped up here and it strains our nerves. By nature we are rather highly strung."

The wolf wanted to laugh as he looked at them, so absurd did they seem, but Kar liked this female immediately.

"What are you?" he growled.

"Borzoi, of course," answered Manov behind his mate, raising his head again, so high that he might have snagged his nose on the clouds. "Can't you use your eyes? Thoroughbreds, raised on the great northern steppes, for our speed and courage. Raised only by the greatest and most powerful of the humans. We are royal dogs and should be treated as such."

Mitya raised her own eyes to the heavens. "Don't mind Manov," she said as humbly as possible, although it wasn't really in her nature to be humble. "We need your help. If you don't help us, we'll be dead before long."

Kar padded closer and thrust his muzzle through the bars to sniff at the dogs, but as soon as he did so, Manov began to growl.

"What did I say?" he cried scornfully. "No breeding. No breeding at all."

"I don't know what you mean by this breeding," growled Kar. "But if it gives you legs and a muzzle like that, I'd rather be a wolf runt."

Manov leaped forward, barking angrily, and when he opened his long snout, Kar saw the sharpness of his teeth. But Kar would not allow himself to be intimidated by this absurd creature. He let the growl start deep in his stomach, rumbling up through his throat, until it exploded into an angry snarl that made Mitya shiver and back away. It was a strange and almost humorous sight—the wolf outside the cage, wild with an instinctive anger; the two borzois within, so refined and inbred that it seemed a gust of wind might blow them over. But suddenly Kar turned and, flicking his muzzle scornfully, he sprang away.

He heard Mitya scolding Manov as he ran, but he didn't look back. Kar was desperately hungry himself and, as he thought of what the borzoi had said and felt the anger in his belly, he wanted to strike out at something.

It was getting dark and Kar had begun to feel guilty about the dogs in their prison, when he came close to the remains of another human den. It was edged by a sheepfold and, as Kar approached, he felt a furious hunger rising inside him. There was no one about, and the sheep had begun to bleat pitifully as they sensed the Varg.

In a single bound Kar leaped over the fence, and almost as soon as he was among them, he felt anger overcome him. He had meant to take only one, but when he began to bite, a feeling mastered him, as liberating as it was violent. Kar swung left and right at the sheep, snarling and snapping blindly as the bloodlust took him. His head was swamped with their scent and, as they tried to get away from him, his anger consumed him.

Kar seemed to wake from a dream as he looked around. Five sheep lay dead already, bleeding on the snow. Kar was startled by his own ferocity and he shuddered. Suddenly he looked up and growled. For a moment, Kar fancied he had seen a wolf in the distance, watching him, yet as soon as he spotted it, it vanished.

Mitya was the first to see Kar again. He was padding toward the kennel in the coming morning, and he carried a haunch in his jaws. Manov tried to hide the gratitude in his eyes as Kar threw them the meat and lay down to watch them feed. That night found the wolf talking with Mitya in the shadows.

Kar told her the story of the legend and his own journey, then he asked Mitya and Manov of their own lives. They began to tell him of the lands to the northeast, that men call Russia, where the borzoi had been born and bred.

Kar growled excitedly as he learned of the sweeping land called the steppes and of the terrible winters that were even worse than those in Transylvania. Mitya told him of the giant landlocked lakes that would freeze as solid as stone, and the vast mountain chains that seemed to go on forever and ever. About humans, too, who always kept on the move and were known to the borzoi as the tamers of horses, though the humans call them Cossacks.

Manov and Mitya had lived for a long time with the Cossacks, and had slept in the open by their burning air, until they had been sold into their current slavery. They had watched the Cossacks' strange, wild ways, and listened as the humans gathered together in the evenings and picked up odd wooden objects, just as Larka had described the Gypsies carrying. These gave off wonderful, haunting melodies as the Cossacks danced and spun around and around with each other in the night.

Politely, Mitya avoided the matter of hunting and the purpose the borzoi had been bred for, but the wolf listened in amazement as he learned how the humans would choose characteristics in their animals and dogs and marry them together to produce more specialized qualities in their young.

"Then it's true," growled the Varg. "The only freedom runs with the wolf."

"I don't know why you say that, Kar," Mitya whispered almost indignantly. "I was suckled in a human den when my mother got sick. It's all I know. Sometimes Manov talks about living out there in the wild, but is wildness the same as freedom?"

Kar gave a low, unsettled growl.

"Out there," Mitya went on, dropping her eyes a little as she stared through the bars, "survival is difficult and your kind are hunted."

"Yes, Mitya," Kar nodded. "But all things are hunted, except perhaps Man, and it makes us strong. At least the wolf can roam where he will and choose his own den. At least he can howl to the mountaintops and hunt where he likes, and can never be tamed."

Mitya and Manov felt an odd stirring in their bellies.

"True." Mitya nodded. "But the humans hunt where they will too. And they are more successful at it than any Lera."

"Are you saying," growled Kar, "are you saying that you want to be like them?"

The borzoi paused thoughtfully. "No, Kar. But for some dogs their greatest ambition is to leave their kennels and go and live in the humans' dens."

"You mean that they live with the humans?" gasped Kar. "But what happens to them?"

"They grow tame," said Manov suddenly, looking at Kar with distaste again. Kar's eyes flickered. To him it seemed that Mitya and Manov were already tame, and he could not imagine what it could be like to live in close proximity to Man.

"But how could they do it? Live in the human dens with their burning air and all their strange smells?"

"They have comfort, too," answered Mitya gently. "And the humans are odd. I like many of their kind. Or at least I find, well, I find I am naturally drawn to them. Sometimes I think I could learn things from them." Mitya paused. A memory was flickering across her eyes. "There was one. A boy who used to look after me. He was kind and did not beat me as some of the others did. Sometimes, as I lay by the fire, he would put his hand on my head and it always felt strange as he stroked me. It calmed me, and he would let me look into his eyes longer than normal. . . ."

Kar cocked his head with surprise, but the strangeness of the idea passed.

"Well, I could never do such a thing as live with Man," grunted Kar.

"Don't be so sure. You are a wolf, Kar, and we are dogs, but we are not so different, you and I. We can talk to each other for a start, and there are many dogs I've met that still have the blood of the wolf flowing strongly in their veins."

"Bad breeding," whispered Manov scornfully.

Kar found the idea discomforting, but he felt that perhaps Mitya was speaking the truth. Despite what the borzoi had said of freedom, though, it was clear that they were desperate to get out of their cage. All night they kept whining bitterly and pushing at the gate, and though from the outside Kar tried to help them, leaping up and pressing on the bars with his long, slender legs, it was no use. Morning found them still together, and in the night Kar had crept back to the sheepfold and brought them more meat. Mitya was clearly very grateful, but Manov still kept looking at Kar angrily. Kar could stomach it no longer.

"Why do you hate my kind so, Manov?" he growled.

"Because of what you do," snorted Manov.

"And what is that? Hunt free and wild."

Manov's eyes flickered. "I was caged with a wolf once," he whispered coldly, "to the north when the humans had been fighting. But she knew only the freedom of killing, and I have never seen a Lera kill with such a will."

Kar's ears came up immediately.

"At first they fed us on mutton and scraps, but then," Manov shuddered strangely, "then the food they brought us . . . *that* I would have nothing to do with."

There was something horrified in the borzoi's look.

"Tell me," growled Kar.

"The humans," he said, "in their fights, they had captured many men, and one night they brought one down to the kennels and thrust him into the cage with us. It was clearly terrified. But the wolf went straight for the human's throat. After that, for suns they would bring down more of their prisoners and the wolf would gorge herself. The kennel floor was littered with human limbs and, as she grew fat, she kept watching the humans greedily, as though she were studying them. I remember her face well," said Manov, "with that torn ear and those terrible scars on her muzzle."

Kar suddenly felt a weakness grip him. "She said she knew of the humans?" he whispered to himself.

"She was a strange one," growled Manov. "She kept muttering about an energy filling everything. About a power that connected all. In the nights she would talk of death and laugh to herself. Then she would mutter things about the past. About some great injustice that had been done to her."

"Morgra," snarled Kar. "It was Morgra."

"One sun I approached her and asked her why she so delighted in killing the human Draggas. Why she hated Man so."

"What did she say?"

"She laughed in my face. 'Hate Man,' she answered, 'I do not hate Man. I feed on him because everything feeds on everything else. But far from hating him, I must learn from him. One sun I shall truly understand his mind. For there dwell the real secrets. The secrets of freedom and of life itself. For only Man's mind may look beyond the slavery of instinct, the slavery of the thoughtless Lera. The Lera that shall be my slaves.' "

"How did she escape?"

"One sun, after they had stopped feeding her, we noticed a child kept coming to the kennel to watch us, a girl. The she-wolf pretended to be ill and sickening, and lay there like a mild dog, whimpering pitifully. The girl seemed moved, and one sun she opened the cage. It cost the creature her hand."

Kar's discovery woke something terrible in the wolf, and in that moment he knew that he must find Larka. But Kar felt guilty at leaving the dogs behind and so, once more, he went to the sheepfold and piled as much food up for the borzoi as he could.

"Don't worry, Kar," said Mitya as he took his farewells of them. "I'm sure our human masters will return, when they think it safe enough and they remember about us. But you have helped us and we thank you."

Manov was staring at Kar haughtily, but as he looked at the fresh meat his expression softened.

"Take a rabbit for us, Kar," he growled grudgingly, "or a deer and get strong again. So it'll be a fair chase, eh, when we get out of here. But in the meantime I suppose . . . we wish you the joy of a free heart. Good luck."

As they watched the wolf padding off through the snow, Mitya turned to her mate. "I wonder, Manov," she whispered gravely, "what it would be like to be truly wild."

Kar wandered for suns and moons, and at first his heart lifted again. To be free was a wonderful feeling. To stretch his legs and run through the grass, to drink at the stream and watch the birds in the wintry sky. But one sun he strayed close to the humans' dens again and, as Kar approached a snowy field, he caught a terrible scent in his nostrils.

The wolf gasped as he came to a pit. It was filled with bodies. They were wolves. There must have been twenty or thirty of them. They were all dead, and the skin had been flayed from their carcasses. But among them, hidden beneath their bodies, there were dead humans, too, Turks that had been murdered by the local people and buried here in this wolf pit, to hide the crime.

The sight made Kar whimper and struggle for breath, and for suns after that he could hardly sleep. It had scarred his mind, and now a terrible wariness woke in him.

As Kar wandered in search of Larka, another feeling grew in his heart. A feeling he was totally unprepared for.

Loneliness. He noticed how the Lera responded to his passing. Most seemed terrified of him and would vanish into the snow or the trees when they caught the wolf's scent on the breeze. On Kar wandered and, as he did so, he began to scavenge. He was forced to hunt even the smallest Lera, and it taught him how hard it was to survive in the wild. The wolf felt the harsh edges of life and saw how, even in the damp, dark places in the forest untouched by the snows, a battle for survival seemed to be taking place that could never cease.

Loneliness gnawed at the Varg's heart and, as his isolation grew, he began to feel that everything was at once his enemy and the enemy of everything else. His burns had healed and his fur grew back, but Kar hardly noticed. He let his coat beome rough and unkempt, for not spending time with his own, he began to forget the habits of the wolf and would no longer sit to groom himself. He thought of Mitya and Manov, safe in their kennel, and wondered if all he had said of freedom was just a silly lie.

In the foothills of the mountains, he saw Balkar roaming through the trees, and he began to think that not only were the Lera isolated from one another, but that the Varg itself was his bitterest enemy. Then one cold sun he came upon a small pack. There was a dragga and a drappa and two youngsters with them. The sight reminded him of his own days as a cub and his tail lifted eagerly. But they were frightened and, fleeing from the Night Hunters, had seen much horror themselves. As soon as Kar neared them they leaped at him and drove him off, without once pausing to find out who he was or what he wanted.

It pushed Kar even further into himself. He began to

talk to himself as he walked, and at night he would sit on his own and howl to the skies. Often voices would come to answer him, the voices of other lone wolves that rose with the same searching longing, but these voices were not talking to one another, they were calling to themselves and their own pain. They were sounding an elegy for their own despair.

He climbed higher into the mountains and came to a cave by a frozen pool set in a bowl of hills that he stopped to explore. It was a strange place, dry and dusty, with a high-vaulting ceiling where bats hung like living fruit from the crevices. Kar felt an odd sense of peace and calm as he entered and, at its back, he found a pile of old straw and dead leaves that some other creature had used as bedding. He scented the place, but could smell nothing of the animal's life, so he lay down to rest.

As the suns passed, Kar settled into his cave, only venturing out to snatch a rabbit or mouse, or to scavenge for winter berries. He got thinner as the air grew sharper and, having nothing and no one to raise his spirits or share his vulnerability, Kar began to grumble and curse the elements themselves. The wolf's conversations with himself became more and more voluble, and Kar even began to fancy that there was somebody else in the cave with him.

One cold sun he found a bone outside his cave and he grabbed it eagerly. It was the shin bone of a horse, but it had no nourishment in it. Kar swung it around proudly and raised his tail, but suddenly he heard a noise in the trees nearby. His eyes grew wary and cunning.

"It's mine," he muttered loudly. "All mine. But I must keep it safe. Safe and secret."

Kar ran into the cave and, at the back of his home, began to scrabble at the dirt, digging a hole to bury his worthless find. He unearthed a large rock and placed the bone tenderly in the hole made by the space it had left. Carefully, he pushed back the soil with his muzzle. When he had finished, Kar felt deeply proud of himself.

That night Kar lay there, playing with the rock between his paws. As he tossed it from paw to paw, though, something strange happened. The flinty stone split apart and there, inside it, Kar saw a shape. It was like the skeleton of a small fish Kar had taken one sun, etched into the stone. Kar growled as he wondered how this thing had got here, how it came to be in the stone and on the mountain.

With the morning, Kar padded outside, over to the edge of the trees. It had begun to snow heavily, and he stood staring mournfully out over the land. The cold melted through his fur and made him shiver furiously, but as he returned to his cave, he looked back. For one flickering moment, Kar's heart beat faster. There were two sets of paw prints in the snow. But with anguish Kar realized that both the tracks were his own.

As winter grew even harsher, Kar lay brooding in his cave. He thought of Fell, and the guilt Kar felt wrestled with all the slights he had suffered from him as a cub. Kar thought of his murdered parents, too, and Huttser's treatment of him. The thoughts made him feel even more worthless, and he was growing so sick at heart that he hardly cared if he ate or slept. Instead, he would root around the floor of the cave and pick up pebbles and chew on them to hurt his teeth.

Kar's mind was filled with shadows, with dark questions that he could not answer. This cave, Kar's prison, was quite as bad as the kennel. Where iron bars had held Mitya and Manov, Kar's own mind had became his jailer.

Kar could not see how strange he had grown, for he would spend hours chewing pebbles and trying to talk to the bats roosting above him. He would walk in circles in the snow and try and fool himself that the prints were not his own, or stand for a whole sun gazing at a log, and asking what its shape meant.

Though he hunted still, he would also lie in wait for the Lera, even when he was not hungry, and spring out at them to scare them. As Kar saw them run for cover, or freeze in their tracks, he would turn around and around, growling and snapping at his tail delightedly.

Kar had no one to tell him that this behavior might be strange, or to look him in the eyes and hold his gaze and remind him of his life as an ordinary Varg. Kar had lost the living pool of company in which to view his own reflection. He no longer knew himself or what he was becoming.

But one sun, when the snow still lay on the ground, but the air had grown much warmer, Kar woke to the noise of growling outside. A gray wolf was standing there in the sunlight, looking around nervously. Though Kar hardly noticed it, he was desperately thin and he had a wound on his right flank, which, although already moons old, had barely healed. When the stranger saw Kar, his tail and ears came down submissively.

"May I shelter?" he whispered feebly. "I'm tired and very cold."

"No," snapped Kar. "Get away."

The stranger shivered, but he didn't move, and Kar began to growl.

"Please," said the stranger. "I need help."

"Help! Doesn't everything need help? Why should I help the Varg when all they do is kill each other?"

"I will die."

"We all die, fool. Tor and Fenris have made sure of that. Now go away, or I will get my friends the bats to bite you."

Kar turned and marched back inside. But later that sun, when he stepped outside again, the gray wolf was still there, lying helplessly in the snow.

"I'll kill you myself if you don't get out of here," growled Kar furiously.

"Then kill me. I'm finished, anyway."

Kar stepped forward, but he paused. He thought he recognized something familiar about this intruder, and Kar suddenly felt strangely embarrassed.

"Please yourself. But don't come any closer. This is my cave."

"Do you have food?" whispered the stranger faintly.

Kar's eyes glinted, and he thought of the bone he had hidden. "So that's what you want," he cried. "To steal my food."

"No, not steal it. But I'll die soon if I don't eat."

"Die, then," snorted Kar, going back inside. Only this time he was grumbling angrily to himself. As Kar tried to get some sleep, he felt unnerved. He tried to push the stranger from his mind, but he couldn't manage it, and he began to talk to himself so loudly and angrily that the bats grew furious at the chatter and suddenly took wing, exploding from the hollow chamber in a flurry of black indignation.

As light began to filter into the cave and the bats returned from their hunting, settling peacefully on the crevices above him, Kar got up and picked up some spare meat. Outside he tossed it almost resentfully to the stranger, but as he lay down and watched him eat, Kar felt a sense of peace descend on him, and he was glad that he had overcome himself. Later that sun he gave the stranger more food and when he thanked him, rather than snapping at him, Kar just nodded. That night the air grew colder again, and it began to snow once more and, as Kar turned to go inside, he stopped. "I suppose you can come inside."

The stranger picked himself up slowly and limped after Kar into the cave.

"How long have you lived here?" asked the wolf, looking around him.

"I don't know. It's fine, though, isn't it?" answered Kar proudly. "And it's mine, so don't you forget it."

"I should say it's rather lonely," said the stranger softly. "It must be lonely being a Kerl."

Kar's ears cocked up in surprise at the word. But the stranger was right.

As he slept that night, Kar was oddly comforted that there was another wolf in the cave, but he had a terrible dream too. It was of Fell and the ice, and angry faces glared at him accusingly in his sleep. Huttser was there and Palla and the old blind fortune-teller. When he woke he was drenched in sweat, and a yawning guilt hovered about him.

"But you must miss company," the stranger said as they lay together in the morning.

"Sometimes," muttered Kar irritably. "But I have my own thoughts."

"I can imagine," said the stranger, looking around him and shivering.

"They're no worse than my thoughts out there in the real world. Besides, I'm cursed."

An odd, melancholy look came into the stranger's eyes. "Like my poor sister," he muttered sadly.

Kar looked up. The recognition he had felt the sun before had woken in Kar's mind again, and he suddenly got up.

"Who are you?"

"My name is Skop."

Kar's eyes opened in astonishment. "Skop," he cried. "Skop. But . . . but don't you recognize me?"

Skop rose, too, now and peered back at Kar through the shadows. Kar did not realize that his singed fur had changed his features, and also he had grown since Skop had left him.

"It's me, Skop, Kar."

The wolves' muzzles were almost touching now and their tails wagged furiously as they examined each other in the cave. Their memories came flooding back with the scent now filling their nostrils.

◆ ◆ ◆

"I had to leave you, Kar. I couldn't look after you properly, and I wanted to help the rebel pack fight Morgra. I made sure you had a good home."

Kar felt no real bitterness anymore. They had spent two whole suns talking together, and already the company had worked its own small miracle on the Kerl. Kar had learned that Skop had never found Slavka and the rebels, but had got lost in the winter and for moons had wandered alone.

"You have suffered, Skop," growled Kar quietly.

"All the wolves have suffered, Kar. The Balkar ambushed me in the mountains. I fought them off, though this wound still won't heal."

Skop tried to lick his side, and Kar winced at the sight of the livid cut. Now Kar had Skop with him, he found a new purpose. As spring came, he went hunting again for game for his friend. The wolf took a young roe deer seven suns later and brought the meat proudly to Skop.

"That's more like it, Kar. You're behaving like a real Varg again. Will you do something for me, though? Will you go outside and look at yourself in the water?"

Kar looked into the rippling water and hardly recognized himself. His muzzle was thin and gaunt. His eyes were sunken and glassy, and the fur around his ears was wild and disheveled. From that moment on, Kar began to groom himself and to eat properly, yet the greatest healer was talking to Skop.

As he listened to Skop, Kar was staggered at his lack of bitterness. Skop hated the Balkar, but the hatred had not eaten him up as Kar had been consumed by what he had seen. Kar realized that Skop had some philosophy that had protected him from his own experience, and as Kar listened and talked, his own heart and mind began to heal. But Skop's wound was growing even worse. It had become infected and caused him terrible pain.

As summer approached, the wolves felt something of the bonds they had known in their pack being gradually restored. They were sitting together outside one warming sun when Skop told him a secret. He had learned from a lone wolf that Kar's brothers had been killed in the Balkar camp. Kar lay there growling bitterly.

"Skop," he whispered at last, "do you know what's become of Huttser and Palla?"

"No. I heard nothing of them. I would like to see them again."

"And Larka?"

Skop shook his muzzle as he looked out toward the forests and the giant mountains. Kar gazed out there, too, and as he did so, he felt a sudden tugging at his heart, but a sense of certainty also, that Larka was still alive.

All that sun Kar thought of Larka, and that night he dreamed of her. But it wasn't a dream of their childhood, when they played together at the Meeting Place. They were walking quietly together and, as they stopped in the grass, Larka suddenly turned and rubbed her muzzle against his. He felt a great sense of peace and of place at her side. When he woke, for the first time in as long as he could remember, he felt happy. Kar's happiness did not last. When he got up, he found that Skop was shaking terribly, although it was hot outside. His eyes were open, but they had a distant look.

"Skop?"

"This wound, Kar. It has poisoned my blood. It won't be long now."

"But you can't leave me, not now."

"We all leave one another in the end," said Skop sadly. "That is Tor and Fenris's way. But maybe we shall meet again. If Tor and Fenris's forests exist."

"But Skop—"

"Don't be sad, Kar. At least I will not die alone, and you have done my heart good. By helping me, even before you knew who I was, you restored my dwindling faith. But promise me this. When I am gone you will leave this place. In my travels I met many lone wolves and many of them were happy, but the life of a Kerl is not for you. Look after yourself, Kar. Love yourself."

"I promise," said Kar, thinking suddenly of Larka.

"Then go in search of your family, Kar, and if you ever see Palla again tell her . . . well, you know."

"I'll heal you, Skop," said Kar suddenly, "I'll—"

"Oh, my friend, it would take a miracle to heal me now."

Kar laid his head on the cave floor as he gazed out at the world. "And there are no miracles, are there, Skop?" he whispered bitterly.

But Skop lifted his head again. "Don't be foolish, my friend," he growled softly. "Can't you see? It's all a miracle."

It took three more suns for the poison to do its work, but when it was finished, Kar noticed with surprise the look of peace that lay on Skop's muzzle. His own heart was choked with pain, though, and the howl that rang through the cave sent the bats wheeling into the air. For a whole sun he stood there, suddenly alone again.

He picked up a few pebbles in his mouth and began to toss them angrily around the cave, and when the bats returned he growled and snapped at them furiously. The loneliness was even more terrible than before. But as he lay down to sleep that night, something else came to his rescue. He dreamed of Larka again, and the next sun he stood staring down at himself in the pool outside.

"I need others," he growled to himself, "for good or bad. That is my nature. I need her."

But as Kar thought of the wolves out there, and of the Night Hunters who had murdered his parents and his brothers, a terrible anger rose inside him.

"I'll avenge you all," he cried. "Whatever I do."

Kar padded back into the cave and looked at the wolf lying there on the floor of the home where he had nearly gone mad. He hated to leave him in that hollow stone grave, but his mind was made up. He blessed Skop for having helped him and wished him a safe journey. Before he turned to leave, Kar looked up at the bats hanging in their crevices. "Guard him, my friends, guard him well."

Kar traveled for several suns, and he began to climb higher and higher into the mountains. On the wide, flat plains to the south, Kar looked down and saw more evidence of Man and their battles: fields flecked with fire, stone dens in ruins, horses thundering through the dust. As he traveled into the woods, he began to notice the Lera again and shuddered at what he saw, as he remembered the words of the legend.

What has happened? thought Kar. *Am I too late?*

But at last Kar came to a place that made him gasp with horror. In the valley of Kosov the dead rebels lay everywhere, their torn carcasses already dissolving into the earth. Kar shivered and passed on, his thoughts even more urgently on Larka.

Kar could not know that the Greater Pack had already been defeated, or that Morgra had used the ancient howl to open the Pathways of Death. He could not know that the power to look into minds had entered the world, or that the Searchers were abroad, touching the Lera and filling the animals with horror and guilt and confusion.

The next night Kar woke suddenly among the trees. Again he had dreamed of Larka. It was a beautiful night with a moon shining through the canopy of leaves, but though the weather whispered of warmth and ease, Kar's heart was heavy. He didn't know what the feeling was. If it were true or not. It had come on him suddenly and, though he thought somewhere that he was imagining it because he had dreamed of Larka, he couldn't shake it off.

It was like a sick feeling in the pit of his stomach, a queasiness, a sense of betrayed responsibilities. But as he lay there and listened, Kar felt a tingling, just as Huttser had felt that sun approaching the cave when Khaz had spotted Morgra's tracks above the den. Something was calling to him. That sense that all the Lera know. Beyond sound or sight or scent: instinct.

"The pact," whispered Kar. "I have forgotten the pact."

14

THE RED MEADOW

They stood begging to be the first to make the voyage over.
Their hands outstretched in yearning for the farther shore.
— VIRGIL, *The Aeneid*

"BUT HE ESCAPED THE FLAMES?"

"Yes, Father," nodded Larka, "of that I'm certain now.
I saw it in the water." Larka shuddered. What else had she
seen in the drizzling rain?

As her parents lay beside her, shielded by the trees,
Larka appeared changed almost beyond Huttser and
Palla's understanding. It was more than the natural dis-
tancing of parent and child. She had grown far more serious with the terrible responsibility that afflicted her.

"So Kar, too, is alive," growled Huttser. "Fenris is kind."

It was ten suns since Larka had saved them from the
combat and seen the vision of her own death at Harja. Her
coming had worked a dramatic transformation among the

rebel pack. Though they all felt something of fear as they watched the odd little party, they had begun to hope again at Larka's coming, and they kept talking of the family and a deliverer.

Seeing how helpless Bran was, they had grown less fearful of the legend of the Man Varg. They could no longer refute the power of the Sight after what they had seen of the Searchers, and some even started to mutter that Larka should find the entrance to the citadel and look into the human's mind herself. They had argued over which wolf would have the privilege of guarding Bran. They all wanted to hunt for it, too, and the little child had begun to grow quite fat. It seemed to have no fear anymore and, as the wolves came up to marvel at it, Bran would reach out with his searching hands and tug at their fur or smile and pat their muzzles.

Larka had gone to speak quietly to Slavka and tried to convince her that her hatred of the Sight was misplaced. As she told Slavka of her own journeys with Skart and what she could see in the water, Slavka's eyes had grown as large as they had done when she had seen the Searchers come. But as Slavka listened to Larka, again that voice crept into her mind. Just as it had done the night before she made Huttser and Palla fight. This time the words were different, though.

"So," they whispered, "at last we have the child too. Wait, Slavka. Wait and watch."

Now Larka got to her feet and smiled down fondly at her parents. "I must leave you now. Tsarr and Skart must tell me more of the rite—of howling to the dead."

"But when you return," growled Palla, trying to reassure her daughter, "at least then we shall face Morgra together, as a family once more."

As Larka turned and looked out on the beautiful day, she suddenly trembled—not with fear this time, but with a strange, tender passion. A passion carried on the breeze stirring around her, for the trees and the grass, for the air and the clouds. For all the things of this world. For all the things that her vision had told her she must lose.

In that moment Larka's heart stirred and beat faster, and she longed to know if the Sight could carry her to the truth of everything, to a union with all, not just the Lera but the insects and flowers, the plants and the trees and the earth. Even the stones themselves. Did they have a nature she could touch too? But as she reached out with her senses and looked out through the trees, Larka felt afraid. But not of Morgra. Not of Wolfbane or the Searchers. She was afraid because somehow to look out on the world like this, and to love it so very much, wounded Larka to her soul.

That night Larka slept near Tsarr and Skart, and dreamed of her vision on the bridge. But as she dreamed, something strange happened. Larka fancied, as she lay there, that she could hear real voices in her head. Not one voice but twenty, thirty voices whispering through the trees. They muttered of the legend, of the Searchers, and the citadel. They spoke of hope and victory. It was as though the rebel pack were talking to her as one mind.

"You are touching the truest power, Larka, of seeing into the minds of others," growled Tsarr as light began to rib the trees. "You were listening to the rebels' dreams. The power has entered the world with the Searchers. It is time, Larka."

"Yes," said Skart, "and you must carry hope with you as you go. But your parents are here to help you return."

What point is there in returning? thought Larka suddenly, but she kept the thought to herself.

"Tsarr," she said to the old wolf, "is there a way to change the future?"

"Perhaps," he answered softly.

Larka lifted her searching eyes, but she shook her head sadly. "Then it is not the future, Tsarr. Then the Sight lies."

"Now it is the future," insisted Tsarr. "All that happens to us Larka, all that marks our journey through Fenris's forests, has it not been made by what has gone before? But if we could return to the past, affect it in some way, then perhaps the future could be different as well. Perhaps they may tell you there how to alter what is to come, in the realms of death."

Larka lifted her muzzle. She remembered something Palla had said of her friend Karma and breaking patterns.

"Return to the past?" said Larka. "Before Morgra ever came, Tsarr, or before my mother's parents ever drove her out? Before the legend ever began?" But for a moment hope flickered across Larka's face.

Skart spoke, "And you must listen to those who love you if they call. Huttser and Palla."

But Larka was suddenly thinking of another wolf. "Kar," she breathed.

Tsarr and Skart began to tell Larka more of the ancient rite of howling to the dead. Tsarr's fur bristled as he described the most important part of Larka's preparation. She must attempt her journey after a kill and lay fresh meat at her side as she howled, for its shadow would follow her beyond, and then the dead Putnar would catch its scent and come at her bidding. Tsarr told Larka that she must allow only one specter to eat, and only after she had commanded it to answer her questions. Then Larka could demand to know how she might affect her own fate and how the Searchers could be recalled. How the Pathways of Death could be sealed once more.

As Tsarr told her these strange secrets, Larka's thoughts turned to Fell. Meeting him frightened her most of all. As soon as Larka mentioned her brother, Skart grew frantically nervous. It was by no means certain that he would come, but the eagle warned her that if she reached the place of the dead she must not let any specter touch her, for then she risked being lost forever.

But of all the warnings they gave her, the one they stressed most was this: All the while she was among the specters, she must listen for those who waited for her on this side and come as soon as they called her back. For to deny them would be to deny life itself.

That sun, Larka padded off on her own to think and to prepare herself inwardly for her fearful journey. Below the camp a plain opened around a wide river that swept out toward the distant trees. The she-wolf could see the water glinting in the sunlight as she crept stealthily from the woods, looking about her all the while. The day was bright and fresh, and Larka's view ran clear into the shadow of the forests beyond. Larka suddenly stopped. As she looked out, she realized there were no Balkar to be seen anywhere, and only a pair of falcons were circling in the blue, as a flock of sheep grazed by the edges of the distant woods.

Morgra, why has she stopped hunting us? wondered Larka.

The she-wolf paused and breathed in. She could scent summer powerfully on the breeze, and the rich textures of swelling life quivered in her nostrils. As she thought of little Bran in his cave and wondered what Morgra was doing, she suddenly felt a desperate pang for the child, and Larka knew that she loved it.

That night the rebels muttered among themselves. They, too, wondered why Morgra was no longer hunting them, and the rumor had spread of what Larka was about to do. Skart became more and more anxious as he perched in the trees, watching Larka with his hard yellow black eyes.

Larka was almost ready to begin her journey, but first she went to see Slavka. The rebels looked at Larka hopefully as she padded through camp, growling a greeting or wagging their tails, but there was little cheer in Larka's heart. She found Slavka lying by a beech tree, guarded by two rebels and by Keeka and Karma.

"Slavka," Larka growled as she padded up.

As the older wolf looked up, Larka was surprised to see that there seemed to be a new openness in Slavka's gaze.

"Slavka." I must learn what you know of these human dens in the mountains. Morgra seems to have stopped hunting and, if those dens are Harja—"

But Slavka interrupted Larka immediately. "Larka," she growled and her eyes narrowed. "First I have something to tell you."

Larka's thoughts were too consumed with Morgra and her imminent journey to notice the glitter of cunning in Slavka's eyes.

"Well?"

"I doubted the Sight, Larka," growled the rebel leader, shaking her head. "I was a fool to do so. Even after you came I wanted to kill the child."

Larka looked up the slope to the cave where little Bran was sleeping. Rar was standing outside, waving his tail proudly as he protected their charge. The child was safe.

"But now, Larka," Slavka went on, "now I see that there is real danger of the legend coming to pass. You are this white wolf the legend foretold. And your parents, Huttser and Palla, . . ."

Slavka lowered her eyes. "I am bitterly sorry for what I nearly made them do. I would serve you, Larka. I offer you the greatest gift I have. My loyalty."

Larka hesitated, but Keeka had got to her feet and her tail was wagging delightedly.

"I would have you on my side, Slavka," nodded Larka, "as would your rebel pack. They never wanted to betray you."

"Then let me help you. There are still a few rebels who doubt you. Let me talk to them, Larka. Let us fight side by side."

Larka shivered at her words, but she needed friends more than ever, and Slavka's bold face, so like her own, suddenly filled her with hope.

"Very well," she said, "you are free to wander through camp, Slavka. To talk to the rebels."

Slavka nodded gravely. "You will not be sorry."

As Slavka prowled away, none of them saw that her face was bright with scorn. But, as she went, Karma turned suddenly to Larka. "Larka," she growled in her deep, rich voice, "you mustn't trust her."

"You're wrong, Karma," said Larka softly. "We must all trust and have faith in one another."

Darkness had descended over Transylvania, weaving its fingers through the trees and stroking the meadows with night, when Larka made her kill. She found a spot away from the rebels in a sheltered hollow, ringed by oak trees, and lay the meat from an old ewe in front of her. Tsarr and her parents stood watching her gravely as she lay down in the hollow, and Skart's hard eyes were studying Larka more intensely than ever.

"This may take suns," whispered Tsarr to Palla and Huttser, "but if they try to keep her, if that time ever comes, you must call to her. Call to her with all your love and never give up."

"I would give anything to save my daughter," growled Palla, thinking back to everything Tsinga had said in the Vale of Shadows, "even if it means my own death."

"It is not your death we need now, Palla," growled Tsarr, "but your life."

The three of them padded over to Larka and, as Tsarr settled a little way off, Huttser and Palla lay down in front of their daughter. They hardly noticed Skart ruffling his feathers next to them. His hooked beak had begun to bob up and down and his talons were digging into the ground.

"Larka," said Palla softly, "if you go . . . if you go there and see . . . him."

"Yes, Mother."

"Tell him we still . . ."

Palla dropped her muzzle hopelessly, and Larka suddenly felt a burning tenderness for her parents.

"Very well, then," she said. "It begins. And as everything begins, it begins in sleep."

Larka laid her head on her paws. The meat lay in the grass in front of her. She was falling deeper and deeper into sleep. Midnight had passed when Larka stirred and her nose twitched. Palla shivered as she heard Larka begin to growl. Suddenly Larka lifted her head. She was still asleep, for though her ears were pricked and her muzzle moved back and forth as though searching for something in the darkness, her eyes were clamped tightly shut.

"It's beginning," growled Tsarr.

The fur on Larka's coat began to bristle, and she lifted her head higher. Her mother and father could see the fine white hairs rippling along her throat. Larka tipped back her muzzle and, though her eyes were still closed, she opened her mouth.

"Fenris," she snarled. "Fenris."

The howl that suddenly rose into the air made the rebels start in their camp. It came from the depths of Larka's belly and climbed angrily into the night. It shook through the trees and hovered in the air. Out of all the calls of the wolf it was like none that Huttser and Palla had ever heard, even that night when the Searchers had come. Rar heard it, too, and it was so strange that he prowled out of Bran's cave and came down the slopes to listen.

"Larka," he whispered to the breeze, "take care."

But suddenly Larka's call seemed to stop. Larka's throat

was still moving, her head lifting, her muzzle opening to howl, but the sound had vanished into silence.

"Now she's really calling," growled Tsarr, awe in his voice. "Now she is howling to the dead."

Larka's head slumped onto her paws. As it dropped, Skart did something extraordinary. He hopped forward and began to peck at Larka's tail with his great clawed beak.

"What are you doing, Skart?" snarled Huttser, infuriated.

Larka looked like carrion as Skart pulled at the she-wolf's fur, but the bird would not be distracted. He plucked and pecked at Larka's tail, jabbing and pulling frantically. Tsarr was standing now, growling angrily too.

"Have you gone mad, Skart?" he cried, but as Tsarr thought of the legend, a terrible notion sprang into his mind.

"No, Skart, it can't be, not you."

Those words were ringing in Tsarr's ears, "Beware the Betrayer, whose meaning is strife." Still Skart went on and, when he turned to face the wolves, there were tufts of Larka's fur sprouting from his beak. Suddenly, overcome with a fury for his helpless daughter, Huttser hurled himself at the eagle.

But the great bird opened his wings and lifted away. Into the air he rose and, as the wolves dwindled to specks beneath him, his anger beat the air. His mind was ringing with one thought alone as his piercing eagle eyes began to scour the land below.

◆ ◆ ◆

As Larka lay in the hollow, Bran was huddled asleep in the cave. The shadow of a wolf suddenly fell across the child's body. It growled, and as it padded through the entrance toward the child, the wolf licked its lips and its eyes glistened angrily. It prowled slowly around the human, and its mouth dribbled as its hot breath stroked the bare skin.

"So," it whispered bitterly, "the greatest of all killers."

But even as Slavka opened her powerful jaws, remembering her cubs and feeling the hate burn in her belly, something new came into her eyes. An emptiness. The wolf seemed to be wrestling with herself, and her legs and tail quivered frantically, but at last the energy went out of her and she dropped her muzzle submissively.

"Very well," she growled helplessly, "so be it."

Slavka was answering a distant voice. A voice that echoed in her brain. Bran opened his eyes and Slavka's muzzle curled into a snarl again. Her ears flattened on her head as she dropped on her forepaws by the human.

"Come, child," she whispered. "Travel with me."

As Bran felt the heat of hate in Slavka's body, he started to wail and great tears came rolling down his little cheeks.

"Hush," growled Slavka angrily, "they'll hear you. Climb on my back or I will snap through your throat."

Still Bran went on crying.

"Come now," Slavka whispered coaxingly, as she licked Bran's face. "Trust me, child. You must trust me now. We'll steal away from this place. I'll take you to those who would care for you properly. Who can really love you."

Bran's sobs began to subside, and Slavka tilted her body closer. For a moment the child's eyes were filled with an instinctive doubt, but so similar were Larka and Slavka that he was confused. Suddenly he turned and started to scramble onto Slavka's back. Slavka shuddered as she felt him clutching at her fur, but she rose. Her eyes were completely lost.

"Now, Larka," she hissed, and it was as though the voice was not her own, "now we shall truly see."

Larka was in a dark place, like a tunnel or a pathway walled with shadows, like the stairway that, in her youth, she had looked up with her brother to the strange castle. She was walking slowly, and around her pine trees tore into the sky. The meat from her kill was in her mouth, and the air was cold and still.

As she walked, her eyes began to grow accustomed to the darkness and she realized, instinctively at first, that there were other wolves in the trees with her, silvery ghosts that haunted the woods. As she saw them, a petrifying fear came over her. At first they did not attempt to approach, but more and more seemed to be following her, drifting after her through the trees.

"Courage," whispered Larka to herself. "I must have courage."

It felt to Larka as if she was holding onto some blind hope, or to a truth that the whole world was trying to deny.

Light began to come, but as it grew, Larka shivered, for there was no heat in it. It seemed to make the woods even more fearful as the air took on a yellowy pallor, while the objects that it lit seemed drained of color, gray and lifeless. Larka felt a terrible gloom enter her mind, and her legs began to tremble. The trees around her were thinning, and Larka saw more of the spectral wolves. Then, suddenly, the avenue came to an end, and Larka gasped.

She was on the edge of a huge meadow, ringed by giant trees. The trees' shapes were as dim and gray as the specters and, at a distance, they might have been forms glimpsed in sleep. The sky was pallid and sickly, and even the grass looked colorless and white, like straw bleached by the sun. Yet there was color here, as shocking as a wound, for the whole meadow was filled with poppies and, though their stalks were gray, their fragile tops, like the wings of mingling butterflies, were a bright and brilliant red.

Larka dipped her head as she looked on that great sea of bloodred flowers. She felt confused, for the meadow was both beautiful and terrible. Then, as Tsarr had instructed her, Larka threw the mutton in her mouth on the grass and howled. The sound that lifted from her own mouth across that strange field made the she-wolf quake. It was muffled and dull, like a cry lost against the wind. But as she howled, Larka realized that shapes were suddenly moving toward her through the flowers.

From every side of the meadow came the specters, drifting through the poppies, their flanks brushing against the velvety flowers. They had the same shadowy quality as the wolves in the trees, and they all looked gray and pale. Larka trembled as she saw the armies of the dead trooping toward her, for now she made out their eyes and, though they were not red as they had been in Kosov, they all had the same lost and glassy look. Yet in those empty orbs Larka saw something else, a look of hunger, and she realized that they were all scenting the cold air. They were being summoned to her by the meat.

"Come," cried Larka in a commanding voice.

Her parents, watching her lying there in the hollow below the rebel camp, saw her lift her sleeping head again.

On came the flow of spectral wolves, and soon the meadow was entirely filled, but still they came. But as they drew closer, Larka began to growl. As the nearest of the wolves closed in on the meat, Larka howled again and cried out, "Stop, you may come no farther. The living commands you."

The wolves all stopped. Their eyes seemed to look through her as they, too, began to growl. A whispering went up through the poppies, and Larka realized they were speaking as one. "Meat," they murmured like a wind, "meat."

Larka shivered again, but she fought back the terrible fear.

"Yes, I bring meat," she stammered, "from the other side. But only one may taste."

The wolves that ringed Larka began to growl again, for they were wrestling with their hunger, but it was plain that they were frightened too. Suddenly one of the specters stepped forward. His face was scarred and Larka realized, with amazement, that she had seen him among the rebel dead in the valley of Kosov. Around him now she began to see other rebels, and the Night Hunters that had died, too, standing calmly at their sides.

"I would eat," he growled, scenting the air hungrily. The wolf's hollow eyes were staring at the meat, as bright and red as the poppies.

"Tell me then first," whispered Larka, "what is this place?"

"This place? We do not really know. Some call it the Red Meadow and some call it the Field of the Dead."

In the foothills above Kosov, Kar was running. Over the past suns he had hardly slept and had kept constantly on the move, running as long as his stamina held out, never once pausing to hunt or scavenge. Instinct told Kar to hurry, but he hardly knew why or where. A voice inside kept whispering to him, like the voices he had heard in the cave.

Kar rested that night in a wide clearing, and as he woke to the dawn, he suddenly heard a cry high above. Among the shifting clouds, he saw a tiny shape wheeling in distant circles. Around it went and around, and as he watched, it grew larger and larger. It was coming toward him.

The bird sailed straight into the clearing and settled on the ground in front of him. Kar was amazed; he had never known such a large bird of prey to approach a wolf before. Its huge eyes seemed to be examining Kar's features, looking for a sign, and then it nodded and hopped forward. There was something in its beak, which it dropped on the grass in front of Kar. The wolf wanted to pounce on the eagle, but he stopped as he realized that what the bird had brought him was fur. Kar cocked his ears. Slowly he pushed his muzzle toward the fur and sniffed at it. In an instant he was on his feet as her scent filled his nostrils.

"Larka," he gasped. "Larka."

Skart nodded frantically and took quickly to the air again. As Kar looked up, Skart swooped over his head, and Kar realized that the eagle wanted him to follow. Kar leaped after him, running as fast as his paws could carry him.

"Larka," he cried frantically. "Larka is in danger."

"And you are the dead?" Larka asked in the meadow.

The wolf paused and looked up. "Not as you might understand it. We are the Searchers. Specters of the dead, shadows."

So distant was that lifeless voice, it was as though Larka was talking to herself.

"Then . . . then you are not real?"

"Perhaps we are as real as your memories or your dreams."

Larka's eyes opened as she stared back. She remembered something Tsinga had said about the power of memories.

"Then this is not where the dead go?"

"Oh no," answered the wolf, turning his head wistfully toward the forest. He paused. "But of that I may not speak. Of that none may speak."

"But tell me where you come from. Is it like this? Are Tor and Fenris—"

"Peace," snarled the wolf, beginning to back away fearfully. "This you may not know. This the living can never know."

The spectral wolves around him had also begun to retreat.

"But what are you?"

"I have told you. We are the shadows of the dead, the dead you have seen. Like your memories."

"But if you are no more than memories you cannot help me."

"No more?" said the wolf, looking at her strangely. "Have you learned nothing on your journey, Larka? We may help you to know the world of the living, but there your questions must cease."

"Very well," said Larka. "The Pathways of Death. May I seal them again? May I call those that have crossed into our world back into the realm of shadows?"

The spectral wolf looked grave. "The pathways are open and, with the Searchers, the true power of the Sight has entered your world. Morgra has used it to send our kind out to do her bidding already. But only once the altar has tasted blood can they be commanded again. Then the pathways can be sealed."

Larka shivered. "Then tell me. I have had visions. But the things I see—are they real? Can I really see the future? The bridge and the ruins that I saw. Do they exist?"

"Oh yes. It is the ancient place of pilgrimage, Harja. Where the altar lies. You will see it again very soon."

"So it is Harja. Father says it lies very close, in the higher mountains. Guarded by a stone face."

"That is true. But there are two ways in. The second is an entrance lost long ago. To the east of the face. A tunnel by a stream that leads right through the mountain. At Harja, the Vision will come if the child is placed on the altar, but only at the moment the moon reaches its zenith. For the legend, Larka, like Tor, is itself a thing of moonlight."

Larka shivered, for again she was remembering her vision on the bridge and the giant moon that had illuminated it. That had illuminated her own death.

"And is it really the gateway to heaven?"

"Heaven," muttered the wolf strangely, and he seemed not to understand.

"But am I to die there?" Larka whispered, dropping her head.

"If you have seen it," answered the specter coldly, "it is almost certain."

"Almost?"

Larka's head came up. The specter hesitated. He was staring at the meat. "These are dark matters, Larka. For most a future is made by the things that have gone before. But for you . . . You alone have visited us. You have commanded us in the Red Meadow. You have made us real again. Perhaps that itself will change what is to come."

"Then there is hope?"

The wolf looked at her strangely. "For the living there is always hope. Must be hope, Larka. But remember. The path is narrow and the farther you journey along it the narrower it may become."

Larka nodded, and the specter came closer. His muzzle was straining toward the meat.

"There is more I would ask. I must face Morgra. But there is one with her. One I fear. I see him only as a great darkness, a terrible evil. Wolfbane. I know he is waiting."

"Wolfbane is waiting," said the wolf coldly. "And you should fear him above all else. For he is more dangerous to you than any other. But to end it, you must face him, and you must face him alone. None can aid you there."

Larka growled.

"One more thing," she said. "Tell me of Man."

The specter backed away a little.

"Does Man have a third eye, an eye that can see more than the Lera?"

The wolf nodded.

"But his power. Where does it come from?"

"The power of Man, beyond his hands and his machines," whispered the wolf gravely, "is the power of memory and of knowledge, and the power of imagination."

Larka cocked her head in surprise. "To remember," she muttered, "to remember those we love and lose. To remember the horror?"

"Not just the memory of his life, but of all human lives that have been," growled the wolf, "and the memory that lies sleeping in all things. Not simply in Man's memories but in the very force that makes up his being. For there lie the greatest secrets of the past, and so of the future too. Not just the past that seems to end in the Field of the Dead. But the ancient past!"

As Larka looked at the Field of the Dead before her, she suddenly felt a great anguish.

"You are called the Searchers . . ." Larka hesitated. "But what is it you really seek?"

In the Red Meadow, the spectral wolves lifted their heads as one. "Justice," they moaned, and their voices shook the poppies. "Justice and truth."

"Very well," Larka whispered to the rebel specter. "You have earned your reward. You may eat."

The others looked jealously at the wolf, but as he stepped forward, he stopped.

"Listen to me," he growled suddenly, and as he did so, a great longing entered his voice. "Wolfbane. You said that you see him as a darkness. An evil. Very well. He believes he knows of the darkness of the Sight."

Larka's lips curled upward.

"But remember the nature of your world, Larka. Where there is color and form, where there is warmth as well as cold. Remember this and, before you fight him, know that without night there is no day; without lies, no truth; without despair, no hope. Beware above all of hate, but call to its opposite too. For all things have an opposite and, if you choose it, with will and care, you may turn one thing into its reflection."

Larka listened to the specter, but she did not understand what he was telling her.

"Now," said the specter, "stand back. For as I eat I must not touch you."

"Must not?" said Larka quizzically. "But on the other side . . . on the other side I was told that you might try to keep me here."

"Keep you here?" said the specter almost sadly. "No. We would not do that, Larka, unless we touched you. For if we did that we would remember our lives and, feeling your warmth, long to have you with us forever."

A terrible pity entered Larka.

"We could not help ourselves, as you cannot help yourself when you need to eat. You, too, touching us, would long to be more than you are now, long to pass beyond the simple dualities of sun and moon, and step after us. To journey beyond the Field of the Dead and see what, if anything, lies on the other side."

As he spoke, Larka did indeed feel that need, but still she stepped back from him. He dropped his head and, as soon as he touched the meat, Larka shivered, for a fearful moan went up among the wolves in the meadow.

As the wolf ate, his pale fur quivered and color seemed to flow back into his veins. His eyes glinted yellow, and his tail was tinged with red. But as Larka watched him, her heart pounded, for she had suddenly seen a she-wolf standing behind him. She could hardly believe her eyes.

"Brassa, is that really you?"

Larka's heart was full of longing. The feeding specter lifted his head immediately. The feast had stained his mouth, and his voice seemed stronger, more real.

"No," he moaned. "You must not name us. You must never name us."

It was too late. Larka was already calling to her old nurse. "Brassa," she cried. "It is you, Brassa."

The she-wolf heard her and, as the specter looked on, a light woke in her glassy eyes. She leaped forward, and Larka, forgetting all that had just been told her, sprang forward too. In an instant their muzzles had met in greeting. They had touched.

Larka saw a flash like lightning and the whole field was suffused with light and color. The still air was warmed by a breeze, and the grass bloomed green around the poppies. The wolves were no longer specters, the trees no longer gray and lifeless. It was as though Larka had suddenly woken, only the color around her was ten times more brilliant and beautiful than anything she had known in life.

"No!" cried Tsarr in the hollow. Larka had suddenly dropped her head. Her breathing had grown shallow and pained.

"Call to her," cried Tsarr frantically, turning to Huttser and Palla. "Call to her quickly. Command her."

Huttser looked desperately at Palla.

They did not know that another wolf was racing toward them, through the woods beyond, as Skart swooped above him in the summer air. Kar's heart was ready to burst as he ran, and his coat was drenched with sweat.

"Hurry, Kar," screeched Skart from the skies. "Hurry!"

They did not see a shape stealing through the forests toward the mountains. The shape of a she-wolf with a child on her back.

"Welcome, Larka," said Brassa softly. "It is good to see you again. You have grown up. But you still have so much to learn, so much to see. Come with us."

Even as she spoke, Larka gasped. Two wolves were coming toward her, side by side.

"Khaz," she whispered. "Kipcha."

As the pair drew nearer, their tails shaking, they looked as healthy as Larka had remembered them in life. Larka's heart surged. She was a cub again, playing by the river. It was like coming home. Then, as they greeted her, she saw another wolf in the distance. It was Bran, and he was wagging his tail too. Behind Bran came Skop.

"Come, dear Larka," said Bran, "there is nothing to fear now."

"Is this true?" sighed Larka dreamily. "Is this real?"

"We cannot lie to you," answered Brassa. "The eyes cannot lie."

"And is . . . is he here too?"

"Come and see, Larka."

Like a sleepwalker, Larka nodded and, without another word, Brassa and the others turned to lead her away through the poppies.

"Larka, Larka."

Suddenly Larka paused. Those voices, disembodied on the breeze, were calling her back.

"My parents," she said wearily as she listened.

"No matter, my dear," clucked Brassa. "No matter."

"Larka, come back."

"Does one such as you obey her parents?" said Brassa as they listened to the distant, feeble voices. "Whatever they ask of you?"

"But they need me."

"Yes, and they love you too. But such things are for their world. Here we are beyond love or hate. Beyond fear and betrayal. Now you have a greater journey. Let us go."

Larka turned to follow Brassa, but again the call came.

"But I can't," said Larka. "To deny them is . . . to deny life."

"What holds you, Larka?" whispered Brassa. "Their love? Their need? That is not strong enough to call back one such as you. Love is a shadowy thing. Like hate. They are just energies, Larka, and part of the vines that bind us to the world. That ensnare us."

Larka remembered her parents' snarling voices the night Fell died on the ice.

"We all must leave our parents, Larka. Indeed, one sun nature would have forced them to drive you out and, for one who seeks the truth, you must go far beyond. They are your parents, yes. But no more. What would you have done if they had died that night when my kind attacked?

Then you would have been alone, as we are all alone. A Searcher must break such ties forever."

"Forever?" Larka trembled.

Tsarr was panicked. Larka lay slumped on her side.

"Help her," he cried.

Huttser and Palla stood looking down helplessly at their daughter. "It's no good. We are lost. Larka has gone."

Suddenly a shape flickered on the edges of their vision. As Kar crested the slope, some of the rebel guards sprang up growling, but Kar sprang past them. He gasped as he saw Larka lying there at Huttser and Palla's feet. Kar began to whimper pitifully as he leaped toward them.

"Kar," cried Palla in amazement, but Kar had no time for the Drappa and Dragga. He was staring down in horror at Larka. She had stopped breathing altogether.

"No," Kar sobbed bitterly. "Larka. You're dead."

Larka felt a wonderful sense of peace come upon her as she drifted through the poppies. Where before the air had been cold and still, now it was filled with a sweet and drowsy odor that made her limbs seem to float. A terrible weight was lifting from her, and the thought of Morgra and Wolfbane was receding into the shadows. She felt a sense of expectation and as the flowers quivered around her, her heart grew calmer and calmer. Still she could hear her parents calling, pleading with her to come back. But guilt had dropped away and, though she loved them, she knew she was far beyond Huttser and Palla, that they could never reach her now.

The spectral wolves were approaching the trees at the edge of the meadow, and as they went on, Larka gasped. Between the trunks, Larka saw brilliant lights, like eyes of sparking fire dancing between the bows.

"Come." Brassa smiled gently. "It is time."

"Please, Larka." Her parents' voices were like a dream. But even as she hesitated, Larka felt her senses reel. There, between the trees, caught in the fire play of dark and light, flickering among the brilliant glow, stood a young black wolf. He looked exactly the same as she had known him in life.

"Fell," cried Larka, her head spinning. "Dear Fell."

"Come," whispered Brassa beside her.

Larka paused and took another look around the beautiful meadow. It had lost all its terror for her. She turned and stepped toward Fell and the trees. But as she did so, the she-wolf stopped suddenly.

"Larka."

Larka lifted her ears. That voice. It wasn't her parents. It was a voice she had wanted to hear for so long, and now it tugged violently at her heart.

"No," gasped Larka. "It's him. I cannot."

Larka felt an agony of doubt and then an almost physical pain. To tear herself away from Fell and the lights was almost too much to bear, but to turn her back on that call was impossible. Memory began to flood into Larka's mind.

"Again," said Huttser as they stood in the hollow. "Call to her again."

Palla looked anxiously at Kar. His sudden appearance had astounded and thrilled her. Kar understood nothing of what was happening, but he could see their desperation, and his heart began to beat violently as he dropped his head and licked Larka's muzzle.

"Larka, dear Larka," he called. "Don't leave me. Not now that I've found you again."

Palla was shaking and Huttser growling. As they stood over their daughter, they felt that to lose Larka would kill them both. But Tsarr had suddenly stepped up closer.

"Look," he cried.

Tsarr had just seen Larka's leg twitch. Palla's ears were straining forward, quivering.

"Again, Kar," growled Huttser. "Call to her again."

"Larka," said Kar softly, "Larka."

"Damn you, Kar, for Fenris's sake call louder," cried Huttser furiously. As Kar lifted his eyes angrily, Huttser looked down guiltily and fell silent.

"Come back, Larka," cried Kar. "Please come back to me."

Suddenly Kar lifted his head to the star-spattered skies. He opened his mouth and let out a call. A howl that seemed to touch the earth and the clouds and the airless void above the firmament. Louder the howl rose and louder. Not a hunting howl or a greeting call, not a howl of mourning or anger. A howl so strange and tender, so full of pain and love that its sound thrilled through Huttser and Palla. It made Tsarr's old bones tremble. It woke the rebels from their dreams and, as the wolves listened to Kar in the night, none of them could resist it.

From all around came the wolves' cries, circling Kar,

shaking the anguished night as the rebels joined the chorus. Voices of longing and loss, filtered through memories of dead friends and battles fought and still to come, like pain struggling toward consciousness and understanding. Wild, primitive, instinctive. A call as old as the world.

In the bloodred meadow, Larka shivered and began to growl. Her limbs were shaking, the muscles quivering along her back.

"You must come," growled Brassa, and now there was an anger in the specter's voice.

Larka looked back at Fell. He was motionless, frozen as he had been on the ice. But suddenly Larka was turning and running, running through the strange flowers, back toward the avenue of trees.

"Kar," she cried desperately. "Kar!"

Kar had no notion of what was happening, but as he looked down at Larka, she twitched violently. The life seemed to be flowing back into her, filling her body.

As Larka ran, a great darkness came down around her. The meadow seemed to be bleeding of color. Only the heads of the flowers retained their vivid red hue. With the paling gray came emotion: hope and fear, anger and tenderness. In the distance she heard another voice. Fell's voice.

"We will meet again," it whispered.

"So I am to die," Larka cried, "but not yet, brother. Not yet."

Larka twitched again and opened her eyes. Morning was coming and, as she looked up, she saw her parents staring down at her and, in between them, stood a handsome young wolf. For a moment Larka didn't know if she was awake or asleep. It was Kar.

The air all around Kar and Larka was loud with songbirds as they lay together near the hollow. As soon as Larka returned, Huttser and Palla knew instinctively that the young wolves had to be alone, and now they stood off, talking quietly among the trees.

"It was you, Kar," said Larka tenderly. "You brought me back."

Kar rubbed his nose under Larka's muzzle. She looked into his eyes, so fine and clear, and remembered what Tsarr had told her in his story about love entering through the eyes.

"My parents couldn't have done it alone," growled Larka softly. "But you. Dear Kar, how I have missed you."

"And I you, Larka. It has been terrible."

Kar could hardly believe how Larka had grown. She had changed so much. She had grown into a beautiful she-wolf.

"Yes, Kar. I wish I could have helped you."

"You did help me, Larka. After poor Skop went it was the thought of you that really brought me back, the memory of you that saved me from . . . from losing myself."

As they lay there, Kar told Larka all that had happened to him. Of Mitya and Manov, and what they had said of freedom and what he had learned of Morgra's terrible secret. As Kar spoke of freedom and the untamed wolf, Larka's heart thrilled, for with summer burning around them, the meadows languid and poppies blushing in the living fields, Larka suddenly felt nature stirring in her and she knew that she loved Kar.

Not as she had loved him—almost as a brother—but for his fine gray fur and his brilliant eyes, for his kindness and the joy she felt now that she was with him again. For the strange feelings that woke in her, too, as he reached forward and touched her muzzle, and how they inspired thoughts of the future and of fine young cubs that could unite them in new life.

Suddenly, Larka looked up. A shadow had fallen across them in the grass.

Rar was standing there, and his body was drenched in sweat. His eyes were full of guilt, for he had been searching frantically through the forests as Larka had wandered through the Red Meadow. But to no avail.

"Larka." Rar trembled. "The child. It has vanished. And Slavka has gone too."

"What should we do, Larka?" whispered Palla that night. The rebels were around them, and again there was a terror in their faces.

"Morgra," growled Larka, "she must be controlling Slavka. That's why the birds and the Balkar stopped hunting. To put us off the scent."

"Then soon she will have the child," growled Huttser, "and Slavka knows how to find the entrance to the citadel, beyond the Stone Face."

They all looked up at the soaring mountains beyond.

"But what are they planning, Larka?" whispered Palla. "It's not a sacrifice, is it?"

The sacrifice Larka had seen in the water was not the child's, it was her own. Larka turned to Tsarr and he lifted his muzzle. As Palla heard the words again, the strange words she had heard so long ago in the forest, she trembled.

> Then the truest of powers will be fleshed on the bone
> And the Searchers tempt nature to prey on its own.
> With blood at the altar, the Vision shall come
> When the eye of the moon is as round as the sun.
> In the citadel raised by the lords of before,
> The stone twins await—both the power and the law.
> Then the past and the future shall finally show,
> To the wounded, the secret the Lera must know.
> And all shall be witness to that which will be,
> In the mind of the Man Varg, then who shall be free?

The rebels started to growl and look into the heavens as the verse spoke of blood at the altar. But as soon as Tsarr finished, Larka looked at him strangely.

"What is it, Larka?"

"The last line," she growled urgently, "repeat it, Tsarr."

"Why, Larka?"

"Don't argue, just tell me."

"In the mind of the Man Varg, then who shall be free?"

Larka could hardly believe her ears, but the words suddenly sent a warmth through her body. That line of the verse, it was different from how her mother had remembered it all those moons before: *In the mind of the Man Varg, then none shall be free.*

"Are you sure that's what the verse says?" growled Larka, looking hard at her mother.

"Yes," answered Tsarr. "Every spore on my journey has etched the words into my memory."

Larka was shaking her head in amazement. *Of course, the power of memory,* she thought. *The power of memory among the thoughtless Lera.* When her mother or the whispering rebel had recited the ancient verse, memory had not served them well.

"Yes, then," Larka said, suddenly feeling a new strength enter her. "There is no time to lose."

"But we are so few," said Palla. "Think of the Night Hunters and Wolfbane."

"I must face Wolfbane, Mother. Whatever I do. And in the Red Meadow they said I must face the Evil One alone."

The night itself seemed to grow darker as Larka told them her plan. If Morgra set the Balkar to guard the entrance to Harja, it would be almost impossible to get through that way. But there was the second entrance the specters had told Larka of. That was the way in. As long as Morgra had not discovered it too. If her parents led the rebel wolves to the Stone Face to create a diversion, they would not have to approach the citadel itself and would not be in so much danger. But Morgra's all-seeing eyes might be distracted just long enough to give Larka a chance.

"Then," said Larka, not meeting their gaze, "perhaps then I can kill Morgra. Or if I cannot, at least I shall play the scavenger once more and steal the child away."

"No, Larka," growled Palla, "not alone."

Larka lifted her muzzle. "Very well, Mother," she said. "Then I shall take Tsarr too."

If what Larka had seen was true and she was to die on the mountaintop, then she needed Tsarr to get the child away. But Larka suddenly had another terrible realization. The specters had told her that if the pathways were to be closed and the Searchers commanded once more, then the altar must taste blood. But that was not what her vision had showed her. She had been on the bridge, not at the altar. Hadn't Tsinga, too, warned that one among them would pay the price? But who else? And if the altar did taste blood again, then would not the Man Varg come? Suddenly Larka could no longer see the way ahead and, once more, the legend seemed to be closing in around her, like a trap.

"Larka," growled Kar suddenly, "I will come with you too."

"No, Kar."

Kar's look silenced the she-wolf. She had tried to drive him away once before. She could not do so again.

The rebel wolves all dreamed that night and, as they gathered in the morning sun, the fear of Morgra and Wolfbane had them by the throat, for as they talked among themselves, they realized that the dream had been the same. Each of the wolves had seen a wolf snarling and tearing at them and, before they had woken, biting and clawing, they had turned to face the creature and seen nothing but the image of themselves.

Yet as they came together and Larka stood before them, the rebels' hearts lifted. Something close to terror was stirring in her own heart, but Larka's eyes looked proud and defiant as she raised her fine white tail like one of the humans' fluttering banners.

"My friends, it is time. I know you have fought long against Morgra and all have suffered terribly. Well, soon it will be over. They have the child, and Slavka knows where the entrance to Harja is. Now Morgra would fulfill the legend of the Sight and bring forth the Man Varg. I must stop her and that I alone can do. But you can help me. My parents will lead you and, with your strength and courage, I can get through."

Gart suddenly stepped from the rebel ranks. "And when the Deliverer has destroyed Morgra," he growled proudly at Larka's side, "and has looked into the child's mind, we shall rule all the Lera. Then the First Among the Putnar will be our slaves, too, and they will suffer for what they have done."

"No, Gart," said Larka. "The legend is not for me. If I can kill Morgra, the Night Hunters must be disbanded. We must go back to our packs and live as free wolves. Without hate."

"Without hate?" said Gart coldly, and some of the rebel wolves began to mutter disapprovingly. "How can we live without hate, Larka? After all they have done to us. After all we have seen."

Larka nodded slowly. "You must try and forget," she whispered, "and forgive. That is the only way to be free, Gart. Or at least forget the hate your memories bring. We must learn to heal our memories."

Gart snarled. "I will never forget, or forgive. For then I would be less than a Varg."

Larka heard Morgra's curse again in her mind: *May the*

past that's dark with crimes, bring revenge in future times. Larka stepped up to Gart and peered calmly into his eyes. The strength of her gaze made him drop his own.

"We cannot really change the past, Gart," Larka whispered kindly, "but perhaps we can change the way we see it. You must escape your history, as Morgra could not escape hers. That is the only way to truly conquer her. Otherwise it will go on forever. We can make a different future. If we have true courage."

"And should we change our natures?" growled Gart.

Larka shuddered, but she raised her head even higher.

"We leave together. Tor and Fenris be with you."

As the rebels gazed at Larka standing there on the mound, three wolves came up beside her. Huttser and Palla were on her right side and Kar on her left. They looked at each other and smiled. Larka turned to lead her family up the slope. It was the same family that had been sundered on the ice all those moons ago. Yet each of them seemed subtly different.

It was as though their characters had finally been picked out by the strange journey they had taken together. As though they had stepped out from the shadows or, as they walked across that landscape and some silent human watcher surveyed the scene, a shaft of sunlight had suddenly illuminated their forms against the complex camouflage of nature that kept them hidden.

"If only we'd all had more time together," Palla murmured as they went.

"I know, Palla," growled Huttser, looking at their children ahead of them.

"But we will give them time, Huttser," said Palla suddenly. "Won't we, when we get through? All the time in the world."

Huttser growled quietly as Larka looked back.

The rebels, with Tsarr ahead of them, followed too. As Skart lifted above them, the little group of travelers rose into the mountains, and Palla padded up beside her daughter.

"Larka," she whispered, wanting desperately to protect her child as she once could, "why don't we just go away? Any true Varg knows when it is best to flee. Your father and I love you, Larka, and we need you. We could go off into the forests and live freely, as Putnar. We do not have to do this."

Larka's eyes were sad, but in that instant she felt angry with Palla. After all that had happened, it seemed that her mother was tempting her to turn away. For a moment she wanted to growl and tell her mother to get behind her.

"Palla, how can we be free if the Lera are enslaved?"

"But Larka, what do you owe the Lera? You shouldn't feel guilty. Why should the Lera be your responsibility? Why should this child?"

"Mother, true responsibility isn't because of guilt or even simple duty," growled Larka softly. "It's because of love. And I love the child. As I love life."

"But, Larka," said Palla desperately. "You have a choice."

In that moment Larka wondered. Did she really have a choice? Any more than the Lera have a choice to eat? So far the legend had marked out almost everything that had happened to her. Larka looked up. She noticed that in the clear blue sky the edge of the moon was already peeping into the day.

"Mother, do you remember the story Brassa used to tell us. Of Tor and the moon smiling down kindly on the world?"

"Yes, Larka."

"But it seems to have hunted us like Fenris, Palla, ever since Morgra came."

"Then this time," growled her mother, sensing the gravity of her daughter's final choice, "let us howl at it together."

And in that instant, Larka felt carried by her mother's strength.

"Yes, Mother, and we must hurry. For this moon heralds the Vision and the great secret, and it is we who are chasing the moon now."

15
HARJA

I fled Him, down the nights and down the days;
I fled Him, down the arches of the years;
I fled Him, down the labyrinthine ways
Of my own mind.

—FRANCIS THOMPSON, "The Hound of Heaven"

"WE MUST BE CLOSE," Brak growled as he sniffed the thin air.

The Night Hunters had reached the higher mountains above Kosov, and the wolves' eyes all had the same hunted look. They moved like sleepwalkers through the shadows. They were traveling out of a huge gorge, and the shadowy peaks and crags looming above them made them feel as if they were passing through a land of ghosts. The slopes were dotted with beech and fir, dwarf pine and juniper trees, while swirling mists hung about their hag-ridden shapes, breaking into floating wraiths in the fading sun.

"The full moon's coming," said Brak. "It should be no more than a few suns now."

"Then what?"

"We shall never see it, whatever they plan. Until the Man Varg comes, and the Vision. She has taken only her favorite Balkar with her." A jealous look had crossed his face.

"I wish I was with her," said the wolf next to Brak. "I feel so much safer when she is watching over us. Protecting us from him."

"Like Fenris himself. But we have strict orders to defend the gully. Something about this other wolf."

"The white Varg?"

"Yes. She leads the rebels now, Fenris take her."

The leading wolves had stopped and were looking up. They had come to the edge of a high rock wall, its craggy sides looming sheer and black above them. But what had caught the wolves' attention was not the precipitous nature of the cliff, it was the strange shape that rose above them.

Overhead the cliff wall had buckled outward, creating a boulder overhang that time and the elements had eroded into the most extraordinary shape. As the wolves looked on, the shape became clearer in their minds. It was the image of an enormous dog. The ears were there, formed by two spurs of spiky granite. The eyes, too, implanted in the sides of the rock by two small hollows. They lay aslant the surface, which tapered down and forward to form a muzzle. It was like the images men carve out of the bare rock to tell of their beliefs. Yet this face had not been made by man, but by chance, eroded by wind and storm and rain. It was only because of the nature of the creatures gazing at it that it looked like a dog at all.

"This is the place," growled Brak. He led the wolves

on below the shadow of that strange face. They had hardly gone any way at all when another of their number cried out.

"Here, over here."

The crack in the rock wall was no more than five tails wide, but it ran like a scar down the entire cliff. By a quirk of nature, the wall abutting it buckled out, so that it was always lost in shadow. But as soon as the wolf stepped through, he called out again.

"This is it all right."

As he entered it, the sides of the fissure opened and, ahead of him, he saw the beginnings of a canyon that grew wider and wider before him. One by one the Balkar followed him in. The canyon became wider still and the ground began to rise. There wasn't one of the Night Hunters who did not feel a sense of foreboding as they climbed through the entrance to Harja. But something else was troubling them. They all felt it. It was as though they were being watched.

"Can you sense it?" whispered the wolf that had been speaking earlier.

"Yes," said another, his shoulders hunching below those towering cliffs. "The Evil One. I felt him probing my mind last night."

Some of the wolves around them began to growl. The fear of Wolfbane haunted them all, both awake and asleep, and they knew only too well the punishment that awaited them if they showed any signs of dissent.

"He's always watching now," growled another, his voice echoing against the mountain. "Even our most secret thoughts. When he comes, I can do nothing but obey. I hate him—"

"Hush. Don't speak like that. Not here."

Suddenly the Varg that had said it began to growl, and the hackles rose on his back. He was standing stock-still and his legs were shaking. The others could smell the sweating fear that had suddenly taken hold of him, and they felt it themselves as they looked on. He was staring straight ahead, his eyes wide and glassy, and the growl that was coming from his stomach grew louder and louder. Then suddenly he closed his eyes and let out a terrible whimper. When he opened them again, the yellow orbs were bleached white. He was blind.

Wolfbane's back arched, and he let out a sigh as his mind released the blinded Night Hunter. His body was tingling, and it was as though he could feel the wolf's pain beneath his claws. He gave a deep grunt of satisfaction at what he had done, shifting the Night Hunter's own energies through his body to burn out his retina. Now that the power had entered the world, it always pleased him to visit his punishments suddenly on the Balkar. When he did so, he felt a strange closeness to them that always magnified his anger, for it stood in such bitter contrast to the terrible loneliness that gnawed at his heart.

Outside his shelter, Wolfbane caught sight of a shape lying in the grass. The she-wolf was asleep and, for a moment, Wolfbane thought of visiting her. But he let Slavka be. He controlled her mind completely now, and he knew that each time he visited her with his own powerful thoughts it weakened her. He felt nothing for the creature, nothing but a kind of grim contempt, but he wasn't ready to dispose of her yet.

Besides, he had already learned much from Slavka's mind. There he learned the depth of experience that had been denied to him. He had learned of the anger and bitterness of Slavka's own loss and the fury of revenge that made her so strong. He had learned of the pride that swelled in her and the violent agony of defeat. As he roamed her dreams, he had sensed how her own desires were betraying her, tearing her apart. He had realized it when he had first whispered to Slavka of another way, of something that would end the war forever, of power. That was the lie that had finally made her his. That she, too, could master the Sight and with it put an end to her own agony.

Then she had come, the wolf that Morgra had long warned him of. Wolfbane had discovered a new and deeper emotion in Slavka then, perhaps deeper than any other—jealousy. The stranger's arrival had driven Slavka toward him, and with her, the creature they had been seeking for so long, the human cub. Was it Fenris's will that she also knew the way into Harja? Poor, foolish Slavka. Her battle with Morgra was to end here, in the fulfillment of Morgra's great purpose.

"Wolfbane," came the cold, suspicious voice in his mind. "Wolfbane, what have you been doing, my dear?"

"Nothing."

"You can't lie to me. You have been using the truest power to . . . play with my Night Hunters. Don't you feel guilty, Wolfbane, at the terrible things you do?"

"One of them," snarled Wolfbane almost jealously,

"showed fear. I could smell it as soon as they entered the gully."

"Very well. But you mustn't waste the power. Leave them be for the while. We have need of them. I have told them to defend the entrance in case—"

"She is coming."

"Yes, Wolfbane, and she will try to stop me. But it is too late. Now we have the child, it will not be long. Every night I look up and see my hopes growing. But now you must do something. Go down to the second entrance and guard it, in case she has discovered it too. Be ready, Wolfbane, for she is strong."

"Then you will help me to take revenge?"

"Of course, my dear, for we were born for revenge," whispered Morgra. "But no more blindings. Not until it is finished. Then you can torment the Night Hunters as you will, and the name of Wolfbane shall sing like a curse through Transylvania."

A shadow fell across the entrance to Wolfbane's shelter, and a great bellow shook the air. A dark shape lumbered slowly across the ancient stones, rising every now and then on its haunches and crashing to the ground again.

The tiny band of rebels were dwarfed by the trees and the mountains around them. Every sound made them start and growl. The wolves' hearing had been heightened by fear so that even the faintest stirring of a fox or a squirrel echoed in their minds. Close to sunset they came to the top of a soaring, high-backed pass that plunged away into a giant wooded gorge, and here Larka stopped to look out. The mist was rolling like a wave across the far slopes, but

Larka was deeply troubled. More than that, she was in terrible pain.

It had begun almost as soon as they had set out. It was like a great pounding in her brain, a terrible, noisy throbbing. As she listened, Larka realized she could hear the thoughts not only of the rebels, but of the Lera all around her. They were everywhere, chattering, snarling, growling, and whispering, and they were full of terror, for the Searchers had been among them. Larka wanted to make it stop, but she could do nothing but listen to their frightened minds.

"Close the eye," she said to herself. "Close the eye of the Sight."

Larka breathed in and tried to relax. She tried to shut out the noises and she found, oddly, that memory was the best balm. The mist on the slopes cleared, and in the distance the she-wolf saw a strange sight. Standing alone above the tree line, on a rocky outcrop, was a single red deer. It was a magnificent royal stag, and its coat glinted russet even in the fading light. It seemed to be watching Larka and, as the wolf looked back, it dipped its proud head slightly and turned away. But among the trees and in the grass, other Lera were watching the wolves fearfully as they went.

On the rebels traveled, down into the gorge and then up again toward the towering peaks beyond. It was dark when Huttser stopped them again. They had come to an unusual hollow, overhung with gnarled trees and hanging vines. A little spring gurgled out of the rocks at their feet.

"Larka," whispered Huttser. "Slavka told me of this place. The rock can't be far now."

"We will part here, then," said Larka. "Skart will show you the way now. They told me the second entrance lies close to the east. I still have time."

"Very well, Larka," growled Huttser, looking gravely at his daughter.

"But be careful, Father. Worry the Balkar. Make them think we are trying to get through that way. But don't do anything to endanger . . ."

"We can look after ourselves, Larka," said Palla gently.

Larka nodded, but as she stepped forward, and they began to take their farewells, both parents and child lied to one another. They agreed to meet back at the spring in two suns' time. Huttser and Palla were oblivious to the fate Larka had seen for herself. In turn, their daughter was too distracted to see what her parents were hiding in their hearts.

"Look after her, Kar," whispered Huttser as Larka turned to leave.

"Yes."

"And, Kar. Take care too."

Kar lifted his tail, and Huttser thanked Tor and Fenris that at least he had made his peace with the young wolf.

"I will, Father," he whispered.

The rebels turned and, as Skart rose into the air, Huttser and Palla led them up and out of the hollow. But as soon as they were through the trees, out of earshot, Huttser swung around to Palla.

"Now we must hurry. Gart knows the plan."

"Then Tor guide us," cried Palla as they began to run, looking up at the eagle soaring high above them in the sky.

THE SIGHT 480

Larka watched her parents go and turned to see Tsarr and Kar looking at her intently.

"Come," she said.

But as Larka began to run, her paws felt like stones, and she knew that every step was bringing her closer to her doom.

It wasn't long before Skart returned to the rebels and, from his agitated flapping, they all knew that the strange rock was close at hand. But they hardly needed to be told. They had already scented the Night Hunters. The scent grew stronger and stronger as they climbed and, by the time they came on the stone face, they were at their nerves' end. As they reached it and muttered fearfully, Skart was standing quietly in front of it, but before they could say anything he lifted swiftly into the air again.

It was Palla who found the entrance to the canyon nearby and, as soon as she began to scent around it, she pulled away. It was plain that there were Balkar very close at hand. That night the rebels waited at the entrance and Huttser discussed his plan with Gart. He had asked him to distract the Balkar to give himself and Palla a chance to slip through. The wolf shook his head gravely, but he could see that Huttser was determined to reach Morgra before his daughter. Palla lay with Keeka and Karma and Rar, whispering quietly and taking her farewells.

The sun was just climbing the sky as the rebels crept through the fissure in the cliff face. The bottom of the canyon opened out and, in the soft stone above, there were numerous caves, shallow but deep enough for concealment. The slopes up to them banked gently, so it was a perfect position for an attack. Ahead, the path of the canyon bent around suddenly, but they could smell Night Hunters past the turn.

The rebels began to fan out in the caves above, and Huttser and Palla found a spot to conceal themselves while Gart, with Rar and Keeka and Karma behind him, padded up the gorge and disappeared out of sight. It wasn't long before they heard the howls and the three rebels came leaping back down the ravine. The Balkar were at their tails. From above, Huttser growled and Palla's fur began to bristle as they watched the rebels' ambush. Their friends rushed down from their caves setting upon the Balkar. Neither of them joined the fray; they were still waiting.

Suddenly the majority of the Balkar appeared at the bend in the ravine, hearing the others' howls. This contingent did not rush so haphazardly into battle. Instead the wolves advanced slowly, fanning out across the gorge. At first it seemed to Huttser that they could never slip past them, and his eyes ranged over the slopes, looking for a way through. But at last he hit on it. From where he and Palla were standing, a narrow path ran along the sides of the slope and down behind the Night Hunters.

"Quick, Palla," he cried, "follow my tracks."

The Balkar were engaged in the fight, and none of them noticed Huttser and Palla as they threaded past them. The pair looked back and saw that the Night Hunters had started to regroup, and that the rebels were being pushed back down the pass, howling and snarling furiously. But Huttser and Palla were on level ground once again, and they bounded away. They did not notice the tiny shadow that had scudded across the ground behind them. Nor the silent wings flapping in the sky above them.

Huttser and Palla sped on up the ravine, the great granite walls rearing around them. They didn't slow until they had left the Balkar and the rebels far behind, and the twists and turns in the rising gorge had long obscured their path. It was only as evening came in that they began to feel a little more secure. But it did not last. They had rested on the edge of the ravine, and as they moved off again, their attention no longer on flight, Huttser began to scent the ground and called Palla to his side.

"Slavka," growled Huttser, sniffing the earth. "Slavka. I'd know her anywhere."

"And here," said Palla, "Morgra has been this way too."

They padded on a little, and Palla paused again. This time, her muzzle was close to the ground.

"What is it, Palla?"

Palla didn't answer. She suddenly lifted her muzzle and shook her head. "It can't be," she whispered. "For a moment . . ."

"We should get on," said Huttser, and he led Palla up the slope.

They rose up and up as the darkness came in, hardly speaking as they thought of the mysterious citadel above, their forms illuminated by the swelling moon. Instinctively the wolves walked together, brushing each other's flanks for comfort.

At last, the path between the cliffs began to bank steeply and the two wolves climbed toward the mountaintop. They stopped together as they crested the slope and came upon the citadel, glittering before them in the moonlight.

"Harja," gasped Huttser. "The gateway to heaven."

All around them stood temples and statues, shining in the moonlight. But now they saw something that made their thoughts quiver. Beyond these statues lay a wide ravine, and spanning its cavernous drop was an arched stone bridge, old and crumbling. Just beyond the bridge, on a kind of raised platform, set well above the rest and fronted by a flat stone circle, was another statue. The statue of the giant she-wolf. Huttser and Palla shivered as they saw the stone children suckling at her belly and, at her feet, a wide, flat dais. The sacred altar.

The wolves wondered now what they were seeing. They could not know that here the Romans' priests and fortune-tellers had worn wolf skins on their heads, and in the trenches below the temples had kept live wolves to which they sacrificed animals during the feast of the Lupercal. They then tried to interpret the future, as Diana, the huntress and the goddess of the moon, looked down on them all. So, among the wolves that had once been kept at Alba Mutandis, their own story had grown up, like a memory. A legend of a place called Harja, relayed through every new generation of cubs, living long after the city itself had fallen into disrepair and been lost to the memories of both Man and Lera.

The Romans had needed a more powerful myth for their origins than the realities of conquest and power. They wanted to participate in all life, both human and animal. They valued the strength and anger of the wolf, its cunning, too, and the way it cared for its own cubs. They saw the wolf not as later peoples that inhabited this land who, putting aside their swords to become farmers and shepherds, had reviled the wolf as a threat to their animals. Nor as some Christians, looking for sin in everything, as a symbol of evil to be judged and put on trial. Instead, they had seen the she-wolf as a great symbol of strength and cunning and fertility.

Palla blinked and marveled. "What now?" she whispered.

"Morgra. We must find her before Larka comes."

They walked on and the place seemed to be deserted. The air was still and dead, and Palla growled quietly to herself as they went. They saw no signs of life among those ancient stones. Then ahead of them on the ground, among the ruins, they saw something moving. Huttser's eyes sliced through the night.

"Kraar," he whispered, "the raven."

He was hopping along on the ground; his wing seemed to be broken.

"What if we capture it?" Palla growled. "Use it against Morgra. If it's her eyes we might blind her a little."

Huttser had had the very same thought, and he was already hugging the ground, trying to steal up on the bird. It seemed completely unaware of them and, as Huttser and Palla drew closer, they could see that it was on the edge of a wide trench.

Huttser sprang, but suddenly the tricky raven opened its wings and fluttered away. Palla had sprung, too, and missing the raven, landed at Huttser's side. But suddenly she realized they were not alone. Before they could turn,

they heard a furious snarling behind them and their bodies were thrust violently forward.

They landed in the deep trench, gasping for breath, the
air knocked from their lungs by the fall. They got up, side
by side, and around them the Dragga and Drappa noticed
stone tree trunks strewn everywhere. But their attention
was immediately drawn above them. The smell of the
Balkar was flooding their nostrils, and it seemed to flow
down over the edge of the trench like a river of fear. Palla
growled. Above them, a little black shape had appeared.
The raven fluttered its wings and its beady black eyes
glinted as it clacked with satisfaction. The Night Hunters
appeared around it.

"Tricked," snarled Huttser.

Before he could say anything more, Huttser sensed
Palla trembling furiously and his tail rose. Two more eyes
had appeared above them. Large and knowing and glinting yellow in the darkness.

"Morgra," whispered Palla, and the strength seemed to
go out of her.

"So we meet again, sister," smiled Morgra. "And this
time you are in my power."

Larka gazed up at the stars, fading in the sky as the night
deepened and the moon climbed higher and higher above
the thundering mountains. The pounding in her head had
become so furious as they sought out the second entrance,
that they had decided to rest for a few hours. Around them
the air was warm and still. The swelling moon shone
down through the trees and its strange power, that tugged
at the distant oceans and made them move against trou-

bled and untroubled shores, seemed to be calling to the elements themselves.

Tsarr was beginning to doze in the grass, and Kar padded up quietly to Larka.

"Larka," he said softly, "why don't you try and get some sleep?"

"No, Kar. I must stay awake and think, for I shall need all my senses about me when it comes. But Kar, will you stay awake with me for a while?"

Kar lay down beside Larka and, side by side, their hearts beat together. About them the moonlit air rustled through the trees and flowers, and nearby they heard the drone of a beehive. The place was like some ancient garden, the garden that mankind dreamed of at the beginning of the world, made by hope, with nurture and care and intelligence, out of the wilderness of the mind. It was so beautiful that Larka's heart ached.

"Kar," the she-wolf whispered sadly, "I love life. But sometimes I think this power to touch it all is too terrible. I am wounded and I don't know why. I try to shut it out, with anger, by trying to hate Morgra, but in the end I cannot."

Larka turned her head to her dear friend, and she felt that her responsibility now for everything was a burden almost too great to shoulder, but she could see that the wolf's eyes were beginning to droop with weariness.

"Kar, dear Kar, stay awake."

"I am awake," muttered Kar sleepily, raising his head and shaking himself.

Larka looked up sadly at the moon, and Kar followed her gaze. Kar had no real words to talk of the living force that pulled the earth and the moon together, nor of the current that flows between all things, but in his bones he could sense its strength, and in the wolves' tales of Tor and Fenris, of the moon's birth, they had tried to make sense of it.

Larka could feel that energy too, and she knew it as the energy of the Sight. For her that glowing orb above them had a very clear meaning, one that made her shiver as she gazed up into the endless night. As she looked up at the moon, she knew that in just one sun's time that uneven sphere would grow round as a dandelion, as it had so many times since her birth, and that the inevitability of its cycle brought the inevitability of her own destruction.

"Kar," she said quietly, "you know I no longer believe in the stories they told us as children. I no longer believe in Tor and Fenris or gods that look down kindly on wolves. Sometimes I don't know what to believe in, Kar. Except..." Larka paused. "Except truth. I believe in that."

Larka whimpered and again the story of Sita came to her mind. Though she found it strangely beautiful, it laid like a weight on her heart too. She turned tenderly to Kar, but he had fallen fast asleep. Larka did not wake him. She could not bear to tell Kar what was to be, and although Kar had fallen into a blissful, unconscious sleep, despite his promise to her, now Larka was just grateful to have this flawed, vulnerable creature at her side.

It wasn't until noon was brightening the sky that Larka led them on, and they soon heard the sound of water. Just as the Searchers had told her, a little stream ran down the rock face, and next to it Larka saw an opening.

"The tunnel," she cried, "they told me it leads right through the mountain."

As soon as she ducked inside, she whimpered with frustration. The narrow cave entrance was almost completely blocked with fallen rubble. Kar and Tsarr began to scrabble at the stones, but Larka ranged angrily back and forth.

"What is Morgra doing?" she kept growling to herself.

Larka's eyes flashed and she padded up to the stream. As soon as she looked into the water, she saw the swirling vortex and her fur began to bristle. Morgra was looking at her, but this time a voice echoed around her and it was as clear as day.

"So, you have come."

"Morgra."

"But what have you come for?" Morgra growled scornfully. "To steal the Vision? You cannot, my child. I am too powerful already. I do not even need to look into the water to see you, and we have mastered the truest power, Wolfbane and I. Tonight is the full moon and nothing can stop us now. You are close, but no wolf shall pass my guards a second time, no matter how clever the ambush or how cunningly they sneak about."

Larka gasped. Her parents must have reached the entrance already and there had been fighting.

Morgra spoke again. Mockingly. "When the legend comes to pass, I will tame all the Lera. All shall be my slaves."

"No," cried Larka, "we are here. The family to conquer the evil. To conquer you and the Evil One."

"You have survived, it is true," Morgra whispered coldly. "But why didn't you try to sneak past my guards too? With your dear parents."

Morgra paused. "You have found the tunnel, Larka. You thought I didn't know of its existence. It is blocked, my dear, is it not? The earth is ancient and quakes here—time has blocked the entrance. But even if you get through, he is waiting on the other side."

"I will find a way."

"No." Morgra laughed. "You are too late."

"Too late?"

"You know what the ancient verse says, Larka. 'With blood at the altar the Vision shall come.' And it shall be their blood. Your parents'. Then we shall put an end to this family forever."

Larka let out a howl and sprang away.

"Larka, what is it?" cried Kar. "What's wrong?"

"Kar, we must hurry. Morgra has Huttser and Palla, and tonight she will kill them. Tonight is the full moon."

"And if we don't stop her in time . . ." snarled Tsarr.

Larka began scrabbling desperately at the stones in front of them.

"But Tsarr," she said, "the Evil One waits. He waits up ahead."

The sun burned above them as Huttser and Palla paced angrily in the trench. The wolves were panting badly in the heat. They had to squint as they looked up at the furious orb and felt its broiling energy burn their eyes, yet there was comfort, too, in the light it brought.

"We never escaped, Huttser," growled Palla. "Not from

the pack boundaries, from the shadow of the Stone Den, from her curse."

Huttser growled up at the sun, but as he did so, a shadow fell across them. Morgra's eyes were smiling as she gazed down.

"So, sister, are you prepared to pay for the injustice of what was done to me? For what must come? For the altar is hungry."

Palla studied her sister sadly, "Why do you hate me so, Morgra? I never even knew what happened."

"You never cared to know. Wolves have no justice."

"And was it out of justice," snarled Huttser next to his mate, "was it out of goodness that you cursed us that night? You killed my friends. You killed my cubs."

"Is it not strange," said Morgra slowly, and her eyes smiled, "that you believe in curses more than I?"

"But you—"

"Your own fear and weakness, your own guilt have worked on you all, Huttser," snarled Morgra. "Your own desperate clinging to life. As Wolfbane worked on the Balkar. That is the meaning of a curse. Nothing more. But the Sight is a true power, and soon I will use it to control all."

"Why didn't you tell us, Morgra?" pleaded Palla. "Why didn't you show us the truth of what happened to you? We would have understood. We would have given you justice."

Morgra began to growl uncomfortably. "Understood? What understanding does the Varg have? All they know is fear. Fear for their cubs and for themselves. Fear for their worthless lives."

"We can all understand pain, Morgra," said Palla, "but can't you remember how to love?"

Morgra's eyes clouded and her tail lowered.

"Sister," whispered Palla.

For a second Morgra seemed to be torn. But suddenly she showed her yellowing teeth.

"Love," she snarled furiously. "Don't you think I wanted to? All my life I have wanted to be allowed to love something. It is too late for love. And you, Palla, by calling me sister you think you can escape. Because you are trapped and fear to die."

"That is not true. But I can feel the hate in you, Morgra. And I can see that it hurts you."

"Enough. Even if I believed you, the time has long since passed when I ached to be understood. You talk of justice, but what justice can there ever be for one such as me, a she-wolf who is barren? Except the justice that I take for myself. I have gone far beyond the ordinary life of the Varg. I have tasted the power of the Sight. And tonight, when the full moon glows above us, I will go even further. The power of the Man Varg will come."

A terrible light glowed in Morgra's eyes, a light that reminded Huttser of that night above the ravine.

"You are evil, Morgra," he growled.

"Silence," cried Morgra. "By what authority do you dare to judge me?"

"You are evil," said Huttser once more.

"Fool. You dare talk to me of evil. You who know nothing of the light, or the darkness of the Sight. A foolish Dragga whose only ambition is to rule his pack and to hide among his family. You think a thing is evil simply because you are told it is evil. You know only how to live in fear and to obey. Well, tonight you shall know of the darkness that is everlasting. When I slay you at the altar."

"No, sister, listen to me. I am to blame. I will be your blood sacrifice. Willingly. Is it not fitting that you should slay me? That your own bloodline should pay the price?"

Morgra was looking down closely at Palla. "You would do this? Without resistance?"

"Yes, if you let Huttser go."

"No, Palla," cried Huttser.

"Morgra, I beg of you. Perhaps somehow it will make amends."

A look of cold amusement had woken in Morgra's eyes. Though she had no intention of letting Huttser live, she suddenly nodded. "Very well, Palla. Watch for me. At twilight."

Morgra turned and vanished, and still the baking sun beat down. Huttser stood there shaking, but even as he looked down he noticed the stone floor of their prison. He was surprised for a moment, for the stone was cracked and broken and, while the pillars around them seemed so strong and forbidding, he saw that what had done this was nothing more than little weeds and grasses. Tiny shoots, drawn by the sunlight, had managed to reach up from the earth and shatter the human stones.

Huttser pleaded with Palla, begged her to let him go instead, but as the sun crept down the sky, Palla's thoughts grew calmer, and Huttser could see that she was resigned. As the sun began to die, the last vestiges of hope seemed to be dying too. Twilight was thick around them once more when they heard a bellowing above.

Then came Morgra's voice, barking out an order, and suddenly there was a thud behind them. One of the stone logs had been rolled over the edge of the trench as the smell of bear filled the air. It lay against the wall, a bridge to Palla's fate. Before Huttser could stop her, the she-wolf sprang up. As Palla disappeared over the ridge of the trench, the great black shape appeared above Huttser. He was knocked backward, and the plinth crashed to the ground beside him.

"Palla, please."

Palla shut her ears to Huttser. Morgra was waiting, ringed by a troop of Night Hunters. They looked like sleepwalkers, for Morgra was controlling their minds completely. But as Palla looked on, she gasped in horror. Everywhere she looked there were birds. The scavengers of the air were perched on the statues: crows and hooded ravens and great squatting buzzards. Their excrement stained the stones.

"So, sister."

Morgra seemed to have grown far older. The fur across her face was now a weathered gray, and the scars stood out lividly. Already the full moon was rising. The giant orb had begun to cast its light across the citadel as the turning earth lifted it above the Carpathians. It rose like an omen over Harja. Morgra turned and led Palla quietly up the slope. But as they approached the stone bridge over the chasm, Morgra stopped and turned to her sister.

"You hate me, don't you, Palla?"

"Hate you?" said Palla distantly. "I . . . no, Morgra, I don't hate you."

Morgra's eyes sparked. "After all I have done? Well, I want you to hate me, Palla. I want you to feel the power of hate, feel what I felt for so long."

"I could never feel that, sister," said Palla quietly. "I am a she-wolf. I have felt life stirring in my belly."

Suddenly a memory came to Palla that gave her hope. "Which is why," she growled, "why you shall never become the Man Varg. For the Vision can only be given to one who knows the drappa's care."

Morgra winced, but then she smiled coldly too. "I know what the legend demands, Palla. Well, then, let me tell you a secret that will help you to hate me."

Morgra stepped closer, and even as she did she looked cunningly at the Balkar waiting for her command. She began to whisper to Palla. Softly. Words that crept like thieves into Palla's mind. At first Palla did nothing. Her eyes grew larger and larger as she listened. Then suddenly she lifted her head and let out a howl, so angry and bitter that for a moment the Night Hunters seemed to be startled back into consciousness.

Larka had managed to break through the rock wall, but high up the tunnel they had entered, banking steeply up the mountain, they found the way blocked once more. Tsarr and Kar were again scrabbling desperately at the rubble, their paws cut and bleeding. Larka was trying to help them, but the passageway was so small that only two wolves could get to the rock face. It was an agony for Larka as she watched Tsarr and Kar work, their fur dripping with sweat as the wolves scooped the scree behind them. They were all frantic, but something else had come to them as they entered the mountain. A sickening fear. Larka and Tsarr knew what it was. They felt it now as an almost physical thing. Like a wall of darkness. A waiting presence beyond the rock itself.

"It's no good, Larka," muttered Kar wearily. "We'll never manage like this."

"We've got to, Kar, if we don't . . ."

Suddenly the wolves felt a strange sensation. At first Larka thought it was Wolfbane. They felt a stillness about them, as though some of the air in the passage had been drawn away. Then Tsarr began to growl. He was trembling, but not from fear. The ground was shaking. Larka felt it, too, coming through her legs.

Tsarr and Kar leaped back as the earth tremor shook the mountain. The wall in front of them gave way in a shower of swirling dust, and they felt a gust of air like a wind. A rock hit Kar and, whimpering, he slunk back past Larka. As he did so, a great scree of rock and rubble crashed to the earth in front of him, cutting him off from the others.

"No," cried Kar desperately. "Larka!"

They could hear his voice from behind the stones, but there was no way through.

"Kar," called Larka, and the she-wolf felt a sense of relief. "We must go on without you."

"Larka, the pact."

But the way ahead was clear, and now Larka sprang forward. Kar turned and began to run, to run with all his strength.

"Wait, Larka," gasped Tsarr. "He's here. Let me face him."

Larka felt it, too, stronger than ever before. That terrible anger.

"No, Tsarr. I am young and I must face this thing alone."

Larka stepped along the passageway as Tsarr crept behind her. It rose even more steeply, and after a while, they began to see a dim blue light in the darkness. But as the light grew, that feeling of darkness grew with it. Larka remembered Morgra's strange words.

"To fight love," she muttered, "to fight love itself."

Every step Larka took was an agony, and now she was aware only of the presence beyond. She no longer knew anything of her parents, or Tsarr and Kar. Her whole body had grown burningly hot. Nearer and nearer Larka came, and the passage began to open. Ahead, she realized that it gave way to a kind of chamber, and she could see the moonlight filtering through the entrance beyond. She stopped and felt a new wave of fear wash over her. Some deeper terror. Some knowledge.

Larka lifted her head and raised her tail. She set her front paws square and snarled.

"Wolfbane. I have come to meet your evil."

Nothing stirred inside.

"Wolfbane. Too long you have filled the wolves with fear. Face me."

Larka shuddered, and fancied something moved beyond. "Come, then. It is time that you stopped hiding in the shadows."

Larka stepped into the chamber. It was a strange place. A cavern. High-ceilinged with great pilasters, like the stone trees, carved into the rock. On the floor of the chamber was a mosaic that formed an intricate human pattern. At each side stood a wolf and two snakes weaving around their throats. In between them was a man and, in his hand, he held a great hammer that was raised above his head in the act of striking flat two sheets of glinting metal. Behind him flamed a blast of the human's burning air that leaped from the doors of a painted furnace.

Larka had no thoughts for the image now. As soon as she entered the chamber she knew he was there.

"Show yourself, Wolfbane."

Suddenly a shadow fell across the mosaic, and a shape stepped fully into the moonlight. Larka's eyes opened in horror.

"No," she gasped, "it can't be. It can't be true."

16

THE SIGHT

Love bade me welcome: yet my soul drew back,
Guilty of dust and sin.
— GEORGE HERBERT, "Love (III)"

A TERRIBLE WEAKNESS ENTERED LARKA as she stared into that face and saw the sliver of green in his eye. Her brother's right eye. It was Fell, standing before the mosaic. The black Varg had grown into a powerful adult, but it certainly was him. He looked back at his sister; his eyes were veiled and wary. He hardly seemed to see her as he snarled quietly in the chamber.

"Fell," Larka cried, gasping for breath again and almost staggering. "It can't be you. You're dead. I saw you, in the Red Meadow."

The white wolf felt as if her whole world was tearing apart. This. She couldn't face this.

"Fell," she stammered, "it's me, Larka. Don't you recognize me, Fell?"

"I am Wolfbane," growled Fell coldly. "The Evil One. I have been expecting you."

"Fell. Tell me what happened. After the ice."

"Who are you," snarled Fell, "that you know of my dreams?"

"Not dreams, Fell. That night on the river, when we were trying to escape the pack boundaries, and the ice gave way. You slipped through, and Kar and Huttser, our father, tried to save you. It was terrible. You were clawing at the surface and we couldn't break through to you."

"Tricks," cried Fell. "It is the Sight that tells you this."

"No, Fell. It is not the Sight. I was there."

"Silence," commanded Fell. "You could not know of my birth. Yet you talk like one . . . like one that had shared my dreams. For suns and moons I was under the ice, before I was born. When I saw images of things of this world. Of wolves calling me. Calling me into being. I was a thing of reeds then. Of cold and of pain. I was death. I was water. But this world had summoned me. Called me to join them. I broke the veil. I was born to the riverbank in splintering cold. I became a wolf, tended to by other wolves. Fed and warmed into life."

"The Balkar," whispered Larka with horror, shivering, as she thought of the water and souls doomed never to find a resting place. "They must have found you when you broke through farther down the river."

"They were my servants. They obeyed me and they brought me . . . to my mother."

"Your mother," cried Larka. "You think that Morgra is your mother?"

"Silence," Fell commanded again, padding onto the mosaic. "You dare to name her? She who summoned me.

She who taught me what I am. The child of her dark power. Wolfbane."

"Wolfbane is just a name," pleaded Larka, "plucked from a story. Nothing more."

"Fool," Fell cried, "don't you know of my power. As your coat is white, so mine is black. But I am the Sight. I am darkness."

Larka was trembling too.

"But how, how can this be? That you have the power too? Why could I not foresee this?"

Larka's own memories were not strong enough to carry her back, back to the sun in the den before Fell's eyes had come, and Brassa had first suspected that Fell possessed the Sight. But she remembered Tsinga's strange words to Huttser, "Can you look into the darkness and predict the future?" Now she understood why Tsinga had gasped in horror that day. But suddenly she thought, too, of Skart. That's why he had looked so guilty when she talked of Wolfbane and evil. He, too, had known all along.

"You can foresee nothing," growled Fell, "but tonight, when the moon climbs to its zenith and Mother looks through the child's eyes and controls all, then she has promised me that she will give me the power to know the future, and the past too. To know all and be free. To be free as Man himself."

As Larka looked at Fell, she felt a terrible wave of pity surge through her.

"Fell," she pleaded, "what has she done to you? Remember the cave, Fell. When we played as cubs. Remember Bran and Khaz and Brassa. Remember the Stone

Den and Wolfbane living at the top. That was a story too. Just a story. Like your name."

Fell's eyes narrowed, but again he snarled. "More dreams. I left the dream world long ago. When she . . . when Mother taught me of the world. Taught me the true glory of the Putnar. Taught me that all life is pain and that to overcome pain is to gain power. I grew strong on her hate and saw many things. I looked into the minds of snakes that slither on their bellies and tasted the flesh of beetles in the night. I ran through rivers of blood and listened to the howls of agony that wake the world. I was the hunter and the hunted too."

"She is not your mother, Fell," cried Larka desperately. "And though she may have tasted pain and injustice, she has become evil. Evil because of her lies and hate. Our mother, Palla, gave birth to us in the den. We slept curled beneath her belly. She gave us life and warmth and love. Remember, Fell."

Fell was shaking furiously. His eyes were lost and empty.

"Palla?" he whispered faintly.

"Yes, Fell. Palla and Huttser. Your family. Come to them."

Fell was staring at the white she-wolf as though looking into his own faint memories. Larka had stepped forward, and now the she-wolf stood facing him on the strange mosaic. There they stood. Black facing white. Brother facing sister, as the eerie moonlight shimmered in the chamber. Fell dropped his head and bared his glittering white teeth. Larka was quite unable to spring. But suddenly there was a noise behind them.

"Tsarr," cried Larka, half turning her head but not taking her eyes off her brother. "Tsarr. Get to the entrance. Get to our parents."

Fell growled savagely, but he, too, kept his eyes on Larka as Tsarr slunk forward. But as Tsarr edged around the mosaic, Fell suddenly turned his head. With the very turn of his muzzle, Tsarr was flung sideways.

"You see, Larka," whispered Fell coldly. "The truest power has entered the world. It is as strong as a wind."

"Yes, Fell, you named me. I am Larka. Your sister, Larka. Huttser's daughter. The pact, Fell, remember the pact we made with Kar?"

For a moment Fell's eyes seemed to clear.

"He told me," muttered Fell bitterly, "on the ice. He told me it was safe. He lied. He is the Betrayer."

"Oh, Fell. Dear, Fell. Huttser could not see from where we were standing. He did what he thought was right."

"You do not know me anymore. I have been so lonely," cried Fell. "There is nothing but darkness."

Fell tried to turn away, but now Larka thought of what Skart had said of healing the mind, and she held him.

"No, Fell," she cried, "for I have you in my eye."

For the first time ever the wolves were glaring deep into each other's eyes without flinching. But something held them in check as they strained forward. It was as if their very thoughts were trying to touch. Closer they came and closer, and now they were looking at each other's foreheads. Suddenly there was a flash in their minds' eye. In front of Tsarr they stood motionless on the mosaic, held in check by their own confusion, but in their minds they found themselves in another place. The poppies around them were quivering red, and everywhere there were spectral wolves staring at them. Waiting. Watching and judging silently.

"Fell," whispered Larka, and her voice drifted through the meadow. "The Sight. It is not for evil. It can heal."

"I am Wolfbane. The hunter. The friend of the dead."

"No," cried Larka, "look around you. Those faces. Brassa and Bran. Khaz and Kipcha. That is truth."

But Larka's mind thrilled with doubt. She had seen her brother here before. Yet what had the Searchers said? "We are like your memories." That was it. Larka had thought Fell was dead. What she had seen had been nothing but her own memory of her brother, as he had been before the ice. So even the Sight could lie.

The shapes around them stepped forward now, summoned by their names. As Fell looked about him in the Red Meadow, he saw the faces from his childhood. The specters of his past. Fell felt his mind beginning to race. Other memories were flashing into his head. Of the Night Hunters. Of the terrible journey beneath the ice. Everywhere he saw death and violence and pain. He saw his own part in it all, and it could never stop.

"Remember," snarled Larka, "but remember right, Fell."

Larka's mind, too, was on fire, and a terrible darkness surrounded her. A yawning emptiness filled her heart. But suddenly Larka thought of Kar, standing between her parents. His face made her heart thunder, but Fell was staring at his sister's throat.

"I died," he cried. "You left me. Left me to the water and the cold. Huttser and Palla, all of you, you all betrayed me. There is nothing but death, death and fear and betrayal."

"No, we thought you were gone."

But the darkness was surrounding Larka too. Death. It was waiting for her, on the mountain. So close she could almost smell it. What did it really matter then, any of it, if it was only death that lay at the end? It was all meaningless. Let Morgra win, for she had suffered too. Everything suffered and nothing was better than anything else. The Putnar, the Lera, the humans, it was all one. Larka felt a desperate longing to be free of it all, to break the bonds of her own misery.

But was the end of the journey, of any journey, just darkness, stretching out beyond the moon and the sun and the Wolf Trail? Part of Larka longed to be with Fell, to follow him wherever he chose to go. Because of the loneliness. For brotherhood. But as she gazed at the brother she had thought dead, her mind pulled away again.

"No," she cried angrily. "That is not love."

The word sounded like a howl through her being.

Suddenly Larka saw another image, so startling in that place that her mind seemed to take on a crystal clarity. It was a spider, weaving its web. Larger and larger the web grew, and flies were caught in its grip. In that moment Larka knew the answer to a question she had asked long ago. That the spider was not conscious of what it was doing, not in the way the Varg was conscious. Not conscious and so how could it be to blame? The flies were struggling for life, but without them the spider could not live, and around the flies the web grew. More and more complex, more and more beautiful. It glittered brilliantly in the sunlight.

"It only seems cruel and empty," cried Larka, "but we give our lives for one another, so that one sun perhaps one of us may know. Perhaps a Lera may truly find an answer. And I shall give my life. Gladly. For you, Fell, and for life itself. One sun your soul will find a true resting place. Huttser never betrayed you. There is love and light and courage. I know now I was meant to prove it to you."

"I will blind you," snarled Fell. "I will kill you."

Suddenly Larka felt a great strength enter her, a strength that made her feel invulnerable.

"You cannot, Fell," she whispered. "I am already dead. For I know my own future. But it does not matter. You will not kill me. You will live. I give myself for you."

"No," growled Fell bitterly. "I am not worth that."

In the chamber, Tsarr was edging past Larka and Fell, but as he crept toward the moonlit entrance, his eyes opened in amazement. Brother and sister still stood there, trembling and motionless, but between Larka and Fell a shape was glittering. Tsarr blinked and growled and, at first, he thought it was a trick of the moonlight, for he had never seen such a thing before. As he looked on, he could see a gray Varg hovering between them.

"You are not evil, Fell," whispered Larka in the meadow. "You have just been robbed of love. Of light."

Fell gave a terrible howl. Larka sprang to meet him, and they struck, rolling over and over in the field of poppies.

Palla's legs were shaking uncontrollably as Morgra led her across the bridge.

"Fell," she kept whispering, "my little Fell."

The Night Hunters, as if held by an unspoken command, waited behind them. Palla's head reeled as she looked into the plunging chasm below them, but suddenly she heard a noise in the night ahead. It roused her from her confusion. It came, strange and mournful across the arched bridge, from the statue beyond. It was the cry of a human child.

Bran was sitting below the stone she-wolf on the altar itself, gazing around it, and the sobs that came from his little body made him shake violently. He was bathed in moonlight, and Palla could see the tears glinting in his blue eyes. Slavka was at his side and her eyes were blank and morbid. Morgra was controlling her too.

Morgra walked toward the altar. She stopped and looked coldly at the human creature below its stone counterparts. Then she turned to Palla.

"Stand next to it, sister."

Palla was helpless. She was overcome by her sudden knowledge, by the moonlight and the citadel and the creature now sobbing quietly to itself. She felt as if she was in a dream, mesmerized by the giant moon, mesmerized by the human stones.

"So, Palla," snarled Morgra as she crept closer still, "now you know that I, too, have felt the drappa's care. The love of a mother. For your own son."

"You could not love him," said Palla bitterly.

"You are wrong. I love his hate," growled Morgra, staring down at the living child and thinking of how delighted she would be to kill it when it was over. "But enough. It is time. The Man Varg waits."

Palla lifted her throat meekly. "Finish it, Morgra."

507 *The Sight*

"It is a pity, is it not, that you must die, Palla. Just as your dear betrayed sister fulfills her greatest dream."

"I have seen enough," Palla whispered sadly, and she felt terribly old. "I have seen too much."

Morgra's eyes glittered with delight. "Would you not see me come to power, sister? Well, you shall," said Morgra quietly, "or at least you shall know of my victory. For I would not slay my own blood."

"What are you saying?"

"The legend," hissed Morgra. "It says that the altar must taste blood. But not that you must die. Not yet. Very well. It shall taste blood, and you shall have your wish too. You shall never see me fulfill the legend."

Palla could not understand what Morgra was telling her. The moonlight seemed to swamp her vision.

"I shall take the blood from around your eyes, Palla," whispered Morgra, "and let you live. I shall watch the beading droplets fall from your eyes like tears, like the tears I shed all those years ago."

Palla couldn't speak. Her eyes were wide now, staring into the ghastly distance.

"Kraar," cried Morgra suddenly, "again I have need of you. Of the tongue of the scavengers."

There was a fluttering behind one of the statues, and suddenly the raven hopped out into the open. Kraar cocked his head, and his little beady eyes peered viciously at Palla as she stood there in the moonlight.

"Blind her," cried Morgra. "Pluck out her eyes."

Kraar opened his wings and lifted into the air as the human cub began to scream. But suddenly it came. The earth had begun to shake once more, and Huttser felt it in the pit. The Dragga sprang back. The quake had dislodged one of the stone columns, and it crashed to the ground beside him. In an instant Huttser was up and out.

"Huttser. Huttser!"

Huttser turned and, up the slopes, he saw Tsarr rushing toward him.

"Tsarr," he cried, "we must save Palla."

As they sprang forward, they were confronted by the Night Hunters and the bear, their jaws barring the way across the bridge. The sky was filled with birds, driven into the air by the earth tremor.

"Now, Kraar!" cried Morgra from beyond the chasm.

The raven had fluttered up on top of one of the standing plinths, and he was poised, glaring viciously at Palla's eyes.

"Do it," ordered Morgra as she swung her head down toward the child. It was still sobbing, but its wails had turned to stifled moans. Morgra felt her whole body grow hot as she glared down at the human in the wash of moonlight. She was summoning the power of the Sight and waiting for the blood. Only then could she reach the child's mind. Again Kraar opened his wings, snapping his beak furiously.

Palla felt the brush of wings on her trembling muzzle and braced herself for the searing pain. But Palla sensed something else above her. A heavy draft of air. There was a furious screech and a shape was moving upward, bearing the raven away in its claws. Above the ancient city of Harja, an eagle soared into the air. In its great talons it clutched a raven.

"Skart," cried Huttser.

The eagle was sailing higher, holding the raven fast.

"Kraar," he cried as he flew, "now I shall answer your question. You think the flying Putnar have no right to wield power over the scavengers. That you are as good as us. But the true Putnar, too, must pay a price for their strength and freedom, and that price is courage."

Suddenly Skart's talons were burying themselves deeper and deeper into Kraar's feathered body. Kraar screeched in terror and pain. Skart's great wings seemed to block out the moon as he wheeled in the sky, and then, swooping low again, he opened his claws and let the raven drop to the ground in front of Morgra. Kraar was dead.

Morgra swung around furiously. "Kill her, Slavka. I command you. Tear out her throat."

"No," snarled Huttser from beyond the chasm, but with the Night Hunters before them there was no way through. Palla seemed to have woken from sleep, and she began to growl, her hackles rising on her neck as Slavka and Morgra advanced. Huttser's courage deserted him. He could not watch, but as he turned away, there was a howl from farther down the mountain. His heart beat faster as he saw where it came from. The rebels were coming up the slope. Gart was ahead of them, Keeka and Karma and Rar, too, fighting as they ran, and at their side came Kar.

"But how?" cried Huttser.

"Your son," growled Gart, "his fury broke us through."

Huttser hardly had time to greet Kar as they locked tooth with the Balkar in front of the bridge. Huttser swung his jaws left and right, with Kar at his side. A Night Hunter swiped at Tsarr and knocked him to the ground with a blow so vicious it opened his side. But even as he fell, they noticed that something strange was happening. Some of the Balkar had begun to disengage and were swaying left and right, growling mournfully, like lost children. But other Night Hunters were still fighting, and Tsarr got to his feet again, his side dripping with blood.

Now Kar cried out. "Get to Palla, Father," he shouted. "We'll hold them off."

Kar and the rebels plunged back into the fight, and suddenly Huttser saw that the way to the bridge was clear. He sprang across and, in spite of his wound, Tsarr managed to follow him. Slavka had been disturbed by the sudden arrival of the rebels, and she stood by Palla at the altar, doubt stealing through her mind.

Morgra snarled bitterly as she saw Huttser and Tsarr behind him. "You," she hissed, her eyes blazing at Tsarr.

"I have come for him, Morgra," cried Tsarr coldly as he ran, "for the child."

Above them Skart was screeching in the sky. Slavka seemed paralyzed as she looked between Morgra and the rebels and, as Huttser reached Palla's side, his mate gazed blankly at him too.

"Huttser," she gasped, staggering forward, "Huttser."

"It is over, Palla. You are safe now."

"No, Huttser. Fell is alive. He is here. He is Wolfbane."

Huttser hardly had time to understand what Palla had said when they heard Morgra cry, "Now, now it begins."

Tsarr had reached the statue—the stone she-wolf, forever suckling those grasping infants—but as he approached the living child, blood from his wound dripped onto the altar.

Tsarr swung around to face Morgra. But as Morgra's mind gave her a silent order, Slavka's teeth were at his throat. Weakened by the fight and his wound, the old gray wolf hardly had a chance. He fell to the ground, and Slavka held him, biting deeper and deeper, the altar wet beneath him, his muzzle right next to Bran. Huttser and Palla moved to help him, but they felt a pulse quiver through the air.

Morgra was staring hungrily at the infant, and she felt a broiling energy that made her swell with power. Huttser and Palla tried to spring forward, but in that instant, both of the wolves were seized to the spot. Thought itself had been turned into energy and, at last, Morgra's hate had become a living creature.

"Now."

It was as though Huttser and Palla had been turned into statues, too, by the force of Morgra's swelling will. Beyond the bridge the Balkar and the rebels could feel it. The Night Hunters had stopped fighting, stopped moving altogether. The crows and the ravens had settled again on the statues, and only Skart was still flying, circling, for somehow Morgra could not reach this creature of wind and air.

"Gart," cried Kar as he stood at the rebels' side beyond the abyss. "What is happening? I can't move."

Even as he said it the wolves trembled. Everywhere silver specters were appearing. In legions the Searchers came again. Out of nothingness. An army of shadows materializing across the mountaintop. They stood watching, waiting, like shimmering sentinels to eternity, judging all they saw. Skart screeched as he saw them, and the moon too.

It was as round as the sun. Huttser and Palla's eyes ranged toward Kar, but still they were held in check as Morgra lifted her head and howled again. But even as she did so, Huttser and Palla were seized not with fear but with wonder.

"Look," gasped Huttser. "It's true."

Palla felt as if her heart might burst apart. Two shapes were moving toward them through the Searchers. Side by side. One white and one black. Below Skart's wheeling shadow, they were the only shapes moving among those ancient stones. Their coats glinted in the moonlight as they came. Larka and Fell were coming toward the bridge.

17
PAST AND FUTURE

I am become Death, the destroyer of worlds.
—J. Robert Oppenheimer, *quoting the* Bhagavad Gita

Huttser and Palla were speechless as they saw their children, but with joy came fear and a grave questioning. They could not move, but their tired, bewildered eyes raked the night.

"So, Larka," cried Morgra scornfully across the gulf. "Wolfbane is revealed at last."

The Balkar trembled, but even as they looked toward the black wolf and the white she-wolf at his side, the strange hypnotic stare seemed to clear a little.

"I am not Wolfbane," snarled Fell. "And I have helped my sister to master the truest power. We are a family once more. The family to conquer the evil."

As Kar heard him, and half turned to see Larka and his dead brother, he felt he was back in his cave, back in a world of dreams and nightmares.

"Come to me, Fell," whispered Morgra, "come back to me. I love you, child."

Fell took a step forward, but growled furiously. "Liar," he snarled. "There is nothing more terrible, nothing more evil than to hate something and call it love."

"It doesn't matter," cried Morgra scornfully. "Your family is too late. Can't you feel it, Fell? The moon is at its zenith and now, Larka, you will truly be united with your brother in my service."

Morgra reached out with her mind, and Larka and Fell were hurled to the side. They struggled to their feet, but there was a terrible weariness in their limbs. It was as though they were wading through sheaves of uncut corn. Larka tried to focus her mind, but as she did so, she heard Morgra's voice in her head. "Darkness. That is what you could never understand. Its power. Its glory."

"Help me, Fell," the white wolf whispered.

Her brother was trembling furiously at her side. "I can't, Larka. I fear it. She will take me back. Can't you feel the strength in her? It's growing like a storm cloud."

Larka and Fell were almost at the chasm, but Fell had stopped. His very will was draining from him.

"Focus your mind on mine, Fell," cried Larka, trying to struggle forward again. "Use the power to fight Morgra's thoughts. Release the energy of your anger, Fell, for you have a right to it. My love will protect you."

But as Larka caught sight of Kar and the bridge where she had spied her fate, she, too, was held fast, filled with sadness. Fell concentrated on his sister, trying to give his energy to her. He looked across the abyss to his parents standing next to Morgra and, suddenly, Fell felt a bubbling hate.

A furious anger swelled in him for the wolf that had lied to him and controlled his mind for so long, that had made him do so many terrible things. The wolf that had shown him the world only through her own eyes and remade it in the image of herself. Larka felt her brother's anger thrill through her mind. Suddenly she was released. She sprang onto the ancient bridge, but as she saw the chasm below, filled with vicious rocks, fear overcame her and she was held again by Morgra's mind. Now they were all here to witness it. Her death. Larka felt pain burn in her legs and she could hardly stand. Morgra's mind seemed to be filling the whole world. Larka looked up at the full round moon.

"We are lost," she moaned. "Morgra has won."

Suddenly there was a flapping of wings just above her head. "The child," cried Skart as he swooped. "The Sight is the key."

"Skart," growled Larka angrily, desperately, feeling bitterly betrayed. "You knew, didn't you? About Fell."

"Yes, Larka," cried the bird frantically. "I visited Tsinga before the Balkar killed her, and she told me what she had seen."

"But why didn't you warn me?"

"Would you have come to this place, Larka," cried Skart guiltily, "if you had known the truth before? Could you have come?"

"But, Skart—"

"Larka. Look into its mind."

"But it is the oldest law," cried Larka, "you said . . ."

"You must," called Skart as he rose again, "the Man Varg. Better you than her." Larka swung her head around toward the little human at the altar, and their eyes locked. But nothing happened.

"No," cried Skart, "look into the middle of his forehead."

The still moon, reflecting the sun on the other side of the world, shone down on the wolves and the strange statue looming above the child, but something had stepped between Larka and Bran, like a veil of darkness. Larka's eyes were misting over again, and she knew that Morgra's own will was reaching into the child's mind, pushing her away. She felt Morgra's energy and her anger, her hate and darkness, and in that moment, she knew that she was not strong enough. That her courage and her love were not enough to defeat Morgra.

But the white wolf heard another voice. It came to her, faint and disembodied and frightened in the darkness as she stood over the void.

"Larka. I have been on a terrible journey, Larka. But you brought me back."

It was true. In the chamber, as he fought with Larka, Fell had felt the Sight filling him, but not as Morgra had shown it to him, plunging him into the blindness of the sleeping mind. As Fell had wrestled with his sister, visions had suddenly flashed before him. It was as if his eyes were opening again, and in that moment, he had known that to kill the body was not the most terrible thing there was, but to kill and maim the soul with hate and lies, to kill the mind and heart that must be free.

Fell had seen Varg pups playing in a summer field and Kar sleeping at his side. He had seen the wonder of trees and a vast glistening delta of thronging birds. He had seen a wolf in a field, and it was lying down next to a lamb. Then, suddenly, Fell had been flying through the brilliant air, alive and free of guilt, the clouds racing by and, beneath the mantle of the air, the sleeping earth. Free of meaning or judgment, peaceful and unknowing.

"Fell," whispered Larka tenderly. "Help me, Fell. But I need your darkness now, your anger."

As Larka felt the force of Fell's angry mind, and her own love for him, she realized the mist was clearing. All that had happened to Fell, all that he had experienced was helping her mind to drive Morgra back. Larka could see the child again, clearly now, and then, suddenly, it happened.

Larka was no longer on the bridge, but by the statue of the she-wolf. She looked down in astonishment for her paws had become tiny hands. She blinked with surprise and gazed out toward the bridge. There stood her wolf body, over the void, and beyond stood Kar and the Balkar. But although Larka knew who Kar was, she felt strangely separate from him, strangely separate from everything around her, from her parents, from Morgra too.

Her sight was not noticeably different, except that the outline of distant shapes had become clearer. But the darkness, too, was greater than before. But it wasn't this that made Larka feel so strange. It was the pulsing energy that she felt in her head. With it came a new clarity, but Larka also noticed that her other senses, her hearing and her sense of smell had changed. They were weaker, as though a wall had come down between her and the instinctive world.

Larka felt cut off suddenly, isolated, but even as she felt this her mind throbbed with longing. It seemed to be swelling in her head, as though the loss of her other senses were forcing her energy up the stem of her spine. In that instant she knew that her most powerful channel to the world around her were her eyes and the sights that lay about her.

She longed to take everything in, to see more and more. To understand. Another force was crying through her be-ing—the will of the wild wolf to survive. But Larka was amazed as she realized that it had been magnified tenfold. Tsarr had been wrong. The child's instincts to survive were not only as strong as the wolf's but far, far stronger. Larka felt a swelling sense of superiority to everything about her. To the wolves and the specters and the stones that human hands had turned into bodies. She longed to know it all and to control it too. To turn her instincts into will and turn that will to power.

"Take it, then," whispered a cold, disembodied voice. There was jealousy in that voice, but a longing too. It was Morgra.

"Show us all the Vision, Larka. For it is yours. You have become the Man Varg."

"No!" Larka trembled.

But her mind was already reaching out with the power of the Sight, searching for the creatures around her, and she wanted to know. To know all.

"See," she whispered. "See."

Larka knew they were all looking, for the Man Varg's mind had come among them. Morgra saw it, and her family, Skart and Slavka and the Balkar, the scavengers waiting on the ancient stones and the spectral Searchers, the guards licking their wounds in the pass below Harja, and the rebels too. Even in the trees and the hedgerows, in the waters and the burrows the Lera saw it. At the delta, the great meeting place, five thousand birds saw it before them. Their eyes were one. Nature itself had become a witness, and in that moment, they stopped fighting one another, stopped fighting themselves, and looked up.

Then the Vision came. At first there was a sea, and out of it came strange fish, pushing forward on their stubby fins. Then those fins began to change into feet, and the creatures began to move out across the land. Forests rose, and among their vast branches were giant moths and huge, swooping leathery birds. There were other giant creatures there, too, stalking across the earth, fighting and preying on one another with such terrible ferocity for their enemies, and such infinite tenderness for their own young, that the earth seemed to quiver.

Then the earth was shaking. Volcanoes erupted in great spouts of brilliant red fire, and the ground trembled and split apart. There seemed to be things coming through the air, coming from the heavens, hurtling down and sending up huge clouds of dust that put out the sun, and the mighty creatures beneath it shuddered and died. But among them, smaller things had survived. Little mammals that set to work in the woods. They leaped from the cover of the woods onto the plains, and there they saw cattle running in terror through the sunlight, and giant speckled horses lifting their necks to the leaves. The sunlight burned around them, and its fury was their fury too. But among all this was a single shape stirring in the dust.

At first it crouched, its back furred with hair like the coat of the wolf. In its paw it held a club and, as the animals watched, it rose on its back legs. Straighter and straighter it stood, and as it did so, it began to change. The fur dropped from its body, and its head lifted higher and higher. As it looked around, the nearby Lera ran in terror from its angry gaze.

Suddenly Larka knew what they were witnessing as they watched this creature that had been an animal and now stood before them, transformed.

"The great secret," she gasped. "You are Lera too."

Before them was a human. The secret was a vision of the ancient past. Of the dawn and ascent of Man.

"So Man is an animal also," hissed Morgra's voice around her. "I knew it, Larka. But he is more than Lera, for only he can understand and control. Man is the Shape Changer, Larka. Man is Wolfbane. That is why the animals must serve him, and be his slaves."

"No," whispered Larka wonderingly. "We are all Shape Changers."

But as Larka watched and the animals looked on, incapable of affecting it, helpless witnesses to the human's birth, it stooped and picked something else up in its hand. It was a branch, and from its tip flamed the humans' burning air. As they saw that flash of fire and the human creature wielding it like a sword, everything began to change around it too.

"In the mind of the Man Varg," hissed Morgra, "then

who shall be free? I shall tell you. None. None shall be free of Man's mind and his power."

Stones rose into giant dens that multiplied and spread out across the plain. There were things of great beauty there, beauty and cunning, but the forests fell before Man, and the earth itself was shaken by human hands, as all of nature seemed to run before him. Man was everywhere, spreading, mating, multiplying, filled with the same desire to survive that gripped all life, but driven by a power and a hunger that not even they could understand. Some of them were crying and wailing, while others snarled with anger and fear. All of them were looking up at the skies, and they longed to know what they were, where they had come from, and where they were going. Larka felt a terrible pity.

But Man's fury and his hunger were as remorseless as the sun. The humans turned their anger on one another, too, at times with such appalling cruelty that they seemed nothing more than mad beasts. Everywhere they were fighting with their burning air, but not simply to hunt and eat and survive, but to know, as though they would cast a light into all darkness, into night, into the heavens and the future itself.

"No," gasped Larka. "No."

"Show us, Larka," growled Morgra's voice. "You have seen the past. Now don't you want to know what will come?"

Among these humans now some seemed to be living in peace with the creatures that shared their world, with the birds and the cattle and the wild wolf. And they had skin like the red girl in the story. Across mountains and vast prairies they rode on horses under giant skies and sang songs of worship and danced with wonder around their fires as they praised the cry of the wolf in the night. They chased great herds of buffalo, and gave one another the names of animals, and for a time, it seemed that man had learned to live in harmony with all the forces of life. But others came, hungry for land and driven themselves, they hardly knew where, to eat up all they surveyed. They raised forts of wood and made war with those who had come before, and soon the prairies were littered with the carcasses of the buffalo, and the voice of ancient song was stilled.

"More," growled Morgra hungrily, "show us more."

Now Larka looked up through the child's eyes at the moon and stars, and she knew that the stories of the moon had been lies. That the stories of Tor and Fenris and Wolf-banc had been lies. And with that knowledge came a great surge of freedom. Larka wanted to journey forever, out into the night, like a bird, like Skart, traveling on and on, past the moon and the sun, past the planets. Like the clear, straight paw prints of the hunting wolf. An arrow of mind, cast by the sprung bow of human thought into infinity. Beyond light and dark, beyond love and hate, into forever.

Larka remembered the spider again, and she knew that just as she could see out into the stars, she could look with the power of this mind down, too, at the smallest of living creatures. That she could look farther still. That she could look into water and see the tiniest of fish. That she could see, even on their backs, the microbes and bacteria that fed on the great carcass of being. That, even as she looked at these tiny wriggling forms, she could see beyond, into the very cells and atoms that made up their shapes.

The tiny atoms were like the stars, too, like seeing planets revolving around the sun. She wanted to reach in, to reach in with her paws, with her hands, and hold those miniature worlds in her palms, to control the very force that bound life into shape and meaning.

"This is true freedom," she cried.

Then Larka's mind flamed. It flamed with power and strength and cunning, and she knew that Man would not only look, but one day try to control the energy that dwelt in all things and the power that gave strength to the Sight itself. Suddenly the animals were looking on a strange column of metal that glinted in a desert. It rose as high as a pine and its center was hollow. At its top hung a metal sphere as round as the sun, and Larka alone knew what it was. It had been made by the ingenuity of Man as a force for war. Like Man's swords or his arrows, his hands had forged this terrible thing out of the strength and cunning of his mind. As the animals looked on, the strange sphere fell.

"The Sight," cried Morgra's voice as it plunged toward the earth. "This, at last, is the Sight made flesh."

As the sphere struck, the earth flashed before them, a burst of light brighter than the sun, a mushroom cloud of dust, and the air itself was fire. A tidal wave of liquid heat swept away everything around it. The humans and the Lera and even the stones within its reach turned to flame as they watched, consumed by the very energy that Larka had seen locked inside the nucleus of the earth, the energy that she had felt through the power of the Sight. About the devastation hung an aura, but not the vivid colors of fear or hunger, hate or love, Larka had seen about the Lera— a sickly glow.

Still the Vision went on and the animals realized that Man had not yet destroyed himself with this power. As the humans fought to survive and their minds brought them success, their dens spread everywhere, and around them bigger dens rose. The world was lit with light that seemed to have been drawn from the very thunderbolts, and peace seemed to have come upon the humans. But in that peace a terrible realization began to dawn on the watching Lera. The world itself was suffering. It had grown black and tired. Then they saw forests consumed by machines, and the seas grew dark and polluted. Smoke and fire were being pumped into the skies.

"The elements," whispered Larka, "what are they doing? Tsarr was right. The humans are losing contact with what they are. They are forgetting their instincts."

Even the air had changed, and above their vision the sky seemed thinner and the sun's heat had a new power. A power that was pitiless. Then suddenly the animals were looking on great mountains of ice. The walls of blue cold rose before them, pure, magnificent, beautiful. But even as they looked, great cliffs of ice crashed from their rocky peaks and thundered into the sea. The seas began to rise as the ice caps melted and the air grew thinner and thinner. Terrible winds began to blow and then, when the seas had swamped the land, and the flowers and the trees and the animals were gone, when everything that Larka loved was gone, even man, a terrible cold settled on the earth. Again the ice came, but this time it was everywhere.

"The fifth element," gasped Larka. "Man will try to control the elements, until the elements control him. This is truly Wolfbane's winter."

Again Larka heard that voice. Morgra. "And now you have seen, you are truly free, Larka. Free to do as you will. For what could you be loyal to after that? What could you love or be faithful to? What but destruction and power?"

Even as she said it, Larka felt Morgra's mind and she knew that she could control her, that she could control them all. That, through the child, the Man Varg could master all the Lera with the Sight and turn them to her service. But the knowledge brought nothing but terror. Larka knew the secret of Man's freedom and so his power—but what they had seen was leading to the death of nature itself.

"If this is their freedom, I do not want it," she cried pitifully. "I am a wolf, nothing more."

"Do not want it?" Morgra's thoughts growled. "It is too late. You have touched the Lera. The trap has been sprung. You are the greatest Putnar the world has ever known."

"Man," said Larka bitterly. "If I don't stop them, they will destroy everything."

"And because there is only death at the end of the journey," cried Morgra triumphantly, "not just the death of each of us, but the death of everything there is, take the power, Larka. Take revenge on the Lera. Take revenge for the anguish of life as Man has always done, because it is he who hates the very thing he comes from, and the thing he is going to."

"No."

Morgra was laughing now. Her laughter seemed to shake the mountain. "But you have shown us their past, Larka, our past, and the future too. What is there left?"

Suddenly, Larka felt a great surge of hope as she remembered what she had learned in the Red Meadow. "No, this may never come about. For I have visited the Searchers, and that may change the future—this may change the future. There must be hope."

Larka seemed to be pushing Morgra's mind away.

"Then lead us against them," hissed Morgra. "Lead the Lera against the humans and wipe them from the face of the earth."

Larka was paralyzed, but for a moment she was tempted by Morgra's great thought. But she remembered her journey with little Bran and the secret, too, that they had learned together. Then she saw a wall of ice before her again, and in its grip, tiny specks of algae as she had seen in the frozen river.

"The still element," she whispered, "that holds all in potential."

Larka threw up her head. "No, Morgra," she cried. "For life is sacred and Man and Lera need each other to survive. Man may come from the Lera, but he has an understanding that the Lera in their present shapes can only glimpse. He can learn and he can truly remember. Perhaps he will find the answer that we all seek."

The white she-wolf closed her eyes. She emptied her

mind, and then she was on the bridge again as Morgra, on the other side, turned toward the child.

"Down, Morgra," snarled Larka furiously. "Down."

Morgra knew she was beaten. Above them the great moon was passing out of its zenith. Morgra grew instantly old and weak, as though she was shriveling up. The old she-Varg slumped onto her paws in front of the statue, and Huttser and Palla could move again.

"Hurry," cried Larka. "Mother, Father. Bring the child to me."

As Huttser turned to the statue, Slavka stood above the child, and their eyes locked.

"Have you not done enough?" whispered Huttser.

Slavka was held by Huttser's anger. He fancied he saw something else in her, too, the flickerings of shame. Huttser crouched down by the creature. For a moment Huttser saw something in Bran's eyes, too, as he looked back at the wolf, as though those little eyes had grown in intelligence with the vision they had all shared. Echoes of those terrible scenes were still moving across its orbs. But now the little human was desperate to reach out for any comfort, and as it recognized Huttser's scent, it began to scramble onto the Varg's back.

"Come," said Larka calmly, her voice echoing across the drop below her. "Bring it back across the abyss. I will protect you."

Silently, Palla and Huttser threaded across the bridge, the child on Huttser's back. They walked among the Searchers and placed Bran beside their daughter. She licked the creature fondly, now safely on the other side.

"Slavka," called Larka, "Slavka. Join us, sister."

As they faced each other again, like twins, the rebel leader growled guiltily and began to back away. In front o the statue, Morgra lifted her head.

"So, Larka. What will you do with your power?"

Larka's ears came forward. "Nothing, Morgra."

"Surely you will kill me."

"No, Morgra, I will not kill you."

"But you are the victor," growled Morgra, filled with anger and confusion. "It is the law. Take your spoils."

"Have you learned nothing at all? Have you not learned that we must forgive and show compassion. I do not want the power of Man, Morgra. I am just a wolf."

"But think of the power to enslave all."

"The secret of the ancient verse," growled Larka. "You hoped it would enslave the Lera. But let me remind you for a final time, it is a question, Morgra, not an answer. 'In the mind of the Man Varg, then who shall be free?'"

Morgra snarled.

"So I shall give you that answer. Those who chose freedom, Morgra, shall be free, just as those with the Sight must choose their own way. As I choose it now. This secret shall not enslave us at all, it shall aid us all, Man and Lera alike. Man's mind is on a journey toward freedom, if he doesn't destroy himself first And this Vision. If we learn from it, so can he The wolves are free of the Man Varg, as are all the Lera. It is over."

Larka turned her head to the Searchers. "Be gone," she cried in a booming voice, "for the past is done with and we must look to a true future now. Or to a present, as wolves. The Pathways of Death are sealed."

The army of silver specters dipped their heads in submission, and their forms began to fade, grow transparent, and vanish into night.

"You think you can change darkness to light," cried Morgra savagely. As Larka had turned, Morgra found she could move again. "That you can alter the law of life, the law of power and survival? But you have not won, Larka. You will never win. There will always be one such as I to fight you, to hate you, as long as the humans build their dens. Forever."

Morgra sprang and crossed the ground in an instant. She was on the bridge too. Morgra and Larka were facing each other above the chasm.

"You," snarled Morgra bitterly. "You."

Larka knew now that with a single thought she could cast Morgra into the void. But she did not use her strength. She could not. Not after the Vision that brought such terrible power. She longed to run free with Kar and have cubs of her own. But if she must fight, she must fight as a wolf now.

"You think you are evil and darkness, Morgra," whispered Larka scornfully, "but even you are not evil. Only what you do is evil, because it thinks to raise darkness above light and cripples and maims. But the truest power of the Sight, Morgra, is to heal."

Morgra was straining toward her. "What they did to me," she snarled. "Your mother's pack."

"They were mistaken, and they were wrong. But because of it you would have the world live forever in hate and guilt and darkness. Like some terrible story we can never escape."

"They betrayed me. The wolf is the Betrayer."

"Don't you know yet who the Betrayer really is?" growled Larka. "Hate is the Betrayer, Morgra, for it feeds on itself. Hate and its mother, Fear."

But Morgra's eyes were burning. "Then I will kill the thing you love. I will kill the child."

Then Larka knew that it must be, as surely as the wolf must hunt and fight and live. As surely as Man must fight. Morgra's jaws opened and, as she sprang at Bran, Larka rose to meet her and protect him. High over the abyss, on the arched bridge, they were fighting, just as Larka had foreseen in the water.

"Kar," cried Larka as they fought, "take Bran to safety."

Even as Larka held Morgra off from the baby, Kar sprang forward and lifted it by the hide around its belly and swung it away from the fighting she-wolves. Around they spun, with Larka forcing Morgra back toward the rebels and her parents. Kar placed Bran carefully by Fell, Huttser, and Palla, and shuddered as he turned to watch. Kar's heart was racing, for as the wolves struggled, they came closer and closer to the edge.

Then they felt it. It came deep from the earth itself, as though the whole world were shaking with anger. It was more furious than before. The ground they were standing on was moving. Around them the statues and the stone trees began to sway and totter and fall and, in a great flurry of wings, the terrified birds took to the air. The whole mountain was moving, quaking, rocking the ancient city, as ancient as that tree in the forest, to its crumbling foundations. And then the stones beneath the bridge began to dislodge, just as Larka had seen it before in the water. First one, then two, tumbling into the gulf.

"Larka," cried Kar furiously.

"Help her," gasped Palla.

Morgra slipped backward and nearly fell and, as Larka saw those stones begin to go beneath them, an anger woke in the she-wolf that seemed to answer the mountain.

But if we are really free, cried her thoughts, *if we can change the future, why must I make this sacrifice? Don't I, too, have a choice after all? Don't I have the right to live and be happy? Why should I be trapped within a legend?*

Larka looked up. Beyond Morgra she suddenly saw a narrow ledge on the side of the mountain.

No, whispered her thoughts bitterly, *because to really love one another, first the wolves must see. They must understand suffering. That's why the stories say Tor sent Sita down to the world. Because of love.*

Yet still something stirred in Larka. Freedom. The freedom of Wolfbane as he was hurled from the heavens for his rebellion, the freedom of Man, and of living animals, the freedom of the untamed wolf.

"A story," she cried. "Is it just a story?"

The little family stood paralyzed as they watched. It went suddenly, the whole bridge. And as it went, Larka sprang. As her springing paws reached out for the ledge, and they all looked on, it was as though time itself had frozen. As a minute particle seen through the slits of a screen can seem to be going in two directions at the same time, Larka might have fallen or reached the ledge.

It was as though her future was nothing but the choice of those who watched, their choice and so, their responsibility. As though they had been given the free will to reach back into the ancient past and to sacrifice Sita herself once more, or to stop that terrible act before it ever happened and escape a legend. So the wolves would not need to resurrect Sita in their stories and pretend there is no death and no suffering. Because love takes responsibility, and in all experience, too, there is a pact between the seer and the seen, the listener and the storyteller, the judge and the judged.

But between Larka and the ledge, between a story and freedom, between the past and the present, stepped reality. What really happens. And, as the family watched, horror woke in their minds. A horror nearly as terrible as that blast of energy. Larka missed, and down they both fell, Larka and Morgra together, spinning toward oblivion. Their bodies broke together on the vicious rocks. Kar felt his heart following Larka into the ravine, and a part of the wolf died with her.

"Please," he cried, "the pact."

Fell's eyes grew black and angry and bright with pain, and Huttser and Palla's minds began to howl. The bridge crashed on top of the she-wolves, and the ravine was now an uncrossable gulf, the air a void of empty silence, stirred only by the sobbing of a tiny human heart.

There they stood and looked down helplessly. Above them in the giant sky, the birds rose like a great soul, released from torment and lifting into the firmament. As they scattered across the skies, the moon was as full as ever. Its light, as pure and brilliant as eternity, shone down as though reflected by that vision of the little sun in the cloud, shone down with neither pity nor sadness on the wolves.

Beyond the chasm, in the grass where old Tsarr lay dead, a statue was lying at his side. The giant statue of a she-wolf and her human cubs—Romulus and Remus, Fren and Barl too. It had split apart, broken by the moving earth itself, and the images of the children had shattered. But the she-wolf lay intact in the grass and, across the void, a real child was stirring.

18
LARKA'S BLESSING

KAR WOKE SUDDENLY AND SHIVERED. He emerged from the agony of his dream and saw Skart's yellow and black eyes gazing into the distance. The eagle ruffled his feathers guiltily now as he watched Fell padding slowly out of the trees. Huttser and Palla lay in the grass, too, with the little human between them, below the mountain that concealed Harja. The wolves lifted their heads as they, too, caught sight of their son. The son that had been brought back from the dead. As the black wolf drew nearer in the sunlight, he addressed Skart wearily.

"What was it all for, Skart?"

"To warn us," answered Skart. "And teach us."

"To teach us what, Skart? Fear and suffering? Loss?

Will that make us better? Doesn't the Varg suffer enough in the world?"

The black wolf turned and walked slowly toward Kar and his own parents, huddled around the human child. Palla growled softly, but there was an emptiness, too, in her look. It was four suns since they had seen Larka die on the bridge.

They had known immediately that Morgra's power was broken, even before she and Larka fell. As the specters vanished, it was as though the Balkar had woken from a terrible nightmare. Huttser and the rebels had wandered among them, and the Night Hunters had looked about them helplessly. But as they gazed back at the rebels, the wolves had all shared the same guilty sadness. Larka's terrible vision had united them. Brak had led them away and, in the mountains, the news of Morgra's death was already being carried on the howls of the rebel pack. Now, no longer the rebels. On the howls of Gart and Rar and all the free wolves.

"Fell," said Palla quietly, "what now. Where shall we go?"

Fell looked down at little Bran. "We must return it to its mother. To its own kind."

"Back to the pack boundaries?" Huttser whispered. "At least there is nothing to fear there anymore."

"No," agreed Fell quietly, "not even the Stone Den. But what is there to hope for either, with Larka gone? I hate to think of her. Up there, pecked at by the scavengers."

"Fell," Huttser growled, "it is only her body, and the Lera must live."

As Fell thought of the flying scavengers lifting into the air, he shuddered, but he remembered then what Huttser had once said of Brassa's body and now, suddenly, he understood.

"The pact. We failed her," whispered Kar bitterly.

"Kar. We have one another. We have the future." Palla's eyes held a grave strength in them. Beyond her own pain. "And she gave you back to me, Fell."

"Did she?" said Fell wistfully. "Yes. But I would not have had her die for me."

For many suns they stayed in the shadow of the mountain, unable to abandon the scene of Larka's death. Their wound was far deeper than any cut. The only solace for Huttser and Palla was the sight of Fell, sitting in the grass or talking with Kar. He had a strange quality about him, slightly distant, thoughtful, and brooding. But he was constantly asking them questions about their journey, and they could see that more and more memories were waking in his mind. Yet they knew, too, instinctively, that he had been somewhere they could never travel.

Of the Sight, Fell said little, though he did remember what had happened to him after the ice. He was almost dead when the river had swept him to the bank where a fallen tree had shattered the surface. There the Night Hunters had found him and, after feeding him, had taken him to Morgra. She had known immediately the gift that burned inside him, and she had had the Balkar scouts who had discovered him murdered. But that is all that Fell told them, for whenever he talked of Morgra, the hackles on his neck rose.

With sorrow in their hearts, at last the wolves left Larka's body to the mountain. Bran rode on Fell's back as they journeyed southwest, crossing the mighty Carpathians and dropping back out of the clouds. Skart flew always above them. They came to strange wooded valleys where the humans' castles loomed like sleeping giants, their fierce crenellated stones touching the skies. They walked again in the shadow of walled fortresses and of brightly painted towns, where colored towers rose over the forests and dark wooden churches squatted eerily among the leaves. They saw, too, everywhere, the evidence of war. Fires that would burn in the night and, in the distance, men riding through the mists on horseback.

The Lera watched them warily as they went, for the wolves felt like soldiers of the future who, returning home from the killing fields of a terrible war, where lives had been cut down like poppies, would seem strange and fearful to those that had sent them out to protect what they thought was good. Strange and fearful because they had been wounded, and so were thought the enemies of life.

They came to the Gathering Place in the valley of Kosov, and then to Kar's cave, where Palla said a silent farewell to Skop's bones. They came to the human dens where Kar had scavenged the pig and, as they journeyed together, Larka's loss ate at each of their hearts. Morgra was gone and the curse lifted, new packs were forming in the mountains, and yet they felt strangely cheated. But of all of them, Kar was the most deeply hurt.

One evening as they were passing through the forests, Palla stopped. She had seen two wolves in the far distance, weaving silently through the pines, traveling southeast. She raised her tail and nodded gladly as the wolves disappeared. It was Keeka and Karma.

Only a few suns later, Fell stopped their march, snarling at something ahead. The others had smelled it too. Ahead, they could see a wide valley, filled with the humans' burning air. The fires flickered along an avenue of poplars, but it wasn't this that had roused the wolves' throats. In between the trees, impaled on long stakes, they saw bodies. Hundreds of them: dead humans. The wooden poles had pierced the humans' hearts, and the blood still dripped on the ground.

"It's like the pit I saw," gasped Kar bitterly. "They are demons."

Huttser noticed the skin of the humans. It was darker than little Bran's, for these draggas did not come from the land beyond the forests. They were Turks who had swept up from the southern lands and met the fury and cruelty of a human who would give his name to a terrible myth. The story of one who walked forever with the dead, feeding on the blood of his own in a lonely castle high on a mountaintop: the Impaler.

But Man's real battles were as terrible as any dark myths. The humans had fought for land and power, driven by other stories that burned in their minds, stories quite as powerful as their shining swords, of a prophet who brought truth to the people of the book, and of a god impaled on a cross.

The smell of blood came stronger and stronger to their nostrils. But none of the wolves felt hungry. Instead they felt tired and sickened. It was as though all they had been through and seen had carried them suddenly beyond their own natures.

So what was left of the legendary family passed away from Man and his wars. Wars that would stretch like a river of blood through history, touching Transylvania and the region of the Balkans, and lighting flames that would flare up again and again. Yet flames that might one day send a light into darkness, too, and only in the remembering of it all, open all men's eyes.

The wolves reached the river where Fell had broken through the ice, and the Varg stood staring gravely into its rushing waters. But this time they plashed through its vigorous current, holding Bran up above the surface, to the far shore and climbed dripping and safe onto the bank. They skirted Tsinga's valley, too, and reached the graveyard where Kar and Larka had fallen in.

"It was all meant to be, wasn't it?" growled Kar angrily, as the family looked down sadly into the earth. "You could never escape the legend, Larka, could you? As you never escaped the grave we fell into so long ago."

But as the family looked down and remembered Larka, they knew another secret—that nothing that was alive could escape.

It was late autumn when they came in sight of the den where their journey together had begun. The willow tree had grown low across the cave mouth, and the boulder on the hill above the den, where they had banished Morgra, had been dislodged from the slope and blocked the entrance. Palla noticed a chink at its side and the boulder looked precarious, for it had landed on a bed of rubble. As Palla pushed with her strong muzzle, it rolled away.

But as soon as it did so, the wolves heard a low, spitting snarl. A family of red foxes had taken up residence, and the mother was guarding her cubs. Palla backed out of the den, and they padded away from the cave. But somewhere in her heart Palla was glad that the place where Larka had been born was giving shelter to new life.

Beyond the den, the wolves stopped and looked up. There, high above the forest, stood the huge castle. It still had a quality that seemed strange and mournful in the fading sun. But it had lost its terror for the wolves, too, and its mystery, and now, as they thought of all they had come through, all they had seen and lost, its once fearful walls looked empty and simply sad.

The wolves crept closer to the village in the night and, as they came through the trees, they saw the humans' burning air. Kar hovered in the trees with Huttser and Palla as Fell crept forward with Bran on his back. As the black wolf approached the human dens, he slunk to the ground, and Bran slid from his shoulders. The child's eyes were frank and trusting as Fell looked down at him and licked his forehead.

"Good-bye," he whispered.

Bran's little hands reached out and clutched the wolf's black fur.

"No," growled Fell, remembering what Skart had told him of Jarla. "You must be with your own. And Larka made a promise."

Bran began to wail as Fell padded away, and suddenly

Fell turned back. Even as the wolf watched, the child's eyes looked angry, and it showed its teeth. Then to Fell's amazement it gave a little snarl.

"Very well," Fell called. "You have lived with the wolf so we will make a pact you and I. The pact of the Putnar. I shall run free and wild and send my calls to you in the night as you search out your truths. And in my cries, I shall remind you of the beauty and the pain of life. In them, you shall hear the icy winds stroking my fur and the snows falling silently on the distant mountains, falling on the animals in the secret places of loss and ignorance, of suffering and fear. And you shall remember to keep the pathways of your senses open to what life is, and what it can be."

The child gazed up at Fell.

"But since it is your success that shall control the world, you must think for the Lera too. For it is from the Lera that you come. So you must promise, too, as Putnar, to protect the wilderness from your own power. For you draw on the wilderness, as the Sight draws on the energy that dwells in all. Promise, to protect life itself."

Even as he said it and gazed down at the child, an image flashed into his mind. It was of Bran, but he had grown into a fine young man. His clear blue eyes carried strength and kindness and justice in them, and though he was a warrior who walked with two great hounds at his side, he used his sword to protect all that was natural, for in his heart he remembered all they had seen together. Fell turned and vanished into the trees.

As the humans heard the wolves' calls, they came from the village carrying clubs and flaming torches, and when they saw Bran sitting there in the dust they were filled with fear. But suddenly a figure pushed through them. She was tall, and great locks of curly black hair tumbled down her back. She hovered there, uncertain. The child had grown, but her instincts knew it. Almost unable to believe her eyes, to believe that it had been restored to her, she suddenly rushed forward and, as she bundled him up into her arms, the sobs shook through her beautiful body.

The leaves fell and winter came once more to Transylvania, biting the land with cold and piling the mountaintops with snow and, because the animals possess the gift of memory but faintly, they began to forget what Larka had shown them. The snow settled on the forest and the slopes. It fizzed around the edges of the river and heaped about the sides of the castle, softening for a time that grim aspect.

Fell was becoming more and more distant. As he watched winter's teeth closing in on the Lera and the forests again, and felt the anger of survival stirring in his guts, more and more his thoughts would turn back to Morgra and all he had seen and done, as though the patterns of the land were shaping the contours of his mind. But they were thoughts he could not share with his parents or Kar, and the evenings would see the wolf standing solitary on the slopes of the valley, etched black against the freezing white.

The pain of Larka's loss tortured Kar. He was losing the will to live. He would howl long and softly to himself, a mourning call, and mutter of Tor and Fenris and Sita. He would ask Palla to tell him the stories of magic and power from his childhood, and somewhere make himself believe that Larka had not gone. That one sun soon she would step from the trees like Tor, to heal his wound. But in his secret heart, Kar doubted that stories could change life.

Kar was lying on his own one wintry night, though, when suddenly he looked up. A she-wolf was coming toward him through the grass. Kar's heart began to pound furiously. It couldn't be. It was a cub's fable. Larka was padding through the stones. Kar sprang forward, whimpering, but even as he did so and saw the scar across the she-wolf's muzzle, he started to growl. It was only the darkness that had made her coat appear white.

"Slavka," growled Kar.

Kar growled again, but there was something in her eyes, a warmth, that touched him.

"What do you want here?" he said.

Slavka looked tired and sad.

"Solace, and perhaps forgiveness."

Huttser and Palla sprang up as Kar and Slavka approached them, but as Slavka began to talk to them they realized immediately that she had changed. Her eyes were clear and certain as she told them how she had found her way down from Harja.

"You have softened, Slavka," said Huttser as they listened to her. "Have you stepped beyond the harshness of survival?"

"We must survive," growled Slavka, "but I was too hard, Huttser. I'll use my instincts and hunt where I will and fight when I must. But as a wolf. No more than that."

"No more talk then of a Greater Pack," whispered Huttser, "or a boundary that can keep everything out."

"The wolf needs to know its boundaries if we are to respect one another," answered Slavka thoughtfully. "And not murder one another as we try to survive. And perhaps we all need to ask Larka's Blessing of each other."

"Larka's Blessing," said Palla in amazement.

"The free wolves," said Slavka softly, "they no longer call it Tratto's Blessing. Now they call it Larka's Blessing."

There was a sadness in Huttser and Palla's eyes but a gratitude too.

"But, Huttser," Slavka went on slowly, "a Greater Pack was a foolish dream. Until, perhaps, the wolves are ready for it. They must choose that for themselves. And now I know there are things in life that we cannot keep out with mere boundaries. Should not keep out."

"What do you mean, Slavka?" asked Palla.

"Larka. She did cross boundaries, not only of rivers and trees, or the markings of power and fear, but borders of the mind and spirit. She crossed them for us all."

"And now she has gone," said Kar.

"Or perhaps she has simply crossed the greatest boundary of all," Slavka said, looking kindly at Kar.

"And she never even learned Bran's secret?" said Palla, shaking her head and thinking back to that terrible day the wolf had been murdered by the Balkar.

"Bran's secret?" growled Huttser.

"Before he died he told me that it's not so terrible," said Palla, "not so terrible to be the Sikla."

Huttser raised his head. "What do you seek here, Slavka?" he asked.

Slavka's eyes were unafraid. "To join your pack. To have cubs again and love and protect them. To live."

Huttser and Palla remembered Morgra outside the den, Morgra who in her very birth had been made the scapegoat. Huttser licked his mate.

"Very well, and we shall learn together."

Kar had a vivid dream that night. Larka seemed to rise out of a swirling mist, and then she was standing before him among the trees, and her coat was shining with a brilliant light. The wolf whimpered in his sleep, and though her jaws did not open, Kar could hear her talking to his sleeping mind.

"Love is what shields us from the pain and fear and loss, Kar," she whispered. "What shields us from ourselves too."

Love, Larka? Kar thought as he felt the bitterness of how she had left him. *The stories command us to love, Larka, but isn't there a law in life that makes love nothing more than a word we use for our own?*

"Perhaps love takes cunning, Kar. I despaired, too, and at the last it made me believe even more in a pack and a mate and cubs. Believe in life, Kar, and freedom. Be true to your own nature, but don't let it turn on itself. And, Kar, love is not a commandment, it is a need, as real as eating. But, like the oriole in the old, old story, love must be free, as free as the birds. Free to leave and free to return."

Larka paused. "But make me a promise, Kar. Promise that whenever you really love someone," she whispered, "you will tell them. You will not keep it a secret."

Kar whined.

"And give Fell a message," Larka went on. "That he must learn to close the eye of the Sight too. To heal himself. For the Sight does heal."

Kar growled and stirred in his dream. "But you died, Larka. We all die," he whispered with sudden anguish.

"Perhaps only when we know that can we truly begin to live. To see the wonder of it all, not the darkness. Though it is all really one. As Man and Lera come from one. But there is something in our thoughts that splits us, and we must beware. As the dragga is split from the drappa. Beware of the dragons that fight in our minds, that throw shadows on the world about us. Trust life, Kar, let it carry you to safety."

"I would sacrifice myself if I could bring you back. Kill myself."

In his dream Larka snarled furiously at him from the trees. "No," she cried, "no more sacrifices. Not in blood."

"But you, you sacrificed yourself."

"I did not escape the legend, Kar. For it was its own kind of trap, as Man's freedom will be if he doesn't learn. But life is not a legend or a story. Reality is far more precious than a story. And to love one another we must begin to see one another properly. Besides, Kar, at times, the greatest courage of all is to live."

Kar trembled.

"So let me give you a blessing. When everything around you seems conspiring to tear out your heart and your mind, or show you that there is nothing but power and survival, look up there, Kar, at the moon in the giant sky. Hold it as a truth, beyond what we are too blind or ignorant to see all around us. Hold it like love, Kar, and remember me."

"Remember." Kar shuddered in his sleep.

"Learn to heal your mind."

"How?" growled Kar sadly.

"By going out there and looking, Kar. By turning and walking out of the cave of your own thoughts. By opening your eyes and feeding your sight on the mists that furl around the mountains and the mighty rivers that thunder to the sea. For it is you, Kar."

"But the humans, Larka, they will destroy it all."

"Not if they learn to love what they really are. Kar, I will show you one last thing before I go. Let me give you a vision of hope."

"Hope. Hope and faith? Like our stories?"

"Kar," whispered Larka firmly. "Let me show you something perhaps truer than a story. And not just truer than the story of Sita, but the story of the wolf Fren too. This is for you, Kar, and it is something far beyond even the stories of the Varg. Look, Kar."

Suddenly, before Kar there stood that army of humans, their heads bowed in shame and fear and confusion. But among them now, side by side, man next to woman, some stood taller, calmly, like guardians. Though their eyes were closed, they turned their heads to one another, and Kar knew that they could read one anothers' thoughts, and that they loved one another and the animals, too, from where they had come. For they had looked into the darkness of their own natures, their own past, and been able to bring light out of that darkness. As Kar watched, he noticed that bees and little butterflies were settling on their shoulders and backs and, suddenly, the strange humans opened their eyes and looked back at Kar. When he saw them, they were so beautiful that he was transfixed. Their eyes. The humans had the eyes of wolves.

"Stay near to the light," whispered Larka.

"Where are you, Larka?"

"I am there. I am in the rain and the skies. I am in the trees and the flowers. I am in the sunlight and in the moonlight too."

Larka and the dream were gone. Kar opened his eyes and looked up into the evening. The moon was as round as it had been at Harja. Again it had come full circle, but as the gray wolf lay in the grass, he suddenly felt that now perhaps there was something new in the world.

So spring came, and the snows melted and the rivers swelled. The wolves felt a force that neither pain nor loss nor suffering could resist, the force of new life, of rebirth, rising through their paws. Life's sap was climbing, and soon a miracle took place no less wondrous than the wolves' pilgrimage to Harja. Kar was lying on the river-bank with Slavka and Huttser when a head emerged from the badger's set in the bank where they had hidden from the dogs. Palla looked exhausted, but her eyes were bright.

"Come, Huttser."

Huttser disappeared into the set, and when he returned to summon the rest of his pack, his face was full of pride. Kar squeezed his muzzle into the den and he could hardly contain his joy. The pups were bound tightly in a bundle, sleeping as soundly as the earth. Two draggas and two drappas. Palla was nestled about them, grooming them tenderly.

"Look," cried Kar, squeezing from the set again, "Slavka, Fell. Come and look."

The pups' eyes opened five suns later. Fell would spend hours watching the cubs as they moved them to the

Meeting Place and, though they found him strange and slightly frightening, they soon got used to his quiet ways and his mournful, searching eyes. Fell hunted for them, too, whenever he could, but Huttser and Palla noticed that he rarely sat with them. He would leave them meat on the edge of the Meeting Place and nod gravely as they took it, then turn away.

Fell spent most of his time on his own these suns, and, though he would smile at the little family, Kar could see that he was still troubled. One evening as the sun sank once more around the castle, Fell came to see Kar as he sat alone by the river.

"Kar," he growled, gazing into the moving waters, "I am going away."

"Going away, but why, Fell? You are a part of the pack."

"A pack?" said Fell. "Like the Balkar? Like the rebels? No, Kar. I am not. I can never be that."

"A family, then."

Fell shook his head.

"You are still in pain, Fell, I can sense it in you."

"Yes. Sometimes I think her curse still hovers over us all. But I must find my own answer. Out there in the wild. Or perhaps," added Fell, lifting his head suddenly, "perhaps among the humans, for I can read their minds, Kar."

"And in spite of what we saw," growled Kar, "they can love too. You can see it in their eyes."

"I think their eyes have been watching us all along, and I have been walking through a dream. I feel as though I was nothing more than the tales Brassa used to tell us as cubs."

"Of Wolfbane, or a human that lives in the earth and cannot die? No, Fell. Those were lies. But we are wolves."

But as Kar looked into Fell's eyes, he shivered, for he knew that the Sight was still burning inside him and that his journey had only just begun.

"What will you do, brother?"

"I am Putnar, Kar," growled Fell suddenly, "so I will hunt. But I will track down lies. And I will hunt for meaning too. And, Kar, remember this, I can see in the dark."

Evening was coming down as Kar lay with the pups at the Meeting Place. Slavka was at his side, and Huttser and Palla were sitting together in front of them. Palla's eyes were sorrowful, but Huttser kept nuzzling his mate.

"He'll be all right, Palla," he growled kindly, "he's strong. Like you. And, Palla, we must learn when to let our children go too."

Palla laid her head gently on Huttser's paws.

"Father," said a little voice suddenly.

Huttser looked down at the cub sitting in the grass in front of him.

"What is it, Larka?" he asked, licking his daughter's ears.

"Will you tell us a story, Father?"

"Oh yes," cried another voice loudly, and a second pup came bounding over and began to scramble on his sister's back.

"Careful, Skop," growled Palla, "and leave your father be. He's too tired for stories."

"Palla," whispered Huttser gently, "don't be angry."

"Oh, please," came two more voices.

Now there were four cubs sitting expectantly in front of their parents.

"Khaz," said Palla softly, "Kipcha. Please settle down. Your father doesn't want—"

"Will you let me?" said Kar suddenly. "I'll tell them a story."

"Oh yes, Uncle Kar," cried Larka. Her coat was perfectly gray.

"What would you like, children?"

"The Stone Den," said Kipcha excitedly.

Kar looked up at the castle. The twilight cast flickering shadows across its walls. Bands of light and dark were stroking its battlements.

"Oh no," said Kar, "there's nothing up there for a wolf. Just empty ruins."

"How do you know?" asked little Kipcha disbelievingly.

"I just know, Kipcha," answered Kar softly, nuzzling the little Sikla toward him as if to protect her from the world. The cubs looked at Kar and they suddenly thought how very grown up he was.

"The Sight, Kar," Skop piped suddenly. "Tell us the legend of the Sight."

"Hush, little one," said Kar, wondering what Huttser and Palla had been telling their children, but as he looked down at the cub, he shivered. He had seen a glint in his eye, a little mischievous twinkle, and for a moment he was reminded of when he had first met Larka by the Meeting Place.

"You are too young, Skop. You have plenty of time to learn of such things."

"Then tell us a hunting tale," whispered Khaz.

"Oh yes," cried Larka, pretending to bite her brother. "Tell us about Wolfbane. Will he come again?"

A note came to them suddenly across the wind, and they all looked up. There, standing on a rock above the castle, silhouetted against the brilliant starlight, stood Fell. The black wolf's howl rose from his lifting muzzle and came loud and mournful to their ears.

In the trees something stirred. It swiveled its head slowly away from Fell and its piercing eyes turned in a circle, once more, to the little family of wolves at their Meeting Place. As it watched Kar, and Huttser and Palla's cubs, those yellow and black eyes blinked slowly. Then the eagle's great wings opened, and it lifted into the sky.

On the mountain high above them, other voices had begun to answer Fell. He turned and, without once looking back, the black wolf vanished into the night.

"No, Larka," whispered Kar as he watched his brother go. "I won't tell you a story of Wolfbane."

The cubs started to grumble.

"But I will tell you a better story."

The children looked up happily.

"It was when Tor, the Varg goddess, mated with the great god Fenris and their mating first brought forth the earth."

Kar paused and his eyes twinkled. "Before they had made the waters and the forests or the Lera to roam in them. Before they had made Dammam and Va who gave birth to Fren, who slew his brother Barl and made all Lera forgetful. Before they had made Man, the strangest Lera of them all. Before they did any of this, they looked out on the universe and they were glad at what they saw."

"Why, Uncle Kar?" cried the cubs. "What was that?"

"Why that was the stars, my little ones," growled Kar, throwing up his proud eyes to the endless heavens. "For in the beginning, there was light."

AUTHOR'S NOTE

It was 1990 when I went to Romania, in the middle of winter, and saw some of the problems of that strange country. Perhaps it was the darkness of their recent history, or the many tales and superstitions, from Dracula to local folklore, that turned *The Sight* in the direction it took.

The imaginative landscape it inhabits ranges beyond Transylvania to an area of Eastern Europe known as the Balkans—hence the name of Morgra's wolves, the Balkar. It also makes direct allusions to Yugoslavia, because of the war that erupted there at the end of our supposedly enlightened twentieth century. It was a war in which so many symbols of the past were used to manipulate and destroy, so a major theme became how all of us are bound up in the past, not only in terms of family myths but the stories we tell to interpret the world, and how that can keep us in negative cycles. How, too, so many of the borders of fear we erect between one another are about competing narratives.

I wrote a large part of *The Sight* in a little house on a mountain in a beautiful region of southern Spain called Andalucía.